❧

Joanna Jemmette was in the theatre in the 1950s but always felt 'there must be more to life than this'. After marriage and two children, she became a priest in the Christian community, which is affiliated to the Rudolf Steiner movement, and has since retired.

Because The Dance Was Long

Because The Dance Was Long

Joanna Jemmette

ATHENA PRESS
LONDON

ISBN 1 84401 512 2

.

First Published 2005 by
ATHENA PRESS
Queen's House, 2 Holly Road
Twickenham TW1 4EG
United Kingdom

Printed for Athena Press

Chapter One

When the train stopped at a station and a man said 'Leek' once, in a little voice, I heard and understood him properly, and getting out of the train, stood on the platform quite overcome by the fact.

I got the letter out of my pocket which had 'Leek' written on it in blue ink letters, and looked across at a brick wall which had 'Leek' written on it in whitewashed ones.

It was quite miraculous really, I thought, that they should be the same.

She could so easily have put an E on it or made the L look like an H, or smudged it, and then I should have started out for some other part of the country and gone on and on, and never come to anything that corresponded, and eventually had to get out in the wild dreadful wastes of a village called Hearken or something – 'Lady it's the best we can do for you' – and actually, I thought, it wouldn't matter very much if I had because she had never seen me and didn't really know if she was expecting me.

The slightness and slenderness of things, the fact that my safe arrival could mean only a little to her and so much to me, made me feel overcome again so I sat down on a bench and re-read the letter. I had done this several times during the day and each time it had cheered me up, because I considered it quite a flattering letter. It said:

> Dear Miss King,
>
> Your letter tells us that you are a young lady of breeding and education. As we are about to embark upon a season of refined plays, my husband and I feel we might benefit by you.
>
> A good wardrobe is essential but with long practise of decisions made through letter alone, we discarded a hundred other applicants in the assumption that you possessed this important item.
>
> If interested please travel tomorrow morning to Leek Town Hall prepared to start at once at lowest.
>
> Sincerely, Lilian Flood (Mrs)

It was written on pale pink paper and had a rose motif in one corner and I thought that I would probably keep it all my life, because receiving it was the most important thing that had happened to me.

A porter put my trunk in the left luggage office and told me how to get to the town hall, and I flapped my way out of the station and into the bright sunlight of Station Road – I flapped because I was wearing brogue shoes that were too big for me. I was wearing a tweed suit too, and a silk shirt and a beret clamped down with a brooch. They were the classiest clothes I possessed and I thought suddenly that if I could have come sitting sideways on a horse it would be perfect.

This made me laugh inside, and with laughing the dazed feeling melted away and I was filled with a wild exultation and my heart circled upwards inside me. I felt the hot sun strike right through me and I wanted to dance, and shout, and sing, and act so that everyone could know that I had arrived.

Instead however, I flapped quickly up the street and thought, *I am absolutely and consciously happy.*

Going along the streets I passed a cemetery and picture houses, and the public baths, and the library and the market and thought, I must look at them, I must look at them hard, these strange places that I have never seen before, because it is the very first time and maybe I will look at them a hundred times more and never notice them again.

They seemed extraordinarily dear to me all these places, dear and familiar and natural; for out of the dream world of seeing it written down once in a letter, and hearing it said once by a man, they built up Leek for me, solid and dependable and real.

There were poplar trees in the High Street, and smart cafés and shops that had branches in Liverpool, and halfway down, standing flat to the pavement, was the town hall. It was large and square, and built of black brick with a row of windows running halfway up across the front of it, and an undersized door set low down in the middle of it.

Three rather drunkenly arranged bills were stuck down low beside the door, and it was at these that I stood on the other side of the pavement and gazed at with awe.

I knew and yet did not know what they would say. With every step that I had taken things had grown up out of the dream world, taking the one shape that I had wanted them to take. Nothing as yet had gone wrong. I had come round corners suddenly, and the pattern had continued until at last I was standing looking at the town hall which had, quite correctly, bills stuck on it. I knew now that they must concern me but I was not sure in what way.

It would be quite in order I thought wildly, that they should say 'Gone away for the summer' or 'Come back September 1st'. I crossed over the road and read them.

They didn't say that but quite simply and wonderfully that the Flood Players were performing a season of refined plays at the town hall, commencing on Monday next with *Flossie's Great Day*.

A great rush of thankfulness and release came over me as I read these words, and I thought for a minute with a kind of light-hearted relish of the expensive ticket, the letter that people had laughed at, and the town that no one had heard of.

I tried the handle of the undersized door but it was locked and dead-looking, so I walked to the end of the building and turned into a thin dark alley that I had seen from the other side of the road. It was cold like a cellar after the sunlight and cobbled with big, round, worn stones, but a little way along there was a door which when I pulled it, opened easily. Inside was a small square hall and a flight of stairs, and immediately I entered my heart started to pound again and my hands to perspire, for floating down from the stairs, very loud and clear on the still air, came the dramatic ringing tones of a male actor.

I walked up the stairs hearing my shoes make little facetious squelching flaps on the marble, and gradually seeing myself reflected in a large gilt mirror at the top of them. In front of it I furtively combed my hair and wished that I could have worn a cotton frock and looked a little prettier.

There was another flight of stairs and at the top of them were two green baize swing doors.

I stood outside these for quite a while because he was just beyond them and the knowledge of this frightened me. I kept saying 'Get a grip on yourself Ann King, get a grip on yourself,' and eventually I did, and gave the doors a bold horsey push and walked through.

The hall was in darkness so that I was only aware of the stage at the other end and the actor walking about on it. His voice was the one I had heard from below, and which now filled the air completely, frenzied and passionate with the things he was saying. Coming on top of my creeping, inside emotions, his visible, tangible ones crushed them considerably and I sat down on a chair and looked at him.

He had a handsome bull-like head covered with bull-like curls, and was shortish and stocky with broad shoulders and narrow hips, and short thick legs. He wore brown trousers and a green nylon shirt with hair coming through it, and from where I was sitting, looked about forty. He was caught up completely with the things that he was saying and very moved by them. He stumbled and lurched against furniture with his voice breaking hoarsely every now and then, and sweat running down his nylon shirt.

There were other people standing on the sides of the stage but I couldn't take them in just then, as I was really quite carried away by him. His face was all screwed up with emotion and just when it seemed he would burst into tears, a sharp Cockney accent rose out of the darkened chairs in front of me. 'Stow it, Willy,' it said.

The man on stage stopped instantly, all expression immediately wiped off his face and sitting down in a chair he took out a cigarette and lit it.

'I shouldn't wonder,' continued the Cockney voice a little less sharply, 'but what that speech shouldn't bring down the house.'

This received no reply from the man but he smiled vaguely towards the darkness, and the people in the wings came out and stood talking in little groups on the stage.

It was quite still now in the hall and waiting, I knew there was not another minute in the world could go by without my doing it, so I rose quickly from the chair and made for the figure sitting in front of me.

'Excuse me!' I began.

It was a shock to me that she was so old. I supposed I had imagined her as fortyish perhaps, but the face that looked up at mine was nearer sixty; wrinkled and ugly with narrow black slit-like eyes, and dyed black hair and a raddled, painted skin.

I began to speak again but she just said, 'Up on stage please, I can't see you here.'

It was dreadfully embarrassing for me being hauled up on to the bright stage and examined. I was painfully aware of the other people's curious, amused faces as she walked round me and pinched the material of my suit, and asked boldly if my hair was naturally fair.

I had meant to be gay and bright and show personality, but I became unable to speak and my hands took over instead and hung heavily, shamefully eloquent by my side while my face burned red.

I thought, in a minute she will say it, in a minute she will say, 'What experience have you had?' and I shall be unable to talk my way out of it after all and that will be that.

'Would you,' said Mrs Flood in a guarded voice, 'stand next to Mr Flood for height please?'

I noticed the other people very slowly. For an hour or so they moved and spoke around me in answer to the screech which came out of the darkness where she had become a voice again, and I hardly saw them. I kept my eyes fixed steadfastly on the piece of paper that she had given me, for it contained the five magical lines that I was to speak in the forthcoming production *of Flossie's Great Day.*

I gabbled these to myself, over and over again, over and over again until they whirled and leaped around my head, and until at last on a certain screech I stood in the middle of the stage and heard myself say them, small and tremulous, to a blonde boy who answered me then escorted me off and whispered, 'Wasn't so bad eh, was it?'

He got me a beer box to sit on in the wings and I looked at him and thought what a nice face he had, and how short he was, and how dreadful that he should be lame. Mrs Flood had not introduced me to anyone except her husband, who was the man I had seen acting from the back of the hall. It had astonished me greatly that he should be her husband, for close up he looked quite a bit younger than forty. It had astonished me too, that with his powerful build and forceful acting, he should have pale blue childlike eyes and a gentle mouth.

I looked now at the other people in the company. There were not very many of them and they were all very small. I supposed that this was with Mr and Mrs Flood being short, but it did look a little odd, as though we might all have been herded together on account of our arrested growth.

Besides Mr Flood and the blond boy, there was a thin, pretty girl of about my own age with black hair down to her waist, a fat older girl, a dark foreign-looking boy and a very, very old man who had not moved once from a corner of the stage where he sat on a travelling rug, and breathed unnaturally.

The thin, pretty girl appeared to be playing, with difficulty, 'Flossie'. The difficulty being Mrs Flood, who pulled her up on nearly every word to tell her that she was saying it wrong. I felt very sorry for the girl, as Mrs Flood wasn't even telling her nicely.

In fact, she was being positively unkind to her with remarks like, 'I don't want Mr Flood here being shamed on his first night' and 'How Mr Flood can go on standing up there and saying nothing beats me.'

The thin pretty girl made no attempt to answer her back, which I thought was wise, but we were all very relieved when Mrs Flood shrieked suddenly at Mr Flood to poke Grandpa to start the tea.

The old, old man woke, moaning a little, and Mr Flood very kindly helped him down some steps to the gas ring.

With the rehearsal broken up the company drifted into a group again, and the blond boy came and fetched me from the beer box and introduced me to them; to the thin pretty girl who was called Rose Hart; to the fat girl who was Hilda Fellowes; to the dark boy Sebastian Day, and to himself Leigh Peters. Grandpa they told me was Bill Irving and no relation.

They were friendly and gay towards me, and when the tea came Leigh Peters gave me a cup first, and the thin pretty girl Rose offered me a cigarette and asked me if I had anywhere to stay and when I told her 'no', she smiled at me delightedly and said what a relief, because she didn't think she could have stood another night at the YWCA on her own.

My tea was hot and sweet and with being very hungry it made me a little dizzy and for a moment the stage swam round me in a kaleidoscope of colour and sound, with the dark boy laughing and showing his teeth; with the girl Rose telling me that Mrs Flood was a bitch; with the clatter and flash of the old man dropping a cup; with the moving fairness of the boy Leigh Peters' hair; with the humming noise of something electrical, and the sharp smacking noise of Willy Flood practising intricate tap-dancing steps down by the footlights.

I fought against it in a panic because it belonged to the dream-world part and Mrs Flood must have fought for me too, because her voice came suddenly close to my ear.

'You're not hard of hearing I hope, Ann King?' she said.

I looked up, assuring her that I was not and apologising fearfully for my rudeness, and she beckoned me over to where she and Mr Flood were sitting, apart from the others on a bench made out of a plank and two pots of paint.

'Mr Flood and me,' she began in a heavy whisper so that I was caught up in a web of isolated secrecy, 'have been considering.'

She fixed me with a narrowed, disapproving black eye.

'Mr Flood and me,' she repeated, 'have been considering that you shouldn't want for nothing on three. Very happy and contented, Mr Flood and me consider you should be on three pounds.' There was a short pause and she nudged Mr Flood and said, 'Eh! Willy,' sharply.

Mr Flood looked up from where he had been gouging holes into the plank with a penknife, gave me a brief and lovely smile and looked down again quickly.

'Just as I said!' said Mrs Flood as though he had come out with a torrent of words. 'Just as I told you Mr Flood and me had decided, three.'

I said, 'You mean... You mean three pounds a week?' and she nodded her head at me in a dismissed manner and I said, 'Thank you very much, Mrs Flood,' and backed nervously away. Three pounds a week didn't seem a great deal of money to me but I reflected that it was a living wage and that she had after all stated 'lowest'.

After the tea break, rehearsal continued and I helped Bill Irving wash up the cups, as my five lines wouldn't come for another hour. I started to talk to him but saw at once that it was an effort for him to answer me back and that he would rather I didn't. Leigh Peters helped him back to his corner and confided to me that he had to reserve every ounce of his strength to get his words out on stage. The rehearsal went on and on. My five lines came round, and then again, and the sun-mote which had wriggled in from a hole in the roof and danced on us all afternoon disappeared, and our voices became lucid and intense on the evening air.

Out among the darkened chairs Mrs Flood flapped and screeched like a bat, at the awfulness of our acting and the shame that was to be visited on Mr Flood's head the following Monday. But up on stage with the lateness of the hour and the fact that we couldn't see her, we became banded together, friendly and well-disposed to share our cigarettes and comment on Mr Flood's acting.

Now and again things swam, and now and again my mind would go back and trace in minute detail my journey. And sometimes it would stick at a certain point so that I could not lose the movement of the train or the knowledge that the man was looking at me, or the fear that I would lose the letter. And even when my mind had moved on to the walking from the station bit, the feeling clung to me, which was silly because I had only been happy then.

'Stow it, Willy,' said Mrs Flood, and in the disconcertingly swift silence with which he obeyed this remark she added, 'Ten thirty sharp in the morning, the lot of you please.'

We ate Welsh rarebits and drank coffee in the window of a snack bar with the sky outside pale green and set with one thin silver star. Then I walked with the girl, Rose, to the YWCA and they gave me the other bed in her room. It was a nice little room with a creeper growing all round the window, and I lay in a narrow bed with crackling white sheets and thought about it all.

Chapter Two

It was not until the first night of the play and the party which followed it afterwards that I really got to know the company, for from the Thursday that I had joined them until then we had rehearsed all the time.

'No talking on stage,' Mrs Flood would screech at us if she caught sight of any overtures of friendliness. And, 'How you can let a minute of studying go by without wanting to kick yourselves that it isn't two, beats me. How you can presume to stand there talking, knowing what Mr Flood and I think, leaves Mr Flood and me without words.'

Outside, the sun shone fiercely down on an unexplored Leek, and inside the town hall we worked hour after hour on the wooden stage of the shut-in, upstairs theatre.

I learned very quickly, as the others had already done, to dislike and to fear and to admire Mrs Flood. She managed every aspect of the company down, from acting and producing to rootling with infinite pains among the market stalls for the endless substitutes of decoration necessary for classy plays.

Her relationship with Mr Flood intrigued me greatly; she obviously worshipped the ground he walked on, but at the same time had him so completely under her thumb that she even doled out his cigarette ration to him – five in the morning and five in the afternoon. 'No Willy!' she'd say when he looked at her with craving eyes, 'You've had your fourth and there's still another hour to go.'

Mr Flood himself baffled me quite a lot. I admired his fierce acting tremendously and I could not help but like his kind, gentle and unassuming nature, yet these two things, coming together as they did, disquieted me somehow. At one moment, watching him act, I would seethe with indignation that he should be so henpecked, but the next, looking into his vague childlike eyes, would wonder if she wasn't terribly necessary to him.

Of the rest of the company, Rose alone I got to know, on account of living with her. She came from Blackpool, she told me, where an adoring fiancé was waiting to marry her. On the whole I liked her, although at times she appeared to be unreasonably discontented with her lot.

'Stagnating, wasting, my youth gone up in smoke,' she announced tragically to me over supper in the YWCA one night. 'I can see it coming on, I can see myself heading for it – the same fate that has overtaken him.'

'Who?' I asked her.

'That handsome, pathetic brute of a husband of hers,' she replied emotionally.

We were not told that there was to be a party until latish Sunday night, when at the end of rehearsal Mrs Flood announced in a rather coy voice that she thought a small port or sherry taken after the show might set a happy family seal on the season. 'Not,' she added firmly, 'but what I won't have to ask you all to contribute; seven and sixpence each, Mr Flood and me thought might be suitable, with –' here she paused for a magnanimous moment – 'Mr Flood and me giving ten.' We were quite overcome by her generosity and it was not until we were walking home, when we indulged in a little calculation, that we realised we had been mistaken.

For Rose and me a party after the show presented the major difficulty of getting around Miss Fluck. The one snag about living at the YWCA was the matron Miss Fluck. She was a great big grey-haired harridan of a Christian woman who insisted on the 10.30 p.m. curfew being adhered to, and who unfortunately was convinced that all actresses had been 'led astray'.

Had we been a couple of decent Leek typists, I think that she might have relented over the party, but the fact that, coupled with our unfortunate calling, she had twice had to wait for us at the door with clanking keys, tended to make her unreasonable.

We pointed out to her that it would only be for an hour or so, and that in a way it was our duty to attend, but she refused to agree with us.

We retaliated by outwardly refusing to eat our cheese sandwich suppers, but that night in the darkness of our room, we made our plans. Our room was on the first floor and a profusion of virginia creeper and a conveniently situated drainpipe had not escaped our notice. We decided that the following night we would have no other course than to come in, retire as usual, then use these natural amenities of escape.

The first night of *Flossie's Great Day*, which was my professional debut, was not quite the momentous occasion I had anticipated, as Mrs Flood went wrong just before I was due to speak and by the time she had righted herself, was several pages on in the script. She apologised afterwards, but it was not the same; I had felt distinctly silly just coming on and standing there, and being hissed at by her to get off.

It was, I reflected, unhappily wiping off my greasepaint, just as well that there was to be a party.

Back at the YWCA Miss Fluck had been feeling her conscience and tinned fruit and ice cream graced the supper table to make up for our disappointment over missing the party.

'Nerve!' muttered Rose as we coldly devoured it.

Unfortunately Miss Fluck's room was at right angles in the wall to ours, so after fishing around in the dark for our party frocks, we crouched at the window keeping sentinel until her light went out.

'God! How long can it take to wind thirty curlers into a head of short hair?' For ten minutes we watched her large form encased in a shocking pink dressing gown launch into battle. First, half a bottle of setting lotion was poured over her head and then, having three gos with each curler, she wound them slowly in. This done, she settled a frivolous piece of pink net around them and turned her attention to her face.

Three different sorts of cream were massaged in, each being left to soak for two minutes; on the last soaking she killed time with a pair of eyebrow tweezers on her moustache. We were fascinated by then and when at last she removed the dressing gown and stood admiring herself in the mirror, we promptly had hysterics.

This however, was her last ritual, and a second later the light snapped out.

A half moon lit the night but even so, the ground looked a hell of a way off. Rose clutched me and we both looked longingly back at our safe beds, but the outrage of my first real freedom being locked indoors by ten thirty was too much and to Rose's great relief – we were going to toss up for first down – I swung a leg over the sill.

It wasn't nearly as easy as we'd imagined and I soon gave up expecting any help from the creeper. The drainpipe was old and rusty and kept moving away from the wall. The only way was to slide; I closed my eyes and did so – success – except that my nylon frock was filthy from neck to hem.

Shaking like a jelly I whispered up to Rose, 'It's easy, but tuck your dress in your knickers.' Rose was one of the smallest and slimmest girls I had seen and with chagrin I watched her lightly and easily nip down the creeper.

'Why on earth didn't you use it?' she asked me as she smoothed down her immaculate dress. Bitterly I pointed out her unfair advantage.

'Oh!' she said brightly, 'It won't be so easy for you shinning up again then, will it?'

It wouldn't. I stopped dead in my tracks as the awful realisation dawned on me, but Rose was tugging at me impatiently.

'Come on, come on we're half an hour late already, we'll just have to get one of the boys to hoist you up.' Or something, I thought to myself as we sped off down the hill. Both the boys were a good deal smaller than I.

At the theatre the party was well under way. We came breathless through the green baize door, where a little earlier on twenty-three people had sat moodily watching the play.

We found the rest of the company gay, and laughing and colourful with the sound of dance music and clinking glasses.

Our contributions appeared to have been well spent and a glorious array of bottles was laid out on the prop table. The others had already been liberally imbibing and the party atmosphere was thick.

We were swooped on by the boys and whirled away across the stage to the strains of Victor Sylvester, played maximum on the Panatrope.

It was a wonderful party with everyone for the first time relaxed and natural. We drank a toast to the success of the season, and Mrs Flood said that but for the fact that we'd only managed to draw in twenty-three people, Mr Flood and her would have been quite agreeably surprised by the performance.

By one o'clock we were indeed in merry mood, and Bill Irving was heard to murmur something about reciting *If*. This excessiveness was not however encouraged, and Mrs Flood suggested that he be put on to tonic water immediately.

We were all of us amazed by Leigh Peters. I had discovered that he was a much quieter boy than I had at first imagined with a tendency to become depressed, but tonight he knocked back sherry after port after sherry, and expanded for the first time and kept us in hysterics with his dry, witty stories.

Mrs Flood let out wild shrieks of delight at these, and kept hitting him on his narrow back and telling him that he ought to go on the Halls. Willy never said much but he sat on the floor grinning happily and rocking back and forth in time to the music. And then someone suddenly put on 'Temptation'.

After the background of Victor Sylvester we were all of us aware of it. Our excited conversation cracked across for a second, and the cold, controlled passion of the tango music beat about our ears. Willy got up from the floor, crossed over to Rose who was sitting on a tea chest, and without a word just held out his hands to her.

We were all of us suddenly silent; we all knew that she must not accept his offer, but that halfwitted, predatory Rose just smiled up into his face and eagerly put her hands into his. He pulled her up and in a second they were dancing away. And oh! How they danced; I had never seen anyone move so beautifully as Willy did then.

His stocky figure was the effortless tool of his feet and Rose the pliable clay of his craft. They danced in Spanish style, back and forth he coiled her on his arm, now letting her fall only to catch her two inches from the ground; now whirling her high across his shoulders, his feet stamping impatiently on the ground. Her blue chiffon dress swathed itself around him, and her long dark hair streamed across his face. It was the most sensual dance I had ever seen.

Greatly daring, I turned my face to look at Mrs Flood. She was sitting on a low stool with her glass poised halfway up to her mouth. Her mouth was wide open and her face wore a dazed expression. She was utterly engrossed with their dancing. I kept on looking at her and slowly two tears trickled out of her wide open eyes and coursed unnoticed down her cheeks, and one of them fell with a plop into her drink.

The record came to an end and we were all of us staring at her now. I braced myself for the coming scene. In the centre of the stage, Willy finished with Rose held close against him. He released her instantly though, and as they stepped apart Mrs Flood rose from her stool. Still clutching her drink she slowly advanced upon them. Willy turned to face her, suddenly, as though he were only now aware of her. He was smiling, with sweat on his face, but his eyes were frightened and a muscle ticked in his cheek.

Mrs Flood however was completely unaware of him. Her goal was Rose, and now she lurched a little as her carpet slipper caught in a splinter. Rose stood frozen where she was, her mouth as open as Mrs Flood's. They drew parallel and from where I was sitting the open mouths looked rather funny, but this was no time for laughing. I don't know quite what we thought Mrs Flood might do to Rose, but when at last she spoke it was certainly not what I had expected. She breathed heavily, the words coming out with difficulty.

'I... danced... with him... like that... thirty years ago... People came from all over the world to see us...' Her voice trailed off miserably and she turned and shuffled back towards her stool. She was all broken and old with dry little sobs. 'My waist... was smaller than yours though... He could span it with his hands...'

And then Willy Flood did the most terrible thing that I hope I shall ever live to see any man do. He crossed over to Rose and put his hands around her waist.

'See!' He said triumphantly, 'I can do it with her, too!'

In the silence which followed, a stillness crept over the stage so that the echo of his voice and the clamouring whirr of the silent Panatrope still lived. I felt the heat ebb away from my body and the glass in my hand become cheap and hard and cold, but I could not move because we were still watching.

Then Rose moved swiftly towards us and the silence became filled with our jumbled voices saying goodnight, and the stillness was broken with the movement of our clumsy feet, which could not take us quickly enough away from the theatre. Outside we didn't say much except Rose, who kept saying, 'It wasn't my fault, it wasn't my fault.' We didn't argue with her; by this time next week the poor girl would surely be back home in Blackpool.

Hilda Fellowes and Bill Irving lived in opposite directions to us; so did Leigh and Sebastian, but they walked us up the hill.

It was just as well that they did as we'd completely forgotten about getting in again. We reached the YWCA just as the moon went behind some clouds, and as we tiptoed across the lawn the sight of the wall rising sheer up before us just about rounded off the evening perfectly. The boys however had cheered up no end at the romance of our situation and appeared to relish the idea of having to hoist me up. Rose easily got up via the creeper again, and I had another tentative try at it, but the tearing noise of it coming away in my hands sent me post haste on to the valiant Sebastian's doubled back.

This gave me a three foot start. I floundered on to the drainpipe and he carefully removed himself. What, I asked myself as I clung there ineffectually, was I expected to do? Swarm nimbly up it as I had enviously watched other girls doing in the gymnasium at school? So much for that little fancy. I was unable to move my trembling arms one inch, let alone my legs.

The boys kept yelling up instructions but it was no good. I suddenly panicked, and the next instant landed in a heap at their feet. No harm done, but at the same time, no question of my trying it again. It was getting past the joke stage now. We peered around a potting shed to see if there was the odd ladder or some such helpful instrument; nothing except a wheelbarrow which Leigh knocked over. Instantly the light sprang on in Miss Fluck's room, and we waited, crouched on the ground with our hearts in our mouths.

Back underneath the window Rose informed us that it had been a coincidence and only nature calling her, but it was unnerving and made me feel very weak and undaring. Looking up at Rose though, I got the idea.

'There's nothing for it,' I told the boys bravely, 'she'll just have to knot some sheets together and haul me up.'

This seemed the only answer but as Sebastian pointed out, Rose wouldn't be able to haul me up alone.

'Obviously,' he said, grinning, 'I'll have to go up and help her.'

He shinned up the pipe in an instant and after a few minutes our sheets writhed slowly down the wall. I knotted the end to form a seat, settled myself on it and signalled to them to start hauling. They were both of them pulling wide out of the window with my weight but inch by inch I began to move into the air. I was able to steady myself with my feet on the creeper and was just about nicely halfway there when it happened.

An ominous ripping noise sounded suddenly from above. Rose let out a terrible scream and at the same time they stopped pulling. With perfect timing as the sheet slipped through their hands and I rapidly returned to earth, Miss Fluck chose to floodlight the scene. Like a quivering pink blancmange she leaned out into the night.

I had just landed lovingly into Leigh's waiting arms, and above us Sebastian was twined round Rose preventing her from following me down. She looked from one little scene to the other.

'You wicked, immoral deceivers,' she gasped at last. 'Men in your room at two thirty in the morning, and my sheets used as the means of their entry.'

It was hopeless trying to explain to her. She refused to allow any of us to speak.

'Get down from that room at once,' she thundered at poor Sebastian, who meekly slid down. 'And now get out of my grounds before I call the police.'

They beat it hot foot but at the gateway paused. 'Good morning, Miss Fluck,' they chorused in a manner which made it just as well that she was an unspoilt Christian woman.

She treated us to one withering stare. 'I'll deal with you in the morning,' she said between gritted teeth, and prepared to shut the window.

'Miss Fluck,' I quavered up at her, 'you'll have to let me in... I'm afraid I can't manage the sheets.'

For an instant I thought that she was going to refuse, but after a few minutes a bunch of keys thudded down at my feet. I started to call out my thanks but the window was slammed in my face and the light snapped out.

The following morning we at least got our say in, but it made no difference. Miss Fluck had no further interest in re-guiding us onto the paths of righteousness; we were to leave that very same day.

I felt pretty low as we walked down to the theatre; much as I disliked Miss Fluck and the YWCA it upset me to think that we had been asked to leave at once. On top of that I kept remembering the scene on stage the night before, and the storm which must now break on Rose's head. Rose however appeared less perturbed by her misfortunes.

'Oh, I don't know,' she said. 'They've got me cheap, and she's got to have someone to nag and now she can really go to town on me, and anyway,' she finished, 'what the hell could she say to me? "When you dance with my husband, Rose, you must try not to make him think that it was me thirty years ago?"'

Rose shrieked with laughter and jumped into the air and pulled off a leafy branch of a tree. I supposed that it was just as well that she took this light-hearted attitude.

She was right too, down at the theatre Mrs Flood was bright and businesslike, and no mention was made of the previous night.

It was a Tuesday morning, and the first rehearsal of the play we would perform the following week.

It was exciting for me too, for all the pent-up excitement of yesterday, which had resulted in only being hissed at to get off, could be released in the much longer part (two pages) of Mrs Flood's mother in a stark drama entitled *Racked*.

It was two o'clock before rehearsal ended and Rose and I were free to look for somewhere to live. Digs were scarce in Leek so we went straight to the police station and, armed with a slender list, set forth. After half an hour we had been through the lot. Only three could offer us accommodation and they were all far too expensive. We had been given two word-of-mouth addresses en route, and these we tried.

The first one, only two minutes from the theatre, was no good on account of our being actresses, and the second was a twopenny bus-ride out of the town in Cockton Heath, and Leigh who was living out there, said it was quite nice.

'We can try it,' I said to Rose doubtfully. 'In fact, we'll have to try it, but the bus fares are going to be something cruel.'

We found number eight, 'The Rooley', all right; a rather gone-to-seed-looking semi-detached house, with a wild garden and straggly net curtains at the windows. We knocked on the door but the house was reverberating to the vicious screaming of a small toddler. We could see it through the letterbox, sitting in a highchair and lashing out with a wooden spoon.

A little girl of about five appeared to be the butt of its temper. She was trying to feed it with something from a saucer but as we watched, a particularly well-aimed blow from the baby knocked her to the ground. The saucer broke and the little girl started to cry. We hammered louder at the door but there appeared to be noone else in the house.

'Let's go round to the back door,' Rose said. 'Maybe we've been given the wrong number.'

The back door was open and led into the kitchen where the children were. The little girl had picked herself up but was still crying because of the broken saucer, and the baby, frustrated with her now being out of hitting range, had redoubled its volume. His (it was now very clearly male) face was puce with anger, and the amount of time which elapsed between each breath was quite alarming.

'Little girl,' said Rose in a winning voice, 'where's your mummy?'

At the sound of her voice the baby's shrieks stopped as though they had been switched off. The little girl stopped crying too, and they both gazed at us, wide-eyed. She was an extremely pretty little girl with golden ringlets and big blue eyes, but terribly thin and strained-looking. The baby, on the other hand, was enormous and far too large for the highchair. It was impossible for him to sit down in it properly; half of him was lodged in mid-air and the other half leaned towards us at a perilous angle.

'Where's Mummy?' Rose repeated.

The little girl looked at her shyly then said, 'Upstairs,' in a rather dull voice.

'Are you sure dear?' said Rose carefully and kindly. 'Isn't she out at the shops?'

The little girl shook her head. 'No, upstairs, she's resting.'

'Oh. Well, do you think that you could run upstairs and tell her that we're here?'

The child looked a bit dubious but eventually pattered off. Rose and I exchanged glances. We wondered how any mother could possibly rest through that noise. I picked up the broken saucer and Rose made cooing noises at the baby. This was a mistake.

She ducked just in time to miss the wooden spoon. The child returned and said would we go upstairs to see Mum. We picked our way through the debris of the kitchen and this time the baby caught Rose a nasty blow on the back. He chortled with satisfaction and the little girl murmured brokenly, 'Oh please don't, Launcelot.'

'What a lovely name,' I said brightly. To her, 'And what's yours?'

'Guinevere,' she replied.

Ooh! I couldn't wait to see Mum.

She led the way up the stairs, which were as dirty and cluttered as the kitchen and stopped on the landing.

'In there,' she said, pointing to a half-open door.

We knocked rather gingerly and were answered by a deep sultry voice, bidding us to come in. I pushed open the door and we gazed round the room in wonder. It was the front bedroom and filled with a dim mauve light from the curtains at the window. Every inch of them was swathed in purple net, crossing and criss-crossing. It was draped in fantastic loops and folds held into place by large purple satin bows. There was no carpet on the floor but two large Spanish shawls had been spread over the stained boards.

In the corner facing us was the dressing-table, one of those hire-purchase glossy redwood affairs with a lot of mirrors.

Pieces of purple net ruching had been tacked around the frames of the mirrors and more purple satin bows drooped from each corner. The two outer mirrors were half filled with an array of cut out photographs of famous American film stars. These were mostly in bright colours and noticeably of the beefcake variety.

A curtain was stretched across another corner and I supposed that this was the wardrobe, for the only other furniture in the room was the bed. This protruded from one of the walls, an enormous ancient double bed with brass knobs and a brass rail. It was spread with a purple satin counterpane, and there lying resplendent in its centre was Mum.

I supposed that she was about twenty-eight or nine, and my first thought was, gosh, what a beauty. She was tall and very thin with a vivid gypsy face and masses of thick dark hair tied on top of her head in Edwardian style. She was clad in a transparent pink negligee, arranged around her so that her long slim legs were in full view.

By her side was a half-eaten box of chocolates, and the whole of the bed was littered with a profusion of highly coloured paper-backed novelettes. She raised veiled, disinterested eyes to us on our entry, but when we told her the reason for our visit they immediately became interested and she swung her legs off the bed and invited us to join her on it.

'The theatre!' said Mrs Winifred Welles with flattering awe in her voice. 'Oh, I should love to have two theatre girls come and stop with me.'

'And we'd love to come too,' I told her. 'We're absolutely desperate now. Can you fix us up?'

'Aah,' said Mrs Welles ponderously, 'that is the question. That is the question!' she repeated dramatically. Then eating two chocolates at once said, 'Larry, I've got the record,' rather thickly through them.

'You see girls,' she said, taking up another chocolate, 'it's like this. There's me in here and the kids next door and the only other room is the attic upstairs.

'It's a bit bare,' she said, 'but I won't charge you much and I would love to have you.'

Rose and I looked at each other, we both rather fancied an attic.

'Can we have a look at it?' I asked her.

'Sure.' Mrs Welles rose, majestic, from the bed and led the

way up the next flight of stairs. Bare was a gross understatement. The room stretched the whole length of the house, indescribably dirty and completely empty save for a narrow iron bed and a small divan resting on one leg, and three little piles of bricks.

'Well—' I began, but Mrs Welles was striding around extolling its advantages.

'Such air, such space, such freedom!' she said. 'It'll clean up lovely and we'll put up a string for your clothes, and would ten shillings each and buy your own food be alright?' That settled it, Rose and I exchanged glances. On three pounds a week the attic was heaven sent.

'It'd be wonderful,' we told her in unison.

Over a cup of tea in the kitchen she told us about herself. It appeared that she was separated from her husband but that he'd left her the house and gave her just enough to live on. 'What a sweet little girl Guinevere is,' I said. 'How old is she?'

'Seven,' replied her mother. 'And what a godsend that child is too. I don't know what I'd do without her, absolutely runs the place. Look at her now.'

We looked. The godsend was struggling under the weight of the still screaming baby (quite able to walk himself).

'Never forgets his walkies,' continued Mrs Welles fondly. She looked darkly at her son. 'I gave up trying to cope with him a year ago. She's the only one that can do anything with him.'

Above the shrieks Guinevere piped up reproachfully, 'Oh Mum, he's awful with me too.'

'Don't be silly, Gwinny,' replied her mother sharply. 'You know he adores you.'

We watched whilst she lowered him into an ancient pushchair in the corner and he adoringly kicked her, savagely.

'A marvel,' murmured Mrs Welles, shaking her head wonderingly as they trundled off down the path.

'But doesn't she have to go to school?' asked Rose.

Mrs Welles drew herself up. 'School! I would no more think of sending a child of mine to one of those personality destroying establishments than I would…' She floundered off, but concluded grandly. 'Anyway, I am attending to Guinevere's education myself.'

'Oh!' I said politely.

On our way down to the theatre we collected our stuff from the YWCA and after the show, Leigh, who lived in the next road, helped us home with them. Guinevere and Mrs Welles, still clad in the negligee, were eating baked beans and chips at the kitchen table. They had thoughtfully saved some for us as we'd had no time to buy anything.

Our attic had been swept out and the beds made up. Mrs Welles apologised for there being no sheets, but told us that we could have hers when they next went to the laundry. She had tied a piece of string across from one wall to the other, and with our clothes on hangers it made an excellent wardrobe. Very happy we were as we fell asleep that night in our strange new home.

Chapter Three

It astonished me to see how quickly we formed a pattern of oneness; how with all our differences we yet became a closely-knit family unit. I supposed that to a certain extent it was inevitable, in that we rehearsed all morning and played all evening, but it was this acceptance of differences, this 'liking-in-spite-of' feeling that amazed me. We might turn white with rage over Mrs Flood's sharp tongue, but no one would ever suggest that she'd be nicer if she were a little kinder.

Hour after hour we would listen to her nagging poor Rose, and hour after hour watch Rose patiently take it, and afterwards we would comfort her with 'Terrible!' 'Shocking!' and 'You were so good too', but it would all be a little vague and automatic because we knew and she knew too that it was Mrs Flood, who was one of us, behaving in a known and natural way. I think this feeling was brought home to me most strongly one afternoon when I was wandering around the town.

The afternoons were a strange and free time when for a little while we could each go our separate ways. I thought of us in the afternoons as like a pack of dogs on extra long leads.

This particular afternoon I had been wandering rather aimlessly through the market with an hour to go till tea, when I had looked up and out of the blue found Willy standing beside me.

We could hardly believe it and were flooded with emotion and happiness that we should have found one another; that out of the tiny little unit of eight, which was scattered so perilously around in the afternoons, two of us should find ourselves standing together.

'Ann!' said Willy, gripping my arm and grinning all over his face, 'Fancy seeing you here!'

'Willy!' said I delightedly. 'Whatever are you doing here?'

We were still staring at one another like long-lost lovers when

Mrs Flood came up and joined in the ridiculousness. 'Fancy,' she said in a gruff, pleased voice, 'seeing you here, Ann! Well, it's nice to know the company gets itself a bit of fresh air in the afternoons.'

Given a hundred yards start, I came to know and be interested in, or aware of, Leigh Peters. Eightpence a day on fares was gross extravagance, and when I discovered that Leigh always walked the two miles home to Cockton Heath, I joined him with alacrity. Rose unfortunately had to indulge in the bus on account of a sudden corn (that was her story anyway).

For the first week Leigh was as silent and morose as always. His expansion at the party, we discovered, had only been a flash in the pan. At first I put this down to his limp but by the end of the week decided it couldn't be that, as the only time he was light-hearted was when he flippantly referred to his 'affliction'. But by the middle of the second week he began to thaw a little in my company, and on the walks home we would discuss the Floods and the general theatre situation quite animatedly. It was, all the same though, a surprise to me when at the weekend he suggested we should take a bus ride into the country together. Rose's fiancé was coming down for the weekend. I told him that I thought it was a wonderful idea.

We caught a bus outside the cemetery, and for an hour watched the chimneys and the warehouses and the yellow scuddy foaming river give way to farmhouses and sheep and little bitten fields, and at last the wide-open spaces that were the moors. We got off the bus at the very furthermost point, where the road ended in a scatter of cottages and a pub that was called Master's End.

We stood on the white dusty road and all around us the moors stretched glorious and free in the hot afternoon sunshine. I had been a little worried about his limp but with a stout stick he walked almost as fast as I. I loved the moors, like the mountains. A great rush of joy filled me as I felt the springy heather under my feet, the wind tugged at my hair and I wanted to run and run and run. I tried to curb myself because of him, but after a few minutes it became an overwhelming desire.

I turned my face to look at him regretfully and to my great surprise he met my eyes with a happy grin.

'Go ahead,' he said, 'run.'

And I did. Leaping and bounding and shouting out to the clouds which raced me above. On the top of a hill I sat down and waited for him, watching with fanatical interest the little black crawling figure become real and masculine and exactly as I had seen it ten minutes before. He joined me, still smiling, and we shared a cigarette in companionable silence.

'Tell me about yourself, Ann,' he said eventually.

I told him, at first sketchily, but as his interest was obvious and the sky swam and the heather glowed, and we were drawn close through our isolation. I told him in detail about myself and my hopes and fears and ambitions, and about my family which had just arrived in Australia. About my three sisters and my mother and father, I told him in detail, reliving as I did so the seventeen tight years I had only just left behind. Sometimes he laughed and sometimes he asked questions, and when I had finished he looked at me soberly.

'How,' he asked me, 'could you come to part with such a wonderful family?'

I thought about this for a while. Now that they had gone and I missed them so much sometimes, I knew that they were a wonderful family.

'I don't know,' I said at last. An awful wave of homesickness engulfed me and I had to play with some heather so that he shouldn't see my tears.

'Look at me, Ann.' I turned my head and his pale blue eyes stared at me hard. 'I'm going to tell you a story,' he said. He held out his hands and pulled me to my feet.

'We'll keep walking and I'll tell you as we go along.' We walked slowly as he was a little tired by now.

'Once upon a time,' he began, 'a little boy grew up in the town of Johannesburg that is in South Africa.' It was the story of his life; the miles passed unnoticed as I listened to the tragic tale he told me.

His first memory, he told me, was of the four walls of the orphanage where he was brought up. At first he had been quite

31

happy there, playing with the other children, and it was only after he was sent to the local school that the fact that he was an orphan and lame into the bargain were driven home to him.

It seemed that he had taken it rather badly, and the other children had taken advantage of his disability. By the time he was fifteen he was nervy and neurotic, described by his masters as vicious and bad-tempered. He left school and the orphanage, a failure at his work and a social misfit.

His first job was bricklaying; he found himself some lodgings and after a while gave up bricklaying to become an errand boy, then shop assistant, then houseboy, then factory hand. He didn't hold any job down very long. The only thing that interested him even then, he told me, was the theatre. He would sit and watch the repertory players every week and long to be among them. They strutted across the stage flamboyant, handsome, confident, everything that he was not, and he envied them from the bottom of his heart.

This was aggravated by the fact that he had fallen in love with an actress. She lodged in the same house with him and although not of the repertory players, she did a very neat striptease act at the local music hall. She was called Louise and he had never been in love before.

He was twenty-three then, but pale and undersized so that he still looked in his teens. For a while it seemed that Louise returned his interest, but before he had been able to do anything about it she announced her engagement to the strong-man act which preceded her on the bill. He gave up his lodgings then and moved into a working- man's hostel.

For the next two years he did a further variety of jobs but now he had begun writing, short bitter essays, a couple of which were published in a Johannesburg magazine. It was one of these, which caught the imagination of the producer of the repertory players.

I gathered that it was a satirical essay on repertory. Anyway, the upshot of a subsequent meeting resulted in Leigh joining the company as stage manager and carpenter. He was happy then for the first time in his life and after a while he fell in love again, with another actress, only this time far above him; the leading lady of the company. He would talk to her sometimes, gravely, without her knowing of his feelings, and she would say to him, 'You are a strange boy but you rest my soul.'

One wonderful night she invited him to dinner at her house and there, after wining and dining by candlelight he took her in his arms and kissed her. It seemed that she rather enjoyed this, for thereafter the relationship altered considerably. He loved her fiercely and never for one single instant allowed himself to think that she didn't love him back. And then quite simply Leigh told me why now, a year later, he came to be over here.

There was a party one night after the show to celebrate his love's triumphant performance in a new play. She was very beautiful that night he said, in a silver, clinging dress. Very brittle and gay. People swarmed round her as though drawn by a magnet. The young author of the play never left her side. Leigh sat outside the circle, happy just to watch, proud with the knowledge that one by one they would all go and that she would remain his alone.

The party went on and on, people were getting drunk now. He noticed with a little frown that she seemed to be returning the author's overtures. It wasn't until four o'clock that people began to leave. He watched them stumble to the door.

'Goo' night Paul, goo' night Bill... Mario, goo' night darling... Goodnight Leigh.' He looked up. She was standing beside her fireplace with the young author's arm around her. For a second he didn't understand.

He said, 'I'm coming up now darling,' and looked pointedly at the author.

She gave a little laugh and said, 'Darling Leigh, how I love you,' and the author gave a little laugh too.

Leigh said, 'Wendy, I—' then he didn't say any more for the author stepped over to him grinning and said, 'Brother, do you want it wrapped up?'

Leigh whitened but, controlling his temper, addressed Wendy. 'Tell him to get the hell out of here.'

She smiled back at him. 'Don't be such a selfish baby, darling, Johnny's written me a lovely part and I'm going to be nice to him.'

'So now, Mr Peters, exit!' said the author bowing to him.

Leigh hit him. He had meant to give him a good uppercut but the man moved and the blow landed on the side of his neck so that he fell instantly to the ground, unconscious. The police were called in, the press arrived, and the young author was carted off to hospital with his life in danger, and in the morning Leigh was asked to leave the company.

At the end of the week he drew out all his savings and took a boat to England. He had been working since then, he told me, at a variety of jobs again, and had only left the last one, washing up dishes, to join the Floods through an advertisement in *The Stage*.

When he had finished I didn't know what to say. I could only think that he must be very unhappy and wondered why he had chosen to tell me his life story. I wanted to ask him lots of things, but somehow I didn't seem able to, and we walked on for quite a while in silence. I felt quite choked with pity for him but he, on the other hand, seemed happier than I had ever seen him. He laughed and whistled, and now and then pointed out flowers and birds with his stick.

On the next dip in the moors we came to a village. We found an old pub and I sat over a shandy whilst Leigh knocked back several Guinnesses and rum. We talked a lot then, suddenly and freely like a tap being turned on, and the rest of the day was one of the most perfect I had spent. It was not, however, until we had reached home and he had said goodbye to me at the gate that I dared ask him the burning question that was in my mind.

'Are you still very much in love with her, Leigh?' I asked him.

'No!' he said. 'No, I got over Wendy on the boat.'

I said, 'Oh!'

And he said, still slowly and smiling at me, 'A jolly good thing don't you think, Ann? It's nice still being as free as the air.'

I looked away from him quickly and murmured that yes, it was nice being free. But inside, my heart knocked about a little and I thought how wonderful it was that the whole of the summer should stretch before us.

It seemed extraordinarily sad to me then that Hilda Fellowes should come out with what she did come out with the very next day. Had it been a week later or even a few days later, I don't think it would have upset me so much. But coming as it did, immediately on top of our day on the moors together, the memory of which was still breaking over me in spurts of gladness, I was both shocked and hurt.

Rose and Leigh and I had walked down from Cockton Heath for the evening show, and leaving Rose in a chemist's shop, Leigh and I had gone on into the theatre together. We were early, but Hilda Fellowes was already making up in the dressing room I shared with her and Rose. The boys' dressing room opened off ours, so Hilda saw us come in together with our arms linked.

Leigh passed through to his room and his door had hardly closed behind him before she said it. She was making up very carefully and addressed me through her inadequate mirror.

'Nice boy, Leigh,' she said casually. 'So unaffected and sincere. Charming wife he's got too, I worked with her all last season.'

It was simple as that. Just a cosy piece of dressing room gossip. For a second my reflection seemed to spin round in the glass and I did not seem to be able to feel the stick of greasepaint I was holding. Then everything clicked back and I said in a vague, controlled voice so that no one would ever know, 'Oh, really? I didn't know he was married.'

'Oh yes,' said Hilda chattily. 'And very devoted they are too. She came down for a weekend and we never saw them except during the show. Mooning and spooning on the beach all day they were.'

'Where is she now?' I asked.

'Bognor!' replied Hilda. 'I read it in *The Stage* last week; soubrette on the pier at Bognor Regis.'

That was all. Rose came banging in and that was all we spoke about Leigh Peters' wife. I felt exactly as though I had been hit across the face, and on top of the hurt, very angry. All through the show I could hardly contain myself, but afterwards on the bus ride home I calmed down and began to ask myself why he should bother to lie to me.

I supposed with disgust that through long experience he had found it easier to strike up relationships by announcing that he was 'free as the air.'

I thought of the pathetic story he had told me and wondered if that was also a tissue of lies. Perhaps, I thought viciously, he finds that the sob-stuff angle helps as well.

All the rest of the week I carefully tried to avoid him, sticking close to Rose and catching the bus with her after the show. But on the Friday night he collared me in the dressing room and asked me outright what the matter was. He closed the door and stood with his back against it, and stared at me with his pale blue eyes and told me that he knew I had been avoiding him.

I suppose I could have said it then, could have repeated to him what Hilda had said to me, and I would have done too. But suddenly, in a flash, it seemed to me terribly presumptive and I thought quickly, what right have I to say I'm avoiding him because he's married? Anyone would think that he'd tried to seduce me or something; we only went for a walk on the moors, after all.

So I mumbled rather shamefacedly, 'Oh, I wasn't avoiding you,' and, 'whatever made you think that?'

He came over to me and took my hand and gave me his smile and said, 'My mistake then. I want specially to be friends with you, Ann. Will you be friends with me?'

I withdrew my hand from his and gave him a rather cracked smile and said, 'Of course!' and agreed to have a drink with him after the show. But at the last minute I made Sebastian and Rose come too.

On the way home Rose said she thought that Leigh had got a bit of a thing about me, and was very surprised when I told her I couldn't stand him.

'Why ever not?' she said. 'He's by far the best of the bunch and you leapt at going for a bus ride with him.'

I told her that I'd changed my mind about him. 'He's wheedling and sly and foxy,' I told her vehemently. 'And I want nothing more to do with him.'

At home Rose repeated this conversation to Mrs Welles, and Mrs Welles looked at me kindly and told me that there was as good fish in the sea as ever came out. And why didn't we draw up a list of our available men and see if we couldn't find me a really nice boy? Rose was rather taken with the idea, so after supper we settled ourselves round the kitchen table and set to work.

Mrs Welles and Rose, both being undernourished, were partaking of a bottle of stout. I should dearly loved to have joined them but was on a strict diet, so instead drew up the list.

It was a very discouraging list.

Willy Flood — Too dangerous.
Bill Irving — 70 and probably impotent.
Sebastian — Noticeable preference for older women.
Leigh — Out.

I read it out to them and they looked at me sadly.

'What you want,' said Mrs Welles bracingly, 'is a real man.' She took a deep draught of stout. 'Like my Mr Goat.'

Mr Goat was her gentleman friend, a foreman at the baked bean factory at Booth, misunderstood by his wife but greatly appreciated by Mrs Welles. He was certainly not my idea of a real man, having a drooping ginger moustache and receding ginger hair. Mrs Welles however, assured us that he had hidden depths.

'Or like my Derrick,' said Rose. Rose's fiancé would of course have been eminently suitable, a big, blond, clean-living youth, but as he was very much in love with Rose, and Mr Goat very satisfied with Mrs Welles, I did not find these suggestions helpful. I told them so and they looked rather hurt.

'Well love,' said Mrs Welles distantly, 'I was only drawing a picture. You are not, of course, Mr Goat's type at all really. He likes them dramatic.' She gave me a dramatic look.

'Hasn't Mr Goat got a nice friend?' asked Rose.

Mrs Welles pursed her lips and thought for a moment, but could only think of Mr Goat's wife's young brother.

'How do you feel about that, Ann?'

I shook my head briskly. 'Far too difficult for Mr Goat.'

'I dare say you're right,' said Mrs Welles regretfully.

We discussed the possibilities of friends of Derrick, but as they were all in Blackpool it was rather pointless.

'There's no getting away from it,' said Rose. 'The theatre is a definite handicap to romance.'

This was quite true. With playing every night our social life was nil. Mrs Welles was now quite disillusioned by us. 'Not a fan between the two of you,' she kept murmuring. 'Not a chocolate or a flower. Not even a nasty suggestion.'

She looked at me and shook her head. It was quite clear that she thought the fault was entirely mine. I was so annoyed at this that I thumped the table and fixed her with a steely eye.

'Mrs Welles!' I said, 'You've seen all our shows haven't you?' She nodded her head. 'You've watched my parts, week after week haven't you?' She nodded again and smiled at me ruefully as realisation dawned.

'Exactly!' I finished grimly. 'Mrs Flood's mother or grandmother for four solid weeks.'

We were silent then with the hopelessness of my situation. Then Rose started being bracing.

'I don't know why you've got this rooted objection against Leigh, Ann. It's very unfair you know, I mean, at least you could give it a sort of chance.'

Mrs Welles followed her up. 'Beggars can't be choosers,' she said pointedly.

A sudden wave of depression submerged me and I crumpled up the horrid list in front of me.

'If it's any interest to either of you,' I yelled from the door, 'I'd rather have that jungle navvy who whistles at me in the next road.'

'Now that's an idea, couldn't we ask him in to tea?'

Mrs Welles' voice followed me as I sailed upstairs. There I lay on my bed and felt very ashamed of my ungratefulness; ashamed too of the ridiculous reason for it. I told myself that I had better snap out of it at once. There I was, I told myself, working in the theatre, doing the one thing in the world that I wanted to do and all I could think of was men.

It was quite disgusting and unworthy, I thought, but at the same time I couldn't help wondering if his wife was Louise or Wendy.

Chapter Four

But after that I didn't think about it any more, as a wonderful and very important thing happened. I was given the coveted part of Cathy to play in *Wuthering Heights*. I never thought for a moment that I'd get it as the Floods cast on looks and not ability and Rose of course looked exactly right, being thin and dark and fey. She was surprised too. Mrs Flood said that she lacked spirit but as she'd been playing madly spirited juveniles for four weeks, that didn't ring true. I could only suppose that it was her latest angle of attack on the poor girl. Willy of course was playing Heathcliffe, and rehearsals were heaven.

Mrs Flood threw herself into the production and surprisingly enough gave me enormous freedom with the part. I had expected terrible scenes, as Cathy was really a better part even than Heathcliffe, but she just said, 'Play it from the heart,' and I did, and she said, 'You'll do!' and never once suggested that I was shaming Mr Flood.

Willy just squeezed my arm and gave me a quarter of jelly babies and went on acting magnificently. Rose was most unselfish about it all.

I knew that she'd wanted to play Cathy very badly and if I had been in her shoes I'd have been frightfully jealous, but she came up to me after the first rehearsal and asked why on earth I hadn't been playing lead all along.

All that week I had no thought for anything but the play. It was to be a costly production and Mrs Flood went really rash and hired period dresses for us from a costumiers. My hair was quite long so I just wore it loose around my shoulders with a fringe. I toyed with the idea of a black rinse but Mrs Flood said that my hair was my best feature and even if she was supposed to be dark, with all that frisking about on those moors no doubt the sun could have got at it.

I was frightfully excited on the Monday night, as it was my

first big part. I think I acted well because afterwards I got what I call my spiritual feeling. I don't get it a lot and then mostly only when I've written something, but when it does come – dear God, it is the most rapturous sensation in the world.

It starts with my body feeling that it is being buoyed up into the air, then my face burns fiery hot and my pupils dilate. There is a throbbing inside me, which is not my heart. The whole of me aches with a sort of love. Everything appears beautiful and things which naturally hold beauty are intensified, so that the branch of a tree across the window or an un-extraordinary evening sky, or the flame of the candle which I use to melt my hot-black, fill me with a longing of frustrated possession. Like when I was a child and taken to the mountains for the first time and people waited for my reactions, and all I could do was kick the car and say over and over again, 'There's nothing you can do about them.'

The thing which has caused my spiritual feeling is not important, I am dimly thankful, but inspiration is unleashed inside me; my mind seethes with brilliance and the old inspiration is just a stepping-stone. I've never tried to explain my spiritual feeling before; there is a lot more to it than I can write down. They say that drugs work the same way. I can understand people taking them.

So there I was, sitting in the dressing room wiping off my make-up in the middle of a spiritual. I was very slow, Rose was already dressed and scratching at the door. I told her to go on.

Tonight I would walk home alone. I looked at myself in the mirror for a long time and decided that I was getting prettier. In the mirror I saw the door open and Leigh Peters come in.

It vaguely crossed my mind that he should have knocked first but in his hands he held a bunch of flowers and his face was smiling at me kindly. My spiritual feeling burned inside me and I wanted to cry and throw my arms around him. I didn't of course, because of my spirituals being just feelings. They begin and end with the impulse; categorical, no actions.

He walked over to me and laid the flowers on my table.

'I was very proud of you tonight Ann', he said. He asked me to come and have a drink with him, and I discovered rather shakily that I wanted to have a drink with him quite a lot. I told him to go on and I'd meet him at our local. I carefully made up my face and put on a clean cotton dress and flat shoes, as he was only my height. I looked to see if there was a note in the flowers but there wasn't so I put them in water and stood for a minute sniffing. Hackneyed though it may be, there is no smell like greasepaint.

I was the last out of the theatre: the summer sky was midnight blue strung with fairy stars. It was warm and still and breathless.

The streets were empty and waiting. A pale shaft of lamplight lay along the murky little passage, which snaked around the theatre and led to the Ship Inn. I'm an actress, an actress, an actress! My heart sang to me as I sped over the cobbled stones, feeling them hard yet soft through the thinness of my shoes.

Where the lamplight ended and the passage was very dark and thick, I could hear the noise of the Ship in residence, a roar of fierce laughter, which came on waves in and out like the tide.

Leaning against the damp passage wall I was sharply aware of free will. There I was, nobody but me knew exactly where, nobody but me really cared.

I was seventeen, it was the night-time and I could do practically anything in the world that I wanted.

There was no one that I could hurt; there was no one who could hurt me. In a couple of seconds I could be in the pub, accepted, unquestioned, or I could turn now, and run back down the passage and catch the midnight train to London. And people in the carriage would accept me too, and I'd make them question me and I'd tell them that my parents were ten thousand miles away, but all they'd say would be, 'Australia? Oh! I've got a sister living in Australia – Sydney too.' And their pink faces as they leaned eagerly forward would not be concerned with me at all.

'When you next write to Mummy, Dear, ask her if she knows a Mrs Fish, F.I.S.H?'

Yet sharply as I was aware of my free will, I knew perfectly well that in two seconds I'd be in the pub. Normally this would have made me feel annoyed with myself, but as I was still in the grip of my spiritual, it just flooded me with an exquisite sadness.

The side door of the pub was suddenly flung open and the passage and I were dramatically floodlit. I couldn't decide whether to be waif or prostitute. I rather fancied the latter but as the two men came into focus I hurriedly decided on a waif.

I hung my head against the wall, shuffled my feet and moaned a little. They passed me by without a second glance.

My spotlight was turned off and now I ran as fast, as fast as I could to the top of the passage and around to the big main saloon bar. I pushed open the door, and heat and the smell of beer smacked me in the face. A lot of people turned and looked at me; six months ago I would have looked back with interest but since then I had learned that being blonde is a dangerous thing, and that I must always be haughty and on guard with strangers.

Any friendliness is always misconstrued. So with hauteur I looked for Leigh. Unfortunately, with his being small, I couldn't sweep my eyes above people's heads. I was just deciding that I would have to be misconstrued and sweep people's faces, when he saw me and yelled to me, squashed against a corner of the bar.

'What the hell have you been doing?' he said. 'I've been here for nearly half an hour, what do you want?'

'Shandy, please.'

He leaned forward to catch the barmaid's eye.

The pub was full and we were standing close together. I looked at him. He was wearing a soft blue and white checked shirt with a dark blue tie and cavalry twill trousers; no jacket. His face was flushed and the light shining down through a glass shade made his hair very pale and colourless.

From my closeness to him I could see that it was extremely fine and clean. It reminded me of white sand and I wanted to touch it.

His prominent eyes were colourless too, and I was fascinated by his eyelashes. They would have been long and rather beautiful but great clumps had been singed out through careless smoking, and the long ones lay singly and unnatural along his cheeks. His forehead was high, his nose straight, he had a pronounced cleft chin and an Adam's apple.

Looking at him sideways he seemed softened and vulnerable; I felt that if I touched his skin it would be warm and moist. My shandy arrived and we cheered each other.

He said, 'Did you enjoy yourself tonight Ann?'

'Oh Leigh, it was wonderful!' I forgot him as the show flung itself before me again. I launched forth at him remembering all the things that had happened, telling him what it was like to play opposite Willy then asking him politely, 'Did you enjoy the show Leigh?'

'I enjoyed watching you,' he said looking at me very hard.

I held his gaze and he said slowly, 'Let's get drunk tonight, Ann.'

My heart thumped inside me, not spiritual at all this time, dead physical.

'We can't,' I said. 'We're going to get thrown out in five minutes.'

He didn't take his eyes off my face. 'We can drink in the little bar at the back, the landlord's a sport. I've often done it.'

I didn't want to get drunk with him alone in a little bar at the back. I liked him as he was now, pressed in a corner with people touching us all round. I didn't want to be alone with him. I didn't want to have to think about his wife and his sob stories. I didn't want to be lied to any more.

I said, 'No, I think I'd better get home, Leigh. Anyway, we can't afford to go on drinking.'

He caught my hand. 'I've got some money, Ann. Please Ann, please.'

His breath smelt thrillingly of beer and his hand, which clutched mine, burnt suddenly hot. I felt frightened but at the same time weak inside. Where I got the courage to do what I did an instant later, I shall never know. On one shandy and the remnants of my spiritual feeling I made my eyes go cold. I withdrew my hand from his, feeling the heat ebb away.

'I won't drink with you, Leigh,' I said quietly. 'Because I don't much like being alone with you. I know we were very friendly on the moors, and it was very nice and I enjoyed it but I'd rather we just left it at that. I'd rather it was just we were in the company together.'

I stopped, waiting for him to ask me what was the matter, to ask me who had put me against him. I would have told him then, just have said quite simply that with my discovering that he was a married man, he must realise that it was the best thing. But he didn't say anything, just put back his head and shrieked with laughter; not amused laughter but wild and maniacal so that everyone in the pub stopped talking instantly and looked at us. He went on and on. I was acutely embarrassed and didn't know quite what to do. In the end I took a deep breath and plunged through the gaping crowd. At the door a drunk said, 'Whoa there, little filly,' and Leigh's laughter redoubled its volume.

Then at last I was blessedly through the door, trembling like a leaf. I forced myself to walk sedately down the street but once I had crossed the bright crossroads and started up the leafy road to Cockton Heath I began to run. I was afraid that Leigh might follow me as he had to come the same way, then I remembered with relief that he was lame and could never catch me up.

As I turned into The Rooley I heard the wonderful comforting sound of Mrs Welles' gramophone being played at maximum volume. The house was flooded with light and I entered the back door never more ready for one of her parties. Guinevere was heating milk on the gas stove, clad in an unsuitable night-dress of her mother's which had been cut down. Five cups from the best tea service were laid out on the table.

On seeing me she climbed off the stool and went and fetched another.

'Coffee,' she explained. 'They're in there.'

'How many?' I asked her.

'Two men and Mr Goat,' she replied sadly. 'They're making an awful lot of noise!'

They were indeed. I helped her with the coffee then suddenly looked at her sharply.

'What have you done with Launcelot? Don't tell me he's sleeping through this.' She looked up at me and her seven-year-old face, which should have been all innocence, flushed, and she dropped her eyes.

'Come on Guinevere, out with it – what have you done with Launcelot?'

Two tears squeezed from under her lashes and she mumbled, 'He's in bed.'

'No he isn't. Where is he? Gwinny, what have you done with Launcelot?'

'Mum give him some sleeping tablets so he won't wake up –

she says he must get his sleep.' She wouldn't look at me and started to cry properly. I knelt down and put my arms around her.

'Gwinny darling, it's not your fault. Anyway, I expect he's perfectly all right. We'll go and have a look at him, shall we?'

Launcelot lay motionless on the bed with his mouth open. He seemed to be breathing alright but he certainly did look a bit unnatural lying there. At the sight of him Guinevere went quite hysterical. 'He's dead!' she screamed. I told her that he wasn't and put her hand across his mouth so that she could feel his breath, but she was still terribly upset so I picked him up and put a blanket round him and carried him into the kitchen. Guinevere took the coffee in and I told her not to tell them that I was in yet.

I looked at the sleeping baby in my arms. It was the first time I had seen his face undistorted by some sort of emotion. Even so, it looked fierce. An iron jaw, a firm hard mouth, and a pug nose. His head was covered with a mass of red-blonde curls, and an array of scabs and bruises where he had banged it against things in rage. I tried to think of him as just an ordinary helpless little baby but there was no getting away from the fact that, at two-and-a-half years old, there was already something very wrong about him. He had a definite vicious streak in him, which was not caused by his having been spoilt.

I was more worried by his condition than I had let Guinevere see, and now that she was out of the room I bounced him about and tried to force some milk down him.

He didn't stir at all so I carried him out to the scullery and held him over the sink and turned the cold tap on his face. His eyes fluttered immediately and he opened his mouth to roar. I hastily withdrew him but he never got as far as roaring, instantly his eyes closed and he was asleep again. Still, I wasn't worried about him any more and took him back upstairs.

Guinevere came back into the kitchen and I told her that he'd just woken up and I'd put him back into bed. I went upstairs with her and we both had another look at him, then I tucked her up too. I dropped in at Mrs Welles' room and combed my hair and put on some more lipstick. Men, eh?

I wondered who she had dug up. It didn't take me long to discover. I opened the sitting room door and there, sitting bang opposite me in the fireplace, was the jungle navvy who mended the road two streets down. My first thought was of the sheer nerve of my landlady. Never for a single instant had I thought she would take me seriously. I was terribly angry but it all melted away as soon as I looked at her.

She was sitting in a low armchair, very beautiful and excited and her eyes met mine with a triumphant 'Look what I've done for you' smile.

She was wearing ridiculous black silk evening pyjamas patterned with red dragons, and a thin chiffon blouse tied high up on her midriff. Her hair was piled on top as usual, but she had made the awful mistake of putting the top of a meat paste pot around the knot. Make-up suited her and it was plastered on thick. She leaned towards me and the twelve bracelets pushed up her arm came clattering down to her wrist.

'At last love!' she breathed, 'A party thrown special for you. Wherever have you been? We thought you was never coming, didn't we Ed?' This to the jungle navvy in the grate.

He said, 'Aah!' and made sucking noises at me.

'Ann – Ed. Ed – Ann,' said Mrs Welles grandly.

Ed patted the piece of grate next to him, his mouth open with anticipation. Mrs Welles gave me a significant wink and flashed a satisfied look at Rose. I crossed over and sat down in the grate. A hairy arm was thrown around my shoulders, but I hardly noticed it as sitting dead opposite me was Rose – not even sitting, but sprawled abandoned across what looked like a blueprint of Ed.

'Steve,' said Mrs Welles, noticing my gaze.

Steve said, 'Hi!' and Rose kicked her legs at me.

The gramophone was churning out Johnny Ray numbers, with Mr Goat supplying the vocal. It was a sort of cabaret turn, which I had interrupted, but now that I was firmly established with a beer and Ed, attention was switched back to him.

He was frightfully bad and frightfully funny. To see the sedate Mr Goat with his collar awry, squeezing tears from under his ginger lashes while his voice broke with passion, sent me into fits. No one else was laughing and as he came to the end and gave me a frozen look, I realised that it was meant to be a serious take-off.

Mrs Welles, who had been looking at Steve and not Mr Goat,

on hearing my laughter, said automatically, 'He's a caution.'

But Rose with a breathy gasp in her voice murmured, 'Oh Mr Goat, you're divine!' Immediately everything was all right and a lot more bottles were opened.

I wondered then if Rose weren't sharper than I thought. By a neat piece of tact she had just saved the situation. I looked at her but she was looking extremely vacant. Perhaps she really thought he was divine.

'Where have you been, Ann?' she yelled at me.

'Having a drink with Leigh,' I yelled back.

'What!' she said theatrically. 'Oh, Ann!'

Mrs Welles made a hurried coughing noise and asked loudly for another drink. It was clear that she thought I was damaging my chances by such indiscreet conversation.

I turned to have a look at the symbol of my chances and then wished I hadn't. Stripped to the waist and two foot down in a hole in the road, he had seemed rather attractive, but now I could see the orange-peel texture of his unfinished face, his broken, blackened teeth and the hair growing out of his ears. Seeing me looking at him gave him ideas.

'I fancy you,' he said thickly.

'Well now, isn't that nice?' Mrs Welles was watching us like a hawk. 'She only said the other day how much she fancied you – didn't you Ann?'

Emboldened, Ed put his face against my hair.

Mrs Welles sighed and grabbed Mr Goat's hand. 'Paul!' she said mistily, 'Look at that picture! Look at that Emblem of Youth! Youth' she repeated, sinking her voice, 'There's nothing, nothing in this world like youth,' then sharply, 'don't you miss it, Paul?'

Mr Goat winced and put on a dance record. Rose immediately sprang up, pulling Steve with her. He was a little more refined looking than Ed and danced rather well. Rose was always carried away by dancing and, given an undesigning partner, was a joy to watch. But Steve, mistaking her abandon for advances, grabbed her after only a couple of steps and rained animal kisses on her face.

'Ooh, he's a caution!' shrieked Mrs Welles with high delight as the ill-fated Rose was dragged back to the sofa.

'Give us a kiss,' Ed said to me, his imagination fired, but with a coy 'Naughty, naughty,' I skipped up from the grate to change the record. All the time I was thinking about Leigh. I supposed he'd be home by now. I looked at my watch; it was twelve thirty. I imagined him dragging home on his lame leg and wondered what he'd think about. In a way, I was enjoying the party. I had no desire to go to bed. I loved the loudness of the music, the shrillness of Mrs Welles' voice, the strong taste of the beer, the stupidness of Ed and Steve. There were a lot of bottles still unopened; I decided that I would get drunk without Leigh.

After three more bottles I didn't mind Ed's arm around me. I wondered vaguely what Leigh would think if he could see me; probably that I was drowning my love for him. This made me giggle, from my safeness, the whole incident at the pub now seemed rather funny. Ed made another lunge at me, which I neatly intercepted. He was so stupid that the game was rather fun.

'Give us a laugh Steve,' said Mrs Welles, directing a look at the heaving mass on the sofa. Steve's head separated itself, dark with anger at the interruption.

'Aaw, give us a break Win,' he muttered, but Rose's face came up for air and we were all of us staring at him. Mrs Welles wanted a laugh so he must perform. Ed got him a nice helpful beer and I took him a cigarette.

He straddled his legs over the arm of the settee and launched forth on a rather questionable story. We shrieked with laughter. Mrs Welles thought she was going to die. Ed fell off the grate and set fire to the carpet, and Mr Goat's false teeth were on view to all. I wondered how Mrs Welles felt about the latter. Did he take them out at night or not? I decided that he was made to keep them in, as Mrs Welles was a great one on appearances.

Once started there was no stopping Steve. Story after story came out, each one bluer than the last.

By two o'clock we were so weak that we had to turn on the gramophone to stop him. We lay around then, silent, just drinking. I was steadily having more difficulty with Ed. He was very strong and the play was rapidly turning into a wrestle. Mrs Welles kept on saying, 'Give over Ann,' and clucking at me with annoyance. It appeared that Mr Goat was also being uncooperative and she was having as tough a time with him as Ed was with me.

They exchanged a sympathetic glance. At half past two she gave up the unequal struggle and decided on action.

'Bed,' she announced firmly, sweeping us all with her eyes.

'Good idea,' I said straightaway and dead keen.

She looked at me, delighted surprise on her face. Immediately I'd said it I realised what I'd done.

Mr Goat paled and Ed's arm tightened on me and he looked me triumphantly in the face and told me that he'd never picked a loser yet. I glanced a desperate look at Rose and signalled to her to come outside with me. In the corridor I clutched her.

'What the hell are we going to do, Rose? We've got to get rid of them.'

'Well,' she began dubiously, 'it's going to be awfully difficult. Steve's quite nice really too… Couldn't we…?'

I shook her with rage. 'You're drunk Rose! He's frightful – so's mine, they're both absolutely frightful. You're just being weak and I'm not going to let you see.' I shook her again. 'So long as we back each other up we'll be alright. You've got to back me up, Rose. Think of Derrick,' I said tragically. 'The man that loves you, the man who you're going to marry.'

That did it. 'Alright,' she said reluctantly. 'But it's going to be difficult. You see, Steve's sort of got the idea…'

I looked at her coldly. 'I should think so too, the way you've been carrying on.'

'What are we going to do, Ann?'

The door opened and Steve's voice shouted, 'Oi, you two!'

'Coming,' Rose said sweetly as I yanked her into the kitchen. I was doing some thinking.

'If we go in there again we'll be lost.' Rose nodded.

'There's nothing for it, we'll just have to go upstairs and lock the door and yell 'goodnight' on the way up.'

We crept upstairs and on the first landing I nudged her. 'Goodnight,' we chorused over the banisters and fled up the attic stairs. I slipped the latch down and we heard them pounding up after us. A minute later they thudded against the door.

'Oi! Oi! What's the hurry, we're coming open the door.'

We crouched on the floor.

'Come on, open up!' They muttered for a minute then one of them kicked the door. 'You don't want me to kick it down, do you?' he said, wheedling. We removed ourselves to the other side of the room.

Mrs Welles voice sailed up from the landing below. 'What's the matter? Stop that bloody noise.' There was the sound of Ed and Steve going down to her, then they all three came up again.

'Rose! Ann! Open the door. What's the matter?' Mrs Welles' voice was sharp.

I took a deep breath and went over to the door. 'Mrs Welles,' I yelled through it, 'will you tell them to go home? We're tired, we want to go to bed. Tell them they're being a nuisance.'

One of Mrs Welles' eyes gleamed at me through the keyhole. 'I don't know about that,' she said tartly, 'I should say some other people were being the nuisance.'

I addressed the eye. 'If you don't make them go they can sit there all night, because we're not coming out.'

There was some more muttering outside, this time heated, then, 'Go on, go!' we heard Mrs Welles shout above their angry voices, then the flip-flap of her mules going downstairs.

They didn't go. They were yelling at each other now and an instant later there was a thud followed by the noise of someone falling downstairs.

'Ooh, a fight!' gasped Rose excitedly, 'I hope Steve wins.' It was exciting; we ran to the door and listened. A terrific din was going on, on the landing. We could hear the biff biff of them hitting each other and the shriek of Mrs Welles trying to stop them. Of Mr Goat there was no sound.

After a while they crashed down the next flight of stairs, out of the front door and down the garden. We ran to the window and watched them. Ed was being supported by Steve. 'My hero,' breathed Rose. That did it.

I collapsed on the floor in hysterics and Rose followed suit. We heard Mrs Welles flip-flap upstairs again. 'Brace yourself,' said Rose, but the voice through the keyhole was excited and confidential.

'Want a fag, girls?'

I unlocked the door. Mrs Welles had changed into her negligee.

'My God, what a night,' she said with satisfaction and threw herself on my bed. 'What a night,' she repeated. 'And I must say you girls put a bit of pep into it. Their faces!' She giggled at the memory. 'Just like my NAAFI days!'

'I do wish I'd seen the fight,' said Rose.

Mrs Welles smiled with relish. 'Steve started it,' she said. 'He told Ed he hadn't worked hard enough on you, Ann. He said he'd spent the whole night on Rose, while Ed just gazed into your eyes. I must say I shall never understand you either.'

Mrs Welles looked at me as though I was a curio. 'There you were, begging us to find you a man, and then, when I literally go out on to the streets to find you one – and a showy one at that – what do you do? Calmly tell him that you're tired and going to bed.' Mrs Welles looked at me sharply, but refrained from adding the last word that was on the tip of her tongue.

I opened my mouth to protest but was silenced by a clank of bracelets. 'Not that I've given up. Oh no – I never admit defeat.' She flung back her head looking undefeated.

'It's all grist to the mill,' she said darkly as she stalked to the door.

'Don't go, Win,' said Rose.

She came back and sat on the bed. 'And as for you, Rose,' said Mrs Welles, 'you're not always going to have those looks, you want to start practising a bit more fire.' She gave Rose a fiery look.

'Where's Mr Goat?' I asked her.

'Sleeping!' replied Mrs Welles shortly. 'That man needs a powder.'

I lay back on my bed and watched the pinpoint of my cigarette. Mrs Welles and Rose started discussing making Rose a new dress. How beautiful they both are, I thought watching them, and how alike.

They were the same type, thin and dark and vivid-looking, but where the vividness carried on in Mrs Welles' personality, it ended in Rose's face. I found her extremely interesting though.

On the surface she would appear to have no thoughts, feelings or emotions at all; she was never really excited and never really sad. With her fiancé, as with us, she was good-tempered and amiable; all of us, that is, with the exception of Willy Flood.

I had thought at first that she might have a crush on Willy, as she had always been loud in praise of his looks and talents. I was never more mistaken. Ever since the night she danced with him on stage she had become very antagonistic towards him.

I couldn't understand it at all, as in many respects Willy's personality was similar to hers. I asked her why she disliked him so much; she said she didn't dislike him, but despised him for the way he kowtowed to Mrs Flood. I pointed out to her that we were all a little frightened of Mrs Flood.

'But he likes it,' she explained. 'He's proud of being under her thumb. If there's one thing I can't stand it's a mummy's boy. Why, he practically smoked his cigarette ration through a feeding bottle.' This was quite true. Willy was treated and acted as though he was six years old.

'Of course he's not very intelligent,' I went on, trying to draw her out. 'And maybe he's ashamed of it.'

'But he is intelligent,' she began – then broke off. 'Oh why the hell are we discussing him anyway? He bores me.'

I drowsily watched her now, brushing her hair. Their voices came to me dimly as I lay in a delicious coma between sleeping and waking.

'…pink I think Rose, with a blue underskirt…'

'No, blue with a pink, I should say, Win… either though would do with my colouring.'

'Yes, do with mine too,' murmured Mrs Welles thoughtfully.

'So it would,' said Rose innocently. 'Why don't you make one too?'

A second later I was wide-awake. We all of us were, straining our ears in the darkness. 'Did you hear it?' asked Rose. Mrs Welles shushed us up and we listened again. It came again, quite unmistakably, a dull thudding noise from the depths of the house.

'They're back!' Rose quavered out the words.

'Not for long they're not.' Mrs Welles rose grimly from the bed and made for the door. We crept behind her. At the top of the stairs the noise came again, a sinister noise, shuddering and unviolent, not a bit like the boys.

'Better get Mr Goat,' I said.

Mrs Welles looked a bit dubious but frightened too, and after a second's hesitation went into her room. The noise was repeated at irregular intervals but never any louder. Rose and I poked our heads round the children's door. They were sleeping deeply.

'When did you last see your father?' said Rose sepulchrally and for no apparent reason. Rather bad taste too, I thought as I wondered when the poor little things last had seen him.

Mr Goat was pushed out on to the landing wearing one of Mrs Welles' more masculine negligees. I noticed with horror that his teeth were out.

'What'th thith, what'th thith?' he lisped angrily.

Mrs Welles hit him and we listened again for the noise. It came clearly now from the kitchen. We crept downstairs in single file, with Mrs Welles bravely leading, Rose next, then Mr Goat with me encouraging from behind.

The kitchen was in darkness and no one put on the light. The noise was louder now; something was throwing itself against the door and every now and then a moan escaped from it. We were all of us dead scared; we stood in the kitchen for about a minute not doing a thing, then Mrs Welles' nerve failed her.

'Go on Ann,' she said. 'You open it!' I was paralysed. Mr Goat nipped behind me quick, 'Yes, go on Ann!' he said giving me a shove. Their white faces stared at me, why pick on me? I thought dimly. Then, you know you've got to do it Ann, you should be proud they picked on you. Very slowly, I walked to the door. The noise came again and I froze with fear.

'Go on!' Mrs Welles' voice behind me was a numb shriek. I put my hand on the latch and opened the door, and at my feet with a thud, rolled the body of Leigh Peters.

Mrs Welles and Rose and I screamed simultaneously. 'What is it?' Rose shrieked.

'Leigh,' I replied.

'Dead?'

'I don't know.' I thought he was dead.

'For Christ's sake put on the light, Goat,' snapped Mrs Welles. The light went on and we crouched around the body on the floor.

He was in pyjamas, with a great cut running down the side of his forehead and blood all over his face.

He moaned again and I realised that he wasn't dead. Mrs Welles knelt down and felt his heart.

'What's the matter with him?' I asked. 'Has he been attacked or something?'

She looked up at us from the floor. 'He's dead alright,' she announced triumphantly – Rose screamed again – 'Dead drunk!' He was; I could see now where he had been sick. We took him into the sitting room and laid him on the sofa. Rose got some hot water and I bathed his cut.

'There's nothing you can do for him now,' said Mrs Welles. 'You'll just have to leave him till the morning.'

I felt rather awful about leaving him but saw her point, so we covered him up with two blankets and shut the door. Mr Goat went back to bed and we three went back to the attic. We discussed what had happened until nearly dawn. Rose said he had sleepwalked, his love for me unerringly bringing him to our house. Mrs Welles thought he'd been with some girl who'd chucked him out; we were all of us foxed by the pyjamas.

I fell asleep, troubled by awful dreams where Leigh was chasing me and Ed was hitting him on the head with a club.

I awoke feeling absolutely frightful. My throat felt as though it had swallowed a haystack, my eyes ached, and I itched all over; I didn't like to think why. I lay in bed waiting for Rose to wake up whilst the whole of the night before flooded my brain.

Someone was coming upstairs; there was the rattle of china followed by the blessed sight of Guinevere carrying two steaming cups of tea. Rose immediately woke up and we gulped it in silence. Guinevere eyes lit up with fear.

'Did you hear us last night?' I asked her.

She nodded silently. Rose cleared her throat.

'Well dear, you know what Mummy's parties are.'

'There's a man on the sofa,' said Guinevere, 'he's cut!'

Rose and I leaned forward eagerly. 'Is he awake?' we asked in unison.

'Yes, he's smoking a cigarette.'

My heart lurched. Last night we had laid a limp body on the

54

sofa, now it was smoking… Leigh Peters… Alert, awake… Now we would know.

'Where's Mummy?' said Rose out of habit.

'Asleep,' answered Guinevere. 'And Ann,' her lip quivered, 'Launcelot's still asleep too. He won't wake up, not even for food.' There was shock in her voice; food was the one thing that Launcelot would respond too.

'I hung a piece of bacon over him and he didn't even move.'

'Go on,' said Rose with disbelief. I told her about the sleeping tablets and she tried to look contrite but there was no love lost between them. Rose was at present Launcelot's *bete noir*.

I groaned. The room was spinning round a little. First Leigh to deal with, then Launcelot then, 'Rose,' I screamed, 'rehearsal!'

We shot out of bed like bullets. Fortunately it was far earlier than I had imagined, nine o'clock, and rehearsal was not until ten thirty. Rose cursed me as I discovered it on the way downstairs.

We looked in at Mrs Welles who moaned 'Take it away' in her sleep. Of Mr Goat there was no sign. In the kitchen, Guinevere made some tea and we discussed what to do about Leigh. I had a curious repugnant feeling about going in and seeing him.

'Well, one of us will have to,' said Rose briskly. 'We've got to get him down to rehearsal.'

We sent her in with a cup of tea. Guinevere got confidential. 'He's been sick on the carpet,' she told me. My head swam again.

'He's dreadful Ann, absolutely dreadful,' Rose said excitedly, 'I mean, quite mad! I went in all pleasant and matter-of-fact and said, "Tea, Leigh," and he drank it and then I said very casually, "Don't forget rehearsal," and do you know what he said?' – her voice was indignant – 'These were his very words.' She flushed, '"My beautiful Rosette," he said, "I'm sorry, but you're not my type." Not my type! And all I bloody well said was, "Don't forget rehearsal."'

I poured her another cup of tea. 'Didn't he say anything else? Didn't you ask him about last night?'

She lit a cigarette. 'Well that took my breath away for a minute but I remembered that it's better to humour them, and asked him if he wanted something to eat. "Yes," he said in a poetical voice, "Ann, where is she?" I thought that was supposed to be a joke and laughed.'

'Yes, yes, and what next?' I was breathless with interest.

'Well,' she paused, looking sad that the only man I could attract should be mad. 'Well then Ann, he said, "laugh and the world laughs with you – cry and the world cries with you too," and started pretending to cry. And then –' she paused dramatically, 'He asked me to cry with him!' Guinevere and I gasped suitably.

'And at that of course,' continued Rose, 'I left him. Quite mad!' she said with finality, draining another cup of tea.

Guinevere buttered us two pieces of bread and we speculated on what to do with the madman. Rose refused point blank to speak to him again. She'd tried and he'd been told in plenty of time about rehearsal. I had no desire to see him then either, so we appeased our consciences by Rose shouting, 'I do think ten thirty rehearsal is early, don't you?' loudly outside his door.

We caught a bus down to the theatre and decided to tell Mrs Flood that his landlady had come round to say he was in bed.

'Not that that will make any difference,' said Rose gloomily. 'Remember that night she forced Bill Irving to go on with a temperature of a hundred and three?'

Mrs Flood duly exploded but she was so thrilled with the success of the previous night's show, that the rehearsal for the new play was abandoned, and she just grilled Willy and I through our big duologues all morning. As we finished at two o'clock she fixed me with an eagle eye.

'I shall hold you responsible for his appearance tonight, Ann King.'

'Old cow,' said Rose as we went extravagant with a bus home. We bought fish and chips at the bus stop and ate them en route; a hectic afternoon lay before us with no time for meals.

Rose thought that in view of his madness we ought to get a doctor in. 'It's probably only loss of memory,' she said authoritatively, 'but I know these first stages.'

I nodded at her, commiserating. Mrs Welles and I had received lurid details of her first fiancé who was now in a Home. The kitchen door was open, the wireless blazing, and the first thing we saw as we entered was Leigh and Mrs Welles tucking into eggs and baked beans.

He was wearing the communal masculine negligee, but apart from that looked extremely healthy and normal.

'Hi,' he said, waving a fork at us.

We preserved a dignified silence and sat on the copper. Mrs Welles winked at me with the leisurely manner of someone who has had the news first.

'Aren't you going to ask him any questions?' she said coyly.

'I'd rather hear it from you,' I said coldly.

Mrs Welles looked thrilled, dislodged a baked bean from her teeth and leaned back in the chair.

'Well…' she began, but Leigh interrupted her.

'Perhaps I'd better explain, after all…' He was silenced immediately.

'Leigh!' said Mrs Welles, 'My poor boy! We can't have you being upset again.' She gave him an upset look and turned to us.

'The suffering, humiliation and degradation that that boy had been through, you two will never know, will never be able to understand.' She weighed out the words at us accusingly.

We were isolated, by our inferior position on the copper and by the fact that she could know and presumably did understand. Rose made an irritated noise and I removed myself to the grate, and we both said, 'Come off it, Win,' but it was to no avail. It was three thirty before she finally condescended to give us an account of the adventures of Leigh Peters between the hours of 11 p.m. last night and this morning.

It seemed that after I had left him in the pub, he duly went into the little bar at the back and got drunk with the landlord. Paralytic he was, and quite unable to walk home. The landlord piled him into a taxi and directed the man to see him into bed, which he did, as Leigh luckily had his own key. The taxi driver undressed him and he fell on to the bed in a coma.

He didn't even remember lighting the cigarette. The next thing he knew he was fighting for breath, choked with smoke, the room lit up with flames, and his landlord was beating the bed with a rug. After that he was clouted on the head, lifted bodily up, taken downstairs and thrown out into the street.

He thought he must have lain there for some time. After a while he began to realise what had happened; all he could think of was finding us. It took him about an hour, he said, to get into the next road. He imagined he must have collapsed again when he found our door.

Told in Mrs Welles' inimitable style, both Mrs Welles and Rose were very moved by the end. I was rather, as well. 'And his clothes!' she went on, 'Thrown out into the road after him, they were. I found a few of them left on the hedge just now – but most of them have been pinched.'

I gazed at Leigh and he gazed back at me.

'What are you going to do Leigh? Where are you going to stay?'

'Where is he going to stay?' said Mrs Welles at once. 'He's going to stay right here, of course.'

'Yes, but where?' said Rose blankly. 'I mean, we haven't got the room have we?'

Mrs Welles' face switched into a winning smile and she offered Rose a cigarette.

'Now listen Rosie, love,' she said. 'And you too Ann – everything's been arranged, see!' She made a complete sort of gesture with her hands. 'Me and Leigh have been chatting all morning and we've got it all worked out, haven't we Leigh?'

Leigh implied with his head that they had.

'Now, you know the attic, girls,' continued Mrs Welles carefully, watching our faces. 'And you know that piece of string we've stretched across for you? Well!' She gave a gay little laugh, 'Well, you wouldn't recognise it any more now, would they Leigh?'

Leigh gave a gay little laugh.

'Oh no!' said Mrs Welles. 'You most certainly wouldn't recognise it any more now.' Her voice got cosy. 'We've hung it with two nice big blankets,' she said. 'And there on the other side, guess what?' She gave another little laugh.

'Yes, you've guessed it! We've laid out a lovely big mattress and made a sweet little bedroom for Leigh.'

Rose said, 'What!' and I said, 'Oh!' and there was a long silence.

Leigh got up and made for the stairs. 'Just another little boarder for the dorm.' he said brightly.

'Oh, he's a caution,' screamed Mrs Welles, but as soon as he was out of sight she turned businesslike and sharp.

'Okay with you girls? I need the money and he couldn't afford anywhere else.'

'Well, I suppose so,' began Rose. Mrs Welles went over to her and clutched her arm.

'I knew you wouldn't fail me, Rose,' she said huskily.

Guinevere appeared round the door with some shopping and Rose put on the kettle. I sat on the copper and thought that I had never known a room so rife with atmosphere. You could cut it with a knife.

Rose was humming in the scullery, Guinevere was unloading groceries, and Mrs Welles was lighting a fresh cigarette from her butt. Then I remembered Launcelot. 'Where is he, Gwinny?' I called out.

Mrs Welles raised a hooded eyelid from the cigarette-grafting operation. 'If you're referring to my son, Ann,' she said coldly, 'he's sleeping quite peacefully upstairs, thank you.'

I was piqued at her tone. 'Yes,' I said, 'I expect he is, it takes some time for a handful of sleeping tablets to wear off, doesn't it?'

As soon as she knew that I knew, Mrs Welles changed her tone. 'I had to give him them, Ann,' she said. 'The poor little mite would have got no sleep otherwise.'

'But he won't wake up Mum,' moaned Guinevere.

'Stop that,' said her mother sharply. 'And go and bring him down – and goodbye peace,' she murmured *sotto voce*.

Guinevere staggered down with the still unconscious Launcelot and we laid him on the table and looked at him. We tried food again, and Mrs Welles smacked him with relish, but he didn't move. I suggested the water again and we carried him out to the sink.

We turned the tap on him and he immediately fluttered his eyes.

'Don't overdo it,' shrieked Mrs Welles as he opened his mouth to roar. 'So long as he flutters he'll be alright. Now take him back upstairs.'

But Rose and I were firm. We turned the tap on harder until at last the familiar roars of Launcelot rent the house.

Rose and I walked down to the theatre alone. Indeed, Leigh

had not even come down from the attic. 'Probably hanging up his pictures,' said Rose gloomily.

I was flooded with a dreary depression. I remembered ironically how only twenty-four hours earlier, I had walked down the same hill with my heart alight with happiness and excitement and expectation.

How I had sat in the dressing room with butterflies hatching in my stomach and my only worry in the world was that I would act well.

'Rose,' I said, 'what are we going to do? I suppose we'll have to leave.' I didn't want to leave a bit. I loved the attic. I loved Mrs Welles. I loved the whole dramatic life of number eight. A wave of possessiveness surged up in me. Why should I give it up to Leigh Peters? And then I thought of him living in the same house, lying next to me in the same room.

'Where can we go Rose?'

'I'm not going, Ann.' She spoke decidedly. 'I couldn't afford to anyway, nor can you come to that. A twopenny-halfpenny little nitwit like Leigh Peters isn't going to get me out of my digs. I only wish I was in your shoes. God! What a situation! He's madly in love with you, sleeping in the same room as you, and you couldn't care less about him! You'll have a whale of a time while I just have to put up with rudeness, I don't know what you've got to worry about.' She looked at me out of the corner of her eye. She knew perfectly well what I'd got to worry about. 'Go on Ann, be a sport. I did you a good turn last night. You said it would be alright if we stuck together.'

'Okay,' I said weakly, but at the same time my depression melted as though it had never been, and relief and excitement started up in me instead. 'But we'll change beds mind.' At present I was sleeping on the string side of the room.

'Of course, of course!' Rose was beneficent with gratitude.

'Oh Ann, it really is rather exciting, isn't it? Anything could happen! I mean –' she went on hurriedly, 'suppose you go and fall in love with him! Well, you'd be frightfully grateful then, wouldn't you? I mean, sort of on a plate…' She trailed off.

I fixed her squarely with an eye.

'Look Rose, I dislike and despise Leigh Peters more than

anyone I've come across, I'm a bit frightened of him too. Therefore –' I said carefully and slowly, like talking to a child, 'there is going to be no romance. No romance, savvy? And you and Mrs Welles had better get that into your oversexed heads right away.'

Rose went huffy and we continued in silence. But not for long.

Every time we walked down to the theatre we had to pass the YWCA.

This afternoon Miss Fluck was weeding the front flowerbed with a large expanse of directoire knicker showing.

Rose grinned at me. 'I'm sure she'd love to have you back dear, wouldn't you like to go?'

'Quits!' We started off again on our home life.

'I suppose she really is broke, Rose, ten bob from each of us, Launcelot's family allowance, and what the husband gives her – if he does.'

Somehow I had never thought of Mrs Welles being broke. There was always food in the house and, often as not, drink.

'Well, I doubt if she gets anything from Goat.' Rose's voice was disgusted. 'Christ! She goes on about you enough but frankly I couldn't touch Goat with a barge pole.'

'Nor me,' I said fervently. 'I suppose she's in love with him.'

'Rot!' said Rose. 'She just lacks opportunity, that's why she's always on about you. Given our circumstances she'd be in mink by now.'

It made me sad to think of Mrs Welles, who was obviously cut out for mink, being fobbed off with Mr Goat.

'We'll keep our eyes skinned for her,' I told Rose. The more I thought about Mrs Welles not having money, the more I realised how essential it was that she should have. I had been naggingly worried about Guinevere and Launcelot for some time, and had a sudden picture of her growing old and losing even Mr Goat.

'There's no time to be lost,' I told Rose agitatedly. 'Promise to hand over anything you find.' As Rose very much fancied a mink herself I thought it just as well to get that point cleared up right away. 'Promise, Rose!'

'I promise,' she said smiling, magnanimous with youth as her asset number one.

The municipal theatre in Leek, with not really being a theatre but a town hall, had its inconveniences. Mrs Flood said the fact that it was a town hall lent tone; be that as it may, it did not alter the difficulty of there only being one dressing room.

This had been divided into two by a wooden partition built by Leigh, and the Floods occupied one half and Rose and Hilda and myself the other.

The men had to dress in a tiny room up a short flight of stairs, leading off our half, which held the communal lavatory. Conversation was therefore not private and everyone was always being madly indiscreet and wondering if they were going to get the sack.

A perilous balcony ran across the front of the dressing room with French windows leading out on to it from each half, and really urgent conversations could be indulged there. But as it was extremely high up and had an extremely low rail and overlooked the main street, even a placid argument attracted a large crowd hoping for a suicide. This intrigued Rose and I greatly at first, and on one occasion we staged a magnificent quarrel where I screamed and pretended to faint.

An enormous crowd gathered and people kept yelling up 'Don't do it!' and calling Rose terrible names.

We were thoroughly enjoying ourselves but then the shout went up, 'They've gone for nets' and we hastily went in. Rose and I sat on one side of the room sharing an inadequate mirror, and Hilda Fellowes crouched by the grate where, for no apparent reason, another mirror was fixed very low down. She sorely felt this position of degradation, although we had both offered to change with her.

We were still discussing Leigh Peters, but switched off hurriedly. Rose eyed the French windows longingly.

'Where's Leigh Peters?' said Hilda Fellowes, addressing me. 'I thought Mrs Flood told you to see that he came down?'

She smeared greasepaint heavily over her face. 'Sick!' she mumbled through the efforts, 'I expect he's lying sozzled in some pub by now.' Her rather pig-like eyes lit up malevolently. 'And then you'll both be for it!'

As she finished speaking Leigh Peters banged through our

dressing room and up the flight of stairs. I stood rooted to the spot, gazing at Hilda Fellowes, while the viciousness of her words still rang in my ears. I had known that she didn't like me, but that her virulence should have been directed at Leigh I found shattering.

'Charming!' 'Such a nice boy!' 'So sincere!' The epithets with which she had described him to me when she had told me that he was married, jarred oddly against the viciousness.

At that moment my mind was entirely innocent; I neither understood nor speculated nor analysed. I was aware only of the shock of her words and the unaccountable elation they produced in my heart.

We settled down to making-up. It was the half-hour of the day I loved best, quiet and dedicated, where with a few strokes of greasepaint I could change myself into someone else. A thousand different people I shall be before I've done, I told myself, and this week as glamorous and exciting as I could ever want, the bewitching Cathy. I tossed my head and gave Hilda Fellowes a 'Fie on't' look through the mirror.

The show went well again. We caught a bus home, suddenly dead tired; it was all I could do to get down a plate of baked beans, and we fell into bed. Hours later I woke up. Moonlight streamed through the window. It skirted Rose who lay soundlessly on my right; but where a ludicrously draped grey army blanket hung impotently across a piece of string, it lit up the sleeping form of a man. He breathed heavily, twitching and turning in his sleep.

Chapter Five

He settled in so quickly and with so little trouble that it was positively slighting. I hardly spoke to him for the first few days and, far from being a nuisance, he practically ignored me.

He always came up to bed much later than us, and in general conversation at meals etc., always addressed Rose or Mrs Welles rather than me. He got on very well with Mrs Welles and also with Guinevere, for whom he developed a great liking. He was horrified to find that she could neither read nor write and offered to relieve Mrs Welles of the responsibility and undertake her education.

This mostly consisted of teaching her French, which he seemed to know very well. He rather fancied her growing up bilingual and thought that she stood more chance, knowing no English grammar. Unfortunately Guinevere was frightened of him and not over receptive, but she was an obedient child and sat mumbling 'Je suis, tu es' after him by the hour. Mrs Welles of course was thrilled, but after only one little week got the idea that Guinevere should be speaking French like a native. 'In French please Guinevere,' she commanded whenever the poor child ventured a remark.

But whilst playing in *Wuthering Heights* I don't think I would have noticed much if he hadn't ignored me, for on the Thursday I acquired a fan. It was terribly exciting and happened in true *Gaiety Girl* style.

Wuthering Heights had been going like a bomb all week and on the Thursday night people had to be turned away. They were the most wonderful audience I had ever played to. They laughed, they cried, they cheered and in the right places you could have heard a pin drop. In the second interval the note came round. It was beautifully written on an expensive piece of notepaper.

Dear Miss King, (I read)

I am enjoying your performance so much. Perhaps you would do me the honour of sharing a drink with me afterwards, when I could discuss my favourite character with its very fine interpreter.

E Dropsey.

I showed it to Rose excitedly.

'What have you got to wear?' she said briskly.

We had a look at the limp cotton frock I had come down to the theatre in and Rose clicked her teeth with annoyance.

'Never prepared,' she murmured. 'It's just as well I happen to keep my velvet down here.'

Rose's black velvet coat was lovely, voluminous and dramatic and capable of covering a multitude of sins.

'Rose, you're a marvel!' I told her as I scribbled an answer on the other side of the notepaper. 'Thank you, give me about ten minutes grace and I will meet you at the stage door.'

I tried to have a look for him in Act Three. I guessed he would be pretty near the front so scanned the first two rows which were quite visible from the stage. There only appeared to be six men, and I quickly decided who it must be. Two obviously married couples, an old, old man, two very young youths, and sitting at the extreme end of the front row, a handsome, distinguished-looking man of about thirty. He stood out amongst everyone else as he was wearing bright tan and white shoes.

I caught his eye and he gave me a luscious wink. I was convinced then, and my heart leapt with anticipation.

'He's really smashing,' I told Rose as we removed our greasepaint, and I carefully applied a street make-up. Rose said she'd noticed him too and had to admit my luck was in.

'Never took his eyes off you,' she said. 'And judging by the shoes, he's got money. Probably a car too.' She looked at me with envy. Rose had got a thing about men with cars, on account of her fiancé Derrick having a motorbike on which she was forced to spend her weekends.

Hilda Fellowes was outraged at this conversation. 'No wonder the theatre has got such a bad reputation,' she said buckling her camel-hair coat, adding tartly, 'Here we are, struggling under great odds to bring a little culture to Leek, and all you can think of is picking up some wolf who you've never even seen before.'

She marched to the door. 'I'm afraid I put a higher price on myself than that.'

'I don't think you'll get it,' I yelled after her. 'The market's too crowded in the theatre.'

'Nerve!' muttered Rose. 'Of course we all know what's the matter with her...' She broke off as Leigh and Sebastian and Bill Irving all crossed through our room.

'I've got a fan,' I told them proudly. 'He's waiting for me at the stage door. Have a look at him as you go out, he's really something.'

They smiled at me delightedly and Sebastian winked and produced a flat, empty whisky bottle from the inside of his jacket.

'Get it filled for an old actor-laddie,' he said hoarsely. 'Slip it under your garter and wait till he's in the gents.'

I was standing swathed in Rose's coat with no other colour showing. A symphony in black I described me to myself, and felt that I looked rather mysterious.

I saw Leigh looking at me, then he leaned over and picked one of the flowers he had given me out of the vase on the dressing table, and tucked it in the black velvet Alice band I was wearing around my hair. It looked wonderful, pale pink and the one touch of colour that I needed.

'Goodnight... Don't do anything I wouldn't do... Don't get drunk...'

I looked up sharply.

'Speak for yourself Leigh Peters!' He made a face at me and I smiled back. It was the first sign of friendliness we had shown each other since he had moved in. Rose trooped out with them and I waited a few minutes so that I could make an entrance. I gave myself a final check in the mirror, then locked the door and sailed downstairs.

On the turn before the final flight, I combed my hair again then, re-swathing Rose's coat, turned the corner and stood looking down on the stage door. I looked again, I blinked my eyes, and I felt my face sort of freeze up. Directly beneath me, and leering up at me from toothless gums stood a hideous old man.

His right arm was extended under the clutch of an enormous box of chocolates. It was quivering violently; I could hear the cellophane paper rustling.

I regained my composure immediately. Angry disappointment flooded me, and still I couldn't be sure there wasn't a mistake. I walked slowly down to him looking past him, through the open door on to the cobbled passage for the tan and white shoes.

'I got your note m'dear,' said Mr Dropsey. There was no mistake.

I held out my hand to him.

'Delighted to meet you, Mr Dropsey.'

He transferred the chocolates with difficulty to his left arm and gripped my hand.

'Miss King m'dear!' he breathed.

We walked down the passage to his car, which was parked in front of the theatre. It was a Rolls Bentley and my heart lifted a little as I noticed the chauffeur at the wheel. He leapt out and helped us in, and tucked a communal rug around our knees. I hastily indented the space between us with my handbag.

'*Cercle Rouge* please, Withers,' said Mr Dropsey into the dividing glass. I leaned back against the cushions and we purred off. Mr Dropsey swivelled round so that he was three-quarters on the seat and could face me. He dropped the chocolates on to my lap.

'For a clever little girl,' he said fatuously.

I thanked him and told him I was glad he'd enjoyed the show.

He looked rather surprised. 'My dear, it was quite the most shocking production of *Wuthering Heights* I have ever seen.'

I said, 'Oh!' coldly.

'Quite disgraceful,' he continued. 'But then of course these companies ought never to be allowed. What in heaven's name was that fat oaf doing blundering about as *Heathcliffe*?'

That did it. I considered Willy's *Heathcliffe* quite brilliant. I stopped leaning back in the cushions and sat up, pushing the chocolates as far off my knees as possible.

'Mr Dropsey,' I said, 'I think you are labouring under a misapprehension. I agreed to meet you because I thought that you had enjoyed the show and wanted to discuss the play with me, but in view of your present attitude I'm afraid I must ask you to drive me straight home.'

The speech came tripping off my tongue as though we'd been doing a season of Oscar Wilde. If I had had a fan, I'd have rapped on the driver's glass compartment.

'Now wait a minute, wait a minute little girl,' said Mr Dropsey swivelling further round so that only half of him was now on the seat. 'You've got me all wrong.'

I stared out of the window at the Leek women's public baths.

'It's you that we're going to talk about, you and your wonderful performance, which saved the play, which made the play, which magnetically drew me in, after Monday's show, again tonight.'

I turned my head a fraction. Mr Dropsey continued down my left ear.

'I was only letting you know how bad were your companions, that I could begin to let you know how great was your triumph.'

I was partly mollified but I wasn't going to let the crack about Willy pass. I addressed a cemetery we were passing.

'Mr Flood who plays Heathcliffe is a very fine actor. He has taught me everything I know. Should you have enjoyed my performance then it is entirely due to him.' I was still being madly Edwardian. I tossed my head and felt Leigh's rose slip and droop over my left ear.

Mr Dropsey's voice came back rather muffled through the petals.

'Such charming, innocent modesty; dear me, I haven't the heart to disillusion – or should I say illusion!' He gave a teetering laugh.

We were out of the town by now but still in a built-up area. A couple of minutes later we purred to a standstill and the chauffeur shot out of his side and round to ours to open the door.

A single handsome gold and white door stood in the wall, lit by a square dim red light, which arched above it from a wrought iron bracket. *Le Cercle Rouge* was written around it in black with a word on three of the squares. As we got out of the car the gold and white door opened, and a bland looking commissioner stepped out into the road.

'Good evening Mr Dropsey, sir,' he said deferentially, then giving me the once-over, 'Madame,' – less deferentially.

I led the way down a white-carpeted staircase, feeling rather frightened. I had expected a drink in the lounge of some smart hotel, but a nightclub... I clutched my velvet coat tighter around me, for that was what it was. At the bottom of the staircase a waiter sprang forward.

'Table for two, Mr Dropsey sir? Aah!' He snapped his fingers. A lesser waiter in the distance looked up and nodded, and we followed the important one across the little semicircular room to a seat by the band – only a quartet, but they throbbed away sensually on a gold platform.

In the centre of the room a fountain played; the water cascaded down bright pink and ran away under a glass floor where there were imitation water lilies and false fish floating around. Set in the ceiling directly above the fountain were three pink and blue fluffy clouds, which moved around. The walls were covered with embossed red velvet, and dark red lamps glowed on all the tables. I had never been inside such a grand place before.

'And what's the little girl going to eat?' asked Mr Dropsey as a waiter hovered with a menu.

I hadn't realised that we would be eating, but I wasn't going to let him see that. I studied the menu, outwardly carefully, but inwardly wildly, then with relief found the dear familiar word, melon.

'Melon, I think, and er –' I paused just long enough, 'steak.' I knew I'd be safe with steak.

'And to drink?'

'Champagne please,' I said boldly.

The waiter still hovered. 'Would madame care to remove her coat?'

'Yes!' said Mr Dropsey. 'Give him your coat, m'dear.'

It was stifling hot, but I thought of my limp cotton frock underneath, and its childish puff sleeves; the two women sitting nearest to us were respectively strapless and backless.

'No, thank you,' I told the waiter superciliously.

He gave a funny little laugh and daringly raised an eyebrow at Mr Dropsey.

The room was not full and whilst we waited for our food I took stock of the other patrons. I was surprised to see that there were a lot more women than men, and even more surprised to see that most of them were unaccompanied by a man. I could understand a couple of dowager gals on a night out together getting through a mountain of food, but these girls were young and extremely attractive.

Strapless and Backless sitting at a small table to our right and sipping Coca-Cola were quite beautiful. I was just about to comment on this to Mr Dropsey when a waiter came across and tapped Backless's bare back. I watched her get up and follow him to two tables up where a man was sitting alone. They were introduced and she sat down beside him.

Realisation dawned and my face burned at my naivety.

Our food and champagne arrived, and Mr Dropsey embarrassingly insisted in front of the waiter that the little girl wanted the cork. I didn't want the nasty cork at all, but the waiter nauseatingly cut a slit across it, stuck sixpence in it out of his own pocket, and handed it to me as though he was giving me the fairy off the top of the Christmas tree. I thanked him and pretended to put it in my handbag but dropped it under the table.

During the meal, which was first class, Mr Dropsey endeavoured to draw me out. I told him sketchily what I had done and what I hoped to do, and he told me that he was in lampshades, a widower and that I must come out and see his house one day.

These confidences exchanged, I returned to eating, and Mr Dropsey (who had only picked at some smoked salmon) to drinking. Suddenly the band, which had been playing popular tunes, went into a classical piece of music. Mr Dropsey put down his glass with a clatter, seized my chin with his hand and turned my face to his.

'Aah!' he breathed, fixing rather bloodshot eyes on mine. '*La Fille aux Chevaux Blancs*. The most beautiful thing ever written, he might have written it especially for you.' He removed his hand from my chin and fingered a clump of my hair. The rose slipped a little further and a shower of pink petals fell on to the back of my coat.

They really did look rather beautiful, and with the sad sweetness of Debussy surging around us, I was suddenly sharply aware of the atmosphere – his atmosphere. I removed my hand, which was still clutching a fork-full of steak and slowly, with the forefinger, traced a pattern between the petals.

I could feel his eyes watching me and when at last I slowly raised mine, fluttering the lashes a little, his face was wobbling with emotion. I was fascinated by it. It was a round face of a mottled puce hue and very loose. Underneath his eyes, which had sunken back with age, the skin was draped and looped in folds, like the net curtains in Mrs Welles' bedroom.

His mouth was rather sunken too, but he had been born with prominent gums and the lips clung around them like an old creeper. He had had bad luck with his teeth too, but on account of the prominent gums, had disdained false ones. Two lower stumps and one long intact upper remained. At the back I was glad to see he had been more sensible, a dull gold glitter shone when he smiled. His mouth was his last feature.

The rest of him fell away in a further wealth of folds painfully checked after a while by a stiff white collar. I supposed he was about seventy.

The emotion he was expressing started in a twitch somewhere about his temples, then rippled along the folds of flesh with the inevitability of the trucks of a goods train shunting into one another. I gazed at him while he still clutched my hair.

'Hi, Teddy darling,' said a pampered voice.

Mr Dropsey let go of me in a hurry and we both looked up.

Backless had waltzed up to the table with her escort. She blew Mr Dropsey a kiss.

'Neglecting us tonight, darling?' she said, eyeing me with distaste.

Mr Dropsey picked up his champagne and took a steadying swig. 'Hallo Celeste,' he mumbled.

'Woofy – Teddy, Teddy – Woofy,' said Backless, bending down to her partner a little; he only came up to her shoulders.

'How do?' said Woofy, looking at me. He gave Mr Dropsey a wink. 'Coals to Newcastle, eh!' Backless shrieked with laughter at this.

'Miss King,' said Mr Dropsey, indicating me with dignity.

Backless swaggered forward with extended hand. 'Oh, Miss King!' she mimicked with a refined accent. 'This is an honour.'

I refused her hand and Woofy yanked her back on to the floor. Mr Dropsey appeared a little shaken by the incident and slopped champagne on my coat whilst refilling my glass.

'Quite a character, Celeste,' he said, laughing nervously.

There was a sudden rumble on the drums and the little red lights and the cloud switched off.

'And now,' said a voice through the microphone, 'it is cabaret time, and tonight we have for your pleasure that very popular young French singing star, Monsieur...' The popular young French singing star's name was never known as, at that moment, something went wrong with the microphone and a loud booming noise hurt our ears. There was a click and it returned to normal.

'Sorry about that,' continued the voice, not bothering to repeat itself. A spotlight hovered on to a space in front of the fountain and a rather cross-looking young man emerged from behind the gold platform carrying the microphone.

Once under the spotlight he formed his face into a heartrending little boy look and addressed us with a beautiful foreign accent.

'Ladies, gentlemen,' – helpless hand gesture and intensified little boy look – 'Here I am,' – whimsical shoulder movement – 'So!' – roll of eyes which cleverly concealed cue for band – 'Here we go!'

The band and he went into *La Mer*. He sang well with a lot of breathiness and catching in the throat, which was just right for a nightclub. After that he did a selection of Maurice Chevalier numbers and then with us nicely softened up and receptive, finished with *September Song* sung in the pathetic broken English. Unfortunately the microphone started going wrong again and the effect was lost. He finished cross and not a bit heartrending, and wouldn't take a bow.

Mr Dropsey ordered another bottle of champagne and picked his two lower stumps with an ivory toothpick. I chain-smoked a box of black Sobranie cigarettes.

'M'dear,' said Mr Dropsey between picks. 'Did anyone ever tell you that you were a very beautiful little thing?'

I had had this remark made to me before and was still pondering on the correct reply. As it was I said, 'Oh, Mr Dropsey,' coyly.

Evidently it was considered a suitable rejoinder. Mr Dropsey extracted his toothpick, laid it on the table and put his hand on my knee. 'Tell me I'm going to see you again, little girl,' he breathed. I had been waiting for this question all evening; never had I enjoyed anyone's company less than Mr Dropsey's, and about an hour ago I had decided on my answer. I was going to be sweet and firm and tell him about the boy I was engaged to in the company.

'Mr Dropsey!' I began looking at the champagne bottle – and then I didn't go on, just looked and looked at the champagne bottle whilst the idea smacked me between the eyes. I cursed myself for being such a blind fool and shuddered as I thought of what my selfishness had nearly lost. It bubbled back at me innocently from the bottle – money. I felt the weight of it from the gnarled hand pressed into my knee – money. I saw Mrs Welles sitting round the kitchen table eating chips out of newspaper like a duchess her caviar. 'Go on Rose,' she'd be saying, 'tell us what the note said again?' My heart lurched with love for her. I would secure the prize at my side and hand it to her in a Rolls Bentley. I kept staring at the champagne bottle. Mrs Welles laughed back out of it clad in a shining mink.

The pressure on my knee increased. 'Yes, yes m'dear?' said Mr Dropsey eagerly.

I gave him a dazzling smile and put my hand over his. 'I'd love to see you again, Teddy,' I said with the trace of a lisp.

I was suddenly ecstatically happy. 'More champagne please,' I said, grabbing the bottle myself. He caught my mood and in an excess of abandon, picked up his toothpick in mistake for the swizzle stick and swirled it around my glass.

We stayed for about half an hour longer over a couple of liqueurs and then I suggested that we went. He demurred rather half-heartedly, but he'd been yawning for quite a while by then, and with a little more persuasion asked for the bill. I discreetly retired to the ladies' but I needn't have bothered as he just scribbled something on the paper and followed me out.

The manager, several waiters and the commissioner bade us goodnight, and Withers emerged from some shadows and opened the car door. The rug was tucked round us again, but this time when I tried to indent it with my handbag, Mr Dropsey had got there first, and it just lodged on top of his hand. I gave him my address, and reassuring myself by the feel of the chocolates on my right, submitted to Mr Dropsey's clutchings on my left.

I felt rather like a girl in occupied France obtaining food for her family and wished I had a rosary to finger. All the time I was thinking, and when we discussed our next date for Sunday I arranged that he call for me at number eight, to take me for a spin in the country.

We were soon home. I leapt out of the car quickly but was nice to him through the window. 'Goodnight Teddy darling, and thank you for a wonderful, wonderful evening.'

He waited until I had disappeared round the back of the house, then I heard the car move off.

The light was still on in the kitchen, I opened the door softly and there was Leigh Peters, sitting in Mrs Welles' chair with his arms on the table and his face buried in them, fast asleep. I shook him gently.

'Leigh, you silly boy, wake up!' He opened his eyes drowsily. 'What did you want to wait up for?' My voice was matter of fact but inwardly I was rather touched. He yawned and looked at his watch.

'It's three o'clock, what the hell have you been doing? I've been worried stiff about you, I thought you'd just gone for a drink.'

'I've been to a nightclub,' I told him grandly. 'I've had a wonderful time.' He grinned and got up from the chair.

'What with, Grandpa or the chocolates?'

I put the chocolates on the table and blushed a little as I remembered how I'd told them I was going out with Tan-and-White Shoes, and asked them to look out for him at the stage door.

'Well!' I said defiantly, 'No one could have given me as expensive a night out as I've had with Grandpa.'

'Go on up to bed,' Leigh said, 'and I'll bring you up a cup of tea.'

'No, don't bother Leigh.'

'Go on!' his voice was firm as he held the kettle under the tap. 'It'll settle the champagne.'

How kind he is, I thought as I crept upstairs. He may have a thousand other faults, but how very kind he is.

I lay in bed smoking a black Sobranie and he brought me a cup of tea.

He took his over to his mattress and undressed behind the army blanket. We didn't talk at all.

'Goodnight Leigh, thank you.'

I was asleep before he had started on his cup.

Mrs Welles was not up when we left the next morning but I told Rose all about it during rehearsal. She was as thrilled and excited about the idea as I. I told her everything that had happened the night before, and she was very thorough and made me remember the minute details, like the material of his suit and whether there was a rug on the floor of the car, so that we could assess his full value. On totting up we decided that it was Mrs Welles' big chance.

'We'll have a really serious confab with her this afternoon,' Rose said as I missed my entrance for the third time.

I had been in a state of giggles all morning, partly because we were rehearsing *What the Butler Saw*, and partly because the whole of the company had been sending me up.

I had purposely waited until everyone had gone last night before making my entrance, and they of course, one by one, had all passed the grinning, toothless spectacle of Mr Dropsey and the chocolates.

Sebastian would keep stumbling up to me, clinging on to a brace with a terrible lecherous expression on his face and saliva running down his chin, and then do a sort of collapse. 'It's no good. It's no good!' he kept quavering brokenly, 'I've left me little black pills at home.'

But the final straw came at the end of the morning. All through rehearsal Mrs Flood had been suspiciously nice to me and hadn't even mentioned my missed entrances. We were just preparing to leave the theatre when she shrieked down at me from the dressing room.

'Ann, come up here a minute, Mr Flood and me want to talk to you.'

'Delayed action,' said Leigh, as I turned pale. 'I've been watching her all morning, her zip came undone when you took one of Willy's lines in Act Three.'

I wobbled upstairs; a visit to the holy of holies could herald but one thing, a scene.

'Now don't go under,' said Sebastian bracingly. 'Try and study it from the psychological point of view, she's extremely interesting material.'

I knocked on the door and Willy let me in with a grin. Their dressing room was quite fascinating but as my visits were always short and extremely emotional. I was having to study it in a sort of serial form.

Willy motioned me to a theatrical basket and I sat down on its uncomfortable lid. Opposite me Mrs Flood sat at the dressing room table wearing her fur. I called it her undyed lion as it was yellow and rather bitten, but Mrs Flood was inordinately fond of it and wore it on most occasions. Willy sat down on a low stool with 'Willy' written across the seat and lit a cigarette.

For a moment nobody spoke and I was able to get in quite a bumper edition of study. On my last visit I had been rather sunken and cowed and hadn't been able to take in much, beside the fact that Mrs Flood had twenty-three pairs of shoes and had got through twenty-one bottles of British sherry; but now I looked at the wall above her head. It was covered with rather crude, highly coloured watercolours all done by Willy.

He was supposed to have a passion for painting, but once when Mrs Flood presented him with a very expensive camel-hair brush, he threw it on the floor with rage and trod on it. He had to come and borrow some secotine from Leigh to mend it.

'I wouldn't mind,' he confided to him, 'if she'd only let me do a few portraits, I'd love to do say Rose's or Ann's head, but she won't hear of it, just endless bloody views.' Remembering this, I was surprised to see that there was a figure in each picture, painted suitably or unsuitably somewhere into the landscape.

I looked harder and saw that it was the same figure in each; that of a rather sexy-looking dark young girl. This staggered me until I read the captions underneath. 'My wife watching the sunset'. 'Lily Flood in the hayfield'. 'Lily and the moon'. Under every picture was a similar title. Mrs Flood followed my gaze. 'Clever boy, isn't he?' She leaned over and ruffled Willy's curls and gave me a dazzling smile.

'Sherry, Ann?' I saw then that they were both drinking.

'Thank you, I'd love one!'

Mrs Flood uncrossed her legs and rehooked a bedroom slipper that had fallen off. 'Get me a glass, Willy.'

Willy crossed to a packing case, delved amongst its depths and produced a glass wrapped in sawdust shavings. I realised then the extreme honour that was being bestowed on me. Mrs Flood poured me a small measure and we all toasted each other.

'Mr Flood and me want to talk to you Ann,' began Mrs Flood kindly. 'It's rather personal.' She poured herself out another sherry. 'Mr Flood and me have thought all along that you're a very good actress, and you didn't disappoint us on Monday. A lot of other people weren't disappointed neither,' – she gave me a rather coy look – 'if you know what I mean... Gentleman and that, eh!' She laughed rather heavily. 'Stage door Johnnies eh! I don't know! Mr Flood and me saw your gentleman friend last night.' She gave another heavy laugh and shook her head. 'I don't know!' she repeated.

There was a long, long pause. Willy hummed under his breath. Mrs Flood swatted a fly on her leg; her voice when at last she spoke seemed to come from a long way off.

'Classy looking gentleman too, expensive clothes. A very wealthy gentleman Mr Flood and me should have said.' Mrs Flood narrowed her eyes and stared into the distance. I watched, hypnotised whilst her bedroom slipper levered itself away from her foot and lodged perilously on the nail of her big toe.

'I should say,' continued Mrs Flood, 'that a gentleman such as the one Mr Flood and me saw you with last night should have taken you to a very nice place, spent a lot of money on you, I should have said.' She looked at me questioningly. The bedroom slipper fell off.

'Yes!' I said. 'He did take me to a nice place. He was very generous.'

'Just as I should have said.'

Mrs Flood eyed the fallen bedroom slipper wearily and tried to rehook it without uncrossing her legs.

'Just as I said to Mr Flood, a classy gentleman like that I said, will always recognise class. It must have made him happy I said to Mr Flood, to discover here in Leek, Living Theatre of a standard of production such as he witnessed last night. Happy too, to watch the likes of Mr Flood,' – here she coughed discreetly so as not to bracket us too closely – 'and yourself.'

There was another pause. Mrs Flood triumphantly regained the slipper and celebrated with a further measure of sherry, which she drained at a single draught. Still staring into the distance she went on.

'But you and me Ann know of course that the standard of production such as your gentleman friend saw last night is very difficult to maintain in Leek. Your gentleman friend is going to be sad, I shouldn't wonder, that we're going to have to do *What the Butler Saw* next week.'

There was another long pause, then: 'I shouldn't wonder,' said Mrs Flood slowly and clearly, 'but what your gentleman friend shouldn't want to do something about it.'

She swivelled round for the first time and faced me.

'Mr Flood and me are very fond of you Ann, we think you show great promise and class of acting. Our only grief is that we can't always train you in the standard of production your gentleman friend saw last night. I was only talking to Mr Flood about it last night; in fact it was the very topic of our conversation as we passed your gentleman friend. "What a shame," I was saying, "that that poor girl can't have a chance to act like that every week." Your gentleman friend must have overheard me. "Terrific, isn't she?" he said to Mr Flood, and then outside Mr Flood got the idea. "I shouldn't wonder," Mr Flood said to me, "but what that gentleman isn't the very answer we're looking for!"'

I looked at Willy; he was reading a science fiction comic and quite oblivious of the conversation.

Mrs Flood continued. 'And then of course I knew Mr Flood

was right, I knew that the wealthy gentleman who appreciated you so much should be told.' Mrs Flood's voice dropped to a tragic whisper. 'Should *have* to be told, of how through painful necessity a great talent is going to be lost. And I know,' – her voice inflected upwards – 'that a gentleman such as the one Mr Flood and me saw you with last night would never fail you.'

There was silence in the room except for a sharp slap, which Mrs Flood gave to another fly on her leg. My inside nearly burst with the desire to laugh but somehow I kept silent.

'Do you want me to speak to him or will you?' I asked her.

Mrs Flood looked sad that I couldn't have wrapped the remark up better, but said that she had given the matter a lot of thought and had decided that I was to feel my way around a bit, and once I had found that he felt the same way as Mrs Flood knew he would, to arrange a meeting between them. I was rather enjoying myself.

'Shall I state the sum we require?' I said cruelly.

Mrs Flood looked rather sick and couldn't fancy the rest of her sherry.

'Ann! Ann!' she said fretfully. 'That's not a nice way to talk. This is a delicate business here we're dealing with, Talent and The Arts.' She looked at me sharply and dead serious, 'And remember that when you're talking to him.'

The interview was over. Mrs Flood leaned back in her chair looking dissatisfied and upset by the whole conversation. I got off the basket and picked my way to the door. Mrs Flood called me back.

'Oh, I nearly forgot,' she said, fancying her sherry again, 'what I really wanted to speak to you about. I've got to go over to Booth on business tomorrow and I want you to sit with Willy at the digs. Okay?'

I nodded; I didn't trust myself to speak.

'That's fine then. I'll give you a list of his food and stuff tonight. We've been gossiping away here for so long that there isn't time now.' Mrs Flood gave me a kind, dismissive smile, and outside I leaned against the corridor in a collapse of giggles.

Back at the digs Mrs Welles was in a high state of excitement and had made us a fish pie to ensure that my memory should be in good working order. Rose had refused to tell her anything until I arrived.

The three of us sat round the kitchen table whilst I regaled them with a detailed account of the previous night's happenings.

Mrs Welles was like a child; she sat with her hands clasped and her eyes shining. She was frightfully impressed that I had been to *Le Cercle Rouge*. 'It's *the* place of the Midlands,' she told me with awe in her voice. 'It's been my ambition since I was sixteen to get taken to *Le Cercle Rouge*. My God, Ann, you don't know your luck.'

I winked at Rose. This was my cue. 'Like to go, Win?'

'Yeah, I'll come and carry your bloody coat.'

'No, really Win, wouldn't you like to go with Grandpa?'

She leaned forward distressfully. 'Why, what's the matter Ann? Isn't he keen or something? What happened, did you do the wrong thing? Or –' She paused for a delicate moment '– or didn't you?'

I was glad she had said that, it gave me the one outlet I was looking for. I had been a bit worried about handing him over, as Mrs Welles could be very proud. Once when Mr Goat had brought her a bumper tin of baked beans for a present, she had thrown it at his head. 'I don't want no charity,' she had screamed at him.

I smiled at her. 'I'm a bloody fool I know, Win, but I couldn't. He's absolutely repulsive and ninety if he's a day.'

Mrs Welles stared at me in an agony of disappointment.

'Ann!' she said in a shocked voice, 'I don't know how you could do it, I just don't know how you could have been so selfish. We all know that you're the little archangel who's saving it for Jesus, but the way you go measuring everyone else with your own yard stick just beats me.' She rapped the table angrily. 'What about Rose and me here, eh? What about my little babies? I suppose it doesn't matter to you that they have to go hungry. I suppose you never realised that some of us can't afford to get to heaven.'

Tears of anger gleamed in her eyes. I gave her a cigarette, well pleased. There would be no difficulty now.

'I haven't thrown him away, Win. He's frightfully keen and he's calling for me on Sunday. The only thing is that it won't be me he'll take out – it'll be you.'

'Why, how do you mean?' Then as realisation dawned, 'Oh

Ann!' We sat all afternoon round the remains of the fish pie, making our plans and disposing of Mr Dropsey's chocolates. Mrs Welles was as thrilled and excited as though she had been through his money already. I felt rather like Mr Dropsey myself or at any rate how he had intended to feel, had I behaved in the expected manner.

I felt exactly as though I had given Mrs Welles the fairy off the top of the tree.

Briefly we decided that, on the Sunday, I was to rush away to a sick aunt and that Mrs Welles, looking absolutely terrific, should receive him, trap him in the sitting room and pounce (Mrs Welles' word). I was a little worried by it; we didn't want to make it look too obvious.

'It's me he's interested in at the moment, remember,' I told her, 'and naturally he's going to be disappointed. I should say your best line would be cloying sympathy and the sweet little woman.'

Mrs Welles gave me a tolerant, amused smile. Mrs Welles was a great one on appearances, and as far as looks were concerned did not consider me a rival.

'There's only one line for a sugar daddy,' she said briskly. 'Keep a smile on your face and keep your big mouth shut!'

Rose and I looked at each other ruefully. The chances of Mrs Welles ever remaining silent could be described as nil.

'What are you going to wear?' Rose asked her.

Mrs Welles looked as though she'd been shot.

'Oh Christ, girls,' she said hollowly.

We stared at her sympathetically, each of us mentally going through her wardrobe. I got up to discarding her sixth negligee and realised there were only her trousers left.

'What about your black satin ones with the red dragons?' said Rose whose mind was running in tune. Mrs Welles withered her with a glance.

'My dear Rose,' she said stiffly, 'we are not dealing with an imaginative young man.'

I offered her the run of my cotton dresses but as she was a great deal taller and thinner than I, it was rather pointless. Rose's were out of the question too. We all had another gorge at the chocolates and gazed out of the window.

'Girls!' said Mrs Welles. 'That's it!'

'What's it?'

'These!' Mrs Welles leant across the table and clutched a handful of limp grey net curtain.

'Oh no, Win!' I told her. 'It's a good idea, but they've had it, they'd dissolve at the first smell of water.'

'No no, not these, clot.' Mrs Welles was excited. 'My purple, upstairs.'

It was of course the perfect answer. I rushed upstairs to her bedroom and yanked the beautiful purple draperies from the window. In the kitchen we swathed them around her.

'I'll run it up tomorrow,' she said, pirouetting and twirling happily. Launcelot emerged outraged from under the table as she trod on one of his bricks. In a sudden rush of motherhood she picked him up and held him against her. 'We're going to be rich, we're going to be rich!' she sang.

Launcelot's face went dark and he tore savagely at the purple net.

'The brute!' said Mrs Welles, putting him down in a hurry.

He retired back under the table and flung a sharp paint box at his mother. It caught her on the shins, tearing another hole in the net.

'Jesus Christ almighty, give me patience,' screamed Mrs Welles. She seized a handful of chocolates, kicked wildly at the underneath recesses of the table, and flung herself out of the room. Launcelot, who had escaped the attack, gave a hollow laugh of victory.

Guinevere and Leigh came in from a walk and over tea we told him of our plans. He shrieked with laughter and seemed to think the whole thing a terrific joke, but then got apologetic and begged to be allowed to help with preparations. Rose told him coldly that he could paint the front gate and weed the pathway. Guinevere was enlisted too, as the sitting room needed a thorough spring cleaning.

'In fact,' said Rose, 'it will be all hands to the happy home tomorrow.'

And then I remembered Mrs Flood.

'I won't be able to help,' I told them. 'I've got to sit with Willy.'

Leigh said, 'You've got to what?'

And Rose said, 'What did you say?'

'I've got to sit with Willy.'

'Sit with Willy?' Rose looked at me oddly. 'Whatever do you mean?'

I told them briefly of my interview with Mrs Flood and, as Leigh was amused, would have been more detailed, but Rose was not interested.

'Yes, yes!' she said, 'But what about Willy, what did she mean about sitting with him?'

Leigh and I looked at her rather surprised.

'Oh, Rose!' I said, 'You know Ma Flood, she's got to go over to Booth on business tomorrow, and she wants someone to give Willy his lunch and keep him company.'

'Why can't he get his own lunch?' asked Rose in a deadpan voice.

'Because he's on a diet,' I told her. We all knew that, we all knew too that he couldn't be trusted to attend to it himself.

I looked at Rose. Her face was flushed with a sort of anger. She stared back at me and I knew exactly what she was thinking. Once during rehearsal she had offered Willy a piece of chocolate. Mrs Flood's voice had come back at her sharp as an arrow.

'Would you mind taking back that piece of chocolate you gave to my husband, Rose?' she'd said. 'Willy hasn't got a very strong will.'

Willy gave her back the chocolate and now Mrs Flood had addressed him. 'Willy,' she said clearly, 'tell Rose what you did one day.' Willy had looked at the ground. 'Go on Willy, do as you are told.'

Willy had looked up at Rose. 'One day,' he said, rather like a child reciting its multiplication tables, 'one day Mrs Flood left me outside a shop while she went into the post office, and I went into the shop and bought six cream buns and ate them all straight off.'

We had all laughed rather politely at this and Willy had laughed too, but looking back now I remembered that Rose hadn't.

She still stared at me then said very quietly, 'God, how I loathe Willy Flood.' She got up from the table and addressed me. 'And if you had any sense of decency Ann, you'd refuse to… to sit with Willy.' She nearly spat out the words.

'What's got into her?' I asked Leigh as the door slammed.

'Probably jealous,' he said grinning. 'Of the great honour Ma Flood has bestowed upon you. For one whole day you will experience the unique sensation of giving Willy his carrots. For one glorious afternoon you will be able to read to him from his Hans Christian Andersen.'

'But Leigh, Rose can't stand Willy.'

'It's not Willy she's worried about sweetie, it's that you should be the chosen one.'

But I couldn't believe it. Rose was not a jealous person, and certainly not of me. However, we both forgot about it on our walk down to the theatre. Our only topic of conversation was of Mrs Welles' forthcoming triumph.

Chapter Six

Saturday morning dawned hot and bright and the family were early astir. There was to be an all out effort of preparation for Mr Dropsey's visit the following morning. Mrs Welles was shut in her bedroom with the sewing machine and the purple net.

Leigh, armed with some red paint, attacked the gate, and Guinevere and Rose made a concerted effort upon the sitting room. There was a short debate on what should be done with Launcelot. Rose was all for me taking him over to the Flood's and, as I was feeling rather guilty about missing my share of the work, I didn't see how I could very well refuse. But as it happened, or rather, as it always happened, the decision was not left with us.

Launcelot took one look at Leigh and the red paint, and attached himself to them like a leech. So at ten o'clock, armed with my writing things and a book, I took my leave alone. They were all so united and happy that I felt a pang of jealousy. Mrs Welles waved at me from the bedroom window and Launcelot grinned at me quite humanely from his rather primitive attempts to paint his pushchair red.

But as I waited for a bus at the top of the road, I felt a growing excitement. I was the first member of the company to be invited to the Flood's home, the only one of us that Mrs Flood had unbent to even a fraction. I had the address written at the top of Willy's diet sheet, and now the bus took me down through the centre of the town past the theatre and out into a rather dismal slum area.

We all knew that the Floods had hired a house for the season, and were frightfully impressed by the fact, but as I got off the bus and gazed up at number 327, Commercial Road, I wondered just what the house comprised. It stood flat on to the pavement and was joined to a row of other houses left and right as far as I could see. The upper window had three pieces of cardboard fitted into the pane frames and the lower window and the front door were completely boarded up. There was neither bell or knocker, and as

I stood staring up at the pieces of cardboard, a woman called down to me from a window in an adjoining house.

'You'll have to go round the back,' she said. 'There's an alley six houses up.'

I thanked her, found the rather unpleasant alley and emerged out into the back of Commercial Road. A sort of dirt path lay along the outside lavatories and coalhods which protruded from each house, and behind it a high brick wall with barbed wire and broken glass stuck along the top.

I carefully counted six houses back and knocked on the kitchen door. There was no answer, so after knocking again I opened it and went in. It lead into a scullery, filthy dirty, with a large sink in one corner. In the centre of the floor was a tin bath filled with dirty water, a lot of which had splashed on to the flagstones. A copper and another pail of water stood against the wall facing me, and from a drunken pulley above my head a wealth of Mrs Flood's underclothes dripped.

The scullery led into a small kitchen, which was obviously unused. A rusty range ornamented one wall and a small deal table and two upright chairs were its only furniture. On the table was laid out Willy's lunch. I checked it with my list. Half a cabbage (to be boiled) three carrots (raw), two Ryvita biscuits and a bottle of yoghurt. A small bottle containing two Dexedrine tablets stood beside them, and these I had been instructed to give him when the pangs of hunger became too terrible.

I called his name from the kitchen and a door opened somewhere above me and he called back from the top of the stairs.

'I'm upstairs Ann, come on upstairs.'

I left the kitchen, passed an open door leading into the darkened boarded-up room I had seen from the front, and felt my way to the stairs. It was very dark; the only light came from the kitchen.

'Where are you?' I called to him halfway up. Willy's voice answered me, very close too, but I couldn't see him. He put out a hand suddenly and touched me. I screamed involuntarily and he shrieked with laughter.

'Will you please put on a light or open a door,' I said crossly.

'I can't put on a light,' answered Willy. 'It's gas, and that means you need matches.'

However, he pushed open a door and I climbed up on to the landing.

Still laughing, he led me into the room.

'It's awfully ghostly this house, isn't it Ann? If I hadn't opened the door you wouldn't have known where you were, would you? If I'd've been asleep and hadn't heard you, I dare say you'd have had to sit in the kitchen. It's horrid in the kitchen too, there's mice!' He laughed again.

'Oh Willy, don't be so ghoulish,' I said.

The room we were in was not very large, but probably the largest upstairs. It appeared to be the living room. A horsehair sofa extended at right angles from the fireplace, and opposite it an armchair. Under the window stood a square table covered with a red plush tablecloth and littered with Willy's painting things.

Facing the fireplace was a small dresser with crockery, books and ornaments intermittently spaced along its shelves. A few of Willy's paintings were hung, but by far the most interesting feature of the room was the wall above the fireplace. It was covered, literally covered, with photographs of Willy. There was scarcely a spare inch between them; every size and shape, they hung.

Fascinated, I walked across to the wall and studied them. They showed him from the age of about sixteen upwards, so handsome he was then that it took my breath away. They showed him laughing, smiling, crying, solemn, naughty, in stage make-up, in stage costume, in expensive lounge suits, in a riding habit, in evening dress, in bathing trunks, in pyjamas, in bed, and three in a row of him stark naked, not holiday snaps on the beach, but three careful studio portraits of Willy Flood aged about twenty-one years, lying stark staring naked on a leopard-skin rug. I looked away from them to him. He was clad in a dressing gown and trousers and had just put a cigarette in his mouth.

'Got a match?' he asked me. 'She said you'd have some.'

I gave him one and lit a cigarette myself. Willy sat down on the horsehair sofa, and I on the chair opposite him. 'You've been pretty widely photographed, Willy,' I said.

'I have my picture taken three times a year, every year,' said Willy proudly. 'And then we bind them in passépartout and add them to the collection. We've got 850 so far.'

'What about Mrs Flood?' I asked him. 'Does she have hers taken too?'

Willy looked faintly shocked. 'No, of course not, not any more, not now she's lost her looks.'

Excitement and curiosity flooded me. My heart began to pound, I had known all along why I wanted to sit with Willy. And Willy was going to play, Willy was going to talk. I leaned forward from the armchair and spoke to him softly. 'But Willy, Mrs Flood is a very fine woman, she hasn't lost her looks, she's really quite attractive!'

Willy's voice sounded sad. 'No, she isn't attractive Ann, she's lost her looks, she's got fat and she's lost her looks.' He paused for a moment and then went on in his multiplication tables voice. 'But you mustn't judge people by their looks, beauty is only skin deep, it's the soul that matters and goodness, and Mrs Flood is good. I have a wife that any man could be proud of. She is good and that's all that matters.' He switched off. 'Thank you though Ann,' he said, 'for saying she is still attractive, she'd like that you see.' He laughed happily.

'We play a game about it, we pretend she hasn't lost her looks and is still young and beautiful, and she plays up and doesn't mind a bit. In fact, she likes me to play it all the time.'

'Yes Willy, go on, go on, where do you play the game?'

'Here in this house, in the bedroom.' He was very excited. 'After supper we have a lot to drink then go into the bedroom and the window is boarded up so I can't see her very well, then she takes off all her clothes and puts on a transparent night-dress and lots of scent and lies on the bed. Then I have to stand for three minutes and think, think back to when she's twenty years old, and with not being able to see her very well and all the scent it's easy. Then we act a beautiful love scene, much, much better than any of the ones we've done on stage, and sometimes I feel really so much in love with her...' He laughed happily. 'She's wonderful, wonderful...'

I felt suddenly cold and frightened. My cigarette had gone out.

I lit it again. Willy still looked at me, his eyes bright with excitement.

'Oh, we have lovely games Ann, her and me. Shall I tell you some more games we play, Ann?'

I didn't say anything.

'Sometimes we play animals,' said Willy breathlessly. 'That's Mrs Flood's favourite game. I'm a naughty dog and run round the room on all fours and Mrs Flood is my master and chases me with a whip, and I make little crying dog noises because I'm frightened of the whip, but Mrs Flood is the master and much stronger than me, and I've got to be taught discipline and she whips me.' He laughed again. 'But I like the love ones better, playing animals hurts really, especially when—'

'Stop it Willy,' I shouted suddenly, I was shaking all over. I crossed over to the window and looked out. After a while I turned to him. 'Would you like your lunch now, Willy?'

'Yes please Ann, and Mrs Flood's left some sandwiches for you on the dresser.'

I lit him another cigarette. 'I don't suppose you're allowed to have it Willy, but is there any tea in the house? I'd love a cup of tea.'

Willy said there was some in the oven in the range. I found it, and a half used tin of condensed milk, and took it up with his lunch. He had cleared his paintings and put my sandwiches on the table. I boiled water on a gas ring in the grate and we sat down to our lunch. Willy ate ravenously and asked me if I wanted my sandwiches.

There were only two, and the plate looked suspiciously crumby; I decided that another two couldn't hurt him. I was weak over the tea as well, and let him have three cups. We leaned back in our chairs with another cigarette.

'You and Rose are digging together, aren't you Ann?' Willy asked me rather shyly.

I told him that we were.

'That's nice, that's very nice, Rose is a very nice girl isn't she Ann?'

'Yes, she's awfully nice Willy.'

'Yes, Rose is a nice girl, but she's a bad actress Ann. You're a nice girl and you're a good actress but...'

'But what, Willy?'

'Rose has got a very good figure, hasn't she Ann? I've got a picture of a girl who's got a figure just like what I should think Rose has got. Shall I show it you? It's in my scrapbook.'

Willy produced a key from his pocket and unlocked the bottom drawer of the dresser. 'This is my treasure chest,' he said. 'I've got all my treasures in here, treasures she doesn't know about, like my scrapbook.'

He lifted a large, rather cheap looking scrapbook out of the drawer and brought it over to the table. The book opened automatically at a certain place and there, laughing up from the black page, was the carefully cut out picture of a naked girl. Apart from the fact that she was dark she didn't look a bit like Rose. She had an enormous unnaturally pointed bosom and fat thighs bulging over black fishnet stockings. Underneath her was printed the name 'Rose'.

'I should think Rose looks quite like that, Ann.' Willy looked at me questioningly.

'Well,' I began, 'she's fatter than Rose…'

Willy looked acutely disappointed. 'Are you sure Ann, I mean, have you really seen her?'

I hastily assured him that I hadn't and could very well be wrong.

Willy brightened and showed me the rest of his scrapbook. On every page there was a cut-out of a voluptuous naked girl and under each one he had printed a girl's name. 'It's how I imagine girls I've met look like,' he explained. 'Do you want to see you?' He turned the pages 'til we came to a cruel-looking blonde sitting astride a large stuffed dog.

'The spit image, I should say,' said Willy, wonderment in his voice.

We pored over the book for about half an hour, and Willy told me where he had met the various names written under the pictures. Mostly they were girls he had come into contact with in the theatre; dancers on variety bills, nudes in a preceding nightclub turn, women he had noticed all over the world when they had toured as a famous adagio act.

I wanted him to talk about those days, not about the girls he had seen, but of their life together when he had been practically a child and she still young and beautiful, and both of them brilliant and sought after. I wanted to know how they had found each other and how she must have moulded him and trained him and taught him, and married him, and how she had tied him to her as securely as though he were held by chains.

And then, much later on, and her dancing days were done, how she had taught him to act, how she had taught him to say things that he could never understand or feel and yet still bring tears to people's eyes. I wanted to know all this but Willy couldn't remember; I asked him and he couldn't remember. He could only, he said, remember girls' names and their shapes.

I wondered next what I should do to amuse him.

Mrs Flood had told me that he liked being read to, so I had brought along a novel, but Willy said he didn't fancy being read to. I asked him to show me the paintings that had been on the table, and saw that they were all practically identical to the ones hanging in his dressing room.

'Ann!' he said to me, 'Could I do a little painting of you?'

I remembered what I had told Leigh, but he looked at me so pleading that I gave in.

'Alright!' I said. 'But only a head, mind, and you must hide it straight away.'

Willy said, 'Of course!' and brought his painting things back to the table. I sat on the horsehair sofa and he arranged my hair so that it fell in a wing across my face. I smoked and looked at his photographs on the wall whilst he painted. We were both quite silent.

I thought on and off about what he had told me. I knew that should I wish it he would tell me more, but my mind, which had previously been like a bad Sunday newspaper, had suddenly shut up.

Perhaps it was because it had been too easy. Perhaps if I'd had to flirt and trap it out of him, I would have gone on. Perhaps what he had told me was not what I really wanted to know. At any event I sat silent on the horsehair sofa and was glad that he was silent too.

'It's finished,' said Willy after a while. 'Look!'

He came over with the piece of paper in his hands and sat by me on the sofa, and I looked at his painting. It was an exact copy of the picture of the cruel-looking blonde. The only difference was in what we were sitting on; (the stuffed dog) had been substituted for (the horsehair sofa). I made my face grow hard and addressed him in a distant voice.

'Willy,' I said, 'this is not a picture of me. Also, it is not a portrait at all. You said you would paint my head. The head in this picture is just a blur, any painting you have bothered with has been directed upon the body.' I looked at him trying to make him understand.

'It's not me, Willy,' I said again, 'and I'm very, very hurt.'

He was immediately contrite. 'I'm sorry Ann,' he said. 'It's just that I've thought about how you looked for so long, that it just came out. She's so like you, Ann,' he said. 'But if you don't see it I wouldn't like to keep it.'

He tore it across, and then again and again until it was in little pieces, and threw them into the grate. I struck a match and set fire to them and we both watched them burn.

'There's nothing like a fire,' said Willy, suddenly philosophical. 'It's so final.'

I agreed with him that this was so, and put on the kettle to make some more tea. In half an hour we would have to leave for the theatre; I was suddenly thankful for the fact. We drank our tea and I remembered the Dexedrine tablets. Owing to eating my sandwiches he hadn't had any hunger pangs, but I made him take them both. Willy didn't mind a bit and confided to me that they had an exhilarating side-effect.

We were down early for the show, but Mrs Flood was already there, all champing impatience in a kimono at the dressing room door. She threw her arms around Willy as though they'd been parted for years. She ruffled his curls and touched his face, and her love for him shone naked in her eyes.

I stood by the door feeling rather spare, then Willy told her he'd had a lovely day and she noticed me. I was dragged into the room and placed upon the theatrical basket.

'Now!' she breathed. I gave her a careful summarised account of the day's events and she smiled at me kindly and lifted her glass, and we both drank a silent toast to the safe passing of another of Willy's days.

Chapter Seven

That night was the last time we played *Wuthering Heights*. We were all of us sad, as it was to be our last piece of 'class' too. Mrs Flood had not been joking when she said that the financial position decreed pot-boilers for the future.

I didn't feel any better when an enormous, anonymous bouquet was sent round to me either; I guessed it must be from Mr Dropsey and it just made me worry about his visit the following morning.

In fact, I'd been worrying on and off about it ever since I'd decided to hand him over. Under an alcoholic haze in *Le Cercle Rouge* it had seemed the easiest thing in the world, but now, looking at the flowers, I remembered that they were sent to me because it was me he liked; me, the absolute antitheses of Mrs Welles.

In my mind's eye I could see their meeting tomorrow, Mrs Welles clad in transparent, inadequate purple net, raping the probably equally inadequate, terrified Mr Dropsey. I shuddered at the fiasco and wildly wondered if we couldn't call the whole thing off. But then, quickly, I remembered the faces of the family as they went about their preparations for the great day, the kill. No, we most certainly could not call it off. I wouldn't miss tomorrow – not for a thousand pounds!

Rose was still a bit off with me, but I knew she was dying to hear how I'd got on with Willy. She wouldn't ask me though, and as I saw no reason why she should be off with me, I didn't tell her. I don't think I would have told her anyway, I don't think I would have told anyone. Willy's conversation with me was very personal.

Back at the digs, Guinevere was still polishing. The kitchen was spotless and we walked around carefully on newspapers. She had laid out some salad on newspapers too, and we ate it sitting gingerly on the edges of the shining chairs. I had another pang as I looked at her. Her face was flushed with overexcitement and not enough sleep, her eyes enormous in her little thin face, and the hollows under them quite frightening.

We kept on saying amongst ourselves how dreadful it was that Guinevere had to work as she did, we kept on saying that something must be done about it, but nothing ever was. She was always there, nipping in and out, mouse-like and worried and conscientious, with everlasting cups of tea to soothe her mother's jangled neurotic nerves.

Leigh had made some sort of a move with her education, but I'm bound to admit that the only time she looked really miserable was in the afternoons, when she was made to sit still on a chair and do as he told her.

Mrs Welles was having an early night on account of her looks, and we weren't late either. There was, Guinevere informed us, a lot of work still to be done.

I was practically asleep when Rose's strained voice came across to me through the darkness.

'Ann,' she said very casually, 'how d'you get on with Willy?'

Dead casual, I answered her back. 'Fine Rose, just fine! Goodnight.'

We were awakened the next morning by the thud of rain falling upon the attic roof. Through the window I could see the grey world wrapped in a sheet of heavy rain. It was 8 a.m. and very cold. I huddled into a dressing gown and went downstairs to start the tea. Leigh and Rose followed me.

'Shouldn't be surprised if he doesn't come,' said Rose, blowing on her tea. 'I mean, it's not exactly the weather to go for a ride in the country, is it?'

We stared at her gloomily.

'Better wake her though,' said Leigh. 'We'd better be prepared all the same.'

I took a cup of tea up to her. The room looked naked without its draperies and Mrs Welles, lying on the bed, looked like a corpse.

She was laid flat out with a cushion under her neck so that her head, encased in an army of steel curlers, could hang over it, thereby lessening the pain. Her face was rigid and stiff under a thick grey cement-like face pack. Two holes had been left for her eyes, and these had been filled in with wet wads of cotton wool.

She looked exactly like the man in the chamber of horrors who had just come out of the other side of the kitchen mangle. I shook her and she woke up, horribly unable to express any emotion.

'It's half past eight, Win.'

Her mouth moved up and down like the section of a ventriloquist's doll. 'My God!' she said with difficulty, 'How I lived through the night I shall never know.'

I guided the cup of tea to her aperture and she made the awful mistake of trying to smile. There was an ominous cracking noise and a wealth of lines creased themselves into the cement. Mrs Welles gave a strangled scream and fell back upon her curlers.

'Oh, Christ,' she moaned in terror. 'I've done it, I'm ruined, absolutely ruined, it says so on the packet. "To crack your pack is to crack your face," that's what it says, Ann.' Her voice rose hysterically. 'I'm cracked up, ruined! Oh dear Christ…'

Her eye pads fell off and she started to cry down her pack. I yelled over the banisters. 'Hot water and a flannel quick.'

Leigh raced up with some water in the washing up bowl and held Mrs Welles' head over it. He couldn't find a flannel, so we soaked the mask for a minute and then I set about tearing it off with my hands. The agonised screams of Mrs Welles rent the house, but after a while it came away.

'Get me a mirror. Get me a mirror,' she moaned in a state of near collapse.

Leigh brought her one. Apart from being a good deal cleaner than usual, I could detect no difference in her face but Mrs Welles, after a detailed ten minutes study of it, announced tragically that it had cracked in three places. We left her massaging hormone secretions into it, and reminded her that it was nine o'clock.

Downstairs Guinevere had got Launcelot up and was giving him his breakfast. Rose had made us some toast and we ate it whilst the rain still thundered down outside.

'Win'll never make it now,' I told Leigh. 'She'll be so preoccupied with the cracks, that she won't even have the interest.'

'Don't you believe it,' said Leigh. 'Money's money, whatever you look like.' And he was right.

A few minutes later Mrs Welles came sailing downstairs with her face beautifully made up and really looking as though it had benefited from its trials.

'It's those hormones,' she said happily as Rose and I unwound her out of the curlers. 'I just got them on before the cracks set.'

We had decided that in order to look as young as possible she should wear her hair loose, and now Rose brushed it out so that it fell in a shining curtain way past her shoulders.

'Show me what you've done to the sitting room, Win,' I asked her.

Rose had told me that it looked absolutely lovely, and I'd forgotten to have a look at it the night before.

'Well, it certainly looks a bit more cheerful,' said Mrs Welles modestly as she led the way.

I don't think I would have described the sight which met my eyes as cheerful, but then it was not intended to cheer me up.

The room had been thoroughly cleaned and the carpet taken up. In its place had been laid the two Spanish shawls from Mrs Welles' bedroom, but as the room was larger than the bedroom, the coverlet from Launcelot's cot had been added. It lay in pride of place under the window. The pieces of purple net ruching from Mrs Welles' dressing table had also been brought down, and these now graced the mirror over the fireplace.

The sofa and armchair had been pushed up close to the fireplace, and purple bows had been liberally tacked into them. Disguising the bare grate was our one wooden tray, with a large coloured photograph of the Queen stuck on to it.

But the most dreadful thing of all was Mrs Welles' little coffee table. It had been placed squarely in the centre of the room, and around each of its four spindly legs, bunches of privet hedge had been tied. Resting on its surface were two small glasses, and a bottle of British sherry with the label carefully removed.

'Why I've never thought of doing this before I can't think,' said Mrs Welles gazing lovingly around her.

We were hurriedly shooed out so as not to soil its pristine glory, and Mrs Welles said she thought it was time Launcelot was locked in the attic. We were all agreed on this as it was reckoned that by eleven o'clock his screams should be well past their prime.

Leigh took him up with half a pound of chocolate biscuits, and Mrs Welles thought that we could all do with another cup of tea.

Rose, Guinevere and I were to be kept firmly out of the way, but Leigh was to witness it all, as Mrs Welles fancied a butler.

I told her that in that case he should bring the sherry into them. Mrs Welles said there was no need to come that Girton patter with her, but at the same time told Guinevere to fetch the sherry into the kitchen.

This was a rash move, as she immediately decided she could do with a pick-me-up. We were all imbibing merrily before I realised that it was 10.30 a.m. Mrs Welles was hastily sent upstairs with Rose to dress and I brushed Leigh's evening dress.

'Anne,' he said as he combed his hair into a centre parting, 'I'm going to enjoy myself.'

'You're telling me,' I said feelingly. 'I feel exactly like Cinderella.'

He looked at me. 'Why don't you and Rose put on macs. and go and crouch under the window? They'll never see you from the little side window.'

'Do you know, I think I will Leigh,' I said brightening. 'And you're right, they'll never see us from there.'

Rose's voice sailed down from the landing.

'Make way, make way, here comes the bride.' She hummed the wedding march and we ran to the stairs to watch Mrs Welles come down. She looked absolutely and completely beautiful.

She had transformed the purple net into a fairytale little girl party frock, with a tight bodice, sweetheart neck, and yards and yards of ballooning skirt. At the waistline she had stitched a posy of imitation daisies and around her neck hung a heart-shaped locket. The earrings, the bracelets, both wrist and ankle, had been done away with, and her dark hair hung unadorned around her shoulders. She looked about twenty-one.

We all gasped and Leigh proposed to her on the spot. She swayed downstairs and Guinevere said, 'Oh Mum!' in a breathy sort of voice.

'Don't you "Mum" me,' returned Mrs Welles tartly. 'And remember, I don't want to see your face around this morning.'

Leigh guided her into the sitting room and sat her on the sofa, which was placed with its back to the light. Rose arranged her skirt and hair around her, and I gave her my cigarette holder.

'She can't just be sitting there doing nothing,' said Rose. 'Haven't you got a piece of embroidery or something, Win?'

Mrs Welles said that no, she hadn't got a piece of embroidery.

'Well, what about my knitting then, you can borrow that if you like.' Mrs Welles said that no, she didn't like, and Rose knew what she could do with it.

Rose got huffy and said she could keep that act for Mr Dropsey and I shrieked, 'Don't you dare!' and Mrs Welles said we were both jealous.

Leigh rushed for the sherry bottle whilst I counted ten, and Rose luckily chose to flounce out of the room. We gave Mrs Welles a small soothing nip and Rose, who was much more interested in the proceedings than having a row, came down with a magazine from the attic. It was five to eleven.

'Okay girls, scarper!' said Mrs Welles, picking up the magazine.

Leigh collected the sherry and we all filed out, shutting the door. Launcelot had been suspiciously quiet, so Guinevere decided she could sit up in the attic with him, as good as anywhere else. Rose and I waited in the hall; as soon as the car stopped we were going round to the window. We held our macs ready over our arms.

At a minute to eleven Mrs Welles came rushing out of the sitting room. 'Nature calls!' she explained briefly as she dragged the kitchen tablecloth over her head and plunged out of the back door.

'Trust Win,' said Rose, 'I reminded her three times before we settled her in.'

Mrs Welles came rushing back and at the same time the scrunching noise of a car drawing up could be heard outside. Leigh, who was watching through the hall window, signalled to us violently to get Mrs Welles back into position.

'It's him,' he mouthed. 'Quick!'

Mrs Welles panicked in the hall. 'Oh Christ, girls,' she said, 'he'll see me through the window, he'll see you settling me in! You must settle me in, I couldn't possibly settle myself.'

'Well, you'll just have to,' I said pushing her firmly through the door. 'Anyway, a coy ruffle or two won't go astray.'

'Girls!' said Mrs Welles huskily. She gave us each a sudden tragic hug, then throwing back her head stalked bravely to the settee.

Leigh made another agonised signal to us, and the front door knocker rapped imperiously. We just had time to see him straighten his bow tie, before dashing through the kitchen and round the back of the house. Under the side window of the sitting room we settled ourselves on our haunches with the macs. over our heads.

It was a perfect vantage point. From where we were the door leading into the sitting room faced us, and at right angles from it protruded the settee and armchair. We hadn't told Mrs Welles that we were going to watch, on account of putting her off her stroke, and now we gazed at her whilst she gave her head a quick scratch with my cigarette holder.

'She looks a real credit,' said Rose proudly, and indeed she did.

She leaned back on the sofa so that her head just fitted between two of the purple bows. One slim leg hung to the ground, and the other was bent up beside her in an attractive if somewhat unnatural angle.

I turned my head and could see Mr Dropsey's Rolls Bentley at the gate. Withers, I noticed, was still standing on the pavement. I wondered why, and then didn't wonder as I looked closer. His hands were covered with red paint which he was wiping savagely on to a large white handkerchief. I looked at the gate; it was swimming in a river of red paint.

'Rose!' I gasped, but she gave me a quick nudge and we both ducked to eye level. Through the window we watched the sitting room door flung suddenly open, with Leigh's arm stretched along it.

'Mr h'Edward Dropsey,' he announced in stentorian tones.

An enormous basket wrapped in cellophane paper and pink ribbon, and Mr Dropsey, came into the room. We couldn't see his face on account of the frou frou cellophane, which the top of the basket was tied into. Evidently it impaired Mr Dropsey's sight too.

He took a quick look around the room, detected a blur upon

the sofa, and in one gambling pounce, leapt across the room and flung the basket and himself upon Mrs Welles.

'My little girl,' he muttered his voice hoarse with emotion, 'My little girl.'

There was a tearing noise, and a stifled moan from the basket, and a second later an overgrown Alsatian puppy burst through the cellophane, and clubbed Mrs Welles heavily upon the face.

I shall never forget what Mrs Welles did then; as long as I live I shall never forget her presence of mind. With her eyes flashing danger signals, she made a high, sweet, happy gurgling sound emerge from her throat.

'Whoops-a-daisy, Boysey!' she said as the brute entangled its paws in her hair.

Mr Dropsey said, 'To heel, sir,' and stared at Mrs Welles with a trembling face. He was still kneeling at her feet, his arms still buried in the folds of her dress. 'Madame,' he said at length in a broken voice. Slowly he backed away from her knees; slowly he got to his feet. 'Madame,' he repeated, 'forgive me.'

Mrs Welles extracted the dog from her hair in much the same way as she would an orchid and threw it on the floor. She was quite magnificent; fluttering her lashes a little she carefully picked a piece of fur from her bosom, and blew it like a coy kiss into the air.

Mr Dropsey backed to the chair opposite and watched, fascinated, its flight through the air. It came to rest neatly in the grate, and now he turned his fascinated gaze upon her. She returned it with a bewildered little smile on her lips.

'Well, well, well,' she said helplessly.

'Madame,' said Mr Dropsey again, 'I owe you an explanation.' There was a long pause, he cleared his throat and dropped his eyes to the floor while his face took on a heightened puce.

'An explanation,' continued Mr Dropsey, 'of my unforgivable behaviour.'

Mrs Welles said, 'Oh, reely,' then, 'oh!' again at beautifully spaced intervals.

'I called here today,' said Mr Dropsey, 'to visit Miss King, whom I believed to be staying here. When your man showed me in and I saw a beautiful young girl sitting upon the sofa, my mind went before me, went without a second glance, went with no other thought than that it could be the little girl who was expecting me.'

'Oh!' said Mrs Welles rather blankly, 'Oh!' Then, 'I think I'd better explain to you too. In fact,' here she picked at one of the purple bows, 'Little Annie asked me to explain to the gentleman she said would be arriving for her. You see,' she went on in a troubled voice, 'Little Annie had a wire from her auntie last night, very sick she is, said the wire, and Annie was to go at once, so of course,' said Mrs Welles, raising matching troubled eyes, 'she went.' Then added quickly, 'At once.'

'I'm so sorry,' said Mr Dropsey, in the sort of voice used by a person suddenly confronted by a tragedy which doesn't touch them, 'is it serious?'

'We don't know,' said Mrs Welles, in the same tone. 'It may of course be... fatal.'

They both looked at the floor, but Mr Dropsey only for an instant. Slowly, very slowly he brought his eyes up Mrs Welles' form. Up her legs, her thighs, her stomach – by the time he had got to her bosom, a small trickle of saliva coursed from his open mouth. He leaned forward in the armchair.

'And what is your name, m'dear?'

'Winifred,' replied Mrs Welles, 'Miss Winifred Welles.'

Mr Dropsey leaned further forward.

'Aah! And are you another budding little starlet?'

Mrs Welles looked rather as though he had made a nasty suggestion and shrank back against the sofa. 'Oh no,' she said in a frightened voice, 'I keep house for Daddy. But Daddy's got to be away on business for a few months, and he wouldn't let me stay here alone, so when two girls from the theatre came looking for somewhere to live, Daddy said it was just the thing for me 'til my cousin comes back from the South of France.'

'Very wise, very wise,' said Mr Dropsey, nodding his approval. 'But you'll be on your own for some time will you, m'dear?'

'Oh yes,' said Mrs Welles. 'Six months at least.'

She picked at the purple bow again, and stifled an exclamation of pain at the cruel angle of her bent leg.

Mr Dropsey gazed at it lasciviously.

The dog, which had been taking an unnatural interest in the photograph of the Queen, defaced it suddenly and savagely. Mr Dropsey coughed loudly and Mrs Welles pretended it hadn't happened.

'Jolly little bitch,' said Mr Dropsey, not making himself very clear. 'I mean,' he went on hurriedly, laughing a little to cover the gaffe, 'the dog, bitch you know, jolly little thing.'

The dog removed itself from the grate and sprang at a purple bow, which Mrs Welles' dangling leg had inadvertently stirred. There was a tearing noise as it missed the bow and sank its teeth into Mrs Welles' leg.

'Jolly little thing,' repeated Mr Dropsey. 'I'd brought her along for Ann, but she's taken such a fancy to you that I don't think there'll be any question of who's going to be her new mummy!'

Mrs Welles gave the dog a concealed kick.

'I've always wanted a little doggie,' she announced vacantly. She leaned forwards, showing a lot of cleavage. 'Thank you, Mr Dropsey,' she breathed, 'thank you.'

'Teddy, please,' breathed back Mr Dropsey, eyeing the cleavage in a maddened manner, 'Teddy, please, to you m'dear.'

'Teddy then,' said Mrs Welles. She gave a long shuddering sigh; the cleavage shook provocatively.

Mr Dropsey, with the air of a priest who was finding things difficult, leaned back in his chair and addressed the ceiling. A pulse ticked in his cheek.

'Funny little thing, Ann,' he remarked. 'Odd little creature. I took her out one night last week and you'd have thought she was seventy, not seventeen!' He laughed, 'Proper little career girl! Well of course,' he went on, 'a career's alright, but it's not much fun for an old fellow like myself when it's a little girl's only interest.' He laughed again and looked at Mrs Welles. 'Eh, Winnie?' he said.

'Oh Teddy,' said Mrs Welles, 'I'm so glad you feel like that because, well, because I'm a bit ashamed of what I want out of life.'

'What do you want, m'dear?' asked Mr Dropsey.

'I want to be looked after,' said Mrs Welles, using the impact of the words to straighten her bent leg. The bone gave a sharp crack and she said, 'Naughty Boysey,' loudly to the dog.

At that point Rose made a terrible explosive noise and I hurriedly had to force her to the ground. When we next looked up the door was open and Leigh had just come in with the sherry. He advanced with two glasses and the bottle, balanced on a saucepan lid spread with a lace handkerchief. It really looked quite good; carefully he lowered it on to the coffee table, but as it touched the surface the bottle gave a violent lurch and an angry jet of sherry spurted through the air. He had forgotten about the handle on the underneath.

For a moment Mrs Welles forgot herself. 'You clumsy oaf,' she screamed, leaping off the settee and just catching the bottle in time. Then she remembered. She drew herself up and pointed a quivering finger at Leigh. 'Take a fortnight's notice,' she said in an icy controlled voice.

Leigh doing a quick character change from the perfect butler to the grovelling, put-upon halfwit, touched his forelock, seized the saucepan lid and shuffled off.

As he closed the door behind him, Mr Dropsey turned a distressed face upon Mrs Welles.

'M'dear,' he said kindly as she poured out the sherry, 'don't you think you were a little precipitate? I mean, the fella's hand just slipped, a genuine accident I should have said m'dear, could have happened to anyone.' He took a sip of his sherry, shuddered slightly, but went on bravely. 'So very devoted and servile too, m'dear. I should think again before you let him go.'

Mrs Welles leaned back against the sofa and gazed remorsefully into her sherry. 'Oh, I shall Teddy, I shall,' she said, 'It's just that I'm such a hot-headed little thing.' She paused for a moment then went on rather brokenly. 'You see Teddy, it's being on my own, having Daddy away for so long, having to cope alone, having the worry of two wild theatre girls tramping around my home, never getting out. It's my nerves, Teddy.' Here Mrs Welles gave a single uncontrollable sob. 'Teddy,' she said, 'oh, Teddy.'

In an instant Mr Dropsey had covered the small space between them and was on his knees by her side. He put an arm round her and stroked her hair. Mrs Welles leaned against him and wept.

Rose and I stared, fascinated as we watched the real tears course down her cheeks in an ever-increasing flood.

I was envious too; acting in the most moving pieces of drama I couldn't produce real tears. But at the same time I knew we were watching no polished piece of technique; Mrs Welles was crying with joy, sobbing her heart out in an abandon of thankfulness at the triumphant ensnarement of Mr Dropsey.

'Don't, little girl,' he kept saying awkwardly, 'don't – please little Winnie, don't.'

He lifted his sherry glass to her lips and Mrs Welles' emotions were diverted. He sat down on the sofa beside her and put a finger on her chin to raise her face to his, but Mrs Welles turned her head into the sofa, and with a quick professional finger ran a purple bow under her eyes to mop up the mascara, then she turned to him and smiled.

Mr Dropsey was overcome, and in a sudden rush of emotion leaned over and pressed his long single upper tooth into her forehead. This primitive rite was accompanied by a sharp cloud burst and Rose and I could no longer hear what they said. As we clung desperately to the windowsill we could only watch them get up from the sofa and make for the door.

They turned to each other for a moment and Mr Dropsey repeated the tooth rite. Then, looking like a couple of Roman soldiers at the aftermath of their first orgy, they went into the hall.

By this time Rose and I were practically fossilised by the elements, but we waited until the front door opened and Mrs Welles, clad in Rose's coat with Leigh holding an umbrella over her, was led by Mr Dropsey to the car. For a moment I felt a sort of pang as I imagined the rug being tucked around her, but Rose was clambering out of the mud and clapping her hands in wild exultation.

'It's worked, it's worked,' she kept crying. She dragged me round to the kitchen. 'We're going to be rich! Oh Ann! You're so clever, it's worked, your wonderful plan's worked and he's really and truly fallen for her.'

'Hook, line and sinker,' finished Leigh, who was taking off his evening dress. We sat round the kitchen table with shining eyes and hysterically went over the whole crazy scene.

Leigh, who had witnessed it all from the keyhole, was besotted by Mrs Welles' performance.

'I've never seen anything like it,' he kept saying. 'She's a natural, born for the stage, born to act. I might have guessed it all along; something must be done about it, to hell with money and men, that woman's got to act.'

We shushed him up. We were far more concerned with immediate gain than Mrs Welles' histrionic powers. Rose went to get the sherry and came back with the Alsatian gambolling at her heels. We eyed it with distaste.

'She'll damn well have to look after it herself,' said Rose.

'And then it'll probably die,' said Leigh.

We brightened at this and Rose gave it a pat.

I still felt a little sad that Mr Dropsey could switch his affections so easily. It was exactly what we had wanted and planned for of course, but he had been my very first fan, and so ardent.

I laughed to myself when I remembered how I had told Mrs Welles to be cloying sympathy, as he would probably be disappointed; so much for that little fancy, he had only maligned me in the first two minutes. I glared at the nasty dog that should have been mine and knocked back a double sherry.

Leigh told us that he had taken her out to lunch, so we decided that it was safe for the children to come down for a while. I went upstairs to fetch them. Guinevere was fast asleep on my bed and Launcelot was engaged in ripping open Leigh's pillow with a framed photograph of Victor Mature. His face wore a smile of sublime happiness. 'I'm hiding fings,' he announced quite amicably.

I was quite startled as he was a child of few words. Indeed, I never remembered hearing him speak a consecutive sentence before.

'Oh really,' I said encouragingly. 'What?'

'Fings,' he repeated coldly, immediately regretting this confidence.

I went over to Leigh's mattress and knelt down beside him.

'Oh, do show me Launcelot, I'd love to see them.'

He gave me the once-over, then burrowing his hand up one of the holes in the pillow, brought out a melted chocolate biscuit covered with feathers.

'Ver's lots and lots more in ver,' he said ghoulishly. He took a bite out of the one in his hand and rammed it quickly back up the pillow.

'Could I have one please?' I asked, wanting him to go on talking.

But it was not to be; his face turned savage and he struck me cruelly with the photograph.

With Guinevere sleeping and Launcelot fairly peacefully occupied, I decided that they were better left. The rain still beat outside in a grey mist and the little attic room was practically dark. I lay down on Rose's bed and watched the drops stream down the window.

The slight sadness I felt was suddenly intensified and a great melancholy filled my heart. I began to think back over Mrs Welles and Mr Dropsey, but then because I didn't want to, further back over all the things that had happened since I had joined the Floods. I thought about my joining them and quite a lot about they themselves.

I wished now, in a jumbled way, that I had got more out of Willy, and wondered and tried to work out their strange relationship; but all the time my mind kept coming back to number eight, to the turbulent exciting life we led with Mrs Welles. Far more dramatically satisfying than my career, which nightly progressed on a little wooden stage at the bottom of the hill.

I felt rather ashamed as I realised what little importance the first night of the new play we were presenting tomorrow should mean to me. And then I thought quickly back to the first night of *Wuthering Heights*, when I had my spiritual feeling and for a brief instance knew why I had chosen to act. I reflected with a start that it was only a week ago, and quickly my feeling of shame gave way to one of a burning ambition.

Ambition to go on playing parts such as Cathy, plays such as *Wuthering Heights*, but tomorrow we were doing *What the Butler Saw*, and a string of other dreary little horrors to follow. No money, Mrs Flood had said, and precious little chance of getting it now, I thought. Our only chance I had impulsively given away.

For a moment I felt a blinding jealousy for Mrs Welles, but

Guinevere on my left stirred softly in her sleep, and I turned and looked at her, and could see the pale exhausted blob that was her face and the tear marks that had washed little white rivulets down her cheeks. I wondered why she had been crying, and then remembered the look on her face when Mrs Welles had screamed at her, 'Don't Mum me.' And she was only seven years old.

I thought back to when I was seven years old, and tried to remember how I had felt. But all I could see was a blur of playing games at school and scampering home with my sister to an enormous tea laid out in front of the dining-room fire and mother plying us with questions about the day's events. The only emotion I remember feeling was wanting the doll that my sister had; my only fear, Friday nights when our hair was washed.

My heart went out in a great wave of love to Guinevere, and I looked quickly away to Launcelot, as there was nothing I could do about her. He had fallen asleep too, clutching a feathered chocolate biscuit, lying on his back, with his mouth open. I felt a bit better about him, as he thoroughly enjoyed and wisely made the most of his unthwarted neglect; we were all agreed that he would undoubtedly enter a remand home at a very early age.

Thoughts spun round my head, leading off from each other with the speed of shooting stars, then quickly came back to my childhood. I liked remembering when I was seven and abandoned myself to a safe wallow of retrospection, so safe, so gentle, so secure that in a minute I recognised the no-man's land between fantasy and fact. Then a minute later I couldn't recognise it at all, and Launcelot had always been my brother.

I awoke very quietly in a delicious coma of warmth. The room seemed quite dark and my eyes focused immediately on the glowing point of a cigarette; the light of it rose and fell to the dry, finished, round sound of it being inhaled. I travelled my eyes over the blanket which was now covering me, and felt with my foot the hard form of the man whose warmth I was absorbing.

Leigh Peters said, 'Hallo Annie,' softly, and looked at me and gave me a cigarette.

'What time is it, Leigh?'

'Eight o'clock.'

'Eight o'clock at night?'

'Umm!'

'Where are the children?'

'They came down hours ago. They're asleep in their own beds now.'

'Where's Rose?'

'Sebastian called round a few minutes ago. They've gone over to the local. I said we'd follow them.'

'Isn't Mrs Welles back yet?'

'No!'

'Oh!' We grinned at each other in the darkness. There was nothing more to be said. Everyone was safe and secure in their little compartments. I had asked him and he had told me. There was nothing more to be said.

A little trickle of fear ran down me because there was only one reason why he was sitting on my bed; only one reason why he had disposed of the conversation so completely. I thought suddenly, only the length of our cigarettes spells civilisation.

I sat up in bed, drawing my legs quickly from under the blanket, and said, 'We'd better go now then, better not lose any time had we?' I felt Leigh's body move slightly, then he drew hard on his cigarette so I could see that his face was questioning and his hand forced.

He said 'No?' drawled and insolent, then when I didn't answer him, 'No,' again, laughing and mock serious to cover up his pique. He held out his hand and pulled me up. For a second while I stood facing him he kept hold of my hands then, bowing elaborately, he kissed one of them and let me go.

I combed my hair and put on some lipstick, and on the way down we looked in at the sleeping children. Outside the rain still poured, and the evening was spread with a premature darkness.

Leigh took my arm and together we jumped the shining pools of water down The Rooley, over the main road and up the cemented incline which led to our nearest pub. The Hope and Anchor was one of the nicest pubs I had ever been in. It was an old gin palace, and thought by the neighbourhood to be rather dubious.

It was full of people laughing and talking and knocking them back, and above it all the insistent jangle of the honky-tonk piano churning out 'Sally'. We threaded our way towards it, and from across the room Rose and Sebastian waved madly. Rose shoved up on the bench and Sebastian, very gay and debonair in a red velvet smoking jacket, shrieked for a waiter.

'Couple of beers, Bob,' he yelled, but Leigh pushed him down on the bench.

'Make it four gins, Bob.'

We all looked surprised and Bob looked surprised too, as he knew actors. 'Celebrating?' he inquired.

'That's right,' said Leigh giving us a wink.

Sebastian hit him on the back and said he hoped it was a boy but that either way gin was the only solution, and Rose said that with a bit of fire inside her she might even be persuaded to sing. We shrieked in simultaneous horror at her and Sebastian said that he'd die for her any day – but not, please not, in an agony of shame at Cockton Heath. Rose, looking nauseatingly coy, said that as an actress it was expected of her and that a man had stopped her outside the ladies' and asked with tears in his eyes that she sing 'Ave Maria' for him.

It was true that we were causing a bit of a stir. As members of the rep, quite a lot of people recognised us, and even those who didn't stared. I supposed we did look a bit different.

Sebastian, with his almost suspiciously handsome looks and bright red jacket; Rose quite beautiful, clad in a white sweater and tight blue jeans, and Leigh and I with our blonde hair; and of course, consciously or unconsciously, we were playing up.

I know that I for one was aware of every move I made, of every expression on my face. And Sebastian too, I noticed, directed his wittiest remarks rather loudly to an admiring party on our right. Rose was a little more personal in her choice, but it was quite plain that she was strongly taken with an elderly foreigner drinking vodka two tables down. I sincerely hoped that the vodka was playing a large part in the attraction.

Our gins arrived and we downed them quickly then clubbed together for a second round. The second one was smooth and melting and intoxicating, making us sing out loudly to the strains of 'My Old Man'. People kept pouring into the bar, shaking raindrops off themselves, stamping, exclaiming, and ordering shorts, as though the elements outside were some terrible war that only by the grace of God they had managed to survive.

'I do wish we had Win with us,' said Rose suddenly, and we all of course immediately fell to discussing her absence, and never, I might add, had an eight-hour luncheon date been so heartily approved. Leigh said he could see them clutching each other at the showing of some Pola Negri film to help Mr Dropsey get the right temperature.

Rose saw them lolling on a chaise-longue in front of a roaring fire in the ancestral home, with Mrs Welles, having carefully got wet, clad pathetically in an outsize male dressing gown.

I rather hoped that *Le Cercle Rouge* was open on Sundays, but Sebastian, who had been thoroughly genned up, said he was sorry but his imagination could go no further than the double bed of a rather dull trust house, with the sheet turned down so bravely, oh! Strangely enough, at this remark, Leigh, Rose and myself all sprang to Mrs Welles' defence.

We looked at each other rather ruefully afterwards as it was very probably the truth, but at the same time, I felt a thrill of pride that they should feel instinctively as I did. Somehow or other, to us Mrs Welles could never be as she must appear to others.

Sebastian had been frightfully keen to meet Mrs Welles all along. I had thought from the beginning that they were suited, and had been meaning to introduce them for some time. But now, as he confessed that his journey up to Cockton Heath on a wet Sunday night had not been without ambition, I was suddenly more thankful than ever that she had not returned. With the acquisition of Mr Dropsey, we could afford to take no risks.

A rather hard-looking middle-aged woman from the party on our right, who had been avidly listening to our conversation, leaned over and asked us what we were drinking. Sebastian said, 'Gin,' with a winning smile, although we were now on beer, and Rose who was still rather taken with the idea of singing for her supper said could she have a teeny vodka please.

The husband of the hard-looking woman went off to get it, and I hoped it would appease her interest in the elderly foreigner; but when he arrived back and we lifted our glasses to him in a cheer, Rose completely ignored the lot of us. Getting up from her seat, she leaned far across the table and flashed a luscious wink two tables down.

We yanked her back in shame, but it was too late. The elderly foreigner lumbered up from his chair and crashed his way towards us with wild eyes. Rose leaned forward expectantly, and we all looked away in disgust, but the next moment we heard her give a gasp of stifled rage, and looking up quickly, watched the elderly foreigner crash back to his table. In her hands Rose held a small white card. We peered at it over her shoulder.

'Repent ye,' it said in thick black letters, 'For the Kingdom of Heaven is at hand.'

Sebastian took it from her, and we laughed so hard that it fell out of his nerveless grip, and the hard-looking woman snatched it up and passed it around her party. They redoubled our delighted yells of mirth and the elderly foreigner, mistaking it for a hysterical mass repentance, got up and took an elaborate bow.

Rose in high dudgeon marched off to the ladies', and the hard-faced woman, who was a little drunk, leaned over and playfully bit Sebastian's ear. The whole of their party, which included somebody's very ancient mother, somebody's brother and a silent woman presumably attached to him, were beside themselves when they learnt that we were actors.

I was greatly amused to see imperceptibly how their attitude changed. Before, they had been admiring of our unabashed hilarity and intrigued by our appearance. But as soon as they knew we were actors, and these peculiarities could be understood, their admiration became rather bantering and demanding. They had paid us with drinks, and now expected an off-stage performance. The ancient mother leaned across the table and poked the hard-faced woman with her umbrella.

'You don't want to do that, Eth!' she said as the hard-faced woman stopped biting Sebastian's ear. 'Actors don't wash.'

Everyone laughed very loudly at this, and all eyes were turned on the ancient mother to encourage further such talk, but she had relapsed, muttering, into her Guinness, the general trend of which, on excited translation, appearing only that she 'could do with another'.

She didn't get it, and now attention was switched back to

Rose, who had reappeared and was standing, very noticeably, alone at the other end of the room. Her face was still flushed and angry, and we watched with horror, as with an exaggerated film star vamp reel, she made for the little wooden platform, where the pianist was happily thumping out boogie-woogie.

'She can't,' moaned Sebastian, clutching me. 'Oh dear God no, she can't.'

But she could. A slight cheer went up, as she and the tight blue jeans co-ordinated themselves in taking the three steps up to the platform, then a hush of expectancy as she exchanged words with the pianist. He looked extremely annoyed at the interruption, and for one wonderful moment we thought he was going to refuse to play, but Rose caught the eye of a waiter, pointed to his empty glass on the piano, and did a further reel over to the microphone.

'Ladies and gentlemen,' she announced in a breathless, ladylike voice. 'I have just received a very special request to sing "Ave Maria" and I hope you'll all like it.'

She looked so beautiful and innocent standing there, that an 'Aah' of pure sentimental satisfaction went up. Rose can't sing. We waited, dumbly praying that the vodka had worked some sort of miracle. Sebastian nearly went blind with his feverish attempts to do a Svengali on her.

But it was to no avail; she was quite, quite terrible. On the first note she pitched her voice about three octaves too high, and at the end of the first bar she forgot her words. To make up for this little difficulty she went into a series of pagan slave-girl gyrations of the body which, performed to the music of 'Ave Maria', was considered even by her appreciative audience to be in rather bad taste.

Little cries and mumbles and mutters went up, and someone yelled out 'Take 'em off,' and then to our everlasting shame, Rose, still wiggling, waved a hand at the offending voice and mimed the actions of a striptease. An animal shout went up from the voice joined by another, and they started yelling terrible ruderies.

An expression of doubt crossed Rose's face. She stopped wiggling, and pretending that she had remembered the words started singing Ave Maria, ave Maria over and over again through the mike.

But it was too late; a second later a bag of crisps thudded at her feet, closely followed by the screw of salt on her face. An angry roar went up from the crowd, and I stood up to have a look at the two men.

From where I was sitting they were both obscured by the piano, but as I got to my feet so did they, I took one look at them and fell back on the bench. It was Ed and Steve.

Rose had stopped singing and stood staring down at the bag of crisps at her feet; slowly her face began to crumple. She looked up and searched for me in a blind terrified sort of way. I stood up and pointed to the ladies' and she gave a sort of gasp and ran off the stage and out of the room. I followed her, threading my way between the tables and knocking over two light ales. Ed and Steve gave a yell as I passed them, and I heard the scrape of their chairs as they got up from their table.

The ladies' was down a long corridor and out in the back yard. I raced along it, crashing the door, behind me, and found Rose sobbing in the yard. I sat down on an empty beer box.

'What did I do wrong?' she kept moaning. 'Why was everyone so horrid?'

I told her that she should never have chosen 'Ave Maria' in the first place, but that it was Ed and Steve who had sparked things off. Rose brightened a little.

'Yes,' she said, 'that's right, they just wanted their revenge.'

I left her there whilst I went to get Leigh and Sebastian and found them in fierce argument with the hard-faced woman's husband as to who should pay for the double vodka the pianist was now imbibing. In the end they agreed to go halves and with much churlish back-chat from the now anything-but-admiring party, we left the room.

I told the boys to wait at the front door and went off for Rose.

"'Allo Ann!' said a voice as I went into the yard. It was Ed. He was standing against the wall just outside the door.

'Where's Rose?' I asked him sharply. She was not on the beer box.

'Rose's alright,' he said softly, 'she's wiv Steve.'

'Where?' He made a lunge at me. 'Where's Rose?' I repeated. He pointed to the opposite wall and we both looked across at the sordid sight of Rose pinioned against the door of the ladies' by Steve.

I didn't quite know what to do. It was obvious that Rose was putting up no resistance whatsoever, but at the same time I knew that she couldn't really be interested. It was typical of Rose as she often was; neither liking or disliking, absolutely passive.

I called her and she said, 'Coming!' in a muffled voice.

'Well, come on then, the boys are waiting.'

'What boys?' said Ed in an insolent voice.

He tried to seize me and we had a little scuffle, then mercifully a woman came through the door and crossed over to the ladies'.

'Would you mind?' she said pointedly to the mass against the door.

Rose broke away and ran over to me, her eyes sparkling.

I grabbed her with one hand and pulled at the door with the other, and then we both fell over backwards as at the same time the door was swung open by Leigh and Sebastian. By this time, Steve had lumbered up. I squinted up from the ground and saw Leigh looking at me. A gurgle of coquettish excitement ran up me. I nudged Rose, and suddenly yelled out, 'Don't let him touch me, don't let him touch me, Leigh.'

Rose caught on straight away. She let out a terrible dramatic scream and announced that she'd been interfered with. Leigh and Sebastian stuck out their jaws in perfect unison and behind us Ed and Steve closed in.

'Okay girls, beat it,' said Sebastian, who had always fancied himself in a gangster film.

We crawled out from under their legs and heard the wham of the first hit. It had the same effect as a factory buzzer sounding at the end of the day. In one frightening swoop people converged on us from all directions. They surged out into the yard with a great hoarse shout.

The landlord and a few waiters kept saying, 'Now, now,' and 'We don't want the Police,' but nobody paid any attention, and while the landlord tried to force his way to the front, the waiters nipped back to the bar and got busy on a bottle of whisky.

Rose and I couldn't see a thing, but we hung around excitedly at the back of the crowd. A minor stir was being caused down our end by the ancient mother, who was trying to get to the ladies'.

She kept lashing out at people with her umbrella and saying that she'd been 'took short', and the hard-faced woman's husband who was accompanying her said, for Christ's sake, couldn't people show a bit of humanity, that mother was ninety-six, and did we want another accident here?

Rose, who had noticed the waiters, extracted herself from the crowd, crossed over to the bar and, leaning against it, announced loudly that she felt faint. She got a double whisky and one for me too.

And then I remembered. I remembered Leigh Peters' lame leg. A real feeling of faintness came over me and I went cold inside.

'Rose,' I said. 'Leigh's leg?'

She looked at me in sympathy and said, 'We'd better have another whisky.'

'We've got to stop them Rose, it's terribly dangerous.'

I went all desperate, and wildly told a waiter he must do something. He smiled at me kindly and said that nobody could do anything at the moment and why didn't we both go home.

'Let's go Rose,' I said. 'I can't bear to see them carrying Leigh out.'

At the door an anguished moan went up from the ancient mother, and we let ourselves out to the triumphant cry of the hard-faced woman's husband saying, 'What did I tell you?'

Outside, the rain had stopped and the moon was up. Mrs Welles was still not home, and without her the kitchen was cold and cheerless. Rose opened a tin of baked beans and we picked disinterestedly at them.

'It must be over by now,' I said at intervals.

And Rose said, 'Yes, it must.'

'I do wish Win was here,' Rose kept saying.

And I said, 'Yes, so do I.'

We made some tea, and sat listless over it straining our ears for the sound of an ambulance bell, but the only sound we did hear, a few minutes later, was the unmistakable laughter of Leigh and Sebastian. They flung open the door, flushed and smiling and wholly intact.

'Are you alright Leigh?' I said in a small voice, and discovered I was trembling all over.

Sebastian put back his head and roared with laughter. 'Tell them Leigh.'

'Tell them yourself,' said Leigh, pouring himself out a cup of tea.

'Well!' Sebastian surrendered himself to a further paroxysm of laughter and straddled the copper.

'Well,' he said, 'no sooner had I drawn back my fist to give lover boy number one a preliminary tickling in the ribs, but lover boy number two jumps up and knocks him to the ground.

'Well, number one's not going to take that lying down so up he gets and knocks number two down, and then with my innocent fists still itching, we are deluged by a spate of righteous Englishmen who know a good clean fight when they see one. So Leigh and I stroll over to a conveniently placed ladder, perch ourselves on the roof of the ladies' and watch the fun.'

Rose said, 'Oh!' coldly, and I felt unreasonably disappointed, and we both said we were going to bed.

But at the doorway Rose couldn't resist it. 'Who won?' she said carelessly to the kitchen at large.

'Yours!' said Leigh, grinning. 'He said that the other one hadn't worked hard enough on Ann, he said he'd really worked hard on you, and all the other one had done was talk.'

'Nerve!' said Rose with dignity and slammed the door.

Chapter Eight

The first thing I remembered in the morning was Mrs Welles. I rushed down to her bedroom and found Sebastian asleep in her bed. Downstairs in the kitchen Guinevere informed me that there was a man in Mum's bed, and was it The One. I said 'No!' and she said 'Oh!' and we both got busy on breakfast.

It was Monday, the busiest day of the week for us, with the new show in the evening. Rose and Leigh and Sebastian straggled down with their heads buried in their scripts, and all of us in terrible tempers at the awful realisation that never in a million years could we know our parts by tonight.

Guinevere asked us in a silence if we thought Mum would be home this morning. And then it sunk in; she'd stayed away for the whole night. Sebastian hit the table triumphantly and said that he wished we'd had bets on it last night, and we all perked up a bit and wondered what had happened. But we wouldn't know yet awhile; we fell out of the house and on to a bus, the burning question being as to how much I could decently allow the butler to see in Act Three.

I usually liked Mondays a lot, but this morning I couldn't enjoy it at all. The handicap of not knowing one's lines obliterates all feeling except the frustrated desire to crawl into a hole alone with one's script. The only ray of hope was that nobody else appeared to know theirs either. We dragged through a terrible rehearsal, with Mrs Flood like a demented dog, and at two o'clock were told that there was to be no lunch break.

We had no money for sandwiches, and with hollow stomachs took turns at the iron while somebody heard us through our lines. Four o'clock was dress rehearsal and we were just as bad, and Mrs Flood threw the book on the floor and stamped on it in rage.

Somehow the curtain went up, and somehow or other we got through the show, and surprisingly enough the audience laughed, and surprisingly enough, by Act Three we weren't too bad at all.

And then, it was over and Rose borrowed five bob from Hilda Fellowes, and we all had a drink at the Ship.

We walked the two miles home. Warm and moonlit it was, with the trees making little summer rustling sounds, and the air thick and bursting and fertile after the heavy rains. Leigh hummed a popular tune under his breath and Rose went quite wild, and leaped and pranced around on the pavement, and pulled off great leafy lengths from the overhanging branches.

We asked her why she was so happy and she picked up her skirts and twirled round and round and said, 'I'm in love, I'm in love!'

Leigh said, 'Oh really, with whom?'

And I said, 'Derrick, of course,' firmly.

The noticeable lack of interest Rose showed in her fiancé was rather worrying, particularly as she was due to be a December bride.

Back at the digs Mrs Welles was still not home. Guinevere was sitting rather lonely at the kitchen table and I reflected that they'd been on their own all day.

'Will she be home today, Ann?' she asked me.

And I could only say that if she wasn't, she must remember that it would only be because Mummy was enjoying herself so much, and she wanted Mummy to enjoy herself, didn't she?

We fell ravenously on to three tins of baked beans and Leigh said that with any luck it could be for the last time. We were just starting on the fourth when he held up his fork.

'Listen!' he said.

We listened, and the tiny purring sound he had heard grew louder and louder until it became an expensive roar. We gazed at one another with shining eyes, hardly daring to breathe. The roar rose to a crescendo then dropped again to a purring halt outside the house. We heard the car door slam, voices, then the sharp tap-tap of shoes coming up the path.

The car drove off, and at the same time the noise of the front door knocker filled the house.

Guinevere said, 'Mum?' in a strangled voice and Leigh leaped up and ran to the door. We heard the little flurry of him letting someone in, then his name, Leigh, said in a throaty mutter, then the tap-tap of her heels along the corridor, then...

Rose fell off her chair and I had to clutch mine. We both tried to gasp and we were both struck dumb. Before us, not two yards away, framed in the doorway with one arm flung above her head, stood Mrs Welles. Breathless, wild-eyed, triumphant, and victorious she stood before us. Her hair hung around her in lank black clumps, and she'd no make-up on at all. One of her shoes was broken, and her legs were spattered with mud.

She looked at least thirty, but at the same time more beautiful than I had ever seen her look before, for clutched around her, with the fierceness of a tiger holding its young, with the bravado of a matador with his cloak, with the wonderment of a mother with her first child; for there, clutched triumphantly around Mrs Welles' form, was a shining mink coat.

The blondeness of it rippled and shone under the electric light. The thickness and the roundness and the depth of it seemed to fill the air. It was a living thing, and the happiness and content of it could almost be felt as it hung in a miracle of satisfaction from the shoulders of someone who'd been cut out for it.

'Like it?' said Mrs Welles.

We just stared.

'Course,' she went on, 'it's the wrong time of the year for a mink really, but as I said to Teddy, with these English summers I said, it's bound to come in useful.'

The words came tripping off her tongue in a sharp blasé voice. She gave the mink a twitch.

'Got a fag, Leigh?' she said.

He gave her one and she lit it. Still we stared at her in an agony of silence. Mrs Welles' eyes snapped a little and she gave us a bantering smile.

'What's the matter with you two, lost your tongues?'

At last Rose spoke. 'Oh, Win!' she said, 'Oh, Win!'

'I thought you'd like it Rose,' said Mrs Welles casually.

'Oh Win!' said Rose again. 'It's... It's beautiful.'

I had never seen Rose so moved in my life. Tears shone in her eyes. She gazed at the coat as though it were a visitation, then like someone in a trance got up, walked over to Mrs Welles and gently ran her hands along the fur. 'Oh, Win!' she said again, then turning, slowly went back to her chair.

For an instant Mrs Welles eyed her cowed back with pleasure, then her eyes met mine in a hard bright challenge. My heart began to beat a little fast but I held her gaze in silence and she was the first to speak.

'Well Ann,' she said, 'what are you looking so peaked about? It's real, you know.'

For a second I didn't answer her, and when I did, my voice was stiff and I looked past her, into the hall.

'I'm sure it is Win, and I'm very happy for you.'

A spasm of anger crossed Mrs Welles' face.

'I don't know what you mean by that I'm sure,' she said. 'Of course, we all know you give your last three minks away, but there's no need to begrudge someone else one. I suppose,' she said, blowing a perfect smoke ring into the air, 'that you're expecting me to act the dog with two heads.' She gave a false smile.

'Let's keep things in proportion Ann, shall we? After all, a coat's only a coat when all's said and done.' She gave the mink another twitch and Rose in a shocked voice addressed her wildly.

'Oh, Win!' she gasped. 'How can you talk like that it's... it's... a mink!'

Her voice rose in a moan on the last word. Mrs Welles gave a tinkling laugh. 'Rose,' she said, 'will you never grow up?'

She detached herself from the doorway and came towards the table. A smell of expensive perfume pervaded the air, and she sat down in Leigh's chair. 'Any more tea in that pot?'

Guinevere, who had been crouched against the copper, ran to get a cup.

'Ta!' said her mother, not looking at her.

Rose stretched out her hand and touched the mink again.

'Don't wear it out,' said Mrs Welles with another little laugh.

A terrible strained silence fell on us. We watched Mrs Welles drain two cups of tea. I looked at Rose and she looked back at me, rather frightened. My voice when I spoke was still stiff.

'Did you have er... a good day, Win?'

Mrs Welles took another cigarette from Leigh and addressed the window. 'Yes, lovely thank you Ann,' she said brightly. 'But dear me, so tiring – shopping, shopping, shopping!' She patted her mouth in a crescendo of little yawns.

'What's your scent, Win?' asked Rose.

'Original Sin,' replied Mrs Welles in an automatic voice. 'Any more questions?' She gave us all another bright glance.

And then I came to my senses. In a rush of temper which surged upon me and nearly choked me, I flung myself off the chair.

'Coming Rose?' I called at the door.

Rose looked from me to Mrs Welles and back to me. She still looked rather frightened.

'Yes. I'm coming Ann.'

We closed the door and heard Mrs Welles laugh behind us. Upstairs in the attic I threw myself down on my bed. Rose came and sat beside me.

'Whatever's the matter with her Ann?' she said in a sort of whisper. 'Why was she like that? Why was she so horrid? I mean, it's not like Win; what's the matter with her, Ann?'

'I don't know.'

Rose's indignation mounted.

'Christ, she was beastly Ann, absolutely beastly, and to you of all people, after all you've done for her. Doesn't she realise that if it hadn't been for you she'd never have met him? Doesn't she realise that by rights that mink coat should be yours? I've never seen anything like it, I've never in my whole life seen such... such...' Words failed Rose, and I finished it for her.

'Ingratitude?'

'Yes, ingratitude.'

For a moment we were silent then Rose sprang off the bed and tugged at my arm. 'Come on,' she said, 'we're not going to let her get away with it, we're going down right now and telling her what we think about her.'

But I didn't move. I just lay on the bed and in a jumbled way tried to work out how I felt. My anger had left me, and physically all I felt was an ache at the bottom of my stomach as though I had once had some trouble with it.

Mentally I was hurt of course, terribly hurt, but far greater than that was the almost overpowering sensation of loss, of being cheated. I owned up to myself then that I had minded about handing Mr Dropsey over, but at the same time I knew it was not the loss of him that hurt me. And then suddenly I did know and I laughed to myself as I realised that Rose had just summed it up in a single word. Where is the sweetness of giving without gratitude?

'Come on,' Rose said again.

'Not now Rose.'

'Oh I give you up,' said Rose rather thankfully. She lay down on her bed and picked up a magazine.

Where is the sweetness of giving without gratitude? A wave of self-pity swept over me. All I had asked, I told myself, was for a crumb of thanks. Sharper than the serpent's tooth is an ungrateful child. Tears pricked my eyelids; I searched wildly for another simile that would unleash them, but I couldn't think of one, and self-pity gave way to annoyance and the tears stopped pricking.

And then for the first time I started to think about Mrs Welles. Rose had said it wasn't like her and it wasn't. Although Mrs Welles was an extraordinary woman, her emotions ran to a fairly even pattern. Gratitude was one of them, and I suppose subconsciously I had known that when I'd given her Mr Dropsey.

At any rate I wouldn't have felt the same way about giving him to Rose. And all the while we had been getting her ready for him, she had been grateful, not in so many in words, as Mrs Welles was not a great one for expressing herself verbally; but by the light in her eyes, by her enthusiasm, by her almost tragic desire to succeed, she had been grateful. And she had succeeded, triumphantly and instantly and beyond any of our wildest dreams... No, it wasn't like Mrs Welles.

'Whatever's the matter with her?' Rose said again.

I tried to imagine what I'd feel if it had been me. I tried to relive Mrs Welles' entrance, but in all honesty the greatest pleasure I could imagine from standing framed in the doorway in mink, would be of its effect on the others, the sharing and the exclaiming and the wondering and the telling of how its possession came about.

'I don't know,' I said again. Then suddenly I wanted to know, and was sick of puzzling it out. I jumped off the bed. 'But I'm going to find out.'

'Oh!' said Rose, 'Oh, good. You don't really want me though, do you?'

I had thought that Mrs Welles would still be in the kitchen

where we left her, but at the bottom of the attic stairs I stopped. Her bedroom faced me, the door was open and a shaft of light from the landing illuminated the bed, and there in the middle of it, lit up in a pathetic furry huddle, lay the figure of Mrs Welles. In the doorway I stood watching her. Her breath came in hard gasping sobs, and little tremors ran up and down the mink.

I walked over to her softly and sat down at the end of the bed.

'Hallo, Win.'

She didn't say anything, but the gasping sobs quickened.

'Want a cigarette, Win?'

Mrs Welles made a muffled noise so I lit two.

'Here you are.' I held it towards a part of the mink which had some hair hanging over it, and after a while a hand shot out and took it.

She sobbed again for a moment without smoking, then slowly levered herself on to her side and took a gasping puff.

'Hi, Win!'

She looked at me then. Her face was swollen and puffed with crying; down the front of the mink her tears had clogged the fur together in little wet lumps, but with one hand she still clutched it fiercely around her, so hard that the knuckles shone white. For a moment we gazed at each other, then her face began to crumple again and at the same time she started to speak.

'It's just like what you said Ann... It's a mink... Just like what you said I should have... Teddy give it me Ann... just like you said...' Her voice broke in a sob and then she was crying on my shoulder and I was patting the fur and... understanding. My heart and throat contracted suddenly as at last I understood.

I understood that getting a mink coat was to Mrs Welles what religion is to some people, what love is to others, what success is, what being a star would be to me. The biggest thing that could happen in your life is not usually something you want to share or talk about, and in religion or love or success, it's not even expected.

I had tried to imagine myself in a mink coat and felt that I would have wanted to talk about it, but I saw now how stupid I had been. It was not the biggest thing that could happen to me, and because we could not understand that it could be for someone else, poor Mrs Welles had had to face us, like a girl in love, the prying, poking ferreting of her family; she had had to face our ravening attempts to lay bare her soul.

But at the same time she knew it must be expected, for she lived in a world where religion and love and success were rated worthier ambitions than mink coats, and the only way out for her was the one she chose.

I remembered the words she had used, which at the time had made me so angry, and which now only made me want to cry.

'A coat's only a coat, Ann,' she'd said, 'when all's said and done.'

For a little while longer she sobbed on my shoulder, and then I relit her cigarette, which had gone out, and she sat up and inhaled it as though it were ether. I asked her if she would like to go to bed, and she said in a rather muffled voice, 'No!' but she thought she could fancy a cup of tea.

I said I'd go and make her one and then added, 'When you came through the door Win, I'd like you to know that I'd never seen anyone look so beautiful in my life.'

Mrs Welles said, 'Get away with you,' and that I knew she looked an absolute fright with no make-up on, and her hair all straight, and could she please borrow my curlers again tonight? She grinned at me then, a rather watery grin, but it was the old Mrs Welles and my heart leaped inside me. The crisis was over; it was going to be all right.

'Rose!' I yelled up the attic stairs, 'Win's having some tea, come on down and join us.'

The kitchen was empty, and just like old times we sat round the table with three cups and the pot. And just like the young girl for whom love had triumphed and who could now talk her head off with preparations for the marriage, Mrs Welles leaned back in her chair, her eyes dancing and excited and we leaned forwards avidly waiting to be Told All.

We sat up till two in the morning hearing how it had been a success from the beginning; how they had lunched together at some grand hotel in the wilds of the country, how they had tramped some wet lanes, then tea-ed quickly afterwards at another grand hotel, sitting high up in a ghostly gallery whilst the strains of Old Vienna were wafted up to them from an elderly female quartet below.

And how it had got into Mr Dropsey's blood and he had seized her suddenly and whirled her round and round the empty tables in a spanking waltz. And had demanded caviar from a suspicious manager, and Mrs Welles had thought it was something to drink and said, 'Make hers a gin please,' and Mr Dropsey had explained that it was virgin sturgeon and pinched her bottom.

Then back on to the wet roads, then drinking, drinking, drinking; one hotel after another, then eating again, dancing again; late at night by this time in another nightclub – no, not *Le Cercle Rouge* but a lovely place which affected Mr Dropsey very happily, because he suddenly said he wanted to give her a present... Then it was later on than ever, and Mr Dropsey had fallen down on to the floor twice and been carried into the car.

Speeding back to the ancestral home, with Mrs Welles being terribly, terribly nice to him and telling him ever so gently just what sort of a present would make her happy. And then, at last when she laid her head on the pillow of the enormous quilted bed, hearing the magic words; hearing Mr Dropsey instruct Withers to go out first thing in the morning and buy a mink coat.

Mrs Welles had paused in her recital at this point, and if she had been a religious woman I feel sure she would have crossed herself. Then she went on to tell us how she had opened her eyes sometime in the afternoon and it had been lying there on the bed. She had stood before the mirror in it for nearly an hour, then fallen asleep again with something brought up on a tray and instructions to wait there till Mr Dropsey returned home from an appointment with his lampshades.

Then out with him for another meal, then suddenly wanting to be home; wanting to be alone; wanting with an almost overwhelming desire to be silent and alone with her mink.

At the end of the recital Rose and I gave long satisfied sighs.

'Just like a beautiful story from *True Romances*,' said Rose, but Mrs Welles thought that sounded rather final.

'More like a beautiful serial I should say, Rose,' she said, gazing wonderingly into the distance.

Chapter Nine

With the acquisition of Mr Dropsey, life at number eight came into its own, and for a fortnight we wallowed in one big sinful delight of money. We didn't see a lot of Mrs Welles of course, on account of the social whirl and 'obligations', but she was wonderful and never forgot us, and great hampers of food arrived round nearly every day. They say that money can't buy happiness and really I had to laugh; I never saw quite so much happiness as in the family just then.

Down at the theatre things weren't going so well. All through *What the Butler Saw* the audiences steadily got thinner and thinner.

Mrs Flood's voice was one long shriek of anxiety. I felt particularly bad about it as night after night she would collar me and with a heavy attempt at disinterest, enquire whether I'd spoken to my gentleman friend yet. Having seen the extent of Mrs Welles' triumph, Leigh said he thought we might still get something out of him, but naturally it would take time and naturally it would have to be done through Mrs Welles; in the meantime I could only keep telling Mrs Flood that he was still away on holiday.

The following week we opened with *Baby Mine*, which got a little better reception. Tuesday picked up too, and then on the Wednesday morning when we arrived down for rehearsal we got the one break which, apart from actual spot cash, we knew Mrs Flood had been longing for.

She stood in the centre of the stage enshrouded in the eerie gloom of a theatre by day, only a sun-mote wriggled in through the tiny crack way up in the roof to proclaim the fierce July heat which burnt outside. She stood there clutching the thick white envelope, her face red with excitement as we all straggled in for the two thirty rehearsal.

'Everyone on stage please!' Her voice was sharp as usual but today with excitement. We crowded round her eagerly, and slowly and carefully she read us out the letter. It was a formal invitation from the mayor, for the whole of the company to open the annual Leek summer fete on the following Saturday afternoon. We were all suitably impressed.

The summer fete was supposed to be *the* social event of the year; and to be invited by the mayor, rogues and vagabonds as we were still often considered, was, as Mrs Flood put it, 'class and prestige such as many another company would pay good money for'.

Nobody mentioned the fact that a week earlier we had been informed that the theatre would be required that Saturday night for a dance to be held after the fete. And nobody expressed any interest in what great person could have fallen through, that we should receive the invitation at such short notice.

No, we had been accepted by the mayor, and Mrs Flood was going to see that he had no cause to regret such rashness. He was coming round at twelve o'clock that morning for a chat and instructions.

'Maybe,' said Mrs Flood, painfully cramming her feet into a pair of nineteen-o-two pointed dancing slippers which Willy had hurriedly been sent to the dressing room for. 'Maybe the plays of late have not been the class that His Worship is at home with, but I shouldn't wonder that with meeting us socially, he shouldn't realise that with a little sympathy we shouldn't be able to rise.' Here she shot me a nasty glance. 'I shouldn't worry too much Ann,' she said, 'if your gentleman friend has ever such a nice long holiday.'

Mrs Flood gave a grunt as the last inch of heel surrendered itself to the torturous confines of *glacé* kid, and handed her bedroom slipper to Willy.

'And now,' she said advancing towards us with difficulty, 'let's see what can be done with the rest of you before twelve o'clock.'

Leigh and Sebastian were sent off for haircuts and Rose was told that if she still wanted to be in employment next week, she would get out of those jeans this instant and see that they never darkened the stage door again. Hilda Fellowes was told to keep her coat on and stay well in the background, but poor old Bill Irving, Mrs Flood thought, was better kept right out of the way.

We all felt rather awful about this but at the same time saw Mrs Flood's point. At seventy, poor old Bill was definitely not a credit to the company, his entire off-stage wardrobe consisting of a pair of old corduroy trousers, a torn cardigan and a white silk scarf. I just passed in a green and white checked cotton frock, but it was to Willy that all the credit went.

From layers and layers of tissue paper in a special basket where it was kept, Mrs Flood took out his blazer. It was her pride and joy, expensively cut in beautiful black barathea with the Harrow school badge neatly stitched to the breast pocket.

At about twelve thirty the mayor and a secretary arrived.

He waddled on to the stage, short, fat and bald, and addressed us in a broad Midlands accent. I only just stopped myself from laughing out loud, he was so perfectly cast. It was obvious from the beginning, however, that he did not approve of the Living Theatre in Leek but he tried very hard and told us quite civilly what we would have to do. A few words from Mr and Mrs Flood to open it, three of us to take over a stall each, then Mr and Mrs Flood and two more of us to judge the bathing beauty competition.

Afterwards, he said, there would be a banquet in the banqueting hall adjoining the theatre, which he would like the entire company to attend. The dance, he concluded gallantly and eyeing Rose, would benefit a great deal by a visit from the younger members of the company. The three stalls, guessing the weight of the cake, the shooting range, and a kiss-me-quick ransom bran tub, no doubt Mrs Flood would suitably allot. The mayor thought, *That's all then… and everyone – Saturday, one thirty sharp at the pavilion please.*

We watched him exit then all turned expectantly to Mrs Flood, but her earlier burst of confidence had gone. She swept us coldly with her eyes.

'The company will be detailed tonight as to what part in the fete they will be taking. Clear the stage please. Act One – Scene One. Willy…'

Mrs Flood jerked her thumb towards her dressing room and Willy, like a well-trained dog, trotted off to take off his blazer and bring back her slippers.

We discussed the forthcoming event with great excitement on the way home. Rose said she thought that Leigh and I would be chosen to judge the competition with the Floods, Hilda Fellowes on the cake, herself on the bran tub and Sebastian on the shooting range.

I thought that was the most likely arrangement too, and hoped so a lot; I didn't fancy being stuck on a stall all afternoon. It looked as if poor old Bill was going to be left out again. 'I bet she won't even allow him to come,' said Rose.

I realise now how little I have said about Bill. It would be silly to say I scarcely ever saw him because I did see him, every day, but that was the way I felt about him. He lived alone and during rehearsals and the show at night hardly ever spoke to anyone, not because he was unfriendly but because he was an old man and had to reserve every ounce of strength to get his words out on stage. We all appreciated this and didn't worry him.

I felt terrible about him when I first joined the company, thinking how cruel it was that he had to work and wondering what would happen to him, but quite early on I had a little conversation with him which made me feel a lot better.

He was living and dreaming, he told me, for next January because next January he would be seventy and could enter the Haven of Rest. He got quite excited describing it to me, a lovely country home standing in extensive grounds paid for by successful actors. Everyone had a beautiful private panelled room, and in the common room (which included a stage at one end for Christmas frivolities), there was Television. We all liked to think of him going there, and whenever he had a particularly long or difficult part to do, reminded him about it.

'I wonder if it will do any good for the company, opening the fete?' I said.

Leigh said that from the prestige and interest point of view it probably would, but that when people turned round next week to look at our bills and saw that we were presenting *She was Poor but She was Honest*, it would all be wasted.

'Very short-sighted of Ma to deliver that crack at you about Dropsey,' he said. 'She'll have to be eating a great deal more humble pie by the end of next week.'

'Old bitch!' said Rose.

As we turned into The Rooley, I reflected upon how strange and miraculous was life, that in ten minutes time we would be sitting down to a meal of cold chicken in the same kitchen of the same house where a fortnight ago we would have been thankful for baked beans. But more than that I marvelled at how quickly you can get used to anything.

'What's for dinner?' Rose had said just previous to my reflecting and marvelling.

'Chicken!' I replied in a rather tired voice.

Actually when we did reach home, all thought of our meal was forgotten. We had no sooner entered the kitchen when the velvety tones of Mrs Welles floated down to us.

'Come on up, kids.'

We rushed upstairs and there she was, laid out on the bed with Guinevere dropping grapes into her mouth and Launcelot fanning her with a plate. She gave us just long enough to take in this tableau then sat up in a hurry, the cotton wool pads of witch hazel falling away from her eyes. A great, evil happy grin spread over her face and, clutching her mink around her (in ten stifling July days we had never seen her without it), she addressed us in a truant-playing schoolgirl whisper.

'He's away. On business. Till Monday.'

We fell upon her with whoops of delight. It was the first time we'd had her home for more than a few hours at a time. Till three o'clock we caught up on the beautiful serial of romance, money, and the social whirl, and then over belated chicken told her about the fete.

Mrs Welles was thrilled. It really was *the* social event of the year, she assured us. She'd been hoping to get to it all along, but with Mr Dropsey being a night bird and liking her to stay in with him during the afternoons, she hadn't seen how she could manage it.

But now of course, with him away and us taking part, it was different, 'Quite different,' said Mrs Welles. 'You wouldn't understand of course but even if he'd taken me... Well, anyway, it was quite different.'

But we did understand, and we caught each other's eyes and smiled.

Mrs Welles was thrilled because at last she could parade her mink without the hampering price tag of Mr Dropsey at her side.

'There's a beautiful baby competition,' said Guinevere, who was sitting on Leigh's knee. 'Couldn't we enter –?'

Mrs Welles withered her with a glance. 'We most certainly could not,' she said.

That night we learned of the parts we were each to take in the fete. Leigh and I, as Rose had predicted, were to judge the bathing beauty competition with the Floods, and Sebastian too, was to manage the shooting range, but over the other two stalls she had made a sad mistake.

Hilda Fellowes was given the coveted kiss-me-quick bran tub ransom, and Rose alone was to know the weight of the cake. She cried all through the show about it, she'd been so sure that she'd get the kiss-me-quick. The rest of us were all pretty astonished too. Rose in a sort of Nell Gwynn costume distributing ransom kisses to the unlucky dippers would have been so right.

Unfortunately we let her know this and Rose, enjoying a particularly clear image of herself thus clad, marched straight up to Mrs Flood, described it, and demanded wildly that she and Hilda should be changed.

Mrs Flood was just making an entrance with Willy, as his mother. She couldn't have picked a more disastrous moment. For a moment I thought Mrs Flood was going to hit her, as her arm jerked up at a menacing angle, but she didn't, and her voice when she spoke a second later was controlled, icy and distant.

'I would sooner,' said Mrs Flood between gritted teeth, 'buy a suit of clothing for Bill Irving to take the stall, than have a strumpet such as yourself flaunting her trade on an innocent money-making charity such as the tub.'

Rose just stared open-mouthed at her and Mrs Flood, who was at that second due to enter, would have swept on stage, but Willy's cue was not for another couple of lines and at that split second Willy was looking at Rose. Mrs Flood stopped short in her entrance and at the same time Willy spoke.

'I still don't agree with you,' he said. 'We had it out all this afternoon and I still don't agree with you, Lil. That Hilda's fat and ugly, no one'll pay to kiss her, but Rose has got a wonderful shape. Look Lil, she has got a wonderful shape. I should think Rose would make a lot of money on a stall like that.'

Mrs Flood's fury was a horrible sight to watch. She took a step towards Rose. 'Get upstairs,' she spat at her, so that little saliva dots appeared on Rose's face. 'And stay there until you're due on stage.'

Willy who was beginning to realise that he'd said the wrong thing said, 'You're on,' furiously, and Mrs Flood, grabbing him, gave Rose a vicious push and made an unsuitable entrance with him on her arm.

I felt faintly ill and looked away from the crumpled heap of Rose at my feet, but a second later she was hissing in my ear, her eyes bright with excitement.

'Wasn't he wonderful, Ann? Wasn't he absolutely wonderful? Just standing there defying her. He stood there and defied her, Ann! It was probably for the first time in his life. Oh, I've been waiting and waiting for the day when I'd see him defy her, Ann.'

I hardly saw Willy's understandable suggestion that Rose could ransom more kisses than Hilda as defiant, but at that specific moment was heartily thankful that she did. For the rest of the evening the actual issue was forgotten and Rose went around in a defiant-Willy-reflected glory.

Late that night when we were both in bed her voice came sleepily to me in the darkness.

'What's a strumpet, Ann?'

'I don't know.'

'Old bitch,' said Rose magnanimously and out of habit.

The following morning we rehearsed as usual and afterwards Rose and I went back to the digs, prepared to settle in for an afternoon of sewing. Mrs Flood had given me an old black velveteen stage drape with instructions to run it up into a smart little something for the fete.

As it had faded into consecutive yellow stripes where the folds had hung, I felt rather depressed about it, but Mrs Flood said that with a bit of trouble I could arrange the stripes to form a kind of animal appeal.

Mrs Welles had said Rose could borrow her purple net. I was pleased about this, as with the morning Rose had got over Willy's defiance and was sunk in a terrible apathy, but it made no difference. Not even remarks such as 'look what it did for Mrs Welles' could rouse her from the thought of her position of degradation behind the cake.

'Green with a ruched bodice, I'd have liked,' she said pitifully to me on the way home.

'It's got a ruched bodice and purple's much nicer than green.' I was patient and bracing.

Rose was patient too. 'No, no dear, you don't understand – Nell Gwynn I mean.'

'Oh for Christ's sake Rose, snap out of it.'

It was whilst I was juggling with the velveteen and the machine, that the bell went. I supposed it was another hamper from Mr Dropsey and Guinevere went to answer it, but a minute later she was back.

'It's a man with a beard,' she said in a whisper. 'I think he wants Mum.'

He did. He was a sad-looking French man with a goatee beard and an eye glass, weighed down with a formidable array of cameras and tripods. He was, he informed me, Medici Studios Ltd., and had been sent round on the instructions of Mr Dropsey, to photograph a Miss Winifred Welles. Mrs Welles, upstairs, was taking it easy with a box of chocolates and a large glossy autographed photograph of Rock Hudson, which had arrived for her with the midday mail. Photography thus uppermost in her mind, she greeted my news of the Frenchman with a dazed smile, and staring glassily up at the ceiling remarked that it was a small world.

Downstairs in the sitting room the Frenchman was creating about no curtains. He had tacked Launcelot's cot cover to one window and was eyeing the Spanish shawls with intent.

'Carpets!' I said firmly and fetched my velveteen from the kitchen vaguely wondering if an hour or two at the window wouldn't help even out the stripes.

Mrs Welles appeared in the doorway in her nicest blue negligee and her hair over one eye. The Frenchman was entranced, his eyeglass fell out of his eye and he stood up and clicked his heels. 'Mademoiselle Welles,' he said gallantly. 'Monsieur had spoken to me of your beauty but had refrained from explaining that it was the face of a Madonna I should be privileged to capture.'

Mrs Welles thought he was taking a liberty.

'Reely,' she drawled superciliously. 'Then shall we get started?'

She was duly draped upon the settee and after a lot of shifting around under some blackout material the Frenchman pronounced that he was ready to shoot. It was at that moment that Launcelot came upon the scene.

The door burst open and he shot across the room and flung himself on his mother's lap. The single spot, which was lighting her head, caught his red curls and turned them into a fiery light. He had thrown himself so that his fat hands clutched at the folds of her negligee and his head was against her breast, only his eyes were turned on the camera, bright blue and wondering and breathtakingly innocent they gazed with complete absorption at the camera.

'Hold it,' shrieked the Frenchman, and the camera clicked.

We didn't need his trembling voice to describe to us the picture he had just taken. Launcelot moved away immediately afterwards, but for that moment the Madonna and Child had been before our eyes, so clear, so bright, so beautiful that the goose pimples ran up my arms and I shivered a little in the stifling room. The Frenchman was even more overcome and had to sit down and have a cigarette. Mrs Welles was rather annoyed at the incident, having no wish to be photographed with her son.

'Beautiful?' she kept saying. 'Beautiful? With that hair? You must be mad.'

'He is beautiful you know, Mum,' Guinevere said suddenly out of the darkness.

'Yes Win,' I said, 'he is.' And of course he was. Subconsciously I had always known it, we all had. It was just that with him being such an evil child one automatically forgot it.

Mrs Welles grabbed him as he collected the maddened Boysey from a corner of the room and scrutinised his face. Launcelot squinted up at her horribly and she put him down in a hurry.

'May we continue?' she enquired of the Frenchman in a brittle voice.

But later that night her interest returned. We were sitting round the supper table and I was telling Leigh about the photograph.

'We supposed that he had burst in to get the dog,' I said. 'But why at that particular moment he should throw himself upon his mother, I can't imagine.'

'An instinctive, heredity feeling for the drama,' said Leigh, who was still very much taken with Mrs Welles' acting talents.

Mrs Welles suddenly thumped the table, her eyes bright with excitement. 'Maybe it's a sign,' she said breathlessly. 'Maybe it's a sign of a brilliant film star career, I mean in front of the cameras and everythink, somethink must have told him inside it was cameras. I mean, we all know that Launcelot and me don't see eye to eye. Somethink must have told him inside that the cameras was trained on him.'

Mrs Welles' eyes crossed a little and she gazed with a foggy, hypnotised stare above our heads and along the dim, distant, brilliant career of her son. I was frightfully taken with the idea but Guinevere made the most practical suggestion.

'Couldn't we enter him for the beautiful baby competition then Mum? I mean if he's going to be a film star it'd be alright.'

'Oh yes,' I said, 'do let's enter him. Win?'

Mrs Welles was still looking foggy. 'A sort of personal appearance,' she murmured.

'Yes, that's right.' Mrs Welles came back to earth with a bump of pleasure.

'We'll get him up really lovely,' she said excitedly. 'Sort of little Lord Fauntleroy and that, you and me can go over to Booth tomorrow Ann, and we'll get him rigged up really lovely.'

Our one worry then was Launcelot's attitude to the project. Should he take it into his head to dislike the idea, everything would of course be ruined. Mrs Welles suggested that we give him just half a little sleeping tablet to dull his senses, and if Guinevere hadn't been looking at me with horrified eyes I think I should have agreed. Half a tablet didn't seem a lot, and it was so galling to think that a three-year-old's will could decide the issue. But Leigh backed up Guinevere.

'Don't be silly,' he said. 'You'll just have to use a bit of child psychology. If there's any dulling to be done you'll get far better results with ice-cream and sweets.'

But as it happened, to our everlasting surprise, Launcelot heartily approved of the idea. A certain amount of artificial aid in the shape of Boysey, Mrs Welles' photograph of Victor Mature (which he had taken an inexplicable liking to) and an expensive box of chocolates was necessary to get him on to the bus, but once inside the children's department of Wolly and Gog, all these were forgotten. In humble awe he trotted around from stand to stand, gazing at the beautiful little party dresses and dashing little velvet suits that were on sale.

It had been explained to him that he was to have some new clothes and he was thrilled to bits. There was one rather awful moment when he decided on a little girl's pink frilly party frock; we pointed out to him that it was hardly suitable, but he shrieked and lay on the floor and was only convinced, when we hurriedly bought it and put it on Guinevere.

Mrs Welles fancied an extremely decorative buster suit she had seen in the window. It was black velvet with sort of Elizabethan knickerbockers spliced with white satin and a white lace jabot. The woman at the counter said that the only black one they had was in the window, that she could get it of course, but would the little boy try on a red one first for size.

It was a rash move; Launcelot took one look at himself in the mirror and refused to take it off. He was so taken with his appearance that he even asked his mother for a comb.

've same tolour,' he said eyeing with pleasure the terrible clash of his hair and suit.

In vain the black velvet was dangled before his eyes, and in vain it was explained to him that it would look the same. It was all to no avail; he refused to take it off. Two assistants tried unsuccessfully and at the cost of personal injury, to hold him down, and after ten minutes of his continuous screaming, a floorwalker said would we mind removing our little boy. At exorbitant cost we bought the suit. We gazed at it sadly on the way home, and then Mrs Welles got the brainwave.

'We'll just have to match up his hair,' she said briskly.

'It's a good idea Win,' I said laughing. 'But we couldn't, I mean there's red hair and red hair.'

'Nonsense,' said Mrs Welles, 'I've never liked it that colour anyway.'

That was the last we spoke of it and never for a single instant did I think she had meant it seriously, but that night when we arrived home she beckoned us upstairs. 'Look,' she said with pride switching the light on over Launcelot's cot.

It was quite, quite horrible. There he lay in innocent slumber with his thumb in his mouth, and there splayed out around him on the white of the pillow was a mass of crimson curls.

'A perfect match,' said Mrs Welles proudly.

We looked at her, too staggered for words.

'It's an old dye,' continued Mrs Welles happily, 'that I'd used on a couple of cotton dresses. Bit of luck there being some left.'

'Will it wash off?' I asked in a hollow voice.

'Oh, I think I shall keep it,' said Mrs Welles. 'As it grows out I can easily get some more for the roots.'

'You can say goodbye to the competition then, Win.' Leigh was rather amused.

'What do you mean?' returned Mrs Welles sharply. 'I should say he stands a much better chance like this.'

And then Rose started. 'It's terrible Win, absolutely terrible, you'll be the laughing stock of Leek if you even let him out of the house like that, let alone enter a baby competition. And if you take him to the fete looking like that, I for one will cut you both dead.'

She flounced out of the room. Leigh moved towards the cot.

'We'd better try and get some of it off, Win. I know you only did it for the good, but it does look a bit unnatural you know. We needn't take the whole lot off of course, we'll just leave him with a pinkie glow.'

How tactful he is, I thought, as I saw Mrs Welles beginning to fancy a pinkie glow. But she wasn't going to give in right away. Launcelot, she informed us, had been highly satisfied with the colour, but if we thought she had overindulged him, then she would take our word for it. But at the same time, she added, she would leave it entirely to us, having no wish whatsoever to participate in her son's understandable reactions to a pinkie glow.

For an hour Leigh held him in a ju jitsu grip whilst I lathered his head, and at last the colour began to come away. I was strongly inclined to wash the lot off but remembering the colour of his suit, left, as we'd promised, a pinkie glow. It was two o'clock before we finally got to bed and by 3 a.m. Launcelot's screams still rent the house.

Four hours later I was awake again. I awoke with the bump of excitement that I have always had since I was a child. This was the day. Today was the day of the fete. Today things would happen. People would say things and do things, life would be rich today. Outside the dawn was all golden and pink and blue; pale and clean it dappled through the silver morning mist, which clung like a great furry cocoon still nurturing its grub, to the infant day.

It will be very hot this afternoon, I thought as I looked at it from the attic window. It will be very hot and people will wear thin silky dresses and cartwheel hats, and their hands will feel like melting butter under the thick stuffiness of white cotton gloves. All except me that is; I alone will be a black haggis pudding aflame with brandy under the wretchedness of my black velvet dress with its animal appeal. I looked at it lying at the foot of my bed, at the long black sleeves which Mrs Flood had insisted were ladylike, and at the yellow stripes which formed the same sort of animal appeal the odd person might get at seeing a zebra crossing.

Then suddenly I had an idea and I laughed to myself as I thought about it. Perhaps, I thought, there will be a fancy dress parade, and if there is I shall enter it. I shall make my face up a dead-pan white, and flaunt the black bits of my dress as mourning. The stripes will still represent a zebra crossing but everyone will know about it, for in my hand I shall carry a big black-edged card saying, 'Keep death off the roads.' How nasty I am, I thought as I couldn't stop laughing, how sordid and morbid I am, but when I had finished laughing I didn't mind about the dress half so much.

Outside, the grub that was morning had burst from its chrysalis; heady and swimming and pale and bright and innocent and tender, it wobbled a little under the responsibility of being a whole day.

Rose, on my right, was snoring, a distressing habit which she had lately picked up but refused to acknowledge. I wished I had a tape recorder and could confront her with the truth. Leigh slept very beautifully. I looked at him now, lying on his back with his cheek turned neatly on the pillow and his hands folded across his breast as in prayer. He breathed heavily only when he had been drinking.

I looked at him and wondered what it would be like to kiss him whilst he was asleep. I wondered if he would wake up still peaceful and neat, or be racked with a terrible passion and tear at the bedclothes and heave and moan upon his mattress. I was rather taken aback at this sudden flight of fancy and looked quickly out of the window again.

A light flapping noise came from the attic stairs and the dog Boysey padded into the room. He looked at me with sad eyes and I heaved a sigh for him. Very early on of course, Launcelot had discovered him and taken to him strongly and his latest desire was to be shut up alone in a room with him. So at about ten o'clock each morning the unfortunate Boysey is gripped by the ears and taken up to Launcelot's bedroom. We all say it isn't right and something ought to be done about it, and it won't be long before the RSPCA are around, but in the meantime turn a deaf ear to the sinister moans and thuds that periodically rock the ceiling.

We comfort ourselves with the thought that the worm may one day turn, but doubt it as, for some inexplicable reason, Boysey dotes on Launcelot. Incidentally, he is a she, but as Mrs Welles refuses to recognise a female sex in anything but humans, Boysey it is.

He settled himself on my foot and proceeded to lick my bare leg with relish. I reflected guiltily that as I hadn't had a bath for a fortnight it was probably very tasty. I found that one of the biggest bugbears of *la vie boheme* was keeping clean. We had no bathroom at number eight and unless the copper was lit (a rare occurrence this), no hot water at all.

There was none at the theatre either and our toilette consisted of forcing oneself to heat kettles, interspersed by an occasional visit to the Leek Women's Public Baths. Leigh's case should have been worse than ours on account of shaving, but very early on he had wisely staked a claim on all hot water left over from making tea.

With Boysey licking me, and the pale new-washed morning all around me, I was filled with a sudden desire to be clean. Cleanliness is next to godliness, I exulted to myself as I stole downstairs. I felt very god-like that morning, and paused in the hall to listen to the church clock strike the hour.

Down in the kitchen I filled the copper and lit it. I filled it right full. There were six of us going to the fete, I was determined that we should all go clean. Whilst it was heating I cleaned up the red mess from Launcelot's hair and put on the kettle for tea. It was wonderful to be alone and doing things in the silent house. I often told myself that the thing I missed most of all in the theatre was never being alone.

But now, as I thought about it again, I wondered. I wondered that from the fullness of my life the thought wasn't sweeter than the action; like the night of *Wuthering Heights* when I had had my spiritual feeling and paused in my flight up the passage and thought about free will.

I had a sudden suspicion that twentieth-century free will was only free thinking. This did not thrill me, so I stopped thinking about it and turned my attention to the tea. I regret to say that I was still very much taken with the idea of waking Leigh with a kiss and noting his reactions. I checked the impulse however and compromised by bending low over him and murmuring, 'Tea, Leigh,' in a husky whisper.

I record now with disappointment that he woke peacefully and neatly and took the tea from me with an inarticulate growl. Rose was still snoring and I made Leigh witness the fact before waking her. She looked quite happy when I gave her her tea, but after the first sip remembered about the cake and pushing the cup back at me, reburied herself, moaning, down the bed.

Mrs Welles was far more sociable and we shared a cigarette and a cosy chat before waking the children. We were both still a little worried about Launcelot.

'As long as he doesn't get hold of a mirror he'll be all right,' said Mrs Welles. 'He'll have forgotten about it when he wakes up and as long as he doesn't see himself, we can kid him it's still bright red.'

'Very true, Win,' I said, putting her hand mirror into a drawer. The only other mirrors in the house were the one on her dressing table and a long one fixed to the opposite wall. These I hung with the Spanish shawls. The one in the sitting room we discounted on account of its height.

Downstairs, the water in the copper was hot and I had a delicious all-over wash before the family came down. Leigh came first, demanding more tea and his shaving water, then Mrs Welles, who had run out of cigarettes. She took one look at the copper and said that she was quite clean thank you, on account of Mr Dropsey's three bathrooms, but Leigh, with a whoop of delight and the hip bath, shut himself up in the scullery. Above us we could hear the thrashing noise of Launcelot preparing to leave his cot.

'Keep your fingers crossed,' said Mrs Welles as we recognised the thump of Guinevere releasing him. A minute later they both straggled downstairs with Boysey.

Mrs Welles said, 'Oh nice!'

And I said, 'Well it certainly looks better.'

Actually it did look rather nice – that is, as nice as pink hair on a three year old can look. We refrained however from further comment and indulged him with unlimited helpings of porridge and baked beans.

So far he appeared to have forgotten about the night before. I thought it better that we didn't remind him about his hair at all, but Mrs Welles insisted on coming out with remarks like, 'Such a nice bright red Launcelot,' and 'just like your pushchair!' every other minute.

Whilst he was eating, Launcelot ignored this and concentrated on his food, but as soon as he had finished he poked Guinevere with a fork and said, 'Det me a mirror.'

The audacity of this remark left us all quite speechless. We stared at him.

'Det me a mirror,' he repeated loudly and clearly. Child psychology went with the wind.

'You don't want a mirror love,' said Mrs Welles in a pleading voice. 'What do you want with a mirror? You saw what a lovely red it was last night.'

For a second, a weary smile of incredible vanity passed over Launcelot's face and he touched his curls self-consciously. Then he got down off his chair and sauntered to the door.

'Crisis over,' Mrs Welles hissed at me in a stage whisper, but in the doorway Launcelot turned and faced us.

'I'll det one myself,' he announced in freezing tones and proceeded towards his toy cupboard under the stairs.

Mrs Welles gulped a little but kept her temper. 'That's right love,' she said in an indulgent voice. 'There's lots and lots of lovely mirrors in there.' She gave me a wink.

We waited for a minute while Launcelot pawed through his toys and then when his attention seemed firmly taken with a lorry, went back to the kitchen. Mrs Welles lit a cigarette with a satisfied smile. 'He'll be all right now,' she said. 'I don't think—'

But what she thought was never known, as at that moment a single heartrending scream pierced the house. We looked at each other without a word then in unison dashed for the cupboard. Inside it Launcelot leaned against the wall, and there, still clutched in his hand with the shining glittering metal underneath part of it held close to his face, was the toy lorry. For a second longer, perhaps, he stared at his reflection then with another shriek he hurled the toy at our feet, and moaning brokenly, collapsed to the floor. Mrs Welles gazed at him almost in admiration.

'I might have known it would be no good,' she said. 'Evil right through. Just like his father!' And shaking her head in wonderment and defeat she seized a box of chocolates from the hallstand and went upstairs.

It was Guinevere however who won the day. With infinite patience and understanding, she got him to go upstairs with her to Mrs Welles' long mirror, and there, with the aid of Rose's Autumn Mist which she let him spray on his hair himself, she eventually persuaded him that his looks were not altogether ruined, and that he still stood a very good chance of winning the competition.

Chapter Ten

By one o'clock the morning had grown strong and fierce and Leek lay in a welter of heat as we walked down the hill and across the town to the paddock where the fete was being held. The paddock was a large field belonging to the vicar, and considered to be one of the beauty spots of Leek. On one side it joined the sweeping lawns of the vicarage garden and on two other sides was bordered by the river.

On the fourth side the vicar (who was said to possess untold private means) had built a really beautiful pavilion. Actually it was a folly (white marble and classic Greek columns), built so that the vicar could sit in it and enjoy the view of the river, but for functions it made a wonderful pavilion.

At one thirty Rose and Leigh and I duly presented ourselves, and as we climbed the marble steps of the folly to meet the others, my early morning excitement returned. The paddock was alive with the hustle and bustle of last minute preparations. Stalls and marquees dotted the green grass in all their pristine glory like clean white mushrooms. Along the towpath of the river, three ponies stood waiting for the children. The sunlight winked on their shining harnesses as they pawed the ground impatiently.

Men in white overalls walked quickly about yelling hoarse instructions to each other as they supervised the reconstruction of an unfortunate marquee. On the river itself another group of men were lowering a flower-decked barge into the water. But dominating the scene like a flock of birds on a sanctuary isle were the ladies. Flittering and twittering, a symphony of mauve and blue and grey, they hopped around their stalls. Little tinkles of laughter and little shouts of 'Vicah' filled the air. He wove in and out of them like a tired black crow and now and again looked longingly back at his home.

Sebastian and Hilda were waiting at the pavilion. Sebastian, like Leigh, wore a plain dark suit, and Hilda, looking self-conscious and enormous, a rather tatty green Nell Gwynn costume. At the sight of her Rose gave a strangled moan, and Leigh and I had to grip her arms quickly. When Rose felt strongly about anything, which fortunately was rare, all caution was likely to go to the winds.

However, she contented herself with telling Hilda that she looked like a cooking apple, and flashed a smile at the mayor who had just come up.

'Into your positions,' he said in a harassed voice. 'They're letting them in now, and I want the opening sharp at one forty-five.' He dashed off behind the pavilion to get into his robes, and his secretary indicated to us five of the gilt chairs arranged on the platform.

The brass band behind us crashed into being and at the same time a flood of people surged through the iron gates. And then the secretary noticed the absence of the Floods.

'Not here?' he said, 'what do you mean not here? They were told one thirty, weren't they?'

The vicar came panting up, took Rose's hand and said, 'Aah, Mrs Flood,' and the secretary with a stifled exclamation of rage rushed after the mayor to report the catastrophe. He came back in a fine temper with his robes askew.

'Bloody actors!' he said, sitting down on a large gilt chair in the centre of the platform. His wife, who was now accompanying him, gave a shriek and tried to drag him off it, but it was too late. The public had seen him. They converged on him from every corner of the paddock, and above them the loudspeaker announced that the mayor had taken his seat and the fete would now be opened.

The vicar sat down in a hurry next to Rose and the mayor's wife collapsed into a chair beside her husband. Behind us, the band gave a sudden dramatic roll on the drums then burst into 'God Save the Queen'. For a second the whole of the paddock stood to attention then slowly, with the national anthem still playing, like a reaper's sheaf cutting through a field of corn, they started to move. They moved so that a gangway began to clear itself between them.

The vicar's eyes, the mayor's eyes, all our eyes were turned on it, and there down the centre of it, with her head held triumphantly high and her husband on her arm, swept Mrs Flood. They were both wearing full evening dress. The national anthem played on and oblivious of it, they swept up the pavilion steps, then with perfect timing as it drew to a close, sank into the two vacant gilt chairs. The mayor sat down too, but his wife pinched him and he stood up again. His face was as red as his robes, and his voice trembled a little under an obvious emotional strain.

'Ladies and gentlemen,' he said. 'We are gathered here together for another opening of our annual fete, and this year I have great pleasure in presenting to you Mr Flood of the Flood Repertory Players, who I'm sure you will all have seen on the stage of the town hall. Mr Flood –' he said, turning a little to Willy. Willy kept his seat and smiled up at him, but on his other side Mrs Flood rose to her feet.

'Thank you, Your Worship,' she said.

The mayor's face took on a heightened puce colour and, gibbering a little under his breath, he sank heavily into his chair.

I looked at Mrs Flood as she stood there addressing the crowds. I looked at her hair that had been carefully done black and set in corrugated iron waves. 'People don't expect actors to have class,' she was saying. I looked at her raddled old face with its ghastly stage make-up. 'That's why I like to meet my public socially...'

I looked at her shoulders and back, which bulged over the ridiculous blue chiffon evening dress with its tawdry glittering sequins, and at the bones of the stays which were pushing against it. 'My husband, who has played to royalty...'

I saw that her eyes were narrow black slits of cunning, that her hands were little wet, pink, flapping fins. I looked at her and I saw all this and I should have been filled with shame but I wasn't. You see, Mrs Flood was happy and I had never seen her happy before. She was so happy that it radiated from her in great waves.

Rose, Leigh, Sebastian and Hilda should all have been filled with shame too, but they weren't, instead they were leaning forward and looking at her with little half smiles on their lips. The vicar's face was beaming, the mayor had relaxed perceptibly, and the crowd was friendly and watching. Willy alone was unaware of her happiness; with tender eyes he was wholly engrossed in the antics of a ladybird upon his knee.

Mrs Flood finished her speech and sat down. The applause which followed was not as good as it should have been, considering her audience's interest, but I understood why. As soon as she finished speaking the radiation stopped and people were left thinking, 'Well, that was a lot of trash,' and, 'Christ, what a sight she looks.' The mayor's wife pinched him and he went red again and stood up and said he hoped that people would spend a lot of money. Then the band struck up with 'The British Grenadiers' and the crowds moved away.

The secretary appeared again and hustled Rose and Sebastian and Hilda off to their stalls, and Leigh and I were free until the bathing beauty competition at four o'clock. We left the Floods talking to the mayor and his wife, and proceeded to tour the stalls; that is, we intended to, but Leigh spotted the tea tent and we spent some time in there first, giggling over Mrs Flood. It's strange how something when shared with somebody else can suddenly become funny.

Most of the stalls, when we finally reached them, were dull, and all of them were expensive. It was rather awkward for us really, as having been seen sitting in the exalted presence of the mayor, we were expected to buy lavishly. 'Nothing you fancy de-ar?' the good ladies would say with a steel edge to their voices.

We hurried along to Rose and found that she was doing brisk business. The cake, which looked suspiciously as though somebody had recently been jilted at the altar, was being passed from one lady's eager hand to another. Rose sat on a stool, wearily recording the guesses. She gave Leigh and I three free guesses each, and asked if we wanted it because if so, she'd tell us the correct weight.

I said, 'Do we want it, Leigh?'

And Leigh said that, in view of Mr Dropsey, he didn't think we did, but what a pity the fete hadn't happened a few weeks earlier.

'Don't go!' said Rose as we prepared to move off. She clutched my arm wildly. 'Ann!' she said, 'I'll give you my pink felt skirt if you'll take over till the bathing beauty competition.' I was sorely tempted. I had always coveted her pink skirt, but I remembered about the Beautiful Babies.

'I can't,' I told her, 'I wouldn't miss Launcelot's appearance for the world.'

We left her but promised to bring her back a cup of tea, and went in search of Sebastian. Sebastian wasn't doing quite so well but was thoroughly enjoying himself. He had taken off his jacket and was standing with his thumbs tucked into his braces, encouraging people to roll up, in a broad Cockney accent. He put on a really superb show for us and caused quite a little crowd to gather. But they didn't stay.

Strangely enough his showmanship seemed to put people off, and even the few who had come prepared to have a go melted away. We had a wonderful time though, and Leigh would have stayed there all afternoon, but after he had shot down his fourth golliwog I was fretting. 'Launcelot's on at three o'clock,' I told him. 'That only leaves you ten minutes to kiss Hilda.'

Leigh threw down his gun and pretended to swoon. 'Why in heaven's name didn't you remind me earlier?' he said. 'Here, have I been wasting my time knocking down golliwogs for you when I could have been experiencing Hilda?'

Sebastian was frankly jealous. 'Hang on to the stall for me Ann,' he said, 'while I nip across with Leigh and have a quickie, I'll only be gone a minute.'

But I wasn't going to miss the spectacle of Leigh kissing Hilda.

'I'll hold it for you later,' I told him as we went in search of her.

We found her down by the river, and Leigh joined the small queue of men whilst I watched how the bran tub worked. It was run on the same principle as the type of machine you can see in an amusement arcade.

You inserted sixpence into the side of the tub and under its glass top watched a steel crane lower itself into the sawdust and claw around for a prize. I watched four men disappointedly secure reels of cotton and bars of chocolate, and then when the next two came away with penny whistles, began to wonder a little.

'How many times have you had to pay a ransom?' I asked Hilda as Leigh came up with a reel of cotton.

Hilda looked at us smugly. 'Well, actually not at all yet,' she said. 'A man came up and twiddled with it just before I started and I've had no trouble at all so far.'

'But Hilda!' I said, 'The whole point of it is the ransom kisses.' I pointed to the big advertisement above her head.

'I can't help that,' she said. 'If the thing happens to give people their money's worth it suits me.'

'But it isn't their money's worth,' I began. 'Their money's worth is –' But Leigh was dragging at my arm.

'Don't you start putting any ideas into Miss Fellowes' head,' he said, 'And besides, it's three o'clock.' It was too; we left her and ran hotfoot along the towpath towards the swinging pink sign which said Babyland.

Babyland was large and disorganised. We paid a shilling each at the gate and were admitted into a kaleidoscope of screaming children, harassed mothers, nurses, dogs, prams, and bored older children.

We had arranged to meet Mrs Welles wherever the competition was to be held, and now picked our way through two crèches, a sandpit, a roundabout and several long queues for the lavatories. We found it eventually, a roped-off section dangerously near the river, and started to look around for Mrs Welles. As she was the only woman wearing a fur coat this was not difficult. She was delighted to see us.

'Thank God you've come,' she said in heartfelt tones. 'I couldn't have stood another minute of it. Now for Christ's sake get me out of here.'

'Now then Win,' said Leigh bracingly. 'If you've stood it so far, you can stand to see Launcelot win, it'll only be for another ten minutes now.'

'Everyone's looking at your coat, Win,' I put in helpfully.

This was true, but whether in admiration, or disbelief that anyone should wear a fur coat in July, I don't know. Mrs Welles however was in no doubt. Whilst we were waiting for the judges to take their seats, she twitched it and tossed it and talked about it loudly.

Guinevere came staggering back from the lavatories holding Launcelot. 'Mum,' she said in an anguished voice, 'whatever are you doing here? You should be over there by the platform with the other mums, here take him, quick.' She thrust Launcelot into his mother's arms.

Mrs Welles put him down on the ground. 'He can quite well walk there himself,' she said, but Launcelot gave a scream and Guinevere picked him up.

'He won't walk there Mum, he's afraid of getting his shoes dirty, you'll have to hold him, Mum – please Mum?' she said, with tears in her eyes.

Mrs Welles shoved him under one arm with ill temper and made for the platform. 'Great sissy,' she hissed down his ear.

Leigh, Guinevere and I pushed after her to the front of the crowd, which was beginning to settle itself on wooden benches. On the oblong platform the judges had already taken their seats; two elderly women and an effeminate looking young man, and around them were ranged fifteen little baby chairs for the competitors.

These were slowly filling up as a nurse at the side of the platform checked the baby's name and allowed the mother to pass through with it.

Mrs Welles was the last one up, and as she dumped Launcelot into the fifteenth chair, she took three quick steps into the centre of the platform and swirled her mink in the style of a fashion model. There was a little amused murmur from the watching crowd, and all eyes were turned on Launcelot as she got into position behind his chair.

He looked so handsome sitting there with the sun glinting on his pink curls, that after a quick look round at the other competitors, I didn't think there would be any doubt about his winning. The only other striking child was a fat little girl with white ringlets and enormous black eyes, dressed rather strangely in black, who was sitting next to him. Her face was quite blank however and she had the appearance of being stuffed.

Launcelot was obviously on top form. His face was wreathed in smiles and he was practising his famous wink, non-stop and with great success. The other mothers kept nudging each other and pointing to him with envy. Guinevere though was a little worried.

'I do hope they start judging from his end,' she said. 'He'll never be able to keep it up if they start the other end.' But Launcelot's luck was in. He was the very first child they examined.

A delighted smile appeared on the effeminate looking man's face as he received the full impact of the wink. They hung over him for quite a long time before moving round the other fourteen. It seemed an interminable time before the last child was examined. Mrs Welles was obviously bored stiff. She had spotted us sitting on the front row and, in between yawns, kept mouthing words at us. Guinevere, with a sudden tragic attempt at humour, turned to me. 'It's a good job they don't take mums into consideration,' she said with a little laugh.

At last the judges finished their tour and went into a huddle to decide on the finalists. Guinevere squeezed Leigh's hand hard, as Launcelot was one of the three they chose. The other two were the little girl next to him and an ordinary-looking child three chairs down.

Back and forth they went between the three children, with the tension rising. It was obvious that the effeminate looking man was all for Launcelot, he kept touching his curls and hoping that he would wink again (Launcelot had wisely abandoned this after the first examining). The two women, though, were being a little difficult. One of them, I think, was determined to uphold the female species with a girl winner, and the other one just dithered.

The third child was soon abandoned and it was now clearly a neck and neck finish between Launcelot and the fat little girl. Her mother was bridling and casting challenging glances at Mrs Welles, and to our great amusement Mrs Welles was bridling back.

At last the judges, after a bit of bickering, went back to their table and got into another huddle. The air was fraught with emotion. You could have heard a pin drop. Guinevere beside me was pale and strained, Leigh was breathing heavily. It seemed to me the most important thing in the world that Launcelot should win. On stage, Mrs Welles put out her hand and clutched Launcelot's.

Then the announcement came through the microphone.

'Ladies and gentlemen,' said one of the elderly women. 'After a great deal of very, very difficult deciding, we think that the most beautiful baby here this afternoon is number fourteen, little Wendy Wool, and it is to her that we have pleasure in awarding first prize.'

Disappointment and indignation poured through me, and Guinevere started to cry.

'The second prize,' went on the elderly lady, 'goes to number fifteen, little Launcelot Welles who…' But nobody was listening; her voice was drowned in the applause for Wendy Wool. The effeminate looking man picked up a large white rosette and with the two women following him, sadly pinned it on the little girl's black dress. Over his head one of the women handed the mother a cheque, then they all stepped back so that Wendy was again on view. It was at that moment, while she still stared blankly before her, and her mother preened herself above that Launcelot acted.

He had been quite quiet during the presentation and I had thought that he hadn't understood what had happened, but now he leaned over and put his face against the little girl's. People thought that he was going to kiss her and a delighted 'Aah' went up, but instead he buried his teeth into the smooth rosiness of her cheek and bit her savagely.

Pandemonium ensued.

Wendy Wool came to life with a jerk and, screaming bitterly, fell off her chair. Her mother, with a matching scream, leaped over it and picked her up, then turning, lashed out at Launcelot with her handbag. Mrs Welles joined the fray and, picking up Launcelot, charged at her, using him as a battering ram. The judges and other mothers tried to separate them but Mrs Welles' blood was up, and while the children clawed at each other from under respective arms, their mothers fought above their heads.

Eventually a tough male nurse came to the scene, and thinking that Mrs Wool looked the stronger of the two, dragged her off. The child's first prize rosette dropped off and fell at Mrs Welles' feet. She picked it up and handed it to Launcelot then, turning, addressed the other mothers.

'I was a mother,' she explained briefly and with a slight tremble to her voice, 'I had to defend my baby.' Launcelot blinked up at her with a watery smile and clutching him to her mink, she made a dignified exit down the platform steps. She joined us, and under staring, accusing eyes we hustled her quickly out of Babyland.

Over much-needed tea she calmed down. 'Of course it was all a big mistake,' she said. 'There was no doubt that he should have got first prize, anyone could see that.'

'I dot the first prize,' said Launcelot coldly, fingering his rosette.

We didn't argue the point further.

After tea Leigh took the children off for pony rides and Mrs Welles and I took a cup of tea along to Rose. We found her ignoring the clamouring hands all around her and talking to Willy and the local photographer who sometimes took pictures of our plays. Mrs Flood was two stalls up talking to the vicar's wife, so I introduced Mrs Welles to Willy, and we chatted gaily for a few minutes and posed in a group round Rose and the cake for a picture.

'Christ, he's a handsome brute close to,' said Mrs Welles as Willy pattered on up to Mrs Flood.

'Fancy him, Win?' asked Rose. But Mrs Welles shook her head. 'I know that type,' she said. 'A beautiful biscuit but dead from the neck down.'

A minute later he passed us again with Mrs Flood. I don't think Mrs Flood would have stopped, but I called her and introduced her to Mrs Welles. I couldn't have picked a better moment. She took one look at the mink and was charm itself.

'So you're looking after the girlies are you?' she said. 'I shouldn't wonder but what they aren't quite a handful, neither.'

Mrs Welles said that we weren't, and that she enjoyed having us, and pardon her saying so but Mrs Flood's frock was lovely.

It was a happy remark. Mrs Flood looked thrilled and explained very grandly that they were banqueting afterwards with the mayor and couldn't get home in time to change. Mrs Welles said that that would be nice and Mrs Flood agreed that it would, and after reminding me about the bathing beauty competition they moved off. Mrs Welles stared after them with disbelieving eyes.

'Ann!' she said. 'You're kidding, they can't really be husband and wife?'

'They are,' I assured her. 'Willy's older than he looks, you know.'

'Love moveth in a mysterious way,' said Mrs Welles, turning her attention on the cake.

'Old bitch,' said Rose from behind it.

I went on another tour of the stalls with Mrs Welles, and this time it was great fun. Mr Dropsey had given her twenty pounds to play around with during his absence. A lot of it had gone on the children's clothes but there was still quite a bit left, and this Mrs Welles was determined to spend at the fete. I was appalled at her extravagance.

Plaster dogs, artificial fruit, binoculars, tea cosies – anything and everything, she bought wildly and delightedly.

'And that lampshade, I must have that lampshade there,' said Mrs Welles, pointing to a hideous pink fluted article. 'Mr Dropsey would like me to have that lampshade.'

I pointed out to her that it was a waste paper basket, but Mrs Welles said it only went to show you how clever Teddy was.

When we could carry no more we staggered back to Rose and unloaded. She was looking brighter.

'The mayor's just come up and told me I can close the stall to watch the bathing beauty competition,' she said. Then she added with a giggle, 'He told me I should be entering it, not stuck behind a cake. He's ever so annoyed about Hilda being on the bran tub. He says Mrs Flood lacks perception of character.'

'Rose, you're incorrigible,' we told her.

By that time it was ten to four, so I left Mrs Welles with Rose and went off to the ladies' to tidy up for the competition. I had never judged a competition before and was looking forward to it.

It was to be held on the same platform as the beautiful babies, and now I realised why it had been erected so near the river's edge. Someone had hit upon the novel idea of having the bathing beauties sail up the river on the flower-decked barge and dismount straight on to the platform. In this way they would surmount the slight oddness of a bathing beauty competition in an inland town, and would also enable everyone to see them. The wooden benches were packed to suffocation when I arrived, and masses of people were already standing at the back. Babyland's roundabout was groaning under a horde of eager youths.

The back of the platform had been draped with a Union Jack and red bunting, and the brass band was already playing merrily. In front of it the gilt chairs from the pavilion had been arranged round a small table.

I found Leigh and the Floods with the other judge, a nervous-looking man who had just published a book about Leek's drains. Mrs Flood was telling us where we were to sit. 'Mr Wynch at the back, Ann and Willy on one side of him and me and Leigh on the other.'

Mr Wynch kept wringing his hands and saying that he'd had no experience of this sort of thing and he was afraid he'd have to rely a great deal on his fellow judges.

'Just you relax and don't bother yourself,' Mrs Flood told him kindly. 'Me and my husband will give you the wink who to choose.'

There was applause whilst the mayor and vicar and their wives took the row of seats above our table, then we filed into our places.

A microphone announced that the barge was just pushing off and we all craned our heads up the river. Crowds lined both its banks and a loud cheer began to spread itself towards us.

For a couple of hundred yards the barge behaved beautifully, but after that it kept nosing into the bank and the rest of the journey was completed rather ignobly with two men on either side prodding it with punting rods. As it drew close to the landing stage the mayor got very excited, and grabbing the microphone from his secretary announced that it was a long time since he had seen such a pretty picture, and that the judges would surely have a very tough time choosing a Miss Leek of Shallot. He was so overcome by the brilliance of this last remark that he spoilt it by repeating, 'I said "Miss Leek of Shallot!"' twice.

The barge drew to a wobbly halt under the platform and the secretary helped the girls dismount. Cat-calls and wolf-whistles filled the air and the band struck up with 'A Pretty Girl is Like a Melody'. Preliminaries for Miss Leek had taken place the Saturday before, and now we had only six girls to choose between. They paraded slowly before us holding little black numbered cards, and I set to work on a close scrutiny of them.

Numbers one and two twirled past us, sweetly pretty in a rather faded English way, wearing modest bathing costumes over modest figures. Number three was a tall redhead with a very good figure clad in an expensive green satin costume, but unfortunately her face was not so good. The crowd, however, cheered her hearteningly. Number four was a blonde, quite nice, but with a tendency to stoop.

Number five was terrific. The crowd gave a shriek of delight as she swaggered across the platform, and I immediately crossed the other four off my list. She was of average height but not of average proportions; above and below a tiny waist, she swelled out like a ship in full sail, and to make matters worse – or better – she was clad in a provocative but inadequate bikini.

Indeed, the bosom part of it was so dangerous that I involuntarily held my breath for her. Her hair was long and black, her face pouting and round, and on top of it all she knew how to show herself off. The crowd was still cheering her while number six (very ordinary) came and went.

Mrs Flood and Leigh went into a huddle whilst the writer leaned back waiting to be guided. I had made my decision and nudged Willy.

'Number five for me Willy, what's yours?'

'What do you think, Ann?' said Willy in an odd voice.

I looked at him, and suddenly a trickle of fear went down my spine. There were beads of perspiration on his forehead and he was sitting with his hands clenched tight on his knees.

'I suppose the same as mine,' I said as lightly as I could.

Willy began to nod his head but stiffened as the girls filed back on to the platform. I knew I should have looked at them again but I couldn't take my eyes off Willy. His mouth was parted a little and he stared at number five, breathing heavily.

'Willy and I think number five,' I told Mrs Flood over the table.

Mrs Flood looked at me sharply.

'I know number five appears to be the most popular,' she said. 'And of course it's entirely up to you, but I do think Ann, that vulgarity and downright indecency are not two attributes the mayor would wish to find in the winner. As for Willy,' she went on, 'well Willy's no judge of a girl anyway, and he'll settle for number three like Leigh and me, won't you Willy?'

Willy still stared at number five.

'Willy,' she repeated sharply.

Willy slowly turned his head to her, and I saw Mrs Flood draw in her breath quickly, as she noticed the perspiration on his forehead.

'What?' he said in a rather dazed voice.

Mrs Flood leaned towards him. 'You like number three, don't you Willy darling?' she said firmly and kindly, as though she were speaking to a backward child. 'That pretty girl with the red hair, you like her best, don't you Willy? Lil'll put her down as your choice, shall she darling?'

Willy turned to have a look at number three then quickly looked back at his wife.

'Oh no Lil!' he said in a troubled voice. 'I couldn't choose number three, she's hardly got any bust.'

Mrs Flood's eyes glittered a little but she kept her temper. 'The bust is not the point,' she began, but Willy cut into her.

'Oh yes it is, Lil,' he said earnestly. 'Very much the point. Look at number five's, a beautiful point. I think…'

Mrs Flood gave a shriek of shame and turned to Mr Wynch in desperation.

'I'm afraid we can't decide, Mr Wynch,' she said. 'Two of us seem to want number five and two of us number three, but as you asked me to guide your decision, I'm sure you will oblige me and settle for number three.'

Mr Wynch blushed and cleared his throat. 'Well actually,' he mumbled nervously, 'I did take a quick look at them myself, and, well, actually… Well, I think I should choose number five myself. The crowds seem to favour her too,' he added apologetically.

This was true; the crowds had been shouting, 'We want five' for some time now. For a second Mrs Flood looked at me, her eyes pleading. 'Are you sure you couldn't alter your choice, Ann?' she said, almost gently.

If I could go back to that moment now, if I could have known then what was to happen, I know most certainly that I would have altered my choice. It mattered not a jot to me who won the competition. In many respects the redhead was a lot more suitable. But at that particular moment, my only feeling was one of protection for Willy's freedom. I wanted suddenly and urgently that whosoever he should care to choose might be the winner.

'I'm afraid not,' I told her.

Mrs Flood took her defeat gallantly. Smiling a little at the girls, she scribbled something on a piece of paper and handed it to the mayor.

He read it with a great delighted grin, and bellowing down the microphone announced that everyone would be very happy to hear that their little sweetheart, number five, Miss Fifi Dawn, was the winner. The crowd went mad with delight, and it was some time before the mayor could continue.

'Now wait a minute, wait a minute,' he said. 'We've got a lovely big blue sash up here, and we want a proper presentation, so if we can have a bit of hush for a minute, we'll ask Mr Flood to make it.'

He leaned over as he spoke and held the blue sash, which had been lying on his lap, towards our table.

'If you don't mind, Mr Flood.'

Willy, with a happy smile, put out his hand to take it, but Mrs Flood was quicker. She all but snatched it from the mayor.

'Your Worship,' she said in a breathless whisper, 'if you don't mind I'll make the presentation, you see, my husband isn't used to this sort of thing.'

The mayor, looking extremely angry at the hold-up, hissed back angrily, 'I'm afraid that's impossible, Mrs Flood. The presentation of the sash is always by a man.' For a full second they stared at one another with hatred, then Mrs Flood handed the sash to Willy.

'Just put it over her head, Willy,' she said.

Willy, by my side, began to tremble a little with excitement, and he clutched the sash so that the perspiration from his hands made an imprint upon it. Then, rising clumsily from his chair, he advanced to where Miss Fifi Dawn had detached herself from the other girls and was standing, swaying a little, under the summer sun.

Mrs Flood gripped the edges of the table hard and the watching crowd grew silent as Willy drew close to her, lifted the sash, and dropped it gently over her head. For a moment they looked at each other, then like a terrible, unbelievable, thunderbolt, the mayor's voice came crackling through the microphone.

'And now Mr Flood,' he said, 'the judge's privilege, a kiss for our lovely winner.'

My heart, which had been beating hard, seemed suddenly to stop, my senses seemed to stop too so that in that split second I was no longer aware of the sun, or of the noise of the river, or of the crowd around us. I was only aware of Willy.

I saw him slowly turn his head to where the mayor was sitting, then lower it a little to look at his wife; for a second he smiled at her, then bending his comely head he kissed Miss Fifi Dawn full upon the lips.

He kissed her savagely, forcing her head back and bending his knees. She tried to resist him, and his arms went around her like a vice and in the struggle, we watched the fastening of her bikini top come undone.

The crowd gave a roar of excitement; I went sick inside as I watched the stupid piece of floral cotton fall to the ground. Behind me there was the sudden clatter of chairs, then the merciful sight of the mayor running towards them. He was tugging at his robes and, as Willy still rocked with the naked Miss Dawn, threw them gallantly around her. The crowd's roars turned into a cheer for him, and with one accord they burst into 'For He's a Jolly Good Fellow'.

The mayor doffed his hat to them, then drunk with success, did the kindest thing that he had probably ever done in his life. He walked over to the microphone, waited until they were quiet, then addressed them in a bluff, jocular manner.

'You don't want to cheer me boys,' he said. 'You want to cheer Mr Flood here. That tempestuous little love scene you just saw saved our winner from a nasty piece of embarrassment.

'Miss Dawn's swimsuit unfortunately came undone, and Mr Flood here, with a very quick mind, did the only thing he could do until I reached her – covered her up with his arms and gave you a nice piece of free acting into the bargain.' The mayor laughed heartily, then blessed sound, the crowd did too.

Willy returned to his chair, and Fifi Dawn, who had been hurried away by one of the girls, reappeared with her top on. She got another terrific reception and the mayor escorted her back into the barge. I looked at her as she sailed away alone amongst the flowers. She struck out her bosom happily and smiled a shallow smile. Only the red mark on her neck, I thought, will remind her of the havoc she wrought in my darling, pathetic Willy's breast.

The competition was over. The crowds moved away. At our table Mr Wynch coughed a little and moved his gilt chair with a rasp. 'Will you excuse me please?' he murmured.

He left us sitting there, alone and ridiculous around the table, like some neurotic tableau of the Mad Hatter's tea party. Opposite me, Mrs Flood still gripped the table. She sat motionless with her head sunk forward. Flies sucked at her neck hungrily, thinking that her petrified form was already a carcass.

Leigh doodled on a piece of paper in front of him. Willy's head was turned so that he could look up the river. I thought, there's no hope, there's no hope. There's no hope for anyone sitting here. I've got to get out of here. I've got to find Mrs Welles. I've got to find Mrs Welles and make her laugh and look at men. I thought, that fool Leigh. That fool Leigh sitting there. I thought, I know exactly what he's thinking. He's thinking, that's love that is, sitting next to me in a heap.

I'm looking at love that's following the classical example. I'm looking at tragedy. I must look hard too, and store it all up. This is an experience. This is all part of life's rich pageant. I might be able to use this on stage one day. I thought, no! No! I'm all wrong. I want it to be that but it isn't.

Leigh is in love with me, Leigh has suddenly realised that he is in love with me. It has come about by what he has just witnessed. He is feeling terrible, grim, but quite, quite sure. In his mind's eye he is seeing a bombed ruin with a tiny flower growing out of its rubble. I thought, I hate him, I hate him, and I hate Hilda Fellowes, and I hate his wife, and then I stood up. 'I'll see you all at the banquet,' I said.

Leigh said, 'Hold on, we're all coming now,' but I ignored him and ran down the gilt steps and through the empty wooden benches and over the rope, and in and out of the people along the towpath. If I run hard enough and fast enough, I thought, there will be no room for any thinking at all. I understand now what people mean by walking it off, only it should be running it off. I understood too, why athletes are all supposed to be a bit dim.

Wouldn't it be funny and Utopian, I thought, if people all took to running instead of drink to drown their sorrows. I thought, damn all these people who stop me from stopping to think, and then drew to a halt. A crowded fete is not ideally suited to indulging the body.

'Ann!' shrieked a familiar voice. I turned, and then everything rushed away and I was just filled with gladness as I watched Mrs Welles come towards me at a tottering run.

'Christ,' she said. 'What the hell's the matter with you, rushing around like a lunatic?'

My heart bubbled again at her normality. 'It's the sun, Win,' I said, putting a ga-ga expression on my face.

'I don't know about the sun,' she said excitedly. 'Jesus Ann, did I say he was dead from the neck down?'

'Win!' I said urgently. I couldn't bear that she talked like that, that she didn't understand. 'Win,' I said, 'you mustn't laugh at him, that was tragedy.'

'Tragedy?' said Mrs Welles. She thought about it for a moment then shook her head. 'No dear,' she said kindly, 'just sex!'

'Did Rose see him?' I asked her as we left the river and went in search of a fortune teller.

'Of course she saw him, she was with me.'

'What did she say?'

'I don't remember her saying anything,' replied Mrs Welles. 'We were both laughing too much.'

We found Madame Tic-Tac, classily situated out of the paddock and under a cedar tree on the vicar's lawn.

Mrs Welles had been on about having her fortune told all afternoon, but as soon as we arrived there she began to get a bit nervous.

'I don't want no shocks again,' she said. 'Last year she said she could see a tinned vegetable in the glass and sure enough two weeks later I met Goat.'

'Oh come off it Win!' I laughed. 'He isn't as bad as all that.'

Mrs Welles looked at me sadly. 'No, no Ann,' she said. 'You don't understand. It was symbols. A tinned vegetable equals baked beans equals Mr Goat.'

However, we both paid two and sixpence and went in. Madame Tic-Tac was nicely got up, with a cocoa make-up, shawls and a frizzy blonde perm. On a round table in front of her was a large, square, green glass ashtray turned upside down. Mrs Welles nudged me.

'Balls is out,' she hissed. 'She says they've found that with a definite shape like a square, they can get a more definite future.'

She sat down on another chair at the table and laid out a trembling palm. Madame Tic-Tac raised vacant, disinterested eyes, which suddenly got interested as they focused on the mink.

'Aah!' she said pawing the air with a nicotine stained hand and accidentally touching it. An expression of reverence crossed her face and she accidentally touched it again.

'Well?' asked Mrs Welles breathlessly.

Madam Tic-Tac drew her hand towards her and stared at it with intent.

'It's been a fight,' she pronounced at last and switched her attention to the ashtray. 'But here,' she continued, 'I can see somethink lovely. Plain as daylight I can see him asking you a question, a question that's going to make you very happy.'

Mrs Welles gave a gasp of delight.

'I can see him not surviving it neither!' said Madame Tic-Tac with matching delight. 'I can see you afterwards still young and alone!'

They looked at each other. Never had two faces expressed so much happiness at the prospect of a bereavement.

'Thanks ever so much, Madame Tic-Tac,' breathed Mrs Welles.

Over me, Madame Tic-Tac was brief and mechanical.

Young love she'd decided, and saw an early marriage to a nice steady boy in a steady job with a home of our own straight away, and a lovely little baby (straight away) to bless it.

Outside, Mrs Welles was ecstatic and wondering.

'However could she have known about Teddy? Uncanny Ann, that's what it is, knowing like what she did. I mean "a question what would make me happy" and then him passing on. It's as if I'd spoken out loud what I was hoping. Not,' she went on hurriedly, remembering that I was there, 'that I'd wish Mr Dropsey any harm, but what's in the book's in the book.'

'Would you really marry him, Win?' I asked her.

'Like a shot out of a cannon ball,' replied Mrs Welles emotionally.

'But Win,' I said, 'what about Mr Welles? You're only separated aren't you?'

Mrs Welles laughed shortly. 'I've got too much on Percival Welles for him to start any funny business,' she said darkly.

People were beginning to leave the fete now and a relaxed orgy-fied feeling began to spread itself over the paddock. The good ladies on the stalls were being devils and indulging latent bartering instincts with their remaining wares. 'All in a good cause,' they told themselves as they haggled delightedly with teddy boys over ancient knuckle-dusters and stilettos, bequeathed by the colonel as *objects d'art*.

'Free rides,' shouted the man with the ponies, hoisting Guinevere and Launcelot up for their tenth ride. 'Got a little nipper like her myself,' he told Mrs Welles as we collected them. 'Golden ringlets just like hers. She's over at Booth General though. Polio.'

'Ransom kisses,' shrieked Hilda, bold with the knowledge that no one would get any.

'Roll up, roll up,' yelled Sebastian. But I steered Mrs Welles away. If Madame Tic-Tac's prophecy was to come true, it would need every ounce of encouragement.

Back at Rose's cake stall, a crowd had gathered for the announcement of the winner. The vicar's wife was seated beside her, busily checking the guesses. Mrs Welles and I had just attached ourselves to the back of the crowd when a voice beside me said, 'Hallo, Ann.' I turned and there was Bill Irving. For a second I didn't recognise him as he was wearing a beautiful suit of morning clothes.

'Didn't expect to see me here, eh?' he said.

I said no, that actually I hadn't, but what a pleasant surprise.

'Thought I'd let the company down, didn't you?' he said.

I said, 'No, no of course not Bill, don't be silly,' and felt awful inside.

'Thought I'd turn up in me corduroys, didn't you?' he said.

'Took your cue from her. "You stay at home, Bill," she told me. "You stay at home and get a bit of sleep. I shouldn't wonder," she told me, "if my husband Mr Flood shouldn't save you a chicken's wing or something from the banquet."' He laughed harshly, unnaturally, because he was seventy years old and had played in tragedy for sixty of them.

'Chicken's wing,' he said. 'She knows what she can bloody well do with her chicken's wing.'

'Bill,' I said quickly, reacting to the crisis as though he were suddenly involved in a difficult role. 'Think of the Haven of Rest Bill, think of January.'

'Aah!' said Bill softening involuntarily, but he struggled against it immediately. 'Chicken's wing,' he said again. 'Chicken's wing. The whole of the company was invited to the banquet, wasn't it? I suppose I am still a member of the company?'

'Of course you are, Bill,' I said. 'Of course you are, and Mrs Flood will be delighted to see you. You look so nice too, Bill, you are a real credit to the company, Bill.'

'Hah!' said Bill savagely. His face was mottled, his eyes bloodshot, I didn't like the look of him at all. 'Hah!' he said, 'thought I was done for, didn't she? Thought I hadn't got a penny or a friend in the world I could look to, eh.'

'Bill,' I began, 'think of...'

But he turned on me, raising his voice in the manner of his barnstorming days, so that the people around us looked at us curiously and sniggered a little behind their hands.

'Where do you think I got this suit from, Ann?' he said. 'Who do you think turned round one day and said to me, "Bill, I'd like to make you a present?" Who do you think said that?'

I told him humbly that I didn't know, that I couldn't guess, and quelled a wicked voice inside me which murmured, 'the ghost of Henry Irving.'

'A man!' said Bill triumphantly. 'A man, a stranger to me, but I am not a stranger to him. Watched me every week on stage, he had. Come every week to see the part I was taking, and last night up at The Ship he introduced himself. Come right up to where I was standing he did and told me he was my humble servant.'

I said, 'How nice Bill, and how gratifying for you,' and wished he would lower his voice a little.

Bill ignored this interruption and continued. '"I am your humble servant," he said, "and I wish I could repay in some small measure the pleasure you have given me. Your humble servant," he said, "who would like in some small way…"' Here Bill drew a trembling breath and staggered a little.

I clutched his arm. 'Bill,' I said urgently 'think of—' but he interrupted me.

'To cut a long story short,' he quavered with dignity. 'The gentleman turned out to be a gentleman's tailor who insisted on giving me this suit of clothing.'

He leaned on me a little then and Mrs Welles took his other arm. 'Keep thinking of heaven Bill,' she said kindly.

'Heaven?' echoed Bill in a shocked, affronted tone. 'My good lady, I think…'

'Win!' I hissed at her angrily, 'For Christ's sake! Not heaven – haven. The Haven of Rest.'

'That's right,' said Mrs Welles, unruffled. 'Haven love. Keep thinking of the Haven of Rest.'

'Aah!' said Bill, and to our great relief the familiar anticipatory, drugged look came over his face.

From the front of the crowd a tremor and a murmur moved towards us, and around us people began to fish for their tickets. I found my three and wondered if Leigh were there and had his. The vicar's wife's voice came to us, teetering and distant.

'And the lucky winner who has guessed the correct weight of the cake,' she was saying, 'is number sixty-nine.' There was another murmur and tremor as people looked at their tickets. 'Number sixty-nine,' repeated the vicar's wife.

'Any good Ann?' asked Mrs Welles. I shook my head and dropped the little pink slips.

'Nor me,' she said following suit.

'Number sixty-nine.' The vicar's wife's voice was weary and bright. 'Will number sixty-nine please come forward and claim.' There was a little more murmuring and movement, then from the back of the crowd a hand shot up.

'Ah!' said the vicar's wife, pouncing on it with relief.

'Ah!' said the crowd turning towards it with envy and admiration. I looked at it too, then watched the singular head and shoulders of its owner wriggle his way to the front. It was Willy. Willy had won the cake.

'No comment,' I said to Mrs Welles as we extracted ourselves from the melting crowd.

By that time it was half past five, and at six o'clock the banquet was to be held. Mrs Welles waited with me for Rose. She was going straight home, she told me, to get a bit of beauty sleep. She looked tired and happy, and contented and excited. Madame Tic-Tac had spoken, she explained, and all she could do at the moment was prepare herself.

'If she can see a difficult thing like a tinned vegetable clear,' she said as Rose came running towards us, 'then "a question what would make me happy" must be very noticeable.'

We said goodbye to her at the paddock gate, and told her that we'd probably go on to the dance, but would come up and see her when we got in.

The mayor had promised Rose that he would give us a lift to the town hall in his car. We piled into the back with his secretary, and I asked rather diffidently how Mr and Mrs Flood would be arriving. 'In the Reverend's car,' he replied shortly, and the drive was a silent one.

All the way I was thinking about Mrs Flood. Ever since the competition I had deliberately tried not to think about her. I had thought about Willy, about Leigh, about Mrs Welles, about anything or anyone that would take me away from the memory of that terrible hunched old figure sitting at the table.

When Willy had won the cake I had looked away quickly from the spot where he was standing, because I had known that she would be there too. But now, with the mayor's cruel attitude swamping the close atmosphere of the car, out of loyalty and defiance and pity, I began to think about her.

I thought, if I was her I wouldn't go. I wouldn't have the courage or the audacity or the bravado or the stupidity, call it what you will, ever to appear in public with my husband again. If I was her, I thought, I would just want to crawl into a corner and lie down and pray that I could die.

But then I remembered that I wasn't her, and thought to myself how thick-skinned and shallow I was to think that I could ever imagine and accept as right, my reactions to another person's circumstances. What could I know, I told myself, I, who had never been in love, what could I know of the feelings she experienced, when in front of a thousand eyes she saw her husband kiss, as he did, another woman?

Probably she didn't feel any pride at all, I thought, probably all she felt was a numb questioning of herself and where she had failed him. Perhaps, when her head was bowed and she was gripping the table, she was thinking, I must use more perfume, I must use more perfume... I must get myself a negligee that is not quite so transparent... I must cement the cracks in the shutters so that there is no excuse at all... I must buy another whip...

'No! No!' I said to myself out loud.

And Rose sitting beside me, nudged me and said, 'Don't be silly, he knows the way.'

But when we arrived at the town hall and found her waiting on the steps with her husband and the vicar and his wife, I felt small and ashamed and thought, you hadn't allowed for that, Ann King, and you... You had forgotten that she is an actress.

She was smiling and magnanimous and inclined her head towards us as we mounted the steps.

Behind us, Mr Wynch's car drew up with Leigh, Sebastian and Hilda, followed by a small flurry of eminent stall ladies with alderman and JP husbands. The mayor, with the vicar's wife on his arm led the way to the banqueting hall. Mrs Flood and the vicar followed, then Willy, clutching an arm of the terrified mayor's wife. She kept casting praying glances into the vicar's back, but Willy did nothing more than laugh once loudly, and say that it felt funny coming into the hall on a Saturday night with no show to do.

The banqueting hall was directly above the theatre. We had

rehearsed in it once when Mrs Flood had put her foot through the stage. It was large and disused and dim, with thick stuffy air and an echo. Around the walls hung the usual portraits of bygone Leek mayors interspersed with fake marble columns. The long, narrow table had reminded me of coffins placed head to foot, and the stiff upright chairs, tombstones.

But today it looked different and rather grand. The room had been thoroughly cleaned and the chandelier polished and lowered. The coffins were decently covered with clean white cloths, and along their pristine surface, silver and glass and candlelight gleamed.

A few embarrassed-looking waiters hovered behind the tombstone chairs and pouncing, directed us to our places. The mayor was put at the head of the table in a very grand tombstone with arms, with the vicar's wife on one side of him and Mrs Flood on the other.

To my amazement, Willy was put next to her, but looking across the table, quickly understood why.

Where he should have been was the vicar, and on either side of him, his wife and the mayor's wife were smiling their relief at the manoeuvre. The mayor called for silence for his first speech and then with annoyance noticed the vacant chair next to Rose.

'Somebody lost en route, eh?' he said moodily and we all tittered politely. There was a pause then, 'Tut, tut, tut,' said the mayor. 'I really think we'll have to begin without him – er – them.' He blushed a little at himself for not knowing if it were a man or woman that was missing, and for not caring either because, male or female, it was bound to be a bloody actor.

Then, a second late, Bill Irving tottered into the room, breathing like a grampus. A perceptive waiter sprang at him and seized his arm, and while the mayor cleared his throat with relief, steered him to the vacant chair, where he collapsed trembling.

Mrs Flood took one look at him and I heard her hiss, 'Instant dismissal,' into Willy's ear.

'And now, ladies and gentlemen,' began the mayor, 'it gives me great pleasure—' but cutting into him as sharp as a whiplash came Bill Irving's voice.

'Your Worship,' he quavered out astonishingly loudly, 'I won't get up because I'm a little out of breath, out of breath and late, Your Worship, because I have just walked from the paddock to the hall. Seventy next January I am, Your Worship, and I have just walked from the paddock to the hall. Most of the people here, Your Worship, including yourself, passed me on the way, but I could hardly explain to you then that I would be late, as you were all in cars.' He spoke the whole speech on one long rush of breath, the words petering out at the end into gasping jerks.

There was a second's shocked silence then, as the mayor made no move to speak, the vicar gallantly launched into a beautiful apology for Bill's victimisation. A shocking thing... Mismanagement somewhere... Could he ever forgive them? But then of course he would understand...

It did the trick. Bill was soon mollified, thankful for even a crumb of kindness, and with Mrs Flood making angry whistling noises between her teeth, the mayor was able to get under way with his speeches.

We ate melon, and plaice, and stew, and fruit salad, and cheese and biscuits, and we drank a good deal of white wine. Over coffee with port, the atmosphere grew warm and relaxed. At that moment I think every one of us was enjoying ourselves, and I thought, looking round at the Flood Players, that at last we were beginning to make up for our unfortunate start.

Opposite me, Sebastian was making an all-out effort with a good lady, dazzling her with his daring black eyes and long lashes, so that her coffee grew cold and untouched in its cup, and her husband began to notice her for the first time in ten years.

Beside him, Rose was happily fancying Mr Wynch, who, with a bit of food and drink inside him was looking a lot less pinched and worried. He had quite a flush on his high, bony cheekbones, and now and again gave Rose a reckless glance. Further along the table Bill Irving thought the mayor's wife looked sympathetic. Snatches of their conversation came across to me.

'Seventy next January... I was standing in the gutter when your car passed me... Actually you smiled at me... Oh yes, it was you alright... Sitting in front with the mayor... No mistake at all dear lady, I recognised His Worship's robes.'

Fortunately the mayor's wife was defending herself with only half an ear. The rest of her, I was amused to see, appeared to be wholly engrossed in Willy who, sitting beside me, was engaged in stuffing himself with an abnormal quantity of cheese and biscuits. She gazed at him as though he was a rather fascinating curio.

I could imagine her thinking that she had never seen a sex maniac before, and now, mellowed with drink, thinking that it would after all have been rather exciting to have had him next to her... To have been in the danger zone... I wanted to hit her silly, fat face, and suddenly came all over protective for Willy again, and stretching down the table past Leigh and Hilda, grabbed a large plate of cheese and biscuits for him.

'Thanks Ann,' he said, rather muffled through his stuffing. 'Any minute now she'll turn round and notice, so I want to get as much down as I can.'

Up until the biscuits Willy had not enjoyed his meal, as he had been denied sugar with his melon, potatoes with his stew, and any fruit salad at all. But now Mrs Flood was in a coquettish, absorbed conversation with the mayor. I listened to her laughing freely and keeping it light, and liberally sprinkling it with flattery, and despite his dislike for her I watched the mayor falling for it. Only very occasionally her voice cracked with the desperate effort of trying hard.

I was feeling cosy and safe between Leigh and Willy and only slightly annoyed that Leigh should be paying as much attention to Hilda on his other side as he was to me.

'Well,' said the mayor, leaning back in his chair, replete. 'I think that a very fitting ending to a right grand dinner, would be a little piece of acting from one of our guests. What do you say, eh Mrs Flood?'

Mrs Flood flushed with pleasure. 'I shouldn't wonder if it shouldn't be very fitting, Your Worship,' she said. 'And my husband here, Mr Flood, knows a lot of little pieces he could be called on to do something from.' She turned to Willy. 'Eh, Willy?' she said.

Willy, caught unawares in the act of eating four biscuits at once, choked and brought one up. The mayor started to say, 'Well, I had thought of one of your young girls...' but Willy, swallowing hard, announced that he'd love to do some acting, and immediately got up from the table.

The mayor clapped his hands for silence and told the table that Mr Flood had kindly consented to do a little piece for them. There was a murmur of approval from the diners. 'Where would you like to perform?' he asked Willy, then as Rose gave an involuntary snigger, immediately wished he had chosen another word.

'Well?' he said testily, obviously already regretting his impulsive suggestion. Mrs Flood had been sizing up vantage spots and now decided on a corner of the room at the other end of the table.

'I think we'll all see him from there, Your Worship,' she said, and pulling Willy down beside her, whispered to him what he was going to do. He whispered something back and she nodded her head, looking well pleased. Willy strode down the length of the table with all eyes following him.

For a moment he examined the spot where he would act, then turning towards us gave us a lovely smile. He looked so handsome, standing there in his dinner jacket, so debonair, so poised and polished that my heart cried out, 'Oh God, why can't you always let him be like that, why can't you let him be inside what he looks like, why must it always be when he's only acting?'

He was telling us what he was going to do. The dream scene from *The Bells*. The famous scene in which Matthias the innkeeper, goaded by his conscience, faces a nightmare dream trial for his murder of the Polish Jew. He gave us the synopsis simply and intelligently, then bowing from the waist turned his back on us for a second. When he turned round again he wore the mad, hunted face of Matthias.

I don't think one person moved a muscle whilst he enacted the terrible scene. I don't think one person was aware of anything but the stocky, tortured figure who, with sweat and tears running down his face, relived the murder before his judge.

When he had finished, falling to the ground and tearing at the rope around his neck, we didn't even clap. Then after what seemed a long while Bill yelled, 'Bravo,' and everyone else yelled, 'Bravo,' and I was aware of Mrs Flood's hand clamped around my arm like a vice.

His face! His face! I was thinking, how can he look like that, how can he say things like that, how can he show us the heights and depths of another man's soul when he hasn't one himself?

They were clapping him now, and he was smiling with the sweat and tears still on his face. Behind me Mrs Flood started to speak.

'It's at times like this I know,' she was saying, 'it's at times like this I know what every single one of his years has been for. It's only a question of time, you see now Ann. It's only a question of time now as he gets there. I've known it all along of course, ever since he was sixteen.

'But sometimes it's seemed like such a long time and sometimes I've wondered why it couldn't have come sooner. Not of course but what he's old now, Ann, he's only thirty-nine is Willy and that's not a bit old really. Not for a man it isn't, Ann, not for a man as looks like Willy, with Willy's talents. That's why I haven't minded the waiting with knowing about Willy's talents. Genius, Willy's got, Ann; that's why I haven't minded the working and waiting, with knowing about Willy being a genius and that.'

Mrs Flood's voice was breathy; hoarse with the drink she had been taking and curiously unemotional.

'And I feel now, Ann, as though the time's nearly come. I feel in my bones as it's only just round the corner, is Willy's time. He's all prepared and all. Every day of his life I've been preparing Willy. Nobody can say as Willy won't be prepared when it comes. I've watched his diet, and his clothes, and his hair, and his teeth, and he's never had to think for himself nor worry has Willy.

'I haven't never let him be taxed with anything, Ann. I haven't never let him out of my sight but only for a few hours, and then only when I could leave him with someone like yourself. He leans on me altogether now, you see Ann. Sometimes I say to myself I shouldn't wonder but what you haven't spoilt him Lilian, him needing you like he does…' Mrs Flood's voice continued; hoarse and flat, like the dull hooting of a boat on a fog-bound night.

'But then who couldn't help but spoil him, Ann? Such a lovely boy as Willy you couldn't help but spoil. He's so simple and trusting and kind and good, and he always does what he's told does Willy... Well, sometimes he'll maybe fret a bit and want to go off on his own to the pictures or something, you know the strong silent he-man! But I'll coax him and talk to him, let him paint a little picture of me or something; I'll amuse him somehow...'

Yes I thought, I know, I know...

'Maybe I'll play a little game or two with him, Ann. He always likes to play a little game or two does Willy. He'll soon come round then. One way or another he'll soon come round. He's a good boy is Willy.' Mrs Flood paused to drain her port and when I didn't say anything she gave a little laugh.

'Of course, this afternoon was a bit much for him,' she said. 'He's not used to a thing like a fete, is Willy. I thought he was looking a bit dazed just before the competition. I tried to tell the mayor and all but no, he must have Willy make the presentation. So then what goes and happens? Willy, poor lamb, gets confused that's what happens, and what with the platform and the crowds and that, he thinks he's on stage, does Willy, and has got to play his part, and with that creature dressed like that and all, naturally he thinks it's well... that sort of a scene. Shocked and frightened he was afterwards Ann, I can tell you, it was all I could do to get him to come on here.' Mrs Flood's voice was bold as brass; it filled me with admiration. Then suddenly she let go of my arm and stopped speaking.

I looked up, following her gaze, and we both watched whilst Willy, with shining, victorious eyes, came towards her.

Chapter Eleven

The dance was well under way by the time Rose, Leigh, Sebastian and myself joined it. After Willy's performance and a few more speeches, the dinner party had broken up, I'm glad to say, on a happy note. The mayor had even offered to give the Floods a lift home, and the vicar, with much pomp and ceremony, had tucked Bill up in the front of his car with a fur rug. Mr Wynch had wanted to come to the dance with us. He had steadily been talking less about his drains and looking a lot more at Rose, and when the party was over and we were all walking downstairs, had got quite frisky.

'Hearken to the music a-calling us,' he said, cocking an ear in the direction of the dance. 'Hearken to the summons which we must obey.'

Rose had looked at him coldly.

'The night is young,' he continued in a pleading, poetical voice.

'Yes, but you're not,' Rose had replied cruelly, and we'd watched him subside like a pricked balloon.

'Why didn't you like him?' we asked her as we went into our theatre which now with no amount of imagination could be called anything but a dance hall.

'Vulgar!' she replied distantly. 'He lights his cigarettes *after* he's put them in his holder.'

'Oh Miss Hart,' mimicked Sebastian, putting a penny in his eye. 'I wonder if I might take the liberty of booking a little waltz, wot with you agad?' And thrusting a pen at Rose he shot out his cuff. Rose wrote a nasty word on it.

The collapsible iron chairs, which formed the seating arrangement for the patrons of Leek Living Theatre, had been stacked along the walls and the floor was a-whirl with the patrons of a Leek dance. They were leaping and screaming to a samba, which was being bashed out by a rakish-looking band installed on our stage.

'Sacrilege,' said Leigh, voicing all our thoughts as we stood surveying the scene.

'I hope the dressing room doors are locked,' said Hilda Fellowes, wishing she hadn't come.

'Dance?' said Sebastian, before she could do anything about it.

Rose, by my side, was wearing a glazed expression and wiggling in time to the music. I had forgotten how much she loved dancing, and nudged Leigh to take her out of the frustration of merely spectating. Immediately I had said it, however, I was filled with discomfort. Leigh flushed and said loudly that nothing would have given him greater pleasure than to dance with Rose, but on account of his affliction she must forgive him.

Mercifully, at that moment two teddy boys came up and jerked their heads towards the floor and Rose and I were swept away. Out of the corner of my eye I saw Leigh limp away towards the bar. My teddy boy and I enjoyed a scintillating conversation.

'Been 'ere before?'

'No, I haven't.'

'Go to The Rooms?'

'Well no, I don't.'

'Didn't think you did.'

'Didn't you?'

'No, I didn't think you did.'

'Oh. Why?'

'Can't dance.'

'Well no, I'm afraid I'm not much good at the—'

'Okay. Okay? No need to make an issue out of it.'

'I wasn't making an issue.'

'Yes you was.'

'Well of course if you'd like to leave me…'

'Relax doll, I don't work it that way.'

'You don't?'

'No, if I'm stuck with a doll I'm stuck, and that's that.'

'Oh, I see.'

'Who's your friend?'

'Oh, just a friend.'

'Smasher isn't she? We both spotted her at the same time, only Alf got there first. Smashing dancer too.'

'Yes she is a good dancer.'

'Smasher! Look when we catch up with them I'll do an excuse

me on Alf and Alf can do an excuse me on some other doll, and you can go off and buy yourself a lemonade. Okay? Here you are then, here's a bob.'

'Oh – thank you.'

Thus ignobly paid off, I joined Leigh at the bar. He was highly amused at my cruel treatment, which in a way was a good thing as it put us back on our old footing.

'Which one was it?' he said as we leaned back against the bar and watched the dancers.

'That one there dancing with Rose,' I said, pointing him out.

'Well, when they've finished dancing, catch Rose's eye and get her to bring him over for a drink.'

I looked at him in rage. 'Are you mad, Leigh Peters?' I demanded of him. 'Ask that ill-mannered brutish lout over to have a drink?'

Leigh laughed up in my face.

'Yes!' he said. 'I'd like to meet the man who knows how to slap Miss King down so that she doesn't know how to answer back.'

I took myself off to the ladies'.

After an hour or so I began to enjoy myself. I danced with Sebastian, and a succession of young men who divided themselves into two groups, the purely material ones who wanted to take me out into the alley there and then, and the higher-thingies ones who suggested the pictures p.m. Monday. I was dancing with one of the latter group when Rose and my ex teddy boy went into their solo.

The band was playing a mambo with which both my partner and I were having difficulty, and it was with great relief that we noticed the couples in the centre of the room begin to clear the floor. The band played hot and fast, and Rose and her teddy boy, alone in the clearing, danced mad and brilliant.

Madder and madder they danced. The cut glass ball, which revolved above their heads, sprinkled them with a thousand facets of light. Around them the crowds clapped time with their hands. I was vividly reminded of the night she had danced with Willy. It had been in this same theatre too, I thought, only on stage, and she had had the same look on her face as she had now.

It was all the same to her, I thought, Willy, a teddy boy, her fiancé, it was all the same to her, and the happiness or tragedy or indifference she left in her wake was all the same to her too. Why must she always settle for indifference? I thought, why can't – and then I stopped thinking as, with everyone else, I watched the purposeful figure detach itself from the crowd and lumber up to the dancers.

I watched, as did everyone else, only with me it was personal – you see, it was Steve. I had barely time to think about his other half before a hand clamped down on my shoulder.

'Excuse me?' said Ed.

'Excuse me!' said Steve, giving the teddy boy a push.

I thought, no, not again, I can't bear it, but there it was – happening.

Steve had got hold of Rose, who looked rather pleased to see him, and the teddy boy, who seemed to be of an indifferent nature, was not offering up a lot of resistance. If only I had let it go at that everything would have been alright, but fool that I was, goaded by the feel of Ed's arm on mine, I yelled out, 'No no, don't let him take her away, you mustn't let him take her away.' That, of course, did it.

The teddy boy, without even looking in the direction of my voice, leapt into the fray. Wham! Wham! went their fists and Ed, thrusting out his chin, let go of my arm and went to his mate's assistance.

I crept round the edge of the crowd without looking at them, grabbed Rose, who was staring at them goggle-eyed, and together we fled to the ladies'. We didn't come out until about ten minutes later when we heard a girl say, 'Pity they broke it up so soon.'

Back in the hall a sedate waltz was in progress and there was no sign of Ed and Steve. Rose said she could do with a drink after that, so we went to the bar and she got us stood a double gin each on her notoriety. We looked for Leigh and Sebastian but couldn't find them, so after another half hour left the dance for home.

Leigh was already home, drinking tea at the kitchen table. 'What happened to you?' we asked him, and he told us that he and Sebastian had taken Ed and Steve off for a drink.

'They had started fighting one another,' he explained. 'The

teddy boy had only got in one little tickle in the ribs, and they were pitching into each other.'

There was a pause, then, 'Who won?' asked Rose disinterestedly.

'Yours,' replied Leigh with twinkling eyes. 'He said he'd got you fixed alright, and you were coming off the floor all peaceful, when Ed had to go and let Ann blow her top off. He said he had been working really hard on you Rose, and all Ed had done was let Ann talk.'

'Nerve!' said Rose, lighting a cigarette before she put it into her holder.

We had some tea with Leigh, then went upstairs to Mrs Welles. She was awake, reading a novel with a box of crystallised fruits and some chicken legs, and ready to hear all about the dinner and the dance. She was thrilled about Ed and Steve.

'That's what I call true love,' she said, licking a crystallised fruit and sticking it on to her hair to see how it looked.

'Never give up. Bash! Bash! At it. How does it look – somethink like a frosted butterfly?'

We told her that it didn't and suggested that she try a chicken's leg, but Mrs Welles thought that it might smell.

'No really Ann,' she said, removing the crystallised fruit from her hair and eating it. 'You could have a really nice time with that Ed. Granted he hasn't got money, but you say you don't want that, and if you don't want that you want the other thing, and boy has that Ed got it.'

'Oh, shut up Win!' I said, embarrassed because Leigh was there. 'You know perfectly well I think he's frightful.'

'Well, what about that Willy then?' continued Mrs Welles unperturbed. 'We all know what he can do, and there you are with him right on the doorstep.'

'Willy's married,' I said with dignity.

Mrs Welles shrieked with laughter, rocking back and forth on the bed.

'That's a good one that is,' she said, hitting Rose in her delight. 'Hear that Rose? Willy's married.'

But Rose and Leigh came to my rescue.

'There are more things in heaven and earth than are dreamt of in your philosophy,' Leigh told her.

And Rose said, 'Besides, Willy's not interested in her.'

'Alright, alright,' said Mrs Welles. 'Take it easy, it's just the thought of being an old married woman again has got me match-making.' She gave a coy little laugh.

Rose and Leigh had been told about Madame Tic-Tac's prophecy, and now we all leaned forward eagerly.

'When do you think he'll speak?' Rose asked in an awed voice. 'I mean, it's only been a fortnight.'

Mrs Welles smiled at her kindly. 'Rosie,' she said, 'when you get to my age, which won't take you so long, you'll maybe have learnt that it's in the passion-racked short spaces of time that you get your best work done.' She leaned back on the bed with another piece of chicken. 'I fancy he'll be down on his knees before next Sunday,' she said complacently.

'Oh Win!' said Rose enviously, then bravely added, 'Congratulations, Win.'

'Ta,' said Mrs Welles, washing the chicken down with a crystallised fruit. She peered at Rose and me, narrowing her eyes.

'Pink, I think,' she said. 'You'd both suit pink, then I can have the kids in blue.'

'Bridesmaids?' enquired Rose with bated breath. 'Oh Win, thanks ever so much, I was hoping you'd have me and Ann for bridesmaids.'

'But Win!' I said horrified. 'The children! He doesn't even know about them yet. He doesn't even know you're married.'

'Neither is he going to know,' said Mrs Welles. 'They're going to be my sister's kids, left sudden on my hands through her fatal stroke.'

'Oh Win,' said Rose admiringly, 'you are clever, I'd have just put them in A Home.'

'I may have to yet,' said Mrs Welles hopefully. 'He'll maybe not fancy the idea of being saddled with his sister-in-law's kids as well!' She gave a shriek of delight at the humour of the situation.

Now although this sounds very callous, and although in my heart of hearts I couldn't really approve of it, I knew that it was the best thing that could happen. I saw now quite clearly that for any lasting results she'd have to marry Mr Dropsey, and that she'd have to manage it pretty soon, whilst he was still in love with her.

He really did seem to be in love with her too. Bouquets of flowers and boxes of chocolates had been arriving for her all over the weekend while he had been away. But at the same time I remembered how quickly he had finished with me, and how friendly, Backless at *Le Cercle Rouge* had been with him.

'Now listen Win,' I said firmly. 'You've got to treat this thing seriously, and the first and most important thing is not to go and get too optimistic. He hasn't said anything yet remember, and it's no good looking at me like that either,' I said as she made a face at me. 'We all know that he's given you a mink, and we all know that Madame Tic-Tac's spoken, but it's no good just leaning back and relying on that. You've got to make an all-out effort, Win,' I said, hammering the words out on the edge of the bed.

'She's right you know Win,' said Rose.

'But I am doing,' said Mrs Welles piqued.

'No you're not Win,' I said. 'You've been slipping ever since he's been away. Look at you now, you said you were coming home for an early night, and here you are guzzling complexion-ruining foods and sitting up reading. You ought to be lying down with a double face pack on you.'

'Well, I was going to put one on,' said Mrs Welles.

'And it's not only looks either Win,' I went on. 'I agree with you that if he is going to speak it'll be anytime now, but you've got to help him, Win. During the next week you can't afford to make even one little slip.'

I was desperately trying to make her see how important her part still was. I hadn't told her about Backless, and I had a feeling that she saw Mr Dropsey as a doting one-woman old fool who she could twist round her little finger. She had definitely been getting rather blasé about him lately. But my feeling began to communicate itself to her.

'Yes,' she said earnestly, 'you're dead right Ann, it is important, but I can manage it. I promise you I'll be the pure clinging vine all week, how's that, eh?'

'That's fine,' I told her encouragingly.

'Oh and Ann,' she said, 'I've been meaning to tell you all

weekend, I mentioned the company to him the other day. "I'd love to have you be patron of the arts, Teddy," I said to him the other day, "and with there being a real live theatre in Leek...?" Well, I told him outright, I said I thought a helping hand would be a lovely gesture.'

'Well?' we all gazed at her in excitement, 'And what did he say?'

'Oh!' said Mrs Welles. 'Oh, he said not to worry my little head about money matters, but that he'd thought about it himself, and as he'd met me through the Living Theatre in Leek, he didn't see why everythink shouldn't be okay. That's exactly what he said, Ann. "Tell them," he said, "that everythink will be okay.""

We found this heartening if a little vague, and decided that she might sprinkle the clinging vine act with a few delicate reminders.

The next day was the first night of the new play, *She was Poor but She was Honest*, and when we got back after the show Mrs Welles had gone.

'The man in the uniform came for her about five o'clock,' Guinevere told us.

This was highly satisfactory, as it had been ever since she met Mr Dropsey. He had never been round to the house again, but always sent Withers with the car to collect her. It had worried us no end at first, as we'd visualised him dropping in whenever the fancy took him, surprising the children and finding out about Leigh.

In fact, for the first few days the children had practically lived in the attic, and Leigh's evening dress had hung ready on the back of the kitchen door. But it soon became apparent that Mr Dropsey preferred to entertain Mrs Welles in his own home, where she would stay for two or three days at a time before Withers brought her back again.

'Did she look alright?' we asked Guinevere anxiously, and Guinevere conscientiously described Mrs Welles' apparel. She had wisely worn the purple net.

'Nothing like wearing the first thing he saw you in,' said Rose sagely as we sat down to supper.

We had a good supper. Fried kidneys and bacon which Guinevere had cooked for us, and we were just starting on cheese and biscuits when there was a knock on the kitchen door. We looked at each other wide-eyed and Guinevere and Leigh made an automatic concerted dive for the hall. But Rose hissed that it couldn't be them because we'd have heard the car, and anyway, Win would never bring him round to the back door.

This was quite true so I went to open it, and there on the doorstep, looking bronzed and jovial, stood Mr Goat.

'Just got back this morning,' he said, pushing past me before I could open my mouth. He looked round the kitchen.

'Win upstairs?'

'N-no, no I'm afraid she's out,' I said, trying to collect my thoughts.

This was frightful. I didn't know quite what to do. As luck would have it, the first day of Mr Goat's annual summer holiday had coincided with the first day of the acquisition of Mr Dropsey. And for two weeks now, lulled into a false sense of security by the plain sailing, had completely forgotten about Mr Goat.

'Out, eh?' said Mr Goat masterfully. 'Oh well, I'll just go on upstairs and wait for her.' He was obviously twice the man he had been on his last visit.

'No! No, you can't,' I shouted at him wildly. 'I mean... I mean she'll be away for some time.'

'Some time?' said Mr Goat. 'What time?'

'Till... Till Saturday,' I said. I guessed she'd be home all right by Saturday.

'Saturday?' repeated Mr Goat in a surprised voice. 'Who the hell's she staying with for that long?'

'A friend,' said Rose. 'A friend who's just had a baby and is very ill, Mr Goat. An SOS came this morning for her, so of course she just downed everything and went. I mean you know Win, Mr Goat, any little thing she can do for anyone and she'll do it without sparing herself.'

'Well,' said Mr Goat, unable to quite agree, 'well... Yes, of course.'

'Saturday you say, eh? Right, I'll remember that.' He pulled on his leather gloves and placed a paper carrier bag he was holding on the table.

'Couple of cartons of baked beans I've brought along for her,' he said. 'I know how much Mrs Welles likes a baked bean, and I know how much it means to her too. Still,' he went on magnanimously, 'I dare say you starving actors will know what to do with them too, eh?' And chortling with delight at the misfortunes of our calling, he let himself out.

'Nasty piece of work!' said Leigh as we sat down to our cheese again.

'It's a good job you said Saturday, Ann,' said Rose. 'I mean, Mr Dropsey'll have been down on his knees by then and she can have a whale of a time getting rid of Goat.'

'Anyone fancy a nice little baked bean with their cheese?' I said, stacking the tins on the shelf that was still half filled with them.

We didn't see Mrs Welles again until the Wednesday, when she popped in during the afternoon for half an hour. She had come to pick up Boysey as Mr Dropsey had suddenly felt like seeing him again.

'How's it going?' we asked her as we noiselessly tried to extract him from Launcelot. (Withers was waiting in the car at the gate). Mrs Welles, closing one eye explicitly, chalked up a stroke on her mink.

'Really!' we chorused at her eagerly. 'Has he spoken?'

'Well, not exactly spoken,' she admitted. 'But hints of a nature such as could only be translated one way. I fancy this'll bring it to a head,' she said picking up Boysey with distaste. 'There's nothing like a dog to help get a man sentimental.'

'Or a child,' Leigh put in slyly, but Mrs Welles chose to ignore the remark.

Outside, Withers was tooting boldly on the horn, so we hugged her goodbye and crossed our fingers for her and told her to hurry back.

Thursday and Friday passed uneventfully except that during Friday's show, Rose's fiancé Derrick turned up unexpectedly for the weekend. We hadn't seen him for four weeks as on his last journey over, he had smashed his motorbike up before he had got out of Blackpool.

Now, however, it had been repaired and Rose fell on him with whoops of delight as he stood in the dressing room, vibrating a little as he always did, through constant contact with the machine. I was very pleased to note Rose's reactions to a sudden appearance, as her continued lack of interest in him had been worrying.

We took him back to the digs for supper and with Mrs Welles still away were able to let him have her bed. He was a nice boy was Derrick, blond and athletic and terribly good looking, and obviously mad about Rose. He could hardly take his eyes off her all through supper, and afterwards Leigh and I discreetly retired early to bed.

We were awakened, however, at about seven o'clock the following morning by the loud sound of him tinkering with his motorbike under the window, and downstairs found Rose disconsolately cutting an enormous amount of sandwiches.

'Another bloody all-day spin in the bloody country,' she said, slapping a vicious amount of mustard on to some chicken. 'Another bloody day of clutching that smelly jacket and ruining my skin.'

'Hey,' bellowed Derrick's voice through the open window, 'what about my breakfast, woman?'

Rose gave an end-of-her-tether shriek and threw a fork at him, which he returned with interest.

'It's no good, Ann,' she said hysterically as I started on the breakfast. 'I could never marry a man who lacks sensitivity, I couldn't Ann, not with being as highly strung as I am myself.'

But over breakfast she calmed down. Either food sharpened Derrick's sensitivity or blunted hers, and afterwards we stood in The Rooley and waved her off, looking quite happy and very smart in Mrs Welles' evening pyjamas.

On Saturday mornings we didn't usually rehearse, so whilst I got on with cleaning the attic, Guinevere took Launcelot in his pushchair out shopping, and Leigh went down to the theatre to get on with his carpentry. He was making Guinevere a doll's house.

I was the only one at home then, when Mrs Welles arrived. I watched the car drive up from the attic window, and dashed downstairs to meet her.

'Well?' I asked her breathlessly as we collided in the kitchen door.

'Oh Ann!' said Mrs Welles fervently as she collapsed on to a chair with shining eyes. 'Oh Ann, it's going to happen tomorrow, he's going to speak tomorrow, tomorrow's going to be the day.'

'How do you know?' I asked her.

'Because he said so. Teddy said so,' she replied. 'Only half an hour ago as I got into the car – he's away on business you see today – and as I got into the car he took my chin in his hand and looked at me dead serious, Ann. "Little Winnie," he said, still dead serious, "you must take care of yourself today, because tomorrow I'm going to ask you a very important question."' Mrs Welles paused dramatically, and I gave an impressed gasp.

'Those were his very words Ann,' she said. '"Little Winnie you must take great care of yourself today, because tomorrow I'm going to ask you a very important question." His very words Ann – as prophesised by Madame Tic-Tac, and the meaning of which even Launcelot could understand.'

It was a solemn moment and we celebrated it with tea.

'It was all I could do,' said Mrs Welles, leaning back with a cup, 'to stop myself screaming, "Get on you old fat-head and say it now," but there, "Love moveth in a mysterious way", as I've always said, and if he feels happier speaking tomorrow it suits me. It might be,' she said reflectively, 'that he's giving me time to prepare my answer.'

She thought about this idea for a moment then shook her head. Imagination had boggled. 'No,' she said regretfully. 'I don't really think that it could have been that.'

At one o'clock Leigh showed up for lunch but immediately afterwards returned to the theatre. 'See you on the green, Annie,' he said to me in a preoccupied voice. He enjoyed carpentering.

Mrs Welles gave a yawn of absolute and conscious happiness. 'What are you doing this week?' she asked me. 'I might pop down with you and have a look-see.'

'*She was Poor but She was Honest*,' I replied, looking at her, my mouth twitching. Mrs Welles gave me a haughty stare.

'How much longer you think you can carry on dishing out unbelievable tripe like that I don't know,' she said. 'We all know that Ma Flood was the sweetheart of the Boer War, but I do think, Ann, that you'd do a little better if you didn't keep hammering the fact home each week.'

'Well, do you want a ticket or don't you?' I asked her, and Mrs Welles condescendingly replied that I could get one for her if it made me any happier, but she thought she would just sit with me in the dressing room.

It was just as we were about to leave the house that Mr Goat arrived. With the excitement of Mrs Welles' infrequent visits we had completely forgotten to tell her that he would be coming round on Saturday. Mrs Welles opened the door and there he was, grinning and expectant after their three week separation. I saw the light of battle gleam in Mrs Welles' eyes and my heart sank that he should have picked the one moment for his dismissal to be clothed in triumphant drama.

'Ha!' said Mrs Welles in delighted anticipation. 'Goat!'

I decided that I was better out of the way so retired into the sitting room, but through the open window their voices came to me plainly.

Mrs Welles was doing the *grande dame* act and phrases like 'growing out of people' and 'worn out gloves,' floated loudly down The Rooley.

Mr Goat was playing up beautifully too, with 'you can't do this to me Win' and 'it's another man, I know it's another man.' He was really getting quite distraught, and there was a sudden scrabbling noise as he tried to push past her into the hall.

Chapter Twelve

We caught a bus down to the theatre and as we turned into the cobbled passage and saw the sign of the Ship Inn swinging a little under the evening sky, smiled at each other and without a word passed by the stage door and went towards it.

'Shandy for me Win,' I said as Mrs Welles ordered herself a double gin. 'I've got to be in in five minutes' time.'

We took our drinks over to the wide window seat and while Mrs Welles gazed at herself in a mirror over the fireplace, I looked along the passage to the bright square of light where the High Street joined it and people and cars passed up and down. Neither of us spoke, Mrs Welles, I think, because her heart and mind were too full of the wondrous words that Mr Dropsey had spoken to her, and I because I felt languid and peaceful and safe and liked just looking down the passage. I watched Mrs Flood and Willy turn into the stage door, she, frowning in a limp floral dress and cardigan, hung with two string bags and Willy's mackintosh, and Willy in a crisp pale green shirt and bow tie, holding a large bloodstained newspaper parcel which proclaimed the Sunday joint.

The pub's wireless finished giving the weather forecast and started on the seven o'clock news, and I said, 'I must go!' but didn't make a move. Our performance started at seven thirty, and we were due in half an hour before. But I thought, well I'm right next door, and I bet half the others aren't in, and allowed Mrs Welles to buy me another shandy.

I watched Hilda Fellowes turn in, then Sebastian and Bill Irving talking to each other, and I gave a contented sigh because in a second I would be united with them all, talking, laughing, acting with them all... I looked up sharply at the clock; it was ten past seven.

'Win!' I said urgently as she lit a fresh cigarette, but she waved a hand at me and said she'd see me over there, and I looked at her face and smiled at the 'beautiful serial' expression it was wearing, and leaving her, ran quickly down the passage.

The theatre was cool and dim. I crossed the stage, laid out waiting for the performance, bounded up the two steps which led to the dressing room, and at the same time as I laid my hand on the door knob, heard a single ear-splitting screech emit from beyond it. My heart began to thud a little for it came from none other than Mrs Flood. I opened the door slowly and fearfully.

She was standing in the centre of the room wearing a kimono and her slippers, and was heavily made up except for her eyes, which were rimless pink slits watering a little under the embarrassment of being surprised without their false eyelashes. Two golden rivulets of British sherry had traced a course from the corners of her mouth, which was still open from emitting the screech. Around her in attitudes of helpless horror stood the rest of the company.

As I came through the door all eyes were turned on me and whilst I stared back at them blankly, Mrs Flood took a staggering step towards me.

'She's to blame,' she said pointing a hysterically quivering finger at me. 'She was there, she could have stopped her.'

'No, no!' said Leigh from behind her, 'It was nothing to do with her. I was there too, Mrs Flood.'

'Nonsense,' shrieked Mrs Flood, taking another step towards me. 'She's her friend, thick as thieves they are…'

An awful fear of her anger and of the frightened faces of the others gripped my heart. 'What's the matter… What have I done?' I faltered.

Mrs Flood's eyes disappeared altogether in a blaze of fury, and when she spoke her breath came in little hissing noises.

'Only let your strumpet friend take a hundred mile ride to Blackpool and, half an hour before she's due to appear on stage, calmly telephone to say the motorcycle on which she and her client were travelling had broken down – that's all you've done,' said Mrs Flood.

I gave a gasp and Mrs Flood sat down suddenly on a chair and put her head in her hands. We gazed at her helplessly and unhappily, and Willy, with the pathetic fear of a child confronted by the sudden weeping of its nagging mother, crossed over to her and put his arm around her.

At the touch of him Mrs Flood raised her head, and as her eyes met his the expression in them made Sebastian and Hilda cough, and Bill Irving shuffle his feet and Leigh look away. But the next second she was on her feet again, all grim purpose and action. Leigh rushed for a script, which she snatched from him and turned quickly to Rose's part, and we crowded round and watched as she leafed through it, looking for the bits when Rose was on stage.

Her idea was for Hilda to double the part of the housekeeper with Rose's part of the heroine, but now as she came up to the big dramatic scene in Act Three, where Hilda had to tell Rose all, the script fell from her hand, and she sat down again under the obvious impossibility of it all.

'It's no good,' she said hollowly. 'We'll have to get someone in.'

'Who?' asked Willy.

'Who?' echoed Mrs Flood, anger at the hopelessness of the remark starting up in her again. 'Who do any of you know?' She swept us with her eyes and brought them to rest accusingly on me.

'Well, Ann?' she said. 'Seeing that you let your strumpet friend get us into this mess, then walk into the theatre ten minutes late yourself, who do you suggest? What were you doing ten minutes late anyway? Didn't you fancy your client enough to go to Blackpool with him? Or did his machine happen to stay intact?'

Her taunting, evil voice lent me the courage to shout back. 'I've been at the digs all day, and Rose is engaged to the boy she's out with, and I'm late because I've been having a drink with my landlady at the Ship,' I shouted miserably back at her.

'What?' said Leigh. 'What did you say Ann?'

'You heard,' I said bitterly.

He crossed over to me and took me by the shoulders. 'Win?' he said urgently. 'You've been having a drink with Win just now? She's in the Ship now?'

I nodded my head. 'She was coming to watch the show.'

'Christ, it's a miracle Ann!' He looked at me and as I looked back at him, understanding suddenly dawned and we both shrieked, 'Mrs Flood!' simultaneously.

Leigh rushed to get her, and I blabberingly explained the miracle to Mrs Flood. 'You remember Mrs Flood... You must remember... the lady at the fête in the mink coat... I introduced you... You must remember, she said how nice your dress was!'

'Aah!' said Mrs Flood, remembering.

Two minutes later we heard them clattering back across the stage, and an excited Mrs Welles was pushed through the door. I rushed to her.

'Win, please please darling Win, could you go on for Rose?' But entreaties were quite unnecessary.

'Take a part?' said Mrs Welles delightedly. 'Ooh yes! Leigh's just told me and I'd love to take a part – what do I have to wear?'

It was twenty minutes past seven. We threw her into a chair and while Hilda slapped make-up on to her face, the rest of us converged upon her with feverish instructions. Above the din of Willy telling her that she'd only got ten minutes in which to learn three acts, and Sebastian telling her that in their scenes to leave it all to him, and Leigh telling her to just pretend it was Mr Dropsey, and Hilda telling her that no, we hadn't got a blonde wig, I tried to make myself up and tell her the story of the play.

'I'm your alcoholic sister, Win, and you're a sweet little thing who I'm selling to a wicked brewer for drink...'

'...Just keep batting your eyelashes Mrs Welles and I'll...'

'...Only you don't know he's a wicked brewer –'

'...hadn't you better start learning some of it up Mrs Welles – you've only got five –'

'...And I send you out into the snow across the fields...'

'The scene you really want to make sure of is your big one with Willy –'

'...across the fields – are you listening Win?'

'...and your big one with me Mrs Welles in Act Three...'

'...across the fields with some calf's foot jelly –'

'...and that frightfully important little cameo duologue with me, Mrs Welles.'

'...calf's foot jelly because I've told you there's a sick man –'

'That's me, me as the wicked brewer, only you don't know –'

'…a sick man up at the big house, can you hear me Win? And you go all pathetic and snowy –'

'…pathetic, you know Win, just the same as when we got you ready for Mr Dropsey, and I'm the butler again, just the same.'

'…and your first scene is just you –'

'No Mrs Welles, I don't think three beauty patches…'

'…just you Win and him trying to seduce you –'

'Seduce, you know Win, just like Mr –'

'It's seven thirty-three,' said Willy looking at his watch and striking his hand in the air as though measuring the starting time of a race. We were off. Mrs Flood gave an anguished moan and shrieked for someone to get her her false eyelashes.

Leigh bolted to change the record to the National Anthem, and I dragged my guise of the alcoholic sister over my head. Mrs Flood and I opened the play. Willy rushed back with her eyelashes and we made a concerted dive for the stage.

'Don't forget, Mrs Welles,' shrieked Mrs Flood. 'Make sure of your big scene with Willy.'

Mrs Welles' voice came back to us faintly. 'I shan't bother myself with any learning, no need Mrs Flood, Ann's just explained and it's right up my street.'

The opening scene was a short one where Mrs Flood as my likewise alcoholic mother and I decide to sell the sweet little thing. The wicked brewer had told us that he will keep us in alcohol if he can have her, and has shut us up in his study for ten minutes in which to reach our decision.

Goaded on by the cruel smell of a gin perfume with which he has liberally sprayed the room, we lose no time in clawing at the study door in a maddened way, saying, 'Take her, take her.' The curtain then comes down on Sebastian as the wicked brewer, standing in the doorway with his foot on Mrs Flood's prostrate body and laughing evilly.

It is all highly dramatic, and as Mrs Flood and I stumbled mechanically through the histrionics, over and over again my heart hammered out a prayer – please don't let us be booed off the stage, please, I couldn't bear to be booed off the stage so soon, please let something happen so that it isn't too terrible. Sebastian laughed evilly, the curtain swooshed down, and as Mrs Flood and

I dashed off stage it rose again immediately on his pacing the study, awaiting the heroine's arrival with the calf's foot jelly.

Leigh was waiting for me as I came through the door. 'Ann!' He said in an agonised voice, 'for Christ's sake get her to take off that mink.'

'She's on,' hissed Bill Irving who was working the curtain.

'She's on,' shrieked Mrs Flood.

She was standing ready to make her entrance, surrounded by the horrified company and firmly clutching her mink.

'Mrs Welles,' said Hilda, jerking at it.

'She's a poor little thing, Win,' thundered Leigh.

'You get the mink coat later,' explained Willy.

'Please, please Win, take it off,' I said.

'Get her on,' hissed Bill Irving.

'Get her on,' shrieked Mrs Flood.

'Win,' I said, thrusting Hilda aside and pulling at the mink myself, 'please, please darling Win.'

Mrs Welles leaned suddenly towards me and hissed confidingly down my ear. 'I can't take it off Ann, Rose's stage clothes didn't fit me, and I hadn't got time to get back into mine, and I've only got a bra and pants on underneath—'

'Get her on,' began Mrs Flood, and at the same time the door was flung open and Sebastian, in a terrible, meaning voice said, 'Did I hear somebody knock?'

And Mrs Flood, cut short in the middle of another screech, seized the packet of soapflakes, which Hilda was holding, emptied them over Mrs Welles, thrust a jar of pickles into her hand and pushed her on.

We all rushed to the prompt corner to watch her make her stage *debút*. Willy and Mrs Flood, Hilda, Leigh and me; all toppling over one another, all strained and white, all wondering whether Leek would take this as the final straw. All wondering what would happen if it did. Over and over again my heart hammered out its silly prayer... Please, please don't let it be too terrible...

My first thought as she came through the doorway and stood screwing up her eyes at the lights was one of surprised relief at her appearance.

She didn't look too bad at all. She had kicked off her high-heeled shoes, and stood in her bare feet with the mink huddled around her like a Victorian coachman's greatcoat, and with her eyes screwed up and the soapflakes clinging to her fur and hair, she really did look quite pathetic.

She is supposed to hand over the calf's foot jelly immediately, but Mrs Welles, ignoring Sebastian's outstretched hand, slowly unscrewed her eyes and looked round the stage with interest; and surprisingly enough it didn't look awful but rather good, as though she were searching for the sick man she had been told about. But Sebastian of course couldn't see this, and pale under his florid make-up he snatched it quickly from her and said, 'Aah, my jelly!' in a loud forbidding voice. Mrs Welles, looking annoyed, snatched it back, and in a high, deadpan voice delivered her first line.

'This-jelly-is-for-a-sick-man-you-shall-not-have-it,' she said.

From above me, Mrs Flood and Hilda moaned, and from beneath me Leigh hissed on to the stage, 'No, no Win, he is the sick man, he is the brewer, give it to him.'

Mrs Welles turned immediately to the direction of his voice, caught a glimpse of our white faces, looked out towards the audience in a panicky way and put her hand over her mouth at the awfulness of having thought that the brewer and the sick man were two different people.

'Give it to him,' hissed Leigh, and Mrs Welles, with another panicky glance at the audience, said in a little trembling voice, 'I-am-wrong-I-can-see-that-you-are-a-sick-man-after-all-here-you-are.'

Sebastian took it, and we saw his face relax as she remained in a dejected, drooping attitude.

'He'll manage as long as she stays like that,' said Willy.

'Doesn't know a word of it,' said Mrs Flood, as Sebastian, talking loudly all the time, deftly dragged Mrs Welles towards the sofa.

'Just as long as she keeps her mouth shut,' breathed Leigh.

I couldn't resist it. 'But Leigh,' I said. 'What about her wonderful acting talents?'

'Acting talents?' said Leigh. 'Look at her face girl, look at her face, look at that range of emotion playing on it.'

Mrs Welles was looking quite terrified and rather sick.

As luck would have it, the part of the heroine, which in its dumb wetness had afforded us great amusement during rehearsal, could, we now saw, be played almost literally and quite credibly, without a word spoken. Mrs Welles, who sat hunched miserably on the sofa waiting whilst Sebastian poured her a wicked drink, had not uttered a word since handing over the jelly, and looking through the spy-hole out into the audience, I realised that nobody was questioning the fact.

Sebastian was rather enjoying himself. He loved acting, and now with the stage as it were to himself, was wallowing in one great big soliloquy, straddling armchairs, twirling his moustaches and hitting the furniture with a whip. Suddenly, as he came up to the seduction scene and started to walk across to her, with effective contrast, he became silent.

'You-are-a-sick-man,' babbled Mrs Welles bravely, thinking that he had forgotten his words, but he frowned at her and still without speaking dropped down on to the end of the sofa and slid up beside her.

Mrs Welles gazed at him in frozen horror. 'You-are-a-sick-' she began again desperately, and then stopped short in mid-sentence as Sebastian, bending over her, slowly ran a hand up her mink. Frozen horror switched off Mrs Welles' face like an electric light and a great delighted smile took its place, and slowly but surely we watched her loosen her mink a little so that one long, slim leg was on view from ankle to thigh.

'Naughty, naughty!' she said in a bold, coy voice.

'Win,' I hissed faintly.

'Win,' said Leigh not even hissing, 'for Christ's sake Win – struggle.'

On stage Sebastian had recoiled from her as though he had been hit, and the audience tittered uneasily. He recovered himself immediately however and muttering something to her under his breath, threw himself upon her in a savage onslaught, as though forcing her to protest, but Mrs Welles, who had always fancied animal passion, surrendered herself with equal savagery and as her arms went around him, pulling his head down to hers, her mink coat fell open unchecked, leaving on view a pair of white nylon pants boldly embroidered with – 'if you've got the key it will fit the lock.'

With trembling hands Leigh managed to get the curtain down.

She wasn't on for the next scene and whilst we hustled her up to the dressing room, and she sent Bill Irving out for brandies all round, Willy, as the hero, combated with the still hysterical audience.

And now it was over and they hadn't booed but thought it funny, we sat round the dressing room with our brandies and laughed hysterically too. Even Mrs Flood said, 'Reely Mrs Welles, you ought to go on the halls,' but at the same time, with a red pencil, she was engaged in cutting out as much as possible of her scene with Willy.

Mrs Welles sat thrilled and excited, looking at herself in the mirror, and perched above her on the dressing table, also looking thrilled and excited, was Sebastian. My heart sank inside me as I noticed that it was not her own reflection that Mrs Welles looked at, but his, and the way his eyes were on her.

By the time she was due on again we had got the play back to a fairly even tempo, and as both Leigh and I were on stage with her after that we were able to carry her along quite nicely. Hilda had stitched her into Rose's clothes and instead of Mrs Flood's undyed lion, we were able to use real mink for the temptation scene. In her scene with Hilda where she is Told All, Mrs Welles really rose to quite remarkable heights. She gasped and moaned most realistically, and now and again came out with remarks like, 'Oh wicked, wicked' and 'Men are all the same,' without even being told to say them.

The play finishes on Willy finding her and carrying her off to a Better Life. It is quite a long scene, but Mrs Flood had shortened it to the extent of Willy just coming on and saying, 'I have discovered my dream,' and holding out his arms. The curtain came down as she pattered towards them, and whilst the audience applauded heartily from the other side, we rushed around Mrs Welles, congratulating her.

She was happy, happy, happy; in the dressing room she sang and did a funny dance and kissed Leigh and Bill Irving and

Sebastian one after the other, and then Sebastian again, and then she laughed long and loud and kissed him again and sent him away.

'This is my happy day Ann,' she said. 'This is my happy day and tomorrow is my happy day too, and after tomorrow it will be all my happy days,' and she got up from putting on a street make-up and waltzed round the room again. Hilda looked at her indulgently and Mrs Welles went over to her and said very grandly and sweetly, 'You must excuse me Hilda, you see, I'm getting engaged tomorrow.'

Hilda smiled gruffly and said, 'Congratters.'

I said, 'Come down to earth, Win.'

From above us the boys yelled, 'Step on it girls,' so we stepped on it and the men came clattering down in a rush and swept us on a bright wave of laughter, out into the clean summer night and up the quiet passage and into the pub.

In the pub we kept on laughing, such happy laughter, and so bright and gay we were, that soon it seemed as though the whole room was laughing with us and the Ship was rocking with us too, as free as its name.

Mrs Welles, who was going to marry money, tossed a five pound note on the bar and ordered a bottle of gin and a bottle of whisky and a bottle of brandy, so that when they said, 'Time gentlemen please,' for the very last time, we came away still laughing with brown paper parcels under our arms.

Hilda and Bill wouldn't join the party, so where the leafy road turned up to Cockton Heath, we said goodbye to them and linking arms, four abreast in the middle of the road, we shouted out songs to the stars as we wound our way home.

At number eight the lights were on and we all fell over Derrick's motorbike, which was lying in several pieces just beyond the gate.

Rose heard our voices and came running out of the front door to meet us. 'Thank God!' she said. 'I thought you were never coming, however did you manage?'

We all piled into the sitting room, and whilst Leigh operated bottles and glasses, we gave her the story. Mrs Welles and Sebastian were the chief narrators, and breathless from singing and drinking I was glad to be able to just lean back in the grate and look at us all. We had kept the room the same as when it had been prepared for Mr Dropsey, but the bunches of privet hedge had long since withered around the legs of the coffee table, and the photograph of the queen had been scratched to ribbons by Boysey.

On the sofa where Mr Dropsey had first seen her, Mrs Welles lay sprawled. Her head rested between the same two bows, but this time at her feet knelt Sebastian. In the chair opposite, Rose was laughing her head off as he unfolded the story.

Derrick was working the gramophone. I was strongly reminded of the party after the first night of *Wuthering Heights*, and I thought what a long, long time ago it seemed since I had run all the way home from the Ship, frightened to death by Leigh Peters; Leigh who I knew so well and liked so much and was no more frightened of than by Guinevere.

I laughed to myself when I remembered how I had nearly left Mrs Welles' when he had moved in the very next day. But was it with a twinge of disappointment I realised that my liking for him now was probably only because of his changed attitude to me. He was kind to me, he was nice to me, I thought that he was even very fond of me, but since that night he had never in any way shown the old interest.

And yet, and yet... I remembered how my heart had bounded when he had woken me in the dark attic, how suddenly at the fête I had known illogically that he was in love with me, how I had wanted to wake him with a kiss... Was it from him or from me that I got the idea, I thought suddenly. But even as I thought it, I knew that it was neither, and my heart started to pound inside me because I knew what the answer was.

It was simple and dangerous and well known to me by now. It was the growing certainty in my mind that Hilda Fellowes had lied to me and not Leigh Peters.

The idea had been in my mind for some time. On many occasions I had lain in bed and thought about it. Knowing him as I did now, I found it hard to believe that he should have lied to me about his whole life, which, if he were married and had been in England last summer, must have been a lie. I found it odd too, that neither Hilda nor he should mention the other theatre company. Granted, he had only been there for one weekend, but in the theatre, people you met just for one weekend, you were likely to greet again as old friends.

I had wondered perhaps if they had had a row, or nursed an old hate, but decided that they were not antagonistic enough for that. The only thing I could think, was that Leigh had simply not noticed Hilda when he had met her before, and that now Hilda took a secret delight in withholding her knowledge from him, for either hurting or protecting me. Or else she was lying. I think I would have believed with complete certainty that she was lying but for one thing.

Leigh had received a letter from Bognor Regis. I supposed that even now, if I asked him he would tell me, but our relationship had long since passed the point when barriers are torn down and swapped for possession.

We were separate and we respected one another, and now I could only wonder and watch and tell myself that if something had gone wrong somewhere, it had mercifully happened early enough for me not to be hurt by it.

Leigh looked across from the bottles, raised a questioning eyebrow and brought me another gin, and I stopped thinking about him as he sat down beside me and said, 'Ssh!' The gramophone was playing 'September Song', which he found very moving and for which he liked concentration *en masse*.

By the time Derrick had finished giving us lurid details of the death of Bubbles, his motorbike, on the Blackpool Road, we were all decidedly merry; but still above the gins and the whiskies and the brandies, like a clear bright light, shone Mrs Welles' happiness.

It was so great that she couldn't sit still but kept leaping up from the sofa and running to change the records, and running to give people drinks and hugging people for no reason at all.

'This is MY happy day!' she had said to me, and as I watched her now, they seemed to me the most beautiful and tender words I had ever heard.

It required little perception to see that Sebastian was by this time quite fascinated by her. He usually talked non-stop and did the fascinating himself, but after he had finished recording the evening's adventures, he grew silent and just watched her and her happiness, and waited impatiently for her to return to him on the sofa.

It amused me to see how the tables had been turned, and at the same time relieved me too. I had been so sure that Mrs Welles would fall for him, really fall for him, hook, line and sinker, and I still think that in any other circumstances she would have done. But tonight, because of the mad way they had met which had made her so unaccountably happy, the full impact of him had been lost.

At one point I think she was happy because of him, but somehow or other she had moved on from there. Perhaps because he had let her see his interest too soon, perhaps because her happy day was to be tomorrow too. At any event, despite the hectic clinches which were now taking place on the sofa, I felt quite safe for her.

Half an hour later, therefore, it was with hardly a pang that I saw Sebastian gather her up in his arms and carry her, picking his way between our sprawled bodies, out of the room. I remember listening very carefully, in an alcoholic manner, to the measured tread of his feet on the stairs, boom, boom, boom, and waiting for the creak which accompanied the last boom from the top.

'Goo dold Win,' said Rose in a rather slurred voice.

'Goo dold Win,' echoed Derrick, spilling some whisky on her.

'If you've got the key it will fit the lock,' sang Leigh, waltzing me round the room. We all gazed up at the ceiling as we heard the bed creak, then raised our glasses.

'To Win!' we chorused drunkenly.

Time and time again I have tried in my mind to go back to that moment, to that last clear moment when we stood in a little semicircle in the centre of the room, and raised our glasses to the ceiling. Time and time again in the hope that I could relive the subsequent vital moments, which followed it up, I see Leigh with his arm around me, Derrick swaying with Rose, and I hear again the creak of the bed. But I was drunk, and no matter how I try, I can only remember through the blur which accompanied and achieved their happening.

I think Derrick put on some old Cockney songs because I remember straining my voice to sing louder than Leigh, and then next I was dancing with Leigh and the room was whirling round and round and I remember the gramophone needle stuck at the same time, and I said, 'That's appropriate,' and Leigh fell over. I remember that he cut himself, because he broke a glass as he fell.

There was some blood and I said, 'Take that record off, Derrick.'

And Rose – I do remember this distinctly – Rose replied, 'He can't, he's in the lavatory,' and the record went on playing 'Early Bird' over and over again.

I think I said, 'Oh dear, that means we'll have to wait hours,' or something like that, because the next thing I remember was seeing Derrick standing in the doorway and thinking, not hours after all. He was smiling and jerking his thumb vacantly behind him.

'Guess what?' He said rocking dangerously back and forth. 'Guess what? I went to answer the doorbell and it was Mrs Welles' dad, and I said, "Go on upstairs," and –' here he covered his mouth in a guffaw of laughter, 'and I've only just remembered what a shock he'll get when he finds her.' He shrieked with laughter again and fell over and we all shrieked with laughter too.

And then Rose said, 'I didn't know she'd got a dad.'

Derrick said, 'Well, I suppose it's her dad, or her granddad – he's ninety if he's a day and he's only got one tooth.'

And then clearly, very, very clearly, I remember he raised his head from the ground and gave a horrible impression of Mr Dropsey.

Somehow or other Leigh and I got out of the room, though with what purpose, what possible purpose other than having to remember all my life the scene which met my eyes, I do not know. A shaft of light from the open door illuminated the bed. Mr Dropsey stood at the foot of it, clutching a knob, and there in front of him, crouched on its surface in attitudes of frozen horror, were Sebastian and Mrs Welles. Sebastian had been thoughtful enough to keep his shirt on.

Mrs Welles looked up and saw us and started to cry. Leigh

picked up the eiderdown from the floor and covered her up.

'Get him downstairs,' he said to me.

In a mechanical way I went up to Mr Dropsey and took his arm. 'Come on Teddy,' I said.

Mr Dropsey turned and looked at me and would have come, but his hand, which still clutched the knob, appeared to be in a rigor mortis grip, and after two attempts to release it he was obliged to bring it with him. I supported him downstairs and put him in a chair in the kitchen, then gently extracted it.

'Would you like a drink, Teddy?' I noticed with alarm that Mr Dropsey had turned puce and was starting to shake. 'A drink, Teddy?' I repeated urgently then shrieked, 'Leigh, quick!'

Mr Dropsey had lurched forward in his chair and was clutching his heart in agony and fighting for breath. The folds of his skin jigged up and down like porridge cooking, and a thick perspiration had broken out on his brow. His long single upper tooth was pressed hard into his chin, as though trying to alleviate the pain.

Leigh rushed up with a brandy and together we forced it between his grey lips.

'Me heart!' gasped Mr Dropsey. 'Me heart!'

There was nothing we could do then but wait, and after a while his puce colour gave way to a ghastly alabaster, and he leaned back in his chair.

'Dad had a heart attack?' said Derrick staggering up.

'Ooh, itsh Mr Dropsey,' said Rose.

I looked at them and knew they were drunk and that I was now sober. Leigh pushed them out of the kitchen and for a moment I was alone with the motionless old grey lump of flesh that was Mr Dropsey. I wondered what I should do with him, whether he should have more brandy, or perhaps coffee, or if we should ring for a doctor.

'Something hot, Teddy?' I said in a brisk nurse-like voice. A belching noise escaped from Mr Dropsey's mouth, which I interpreted as meaning 'yes'.

'Coffee?'

'A glass of hot water,' belched Mr Dropsey pathetically. I heated some and gave it him, and he spluttered a bit but gradually the grey colour gave way to some mottling and his breathing became more even. I knew nothing about heart attacks, but I had a feeling that he ought to keep his limbs going.

'Try and move your arms and legs about, Teddy,' I said doing a few drill movements to show him what I meant.

'Is it usual?' gasped Mr Dropsey. 'Will it help me?'

'Yes!' I said boldly.

Mr Dropsey slowly shot out one quivering arm then the other one, and encouraged by the feeling of the blood flowing to his face repeated the procedure.

'Now your legs, Teddy.'

Mustering up all his strength, Mr Dropsey lifted his left leg from the ground and shot it out sideways under the kitchen table. A terrible human-sounding howl rent the air as it came into contact with Boysey's basket.

'By Christ sir, you poor little bitch,' said Mr Dropsey, and with a great deal of pain and difficulty leant over the chair to look for him.

'Steady Teddy,' I said, as Mr Dropsey's head disappeared under the table for rather a long time. 'I'll get him for you.' I knelt down on the floor to pick him up and there, sitting up in the dog basket with his hand clamped firmly round Mr Dropsey's ear, was Launcelot. He was crimson with rage and obviously just awakened from sleep. Mr Dropsey was making helpless struggling movements.

I thought, keep calm Ann, keep calm, and nudged Mr Dropsey to stop struggling.

Mr Dropsey stopped struggling and said, 'Leave go little boy,' in a winning voice.

Launcelot tightened his grip.

'If you leave go of my ear,' continued Mr Dropsey, 'I shall give you a shilling.'

Launcelot let go of him, but unfortunately the relief of his release caused Mr Dropsey's reflex actions to kick the basket again, and Launcelot, believing it a deliberate second outrage, was goaded to further retaliation. Clawing wildly at Mr Dropsey's face, he clamped one hand around his tooth to steady himself whilst searching for an ear. But whilst he was still searching,

Mr Dropsey unfortunately chose to struggle, and to my horror, with a tearing, grinding, crunching noise, his long single upper tooth came away in Launcelot's hand.

I gave Launcelot one look and dashed to Mr Dropsey's assistance. I just managed to get him upright before he had his second attack.

'Leigh!' I screeched as he lurched forward in the chair again. But he didn't come, and alone I watched the agonised clutchings of the heart, the fighting for breath, the thick sweat and the jigging of the skin. This time though there was no tooth pressed into his chin to alleviate the pain, only a fleshy hole which was pouring blood.

'Leigh!' I screamed. 'Leigh, Leigh, Leigh!' and suddenly he was there and something had snapped inside me and I tore at him hysterically and screamed, 'Get him out of here, get him out of here, he's dying, he mustn't die here, I won't have him die here!'

Leigh looked from me to the writhing, bleeding Mr Dropsey and his face went rather white. He gave me a' push so that I fell over on to the floor and called for Derrick.

Derrick was still drunk but between them they managed to hoist the now motionless Mr Dropsey on to their shoulders. As they staggered and swayed with him, I ran ahead to open the front door. Halfway down the garden path they dropped him, but feverishly I helped them rehoist him, scrabbling at his little thin legs and tearing at his clothes.

His Rolls Bentley stood at the gate with Withers asleep at the wheel. Briefly Leigh explained to him that there'd been an accident, and like some furtive, abortive deal, I watched Mr Dropsey change hands, and Withers, without a word, bundle him into the back of the car and cover him up with the rug. The noise of him starting the car was unnaturally soft.

Back in the house, Derrick poured us each a brandy. My hysteria had gone. Leigh and I sat unable to look at each other, rigid, white and ashamed. I wanted to say, 'Is he going to die? Is he going to die?' But I couldn't say it because of course he wasn't going to die, and I had made a fool of myself, and in our panic we had behaved like animals.

Rose lay flat out on the floor between us, dead to the world, but above us Mrs Welles lay flat out on the bed with the world dead to her.

Derrick lurched around the room refilling his glass, garrulous, inquisitive and giggling.

'Well c'mon, c'mon, spill the beans. You mean to say she was really carrying on with Dad? No kidding, she was really carrying on with Grandpa?'

'Mr Dropsey was... a friend... of Mrs Welles.' Leigh's voice was stiff and small and he stared at the amber liquid in his glass.

'Wash,' slurred Derrick, hitting Leigh on the back and rocking with laughter. 'You've said it chum, wash it ish, 'cos it's all over now. That's right eh? Itsh all over now and she's got shomeone else?'

'Yes,' said Leigh. 'It's all over now.'

'And she's got shomeone else?' insisted Derrick.

'No,' said Leigh. 'She hasn't got anyone else.'

He stood up and made for the door. Derrick said, 'You going up?' and fell back on to the sofa and remained there.

'Are you coming, Ann?' Leigh held open the door.

'What about... What about...?' I looked him in the face, making myself say the words that I didn't even want to think about.

'Win?' said Leigh still in the same stiff voice. 'Oh – she just wants to be left on her own.'

'Is –?'

'No, no. He's gone.'

'Oh.'

We climbed up the stairs. Her door was shut and we passed by it pretending not to hear the sound of her misery which came through it.

Chapter Thirteen

We slept late. It was midday before I opened my heavy eyes. Outside the world was cold and grey. We drank some tea and stared at it through the kitchen window.

Three times we tried to reach Mrs Welles with tea, with cigarettes, with chocolates, but each time, through the locked door, her muffled voice told us to go away.

We watched a man come and take away the pieces of Derrick's motorbike and we said goodbye to Derrick. Rose was sick twice and Guinevere kept asking us what had happened. Underneath the table, Launcelot played with Mr Dropsey's tooth.

And then, with a sudden lightening of my heart, I remembered that it was Sunday and that Mrs Flood had invited me over for tea. Never had the thought of such an innocuous appointment filled me with so much pleasure. It was half past three and I could leave at once.

Outside the house I breathed deep gulps of air. My head swam and I shivered, but for a while the ill and unhappy atmosphere of the house was left behind. I couldn't stop thinking though, I couldn't stop reliving and remembering.

I tried, but it was easier to think than not to think, and over and over again, as I had done all night on my bed and all morning with the others, I abandoned myself to retrospection.

Why, why, why? Why couldn't I have heard the doorbell? If I had heard the doorbell I could've stopped him. Down, down, down the hill from Cockton Heath I walked. Why did we have to let her go upstairs with him? She wasn't really interested, she wasn't keen, she wasn't in love with him, she was only happy. Oh God! She was happy. Past the YWCA squat, smug and secure. If only she was in love with him it wouldn't have been so bad. Pause for traffic. But she only did it for him – over the roundabout – because she was happy and wanted everyone else to be happy. It was only sex.

– Past the theatre – Silly old sex that's like a drink of water to Mrs Welles. Past the bills with their crude red paint, *She was Poor but She was Honest*. Why did he have to come round like that anyway? He'd never come round like that before. He said he was going to be away too, he said he wasn't coming back till the morning... but it was the morning, one o'clock in the morning... Perhaps he couldn't wait, perhaps he had to come straight round as soon he got home, to propose to her.

Down the empty high street, past the Leek women's public baths. Why couldn't I have heard the doorbell?

Past the cemetery and the library and the Regal cinema... Perhaps... perhaps even after he'd seen them we could have calmed him down, spoken to him, let him know that she was drunk, told him that Sebastian had seduced her by force (that dreadful Sebastian, clearing off like that straight away, too.) Perhaps if it had been Boysey under the table in the basket... She said a dog got a man sentimental... But it wasn't Boysey, it was Launcelot, poor little neglected Launcelot who was allowed to sleep exactly where he chose.

Past the shops now, and in and out of the little twisting slum streets. It must have been loose. He couldn't be as strong as all that. It must have been going to come out any minute... But all that blood, there wouldn't have been all that blood if it had come out easily... Into Commercial Road now, numbers one, two, three, four, five... All that blood and those terrible attacks, thirty, forty, fifty. Was he dying? Was he dead? Sixty, seventy, eighty... He was an old, old man, over seventy – one hundred and thirty, thirty-five – why couldn't I have heard the doorbell? I could have stopped him then... One hundred and thirty-seven Commercial Road.

I walked a little further on to the alley which cut through, then carefully counted six houses back. The back of Commercial Road was alive on a Sunday afternoon. Men in shirtsleeves sat on benches at their doors, children and dogs swarmed screaming up and down the dust path. Women in curlers talked with one another and stared at me as they pegged out washing on their lines.

I knocked on the door and after a while heard the flap-flap of

Mrs Flood's slippers on the flagstone floor. She opened the door just wide enough for one narrowed black eye to peer round it, then seeing that it was me, brought the other one into focus.

'Ah, it's you, come on in Ann,' she said, edging the door open another six inches so that I could just squeeze through sideways. 'Mr Flood and me was expecting you.'

I followed her through the scullery, which again dripped a wealth of her underwear, and through the kitchen, which was still as disused; but today the door to the boarded up room was closed and the stairs were lit by a dim gas jet. Mrs Flood was talking about her neighbours as I climbed up behind her.

'A nasty common lot,' she was saying between laboured breaths. 'Not at all the class of neighbourhood that Mr Flood and me are used to. But there, he does like a house to himself, does Mr Flood, he does like a proper home, and in a place such as Leek they're not for the picking and choosing.'

A door on the landing opened and Willy stood looking down on us. 'I'm so glad you've come, Ann,' he said. 'We've got a simply lovely tea.'

It had been laid out with loving care on a little table in front of the fireplace. Jellies and tiny sandwiches, pastries and chocolate biscuits, all neatly arranged on flowered china plates on the snowy white lace tablecloth. And there in the middle of the table, with nine candles flickering merrily from its surface, was a large pink and white iced cake.

I looked at the table and for a moment a wave of nostalgia swept over me, and my eyes were suddenly blurred with tears. It seemed a lifetime ago since I had looked at a tea table such as this, a lifetime ago since my world had been one of gentleness and innocence.

'Like it?' said Willy. His eyes were shining and anxiously watching mine for their reactions. 'Mrs Flood and I did it together, you see Ann,' – he paused for a moment in his excitement – 'it's my birthday!'

'Oh Willy, I didn't know! Many happy returns of the day, Willy.'

I was so pleased it was his birthday that on a sudden daring impulse I went over to him and kissed him on the cheek. I looked round at Mrs Flood immediately afterwards but she just smiled at me indulgently. 'It's my birthday,' said Willy again. 'It's my birthday and I'm—'

'Thirty-nine, Willy darling,' said Mrs Flood firmly. 'Sit down at the table with Ann whilst I make the tea.' A kettle was boiling on the gas ring and we watched whilst she poured the water into a rather dented silver pot.

Willy was eyeing the table with a blissful expression on his face.

'It's the one day of the year I let him off his diet,' explained Mrs Flood as he started wolfishly on a plate of sandwiches. 'His birthday is the one day of the year that Willy can eat exactly what he likes.'

'You should have told me before that you were going to have a birthday,' I said to Willy.

He looked up from a jelly he was eating and opened his mouth to speak, but Mrs Flood gave a gay little laugh and spoke for him.

'We didn't let on Ann,' she said, 'on account of not wanting a fuss. I told Willy just one person for tea; some time ago now I told him he could choose just one person for tea, and straightaway he said, "I'll have Ann. I'll have Ann," he said, "for the person to come to my birthday tea."'

Willy put down his spoon with a clatter and flushed. 'No, Lil!' he said, 'It wasn't me, it was you. It was you said that I should have…'

'Willy,' said Mrs Flood, 'shall I cut the cake or shall you?'

'Me,' said Willy. 'It's my cake, I'll cut the cake, Lil.'

He cut it, closing his eyes and wishing fervently, and Mrs Flood closed her eyes and wished too.

After tea Willy showed me his birthday present from her. It was a musical cigarette box which played over and over again, 'If you were the only girl in the world'.

'Play it again Willy,' said Mrs Flood, and delighted Willy rewound it and opened the lid. The brittle, gay notes came tinkling out again and I looked at Mrs Flood, who had thought of such an entrancing gift, and at Willy who held it against him entranced. They gazed at each other in delight, in surprised wonder that it should bring such complete contentment to them both.

'Play it again Willy,' I said, because I knew that they wanted to hear it again but were shy of mentioning the fact themselves. And he played it again, softly singing the words this time with Mrs Flood joining in. 'If you were the only girl in the world and I were the only boy…'

'We used to dance to that,' said Mrs Flood. 'When we was doing the act. All over the world we used to dance to that when we was doing the act…'

There was a pause. It was their life together. It was what I wanted to hear… What Willy couldn't remember… It was more than anything in the world what I wanted to hear.

'All over the world,' repeated Mrs Flood. 'Paris, New York, Milan, always travelling we was, sometimes it used to get me down, the travelling, but Willy used to love it, he used to love the trains did Willy, he was never so happy as waiting for the train to come in of a Sunday morning.'

'Yes,' said Willy, 'I used to love the trains. I'd forgotten Lil, I used to love the trains. They were so beautiful and fierce, with shining blue and silver engines and they went on and on for days. Sometimes we used to sleep on them. I liked sleeping on them, when it was dark I could look out of the window and watch the sparks flying up from the wheels.'

'Yes,' said Mrs Flood. 'He used to like the act did Willy, he used to like his dancing.'

'Yes, I used to like my dancing,' said Willy. He turned to me. 'Dancing's not like acting Ann,' he said. 'In acting it's always changing, different parts every week, it's always learning, but dancing's the same all the time. We never changed our dancing all the time, and I never had to keep learning. I didn't want to stop dancing. I wanted to travel on the trains and always do dancing…' His voice petered out with the last notes of the musical box.

'Yes,' said Mrs Flood heavily. 'He used to like his dancing.' There was silence in the room. Outside it had started to rain. The drops were thick and slow, they oozed down the window like tears.

'He used to like to come out on to the glass floor of the Lido in Paris with me. He'd have a spotlight on his white silk blouse and his purple cummerbund, and he used to like to hear the nightclub people grow quiet as we danced the adagio. He used to like to know that people had come from all over the world to see us dance.

'And then when they was clapping, clapping us for more, we'd do the soft slipper… "If you was the only girl in the world and I was the only boy". We used to like to do that, straight after the adagio, it come as a surprise, and it always went down well.

'He used to like the hotels too, the big posh hotels with the bathrooms and the lovely food. He wasn't on his diet then, he didn't need to with his dancing.'

'No,' said Willy, 'I didn't need to with my dancing.'

'But best of all,' continued Mrs Flood, with a fond smile at Willy's unhappy face, 'he liked the trappings. He liked to see his name in ten-foot lights wherever we went. "Lily Flood and Willy" it said wherever we went. He loved the parties and the glory, he loved the people who kept praising him, he—'

'No!' Willy interrupted her violently. 'No! No! No Lil, that's not true, you know that it's not true. It wasn't that, I didn't mind about that, I just wanted to dance, even when you got old and people wouldn't have us, except those terrible places, I—'

Mrs Flood cut across his words with a sudden hard bright laugh.

'Dancing's all right for some Ann,' she said. 'But Willy was made for better stuff. I took him away from dancing because he was made to act. You know and I know and the whole world's going to know Ann, that Willy was made to act.'

'I used to like my dancing,' said Willy.

After tea Mrs Flood got out the sherry bottle. She talked no more of their life together and we leaned back in our chairs and chatted pleasantries. I wondered why she had asked me to tea. I was not taken in by the 'Willy's choice' explanation, and wondered what it could be. I was aware, and often to my discomfort, that I was her favourite. Rose was quite nasty about it sometimes.

But knowing Mrs Flood I couldn't see an expensive tea wasted on me purely from motives of affection. Two minutes later, when I *did* find out the reason, I wondered if there was something wrong with me that I had not known all along what it was. We were on our third sherries and Mrs Flood was addressing one of Willy's photographs.

'I suppose you'll have spoken to your gentleman friend by now, Ann?' she was saying. 'Mr Flood and me saw his picture in the paper last week and Mr Flood said to me I shouldn't wonder but what she won't want to arrange an interview some time next week, him being back from his holiday.' For a moment I wanted to laugh; it was rather ironical. It flashed through my mind that he had only just started on his holidays.

I supposed I would have to tell her. Now that it was finished there was no need to prevaricate. It would be quite simple. I should just have to say, 'He's dropped me, Mrs Flood', or 'His wife's found out, Mrs Flood.' Quite simple. Go on, say it Ann. I took a deep breath and opened my mouth.

Mrs Flood was looking at me; her black eyes were no longer cunning but round and liquid like a spaniel's. They were mute, appealing and urgent. The words died on my lips. I didn't say anything.

'Say an interview Wednesday?' Mrs Flood spoke with pathetic disinterest. 'Or Friday? Perhaps Friday might suit him better. It's just that it's… Well… The sooner the better really, things at the moment you know Ann, it's well…'

'It's desperate Ann,' said Willy.

There was a pause.

I had got to do it. I had got to seek Mr Dropsey out in his lampshade factory and ask him if he would please give us the money as he had promised. He would turn his fleshy, toothless mouth to my face and would probably spit at me before having me forcibly removed. But I had got to do it.

I had got to do it because Willy had said it was desperate. Desperate not only for him and Mrs Flood but for the whole company; for the unit or family that we were; for Rose and Leigh and Sebastian and Hilda and Bill Irving – Bill with another four months to go till January… I had got to do it because somehow or other the responsibility had fallen on me, and though my knees already trembled at the thought, I felt at the same time a certain pride that it should be me.

But mostly I had got to do it for my conscience's sake. I had got to plumb the final depths of humiliation before I could shatter her hopes. I had got to be told by him in words that I could repeat to her, that there wasn't going to be any money.

'Make it... Make it Thursday please Mrs Flood,' I said out loud.

We had another drink, but the purpose of my visit had been achieved and when I rose to go, Mrs Flood did not detain me. Outside the rain still fell. Mrs Flood lent me a mackintosh and saw me to the door. The thin sound of Willy's musical box followed us down the stairs but lost itself in the gust of rain which blew in as she let me out.

It was a wild evening. In a couple of hours the wind had risen to a great strength. It lashed the rain in uncontrollable furies, hither and thither. I walked home, one minute struggling to take even a step, the next being carried along a hundred yards at a time. It was pleasant sparring with the elements, exhilarating. At home there would be Rose and Leigh and Mrs Welles.

Mrs Welles would have left her room, the first shock would have passed off and now we would have to comfort her. The wind picked me up for another ride on its wings, as though there were no time to be lost in comforting her.

She was up all right, sitting in a negligee at the kitchen table and holding forth wildly to Rose and Leigh. I stood outside and looked at them for a moment through the window. She was heavily made up, but the black circles under her eyes were heavier, and the thin vivid outline of her face was blurred and swollen. I wondered then at her animation. As I came through the door she greeted me with effusion.

'Ann?' she said, and her voice was high-pitched and excited. 'Thank God you've come Ann, I've been waiting for you all day. Why for Christ's sake did you have to go out to tea today? I've been trying to explain to them for hours but they don't cotton on. You'll have to explain to them for me Ann, you see, it's going to be all right. I've told them you'll see it's going to be all right too, and explain it.

'I've got it all worked out Ann – it's simple! You see, I just go to him all sweet and tell him that he got it all wrong, and that I was in the bath and it was my brother who'd twisted his leg and had kept calling for help, and no one had answered and I'd had to get straight out of the bath and carry him on to my bed, and then he'd come in –'

Mrs Welles paused, desperate and bright-eyed, searching my face.

'Or… or something else Ann, something like that, that could have happened. You're clever Ann, you'll think of something. But I know it'll be all right; I mean, something like that could have happened couldn't it? I know it'll be all right and that he'll believe me.'

Mrs Welles paused to give me a brilliant smile. 'Tell them Ann, tell Rosie and Leigh it'll be all right. They don't believe me you see, they say it's no good, they say it's all over for good but I told them, wait till Ann comes in. I told them, she'll soon tell you it needn't be all over, she won't give in like that. Go on Ann, you tell them!'

I sat down heavily on the copper. I didn't know what to say. I had thought that we would have to comfort her, but there would be no comforting while she refused to accept what had happened. My heart cried out to agree with her, if only to make her happy for a little while, but my mind knew full well what I'd got to do. I didn't know how to say it though. I stared at her while words jumbled madly through my brain, and in the end I could only say, 'I wonder, Win.'

I could not have chosen an unhappier phrase. Sitting at the table Mrs Welles slowly bowed her head into her hands. 'Oh God! Ann,' she said. 'Not you too.'

'Win,' I began, 'darling, darling Win!' But at the sound of my voice, in one single swift movement Mrs Welles drew herself upright and started to shout. She shouted abuse and swear words at us, terrible words which I could only instinctively translate. She said that it had been a conspiracy between us; she said we had done it deliberately because we were jealous, she said that we had staged it just like a play to give ourselves a laugh.

We gazed at her without a word while she railed at us and spat at us and beat the table. Then suddenly, dramatically, and with the impact of a timely injection from a hypodermic syringe, her hysterical ravings were cut short.

'Christ, Goat!' said Mrs Welles.

We had not heard him come in on account of the storm outside. It was unnerving to look suddenly up and see him standing silently in the scullery. His trilby hat was pulled well down over his forehead, the collar of his gabardine mackintosh was turned up, and in his right hand he carried a large expanding suitcase.

Remembering her scene with him the day before, I could not understand his appearance. I looked quickly at Mrs Welles, bracing myself for the scene which now must surely finish him off. I looked at Mrs Welles and could hardly believe my eyes. She had risen clumsily from her chair, and with a great false smile on her face was advancing upon him with a sinuous hip-wiggling walk.

'Paul!' she said, 'My Paul, come home to me!'

It had crossed my mind when we had first looked up and seen him, that Mr Goat's silence was rather unusual. I had put it down to nerves at her reaction to him, but now as she drew parallel with him I could see that it wasn't nerves at all. Without even looking at her, we watched him shove her out of his way with the suitcase and come purposefully into the kitchen.

'Paul,' said Mrs Welles, extracting herself from the gas stove against which she had fallen. 'Paul, what's the matter? Don't be like that Paul; let's talk it over. I was a bit hasty I know, but let's have a cup of tea and talk it over.'

For an answer, Mr Goat swung his expanding suitcase on to the table, knocking two cups to the ground.

'Paul!' said Mrs Welles, plucking at his sleeve as he snapped it open. 'Say something Paul, I can't bear...' But then she didn't say any more as, wrenching open the door of the cupboard above the table, we watched Mr Goat begin slowly and deliberately to take down and pile into the open case tin after tin of baked beans. He piled them neatly and methodically, tin after tin of Smart's Baked Beans.

He paused only twice in his work. Once, to replace a tin bearing a rival product's label, and twice, to adjust the expansion. Nobody said a word; we just sat there whilst our eyes made each fascinating little journey with the tins. Once, when Mr Goat nearly dropped one, Rose moved inadvertently to catch it. It was the only time he spoke.

'Ta!' he said, taking it from her bewildered hands.

When the shelf was clear he snapped shut the case, heaved it off the table and made for the door. Still hypnotised we wordlessly swivelled round to watch him go, pulling on his gloves, turning up his collar and carefully shutting the door behind him.

Only when we could no longer hear his footsteps on the path did Mrs Welles begin to cry.

Chapter Fourteen

During the next few days we did our best to comfort her. The baked bean incident was of course the final straw. It had brought her to her senses in that she now accepted the fact, but she was taking it badly. We were sympathetic and patient, we were kind and constructive with plans for her future life, but nothing as yet could rouse her from her apathy.

She spent most of the day huddled on the bed totting up her losses. In vain we told her that she'd find another Mr Dropsey, in vain we pointed out that she still had the mink. It was all to no avail. By the end of the week she was referring tremblingly to 'My great sorrow'.

I felt particularly bad about it on account of my unfinished business with him. The fact that behind her back I was going to try and extract money from him seemed to me the height of bad taste. But on the other hand I knew that to explain the situation would be worse.

It was very awkward too, as I could not remember exactly what she'd said about his promise. She had just casually mentioned it amongst the news of her expected engagement, and with the prospect of Mr Dropsey as a permanent arrangement, I had not at the time given it undue attention.

I remembered that she had said she'd asked him and he'd said it would be okay, but whether there had been any difficulty about it, and whether he'd specified any amount, etc., I had no idea. His words, 'that's okay' seemed to me to be an extremely slender promise with which to confront him. I did try to do a little delicate fishing, but even a substitute for the word 'money' was inclined to start her off again.

Leigh was a great source of comfort to me. I had told him all about my conversation with Mrs Flood, and he'd agreed straight away that I'd have to make the final effort. He agreed too, that it would be a hopeless and nasty experience, but that was not the point.

We planned opening gambits and conversations and clothes for me, and while I discussed it with him it was not too bad, but as soon as I was alone and thought about it I began to get very nervous. By Tuesday of the following week it was preying on my mind to such an extent that Leigh said I had got to do it at once.

That night I told Mrs Flood that it was important I saw Mr Dropsey the following morning and asked if I might have rehearsal off. She agreed with such alacrity that my heart sank further still, and when the morning came it required every ounce of Leigh's persuasion to get me on to a Booth-bound bus.

Dropsey Lampshades Ltd., lay just outside Booth. It would not, I suppose, be considered a very large factory, but as the bus deposited me outside its imposing gates, I very nearly had to go home. Storey after storey of the building rose before me, and through the long glass windows which lined the front of it, Mr Dropsey's staff were on view.

Hundreds and hundreds of them, men and women and girls and boys, their voices and the sound of their machinery coming clearly to me through the open windows; all standing, sitting and scurrying about as they churned out his lampshades.

Productivity. Industry. The World's workers. Dropsey Lampshades Ltd., enriching our island and supporting our islanders. Hundreds and hundreds of them – men, women, girls and boys, all living, loving, laughing, dying and depending on Mr Dropsey. Mr Dropsey – The Boss, The Guv, Sir. The figurehead that they had probably never even seen. Mr Dropsey, the fatuous old sugar daddy that had been made a fool of.

I very nearly had to go back as I realised the awful mistake of seeking him out on his home ground. Not so fatuous, not such a fool. Mr Edward Dropsey Ltd., strong, rich, revengeful and At Home. I stood at the gate a full five minutes, shivering in the hot sunshine whilst I tried to find my courage. In the end a car swept through the gates, nearly knocking me over and forcing me to run towards the building.

I started to mount the steps up to the main door but had no sooner got up a couple when an irate looking commissionaire appeared at the top of them, and pointed a scandalised finger in the direction of the bicycle sheds.

'Side entrance,' he said, then added with heavy sarcasm, 'if you don't mind.'

'But I want to see—'

'If you don't mind!' he repeated nastily.

I picked my way through the bicycles, found the world's workers' entrance and went in. A sinister array of clocking machines met my eyes and the roar of machinery in my ears. Behind a glass compartment an elderly man sat picking his nose.

'Yus?' he bellowed at me.

'I want to see Mr Edward Dropsey,' I said.

'What, what ye say?'

'I want to see a—'

'Yus, 'ang orn.'

He lumbered up from his chair and disappeared through a door at the back, returning a few minutes later with another man.

'Mister Rorris,' he said letting him through the glass compartment.

Mr Horace was tall, well built, and sharp looking, clad in a natty blue herringbone suit, the buttons of which should never have been fastened.

'Got your cards?' he said, folding his arms and looking at me speculatively.

'Well no,' I said. 'I'm afraid I haven't got a card but—'

'Well, you'll have to get one then quick, how old are you?'

'Seventeen, but I—'

'Okay. Start Monday, half past eight, three pound five flat.'

Realisation dawned. 'No, no, Mr Horace you've got it all wrong,' I began but Mr Horace interrupted me. An angry red had spread over his face and neck.

'Three pound five shillings,' he said in an icy measured voice. 'Do you want the job or don't you? Three pound five flat union rate. I haven't got anything wrong, nothing wrong at all, do you hear? Three pound five flat union rate,' he repeated, his voice getting louder. 'But if I was you I should forget it. Get me? You don't need to bother to come in Monday after all, we're not that short staffed that we've got to take on lip.'

And turning on his heel Mr Horace swung off down the corridor.

Behind me the nose picker addressed me through a hole in the glass in the glass compartment.

'You didn't ought to have spoke like that,' he said. 'You didn't ought to have spoke like that to Mister Rorris. Mister Rorris can get very touchy.'

'Please,' I said wretchedly, 'I don't want a job. I want to see Mr Dropsey, Mr Edward Dropsey, the owner.'

'You don't want to talk like that neither!' said the nose picker. 'Talking like that's not going to get you nowhere. What you want to do is to go on down the road and try Smart's Baked Beans. Ask for Mister Wilting. 'E's the man there, and if 'e's got nothink, you want to try back here in about a fortnight's time. Mister Rorris'll maybe have forgot you by then.'

Out amongst the bicycles again, I decided that I would have one more try at the main door before calling it a day. This time I got to the top of the steps before the commissionaire intercepted me.

'Look,' he said as I told him what I wanted, 'I'm not in the mood see, I'm not in the mood for a laugh. Go on!' he said, advancing upon me so that I was forced to take a step down, 'Go on, hop it!'

A sudden anger at him welled up in me, at him, and at Mr Horace and at the nose picker, at their stupid illiterate presumptive power. I made my voice go stiff and distant and Girton-inflected, and fixed him with a supercilious eye.

'Would you mind removing yourself at once young man?' I said. 'I happen to be a personal friend of Mr Dropsey's, who no doubt will be interested to learn of your rudeness to me.'

It didn't have quite the effect I had intended. A horrible knowing leer came over the commissionaire's face and sucking in his breath he murmured, 'Personal friend, eh?' But at least it got me through the door. 'Well,' he said running his eyes over my body in a familiar manner, 'perhaps you'd better come in after all.'

Inside the shiny contemporary foyer he crossed over to a man sitting at a desk. 'Lady 'ere wants to see the guv,' he said in a meaningful voice. 'Personal friend of 'is, Ted.'

Ted joined him in another insolent scrutiny of me before vouchsafing a reply to the fact.

'Reely!' he said at last, giving the commissionaire a nudge. 'Well, we'll 'ave to ring through then and tell him about it, won't we Jack? I mean, a personal friend's a personal matter, isn't it?'

Three pageboys standing by the lifts gave an unabashed snigger at this remark and Ted lifted the phone with a flourish. He was on the phone for about ten minutes and he spoke to about ten different people, each brief conversation being passed on to the next, through the magical words 'personal friend'. It amused me to see how he adjusted his voice to the various conversations.

With the first ones it was brash and lewd, but by the time it had reached the tenth person it was a discreet murmur, with only just the right amount of emphasis laid on 'personal friend'.

'Okay,' he said to the commissionaire as he put down the phone. 'Miss Dorian says you'd better take 'er up. 'E's in a confab at the moment but she says by the sound of what I've told 'er, you'd better take 'er up.'

The three pageboys, looking acutely disappointed that they were not to have the honour of accompanying me, stepped smartly aside as we entered the lift. One of them gave the commissionaire an envious wink as the doors closed, leaving him alone with me in the confined space. He leaned over to press the button, arranging himself disagreeably close to me, and started to whistle between his teeth.

The lift sped upwards swiftly and silently.

'Known the guv long, Blondie?' said the commissionaire between whistles. I preserved a dignified silence.

'I said, 'ave you known Mr h'Dropsey long, h'madame?' he repeated with a horrid imitation of my Girton inflections.

'Quite a while,' I replied stiffly.

'H'o,' said the commissionaire, 'H'I just h'wondered because I believe 'e 'as such a great many personal friends.' The lift deposited us in another contemporary foyer even lusher than the first. A heavy expensive smell pervaded the air. ''is suite,' explained the commissionaire leading the way towards a handsome white door which he knocked upon. He narrowed his eyes at me meaningfully. 'It's got a bathroom and bedroom and all,' he said.

The door was opened by an efficient-looking middle-aged

woman. 'If you don't mind waiting a few minutes, Mr Dropsey is engaged at the moment. What is the name?'

I told her. The door closed and the commissionaire with a last leer returned to the lift. I leaned back in my chair and gazed at the black wallpaper on the ceiling, which was decorated with small gold stars.

Considering the ridicule and hostility which had first met my simple request, it seemed to me a remarkable thing that I was now ensconced in his private suite awaiting his pleasure. I supposed then that sex really was the most powerful force in life. In all innocence I had established myself as one of Mr Dropsey's 'bits', and as such had been granted concessions that wisdom and age or even a genuine friendship with him would never have achieved.

I hated the idea; I hated it suddenly and fiercely so that my stomach boiled inside. At that moment I felt that should I see sex exploited just once more I should hate it even for its intrinsic value.

Its intrinsic value, which so far had seemed so wonderful to me in its anticipation.

My hazardous progress from the factory gates had temporarily killed my nerves, but now as I sat in the heavy silence of the foyer they returned with a jerk.

Leigh and I had finally decided on the sweet, innocent angle of attack, and I had dressed accordingly in a nauseating white frock scattered with pink daisies, which an ill-advised aunt had given me on my fifteenth birthday.

We had rehearsed a nauseating opening speech too, but now as I went over it for the hundredth time – 'Oh Mr Dropsey I 'spec this is a weal surprise for you, etc.' I was fraught with sudden fears. Obviously, judging by the rest of the factory's attitude, my opening gambit would have to be charged with a lot more sex. Panicking a little, I hastily thought some up.

'Teddy baby,' spoken in a pampered teasing voice, I thought might be better, or perhaps just 'Hi,' gulped at him in a hoarse emotional manner. I tried them both out, plumped for 'Teddy baby' and started practising various inflections. I must have been rather carried away by my efforts, for the white door flew open to admit the secretary.

'Mr Dropsey is still engaged,' she informed me coldly and with a heavy emphasis on his surname.

After that I just fell to comforting myself with the thought that it really didn't matter what I said, I had only got to get it over and my conscience salved and then I should be free of Mr Dropsey and Dropseyland for ever. No more nasty sex and no more nice money, I told myself briskly. In the quietness of the foyer I could hear the raised voice of Mr Dropsey's companion preparing to take his leave.

'Till the twenteh-first then, Teddeh old boy...' Then the sound of an inner door closing behind him. A second later Miss Dorian ushered me inside the white door. I supposed it was her office. Large and airy and cold and contemporary.

I was silently waved to an upright chair until Mr Dropsey's companion had finished setting a bowler hat on to a fringe of white curls. Then, when she had seen him out, Miss Dorian spoke to me. She spoke clearly and brightly using simple words, as though I were a trifle backward.

'I'm going to take you into him now dear and I expect he'll be pleased to see you (this with a false smile), but there's just one thing I'd like you to do for me – don't dear, whatever you do, agree to him cancelling his twelve o'clock appointment. It's only natural that he'll want to dear, but it's a very important appointment, and I'd be ever so grateful if you'd tell him you'll just wait outside – not go away mind – just wait outside till he's kept it.'

I told her that I would do so and she gave me another smile.

'All right then dear, in you go. No need for me to do any introducing eh?' she said with a coy little laugh.

'No – no need at all, thank you Miss Dorian.'

'Right then dear...'

'Thank you Miss Dorian.'

'In you go then dear...' There was an edge to Miss Dorian's voice.

'Yes – yes...' I had got to do it that very second. There was not another second in the world could go by without my doing it. I put my hand on the door, closed my eyes and flung it dramatically open.

'Teddy baby!' I said in a pampered, teasing voice then opened my eyes.

Mr Dropsey sat in the centre of the room, hunched high up on a swivel chair with his back to me. He had obviously not heard me, but with lewd chuckles was engrossed in the perusal of a sheaf of photographs, which he held in his hand. It was unnerving after the emotion-racked hours of our last meeting to be met by his disinterested back. I felt like the proverbial pricked balloon, a quite unscheduled feeling which I crushed immediately.

'Hi,' I said loudly and in a hoarse emotional manner, then added firmly, 'Teddy baby, darling.'

Mr Dropsey shot round on his swivel chair and at the sight of him I gave an involuntary gasp. His toothless gums had been replaced by a very large set of dentures. It was a terrible mistake. They hung from his jaw like overcrowded stalactites in a cave. They were grinning, white and false, dominating his face and obviously quite out of his control. His mouth hung open in helpless misery while his lips tried unsuccessfully to adapt themselves to their new surroundings. Hunched up on the chair with his bald head topping them, he looked exactly like a Japanese war minister.

But if I was taken aback at his appearance, Mr Dropsey was flabbergasted at the sight of me. For one long second perhaps, we just stared at one another, then flushing a dull red, Mr Dropsey shamefully lowered his teeth and uttered a single inarticulate sound. Not loud and irate as I had expected, but low, moaning and terrified.

'Hi Teddy!' I began again, but then I stopped, for in a blind fumbling manner, and completely ignoring me, Mr Dropsey was wildly pressing at the array of buzzers which surrounded him. In an instant the four doors leading out of his office shot open to admit three men, a young girl and Miss Dorian.

They stood respectfully, questioningly looking at him, then as he beckoned them forward, they went towards him. Only when they had arranged themselves into a protective semicircle around him did Mr Dropsey begin to speak.

'Well,' he said at last in a little trembling voice. 'Well, upon my soul this is a pleasant surprise.' The words came out with difficulty, every other one being accompanied by a piercing whistle.

'Little Miss King, eh? Come to visit me, eh? Well! Well! Well!' he said, 'What a pleasant surprise.'

I was so taken aback at his terror-stricken attitude that I was unable to reply, my eyes just riveted themselves on to one of the young men's hands, which was pressed into Mr Dropsey's shoulder.

There was a long pause, then Mr Dropsey cleared his throat. 'What... what was it you wanted m'dear?' he inquired.

Six pairs of eyes bored into me, waiting for my reply. My carefully prepared speeches, my sweet act and my sexy act went with the wind. 'I... I want some money please,' I blurted out unhappily.

A shiver of outrage passed along Mr Dropsey's protectors and one of them started to speak, but Mr Dropsey silenced him with a shaking hand.

'What... er... what would you be wanting the money for m'dear?' he inquired with bated breath.

Again the six pairs of eyes bored into me. I swallowed, fixed my gaze on a portrait of him on the opposite wall and opened my mouth to speak. My heart was knocking inside me with embarrassment. I hadn't bargained on speaking in front of five other people.

I didn't know how to frame my words. I could say 'the promise you made to me Mr Dropsey', or, 'the promise you made to us', but it hadn't been made to me or us, it had been made to Mrs Welles.

'Well, m'dear...?' said Mr Dropsey.

'It, w... it was a promise you made,' I blurted out at last. 'For money for the show – not exactly to me you didn't make it, Mr Dropsey, but to a friend of mine, a... a...'

I got no further, for Mr Dropsey's laugh cut across my speech like a whip-lash, effectively silencing me. In a way it came almost as a relief. His laughing at me had been one of the things I had anticipated. But when I looked up, expecting him forcibly to follow it up, I saw that it was no laugh of ridicule. His eyes met mine frightened and pleading, and the flush on his face had deepened to a magenta hue.

'Come, come, come!' he laughed nervously. 'No need to be afraid of me little girl, no need to pretend it was any little friend of yours either. I remember the promise I made to you. A promise made direct m'dear... And as a promise is a promise I shall be delighted to keep it. Miss Dorian, please get me...'

Mr Dropsey was obliged to break off his conversation at this point as he had become whistle-bound, but he gesticulated to a drawer in his desk and Miss Dorian, still keeping her scandalised eyes on me, searched in it and produced his chequebook.

And then for the first time as I watched him, with incapable hands, pick up his fountain pen and try to unscrew it, I began to understand.

I had been too frightened of him at first, too unsure of myself and too certain of him even to wonder if his reactions could be any different from the ones I had rehearsed for him. I had thought when he had rung for his secretaries that they were to be used for my removal. I thought that the nervousness he had shown had only been embarrassment at the way I had stared at his teeth.

But now as he tremblingly brought his pen to rest against the virgin cheque, I realised with a shock that he was frightened of me. Far, far more frightened of me than I was of him. He was scared to death that I was going to spill the beans, that I was going to split on him, that I had come there to make a scandal.

That was why he had called in his secretaries, to intimidate me, freeze me up, and that was why now, even at the mere suggestion of Mrs Welles' name, he was eagerly writing me out a cheque. I felt my skin go hot and prickly as the word came to me, which summed it all up. Blackmail! Mr Dropsey thought that I had come there to blackmail him, and Mr Dropsey, like a lamb, was paying up.

The wonderful sight of the filled-in cheque was wonderful no more, and the frightened feeling wasn't frightened any more but panicky; the palms of my hands and my forehead became suddenly wet.

'Mr Dropsey!' I said. 'Mr Dropsey I... feel rather bad about it really... I... I mean about taking a cheque from you... I mean... about asking you for money.' I floundered about miserably, hardly knowing what I was saying.

'...I don't think I could take the money from you after all,

Mr Dropsey... I mean not unless... unless – well, I... I feel rather bad about it Mr Dropsey, about reminding you... I mean asking you...'

I stopped speaking and there was silence in the room except for the buzzing of the flies on the window. Then Mr Dropsey spoke.

'M'dear,' he said, and for the first time his voice was normal and brisk. 'You mustn't upset yourself m'dear. I made a promise to you, which at the time I meant to keep. I'm very happy that you've reminded me about it m'dear, and I'm very happy now to fulfil it with a cheque. A cheque, which I might add m'dear goes to a very worthy cause.'

Mr Dropsey gave me a brilliant smile, then carefully blotting the cheque he put it in an envelope, sealed it and handed it to Miss Dorian. 'I've made it out to Mr Flood, m'dear.'

'Thank you... thank you very much Mr Dropsey.'

My voice was so small that I don't think he heard it. His words kept revolving round in my head. At first I didn't think I could have heard right – the wonderful words he had just spoken, that had suddenly made it all right. But when I looked up he was smiling at me with content and almost amusement at my discomfort, and I knew that he had meant it.

It was all right after all, it wasn't blackmail after all, and he had realised I had only asked him for the money because the company needed it so badly. He had kept his promise, that slender, slender little promise he had made to Mrs Welles; notwithstanding all the dreadful things that had happened to him since then, Mr Dropsey had kept his promise.

Miss Dorian handed me the envelope with a smile and crossed through her office to open the door for me.

'Thank you... thank you again Mr Dropsey,' I whispered.

'Not at all m'dear, not at all, a pleasure m'dear.'

Humbled and awed and rather ashamed I took my leave of him.

But oh, how wonderful it was as soon as I got to the other side of the door. How wonderful! To leap across the heavy, silent foyer, and madly ring on the lift, then madly leap inside the golden cage. How wonderful, hugging the cheque against me, to gaze down superciliously on the pageboy's questioning face.

To stick out my tongue at the horrid Ted, struck dumb in mid-telephone conversation as I passed him. Then sweetest, sweetest of all, to push past the hateful commissionaire insolently consulting his watch, and make him an eloquent and daring, oh most daring sign.

Out in the hot sunshine I skipped wildly in and out of the shining executive's cars, all the way down to the wrought-iron gates, where I turned and waved my cheque madly up at the long glass windows.

One of the world's workers saw me and ran to the windows with a hoarse wolf-whistle and in a second he was joined by a crowd of them and they all yelled down at me with cat-calls and laughs, and I waved and laughed back at them and blew them kisses.

I couldn't wait for the slow bus journey back into Leek. I thought of them all struggling on with rehearsal, pretending that it was just an ordinary Wednesday morning, pretending that Mr Flood giving me leave of absence was an everyday occurrence.

I could see Mrs Flood herself getting sharp with nerves and cruelly taking it out on everyone else. No, I couldn't wait for the bus, I just ran and ran up the street to the nearest telephone box. It seemed an age before I could hear the flapping of her bedroom slippers and her laboured breathing coming towards me, an age before the sharp Cockney voice snapped, 'Flood Players speaking,' an age before my words could come tumbling out.

'Oh Mrs Flood, it's me! It's me Mrs Flood, and we've got it, I've got the money for us Mrs Flood, it was easy, he was marvellous, I've got it here in a cheque he's just written. It's probably thousands, Mrs Flood, I mean he was just wonderful, just wrote it out, thousands I should think Mrs Flood – or hundreds anyway. It was so easy and he was so nice, Mrs Flood. He said it was a worthy cause Mrs Flood, a worthy cause, us, he said, me, the company, a worthy cause!'

There was the sharp intake of her breath then the pause, the sweet, eloquent, unbelieving pause – that second of silence, which is the greatest tribute in the world, then –

'Take a taxi cab,' shrieked Mrs Flood. 'Take a taxi cab over right away Ann, I'll pay for it but come right over straight away and tell him for God's sake drive careful.'

'Okay Mrs Flood, straight away, I'll be over straight away Mrs Flood, yes… Yes, I will be – yes really careful – I promise you I will.'

And then I was in the cool, velvet blackness of the cab and gazing and gazing at the thick, white, maddeningly sealed envelope.

The company was on stage waiting in little anticipatory knots for my arrival. They swooped on me in delight as I ran through the auditorium and up the steps, but I shook them off.

'Later… later!' I yelled as I made for her dressing room. This was Mrs Flood's moment.

She was sitting at her dressing table as I had so often seen her before, clad in the undyed lion and the bedroom slippers, with the bottle at her elbow; only this time it wasn't sherry, but two bottles of whisky and two bottles of gin. Mrs Flood's eyes met mine.

'I thought it called for a celebration,' she said huskily. 'Willy's just been over for them.'

Willy was sitting on his stool. 'Oh Ann,' he said breathlessly. 'Is it really true, is it really true that you've got the money for us Ann?'

For an answer I brought my hand from behind my back and held the envelope out to him.

'It's addressed to you, Willy.'

'Oh,' said Willy. 'Not really? Oh Ann, but—'

'But I'd better take it,' said Mrs Flood.

She rose from her chair and came towards me with a podgy, white hand outstretched. Her eyes glittered with a feverish kind of wonder.

For one little moment our hands were both holding it, then – 'Thank you Ann,' she said simply, and I let go, and in one swift movement Mrs Flood had slit the envelope across and taken out the cheque.

I don't think I shall ever forget that moment when Willy and I, with bated breath, watched Mrs Flood slit open the envelope and take out the cheque.

For a second she just held it there, still with the feverish wonder, then roughly she brought it up close under her face, and in a blind animal way moved her eyes across it from side to side, back and forth. Then suddenly she wasn't doing it any more, and Willy jumped up from his stool and I took a step towards her and the hand that was holding it fell heavily to her side.

'What's the matter? What is it, Mrs Flood?'

For an answer the little slip of blue paper fluttered softly out of her hand and fell to the floor. I picked it up and in the silence of the room, the silence that was wrapped like a pall, I read out the words.

I read that Mr Dropsey had instructed the Booth branch of Betterton's Bank Ltd., to pay to Mrs Flood the sum of two pounds two shillings only.

'What is it?' said Willy. 'What does it say?'

Mrs Flood had been staring out of the window unmoving, but at the sound of his voice she looked round. 'Willy,' she said in a little voice and held out her hands to him.

He went over and took them. 'What is it, Lil?' he said. 'What does it say?'

With his hands clasped tightly in hers, Mrs Flood turned round and faced me. She drew herself up to her full five feet, and her voice when she spoke was grand. 'Mr Flood and me was wrong,' she said. 'He wasn't a gentleman after all.'

It was one o'clock, the usual time for our dismissal from rehearsal, but that Wednesday afternoon we didn't leave the theatre until four.

Mrs Flood said nothing more to me in the dressing room, but dragging Willy by the hand plunged straight on to the stage.

'Act One, scene one,' she shrieked at the bewildered, waiting company, and Act One it was, and then Acts Two and Three and then all of them over again.

It was a nasty way of getting her own back on me. We were rehearsing *Wives for a Night*, with me playing one of the wives. It was a dreary little comedy but I had been enjoying rehearsals. It was the first time I had played a dumb blonde and the first time I had got a thrill out of comedy.

In fact, the Monday morning of our first read-through had

been rather important to me, for suddenly as I had read the inane dead-pan lines of Patrice, they had filled me with excitement. Suddenly I had known exactly and absolutely how to say them. Always before in comedy I had thought, well I could say it this way, or that way, and it would still get laughs depending on the audience, and, there must be a hundred different gestures and reactions to go with that line.

All equally suitable – but suddenly with Patrice there was only one way to say her lines and I knew instinctively that it was the right way. Comedy had clicked with me like the cap of a bottle finding the right thread. Leigh called it the beginnings of technique.

It was a very new and precious thing then, this technique. On Tuesday morning I had worried all the way down to the theatre that it had been a fluke, this knowing just how to say my lines, but it wasn't, and I said them again exactly the same with the same inflections, only bigger perhaps, and felt the same mathematical thrill.

Mrs Flood hadn't interrupted me the whole way through the play, and afterwards she'd said, 'You seemed to know what you were doing and it seemed to sound all right, so you'd better just carry on as you feel.'

So when we started that dreadful afternoon rehearsal I tried to, and sure enough, despite the morning's events, like some magic potion that had entered into me, my technique was still there.

It was a nasty way of getting her own back then, when she took it away from me. She wouldn't let me do a single thing that I had done before, she wouldn't let me say a single line the only way that it should be said; she picked me up and stopped me on every line that I uttered, shouting it out herself in an opposite inflection and making me repeat it after her.

She took my little beginnings of technique and threw them on the floor in front of the others and ground them away with her heel. She mimicked me and ridiculed me and told me that I was insulting Willy.

The rehearsal was called entirely for me, that she could avenge herself, and like a bear that has to dance because the ground it walks on is burning, I had to bend to Mrs Flood. I suppose I could have shouted back at her or refused to do what she told me or just walked out, but it didn't occur to me. The only thing that occurred to me as she drove me through Act Three for the third time was whether I hadn't been rather silly after all believing that there could only be one way.

And then at last it was four o'clock, blessed, blessed four o'clock and I was free. It came almost as a surprise to me when Leigh came up and took my arm and said, 'Thank God Ann, now we can talk,' and I realised that he meant about Mr Dropsey.

With the awfulness of my treatment during rehearsal, no one had asked me anything about what had happened. They had just looked at me with kindness and pity and smiled at me with embarrassment.

I remembered that I had rushed past them with the envelope crying, 'Later, later,' and that they must be dying to hear what had happened, but at the end of rehearsal when they did crowd round me, it all seemed a long, long way off.

Mr Dropsey and his cheque suddenly made me want to laugh, it all seemed so meaningless and small on top of the pain in my heart, which hammered out over and over again, 'She can't act! She can't act! She can't act!'

'Two pounds two shillings?' said Bill. 'It's an insult.'

'Two guineas,' said Hilda, 'is two guineas.'

'Can't you alter it?' said Rose. 'Put a couple more noughts on the end or something?'

'She didn't lose so much after all then,' said Sebastian, 'did she?'

But nobody answered him, Hilda and Bill because they didn't know what he meant, and Leigh and Rose and I because we had sent him to Coventry.

Mrs Flood's dressing room door opened and Willy crossed on to the stage holding a paper bag with two bottles of whisky and two bottles of gin in it.

'He's... he's been sent to take them back, Leigh,' I said, and suddenly the pain in my heart welled up in a great big choking lump and I was going to cry, but Leigh's arm came round me like a vice, willing me to stop.

'Don't get sentimental,' he said, and because I was so surprised that he understood that it wasn't Willy and the bottles I wanted to cry for, I stopped.

We walked out of the theatre and up the High Street together, still with his arm around me. I could feel my shoulder bumping into his armpit, which was damp with the heat, and his blue Dayella shirt, which smelt of sweat.

Across my neck I could feel the muscles of his forearm and around the top of my arm his damp finger. We walked awkwardly together because of his limp. We were both terribly aware of the awkwardness but we couldn't break it because we had never been so close together as at that moment.

We ought to have gone home to tea. Tea out was a gross extravagance. I said it out loud, 'We ought to go home to tea Leigh,' and Leigh said, 'I suppose we ought,' but instead we turned into the Madeira Cake, which was the most expensive teashop in Leek. I sat opposite him at a little table spread with an embroidered cloth, and a waitress brought us china tea and a plate of éclairs.

At home there would be Mrs Welles, hunched in her mink, miserably leafing through some novelette; the teacups from the hour before and the hour before that would stand stained on the kitchen table, and as we came through the door, Guinevere, for the millionth time, would pick them up and carry them to the scullery and rinse them through.

I lifted the shining silver pot and defiantly crooked my little finger as I bent it to the cups.

'Miss King,' said Leigh, watching me, 'excuse me Miss King, but where is your sense of humour?'

His voice was gentle and tender. For a split second the smile that he wanted and the lump in my throat that I wanted wrestled for supremacy. Then I gave him a wobbling grin.

'Gone!' I said. 'Gone with the wind, Mr Peters, you are now watching the beginnings of technique!'

And then I told him; every little thing I told him. Right from when he had seen me on to the bus to where Mrs Flood had dropped the cheque. And he laughed and laughed and laughed.

'Tell me... Tell me what Mister Rorris said again?' he spluttered, and I did, and he doubled up on the window seat so that people thought he had indigestion and the waitress hurried up and said should she get us some more hot water. But gradually he made me begin to laugh too. Gradually he made me stop thinking about the awful rehearsal, and gradually we fell to talking not of the result of Mr Dropsey's cheque, but of the reasons for his writing it.

Leigh was inclined to admire him. He said that he would never have credited Mr Dropsey with so much good taste and such a sense of humour. He said that it was a rare example of dignified revenge and he only wished Mr Dropsey could have been there to see Mrs Flood's face.

But I wasn't so sure. It was a nice idea and it was probably just about occurring to Mr Dropsey, but I had been there and seen the whole range of emotions which passed over his face. It didn't seem to me to be revenge he was interested in, not the revenge of Mrs Flood and myself anyway. He had been prepared to pay me money to keep my mouth shut, but because I had been frightened and unaware of my position of a blackmailer, and because when I had realised it, I had not exploited it but become even more frightened, he had paid me the sum of two guineas.

It seemed to me that had I behaved as he had expected, I would have got a great deal more money out of him. I expounded my theory to Leigh, but he pooh-poohed it as melodramatic, and we continued to wrangle happily enough over the complexities of Mr Dropsey's character.

The only other reason I could think of was that Mr Dropsey in all honesty believed that the frightened little girl in the daisy-spattered frock, would be quite happy about the cheque, and that to the dregs of an enterprise such as the Flood Players, two guineas would be quite acceptable. But Leigh stuck to his theory; whatever the reason was, we should never know.

Leek High Street was rather beautiful in the late afternoon. The lime trees along its pavements, which by day hung stiff and motionless in the shimmering air, now cast long fingers of shadow horizontally across the road, continuing vertically up the buildings. The first evening breeze moved the tops of the branches so that the tip of the rigid silhouette softened and dappled itself along the panes of some upstairs windows. The street was only moderately full, most of the shoppers had gone home and the rush hour had not yet started. Leigh and I had grown silent and were watching the scene.

He had his back to the bay window but had swivelled round

so that he was in profile, with one knee crooked up on the window seat. A shaft of sunlight fell across his head, making the outline of his face glow like a saint's in a stained glass window, and his blonde hair appear as a dazzling halo.

He is beautiful, I thought. His body is small and he is a cripple but his face is quite beautiful. Not handsome-beautiful like Sebastian and Willy, nor pretty-beautiful like Rose, nor vivid-beautiful like Mrs Welles. The largeness of their eyes and the distinctive modelling of their bones set their beauty.

They will always be beautiful and not a hundred black and seething emotions inside them can ever really mar it. But Leigh, I thought, is beautiful because of what he is inside and because he has no striking features, but neat, regular mobile ones and a translucent skin, what he is inside can come through to advantage.

If he were cruel and evil he would be ugly I thought, but because he is a good man he is beautiful.

I thought of this in a jumbled and incoherent way. I was still in a rather emotional state of mind and terribly aware of his kindness to me. The lump in my throat came up again as I relived the sudden pressure of his arm round me when I had wanted to cry.

'Leigh,' I said softly, but when he turned his head to me I could only mumble, 'Oh nothing!'

I can remember so plainly the tick-ticking minutes of that hour. We hardly spoke at all. I watched the long, thin shadow of the poplar tree fall suddenly across the tablecloth, black on white like some river cutting through an expanse of desert sand. The little knobbly embroidered flowers, which bordered its outline, were cacti. I heard the tinkle of silver spoons upon bone china and the distant affected ripple of women's voices.

I saw for the first time in my life Leigh's sunburned hand make the casual and unforgettable movement of piling sugar lumps one upon the other, and in my heart and in my mind and in my bones and in my soul, I felt the terrible aching sadness that is called love.

Chapter Fifteen

I didn't know then though that it was love. I didn't, as I sat touching the embroidered flowers, say to myself, you are in love Ann, you are in love with Leigh Peters, this is it Ann, this is love.

I couldn't know that it was love because, in my mind, loving Leigh Peters was not a possible thing. I only know now that it was love because it had a beginning and an ending, and afterwards, although we were terribly adult about it, it was never quite the same. I am aware too that it was mostly brought about by my state of mind, bitterly conscious of the fact that had I been less desperately unhappy or Leigh less unbearably kind to me, it would probably never have happened.

But I didn't know, until Sunday when it was all over, that it had been love. Sunday was the ending, Wednesday the beginning; only four days, but if I could wish any part of my life away it would be those four days.

All the time Mrs Flood was cruel to me. No one had ever been deliberately and consistently cruel to me before, and I found out that I couldn't take it. Everyone kept telling me to stand up to her and give her as good as she gave me, but somehow I didn't seem able to.

With every fresh contact I had with her during those four days I went further under. She crushed me completely. At night, during the show when I was on stage with her, she did everything that she could to confuse and ridicule my acting. If I was speaking she would mutter at me under her breath or, with ridiculous actions, rivet the audience's attention on herself. When she was speaking she would put in whole chunks of her own creation with pointed unkind references to me.

But all the time while I suffered her Leigh was there too. I had only got to turn my head to the prompt corner and his eyes would be there to comfort me. Sometimes he would pull faces at me or wink at me, and sometimes he would be very bold and mimic

Mrs Flood. He was always there though, always watching me on stage and always waiting for me when I came off. I clung to him as I had never clung to anyone in my life before.

In my unhappiness his kindness seemed to take on a sort of saintliness. I would stand in the wings and watch his floodlit profile and gold hair almost with awe, and then when he came off stage and made straight for me, my heart would start knocking inside me with love for him, only I didn't call it love then, I called it gratitude.

At night when he lay on his mattress not ten feet away from me I would think about him, and in my mind's eye relive all the things we had done together since I had known him.

And clearest of all, as vivid as if it had only happened yesterday, was the memory of the first time we had been alone together, when he had taken me out on the moors and I had laughed and danced in the sunlight. When I had been intoxicated with freedom and beauty, and when he had lied to me and told me that he was as free as the air. It wasn't that I minded him being married, I told myself as I cried into the pillow, it was just that – that he had lied to me.

So Wednesday and Thursday and Friday passed by and then at last it was Saturday night and the curtain had come down and we were free until Monday. And as usual on Saturday nights, we dashed off our make-up and assembled in the Ship for a drink. I didn't want to go, I wanted to go straight home as, on top of Mrs Flood, every minute of the evening had been fraught with the memory of the Saturday before and Mrs Welles.

'Remember this time last week? Remember when she wouldn't take her mink off? When she showed her pants, when she bought us brandies?' I didn't think I could bear to go back to the pub when they would remember how happy she had been. But in the end I did go because Leigh said he'd got to have a drink. We leaned on the bar with Sebastian and Rose and drank a dismal beer.

Sebastian said, 'Well, Sunday tomorrow,' and rubbed his hands in a hypocritical manner.

And Rose said, 'Why don't you drop dead?'

And through the silence which followed, Leigh spoke the

words that were to shape the fourth and last day. He was draining his glass while Rose was speaking. I watched the contortions of his Adam's apple. Then he settled his glass with a thump on the bar and looked me full in the face.

'Annie,' he said. 'We're getting out of here tomorrow.'

'Where to?' asked Rose.

Leigh was smiling with a great happy grin on his face. 'I don't know,' he said. 'Anywhere, everywhere, we'll just take a bus, any bus.' He stopped short suddenly. 'Oh no, but I'm wrong,' he said. 'Only one bus we'll take, only one bus, Annie,' – he caught hold of my hands – 'the bus to the moors,' he said. 'You remember the moors? We only went there once and we promised we'd go there so often, every week you said you'd like to go to the moors, Ann.' He let go of my hands and said, 'So you changed your mind? Well, you can change it again.' He was pleading with me. 'Two to the moors, Annie?'

My heart circled upwards inside me, making the blood course through my cheeks. I wondered why out of all the Sundays that had been he should pick this one. Perhaps it was then that I got the first trickle of awareness, the sixth sense feeling which immediately coiled itself in a heavy red ring and lay around that Sunday.

I answered him carefully and casually and looked at a woman whom I thought might be Madame Tic-Tac.

'I'd love to go to the moors Leigh, what a wonderful idea.'

We didn't start until after lunch. Leigh had planned that we should walk all afternoon, have tea somewhere, find a country pub where we could spend the evening, then come home on the last bus.

The afternoon was pale and warm and still when we set off down the hill into Leek. I wore my green and white checked frock, sandals, and my hair tied on top in a pony's tail. Leigh had on black jeans and a black shirt and around his shoulders a sweater and my cardigan.

Outside the cemetery we boarded the single decker bus, which would take us to Master's End. It was the most wonderful and terrible journey I had ever made because, for one whole hour, I experienced for the first time, the agonising pangs of desire. I had been kissed before and felt a nice little glow and once someone tried to go further with the result that I didn't even get a nice little glow, but now, with only our arms and thighs touching, I was flooded with a frightening desire. I was trapped with it in the bus.

I couldn't move, I couldn't speak, I couldn't break it in any way, I could only wait for the next wave to engulf me. It came in inexorable waves, starting with the steady beats of my heart vibrating faster and faster, then my blood heating and thickening, then the sensation that my face was melting, melting, leaving only the gross outline of my swollen mouth... and then suddenly it had passed beyond the limits of pleasure and I felt only the sickening physical uprush of nausea so that I was forced to turn my head and press it hard against the window. The nausea would then retreat, and I would wait for it to start all over again.

There was nothing I could do about it. I knew that Leigh must feel the fiery heat from my body, and the thought that he might understand it filled me with embarrassment. But the curious and rather horrible thing about it was my feelings towards him.

Looking back I should like to have been able to say, 'Well, of course that was when you knew you were in love.' But it wasn't. My desire was completely detached and self-sufficient, I wanted nothing from him except that he didn't move or speak. I wanted no tenderness or kisses; I didn't even want to go further. It was a complete thing in itself and although brought about by him, purely personal.

The bus conductor shouted, 'Master's End,' and with a jolt of disappointment I felt the reverberations of the bus cease and Leigh's body separate itself from mine.

For a second the whole of one side of me was suddenly exposed, vulnerable, uncomfortable, and shocked, like a newly-delivered baby. Then my desire left me as abruptly as though it had been a current switched off, and I clambered quickly after him with shame in my heart and slightly trembling limbs.

Master's End was just a scatter of cottages and a large pub. The road ended bang against the doors of its saloon bar, which, as we dismounted, were in the act of being closed. All around us the moors came down in purple stretches. North, east, south and west as far as we could see.

Still and silent with the aching silence that heat will bring, they lay at our feet. We sat down on a bench outside the pub and Leigh consulted his map. We could have taken the same track that we took before, and Leigh pointed to where it wound its way, a thin white chalky ribbon disappearing suddenly into a fold of the moors. But for some reason this time we both preferred a rougher track which lay above the pub and was visible only to the top of the hill we were on.

We walked without speaking. Leigh never spoke much. I could prattle away at him for hours and he would only just nod or smile or bring out the odd ejaculation. But because I knew he was always listening and sympathetic, I liked his silences and on several occasions had unburdened my soul to him.

But as we climbed the hill even the little everyday things that I longed to say because I knew he must be expecting them lay choking in my throat. I could only watch the small, black limping figure in front of me and remember how I had felt at the touch of it. I was glad when the hill grew steeper, when the great blocks of stone stumbled in our pathway, when our walking became climbing, hard and physical with no room for any thought at all.

I abandoned myself to the thrilling sensation, letting my senses magnify and close in on me, everything else blocked out, just the seeing and the hearing and the smelling and the touching. Above me Leigh's body was like a little black beetle, crawling along so slowly with his stick getting in the way.

I felt a sudden defiant exultant thrill of power because I was stronger and healthier than he. Straining my body, I scrabbled and tore at the rocks until I had passed him, swinging myself upwards with a lunatic strength and lodging my feet in perilous footholds until I stood high and remote on the skyline, while he struggled below me. And there for a brief instant, as I had unconsciously intended, the old freedom returned.

I clung to it childishly and desperately; the doubts, the uncertainties, the strange new feelings melted away as I laughed down at him and he crawled towards me. It was only Leigh, dear silly old Leigh who had always been keen on me. Leigh whom I liked and admired and because of my safeness had occasionally flirted with. I strutted and posed and pirouetted on my rock to insist to him that it was just the same. But as he grew nearer and nearer it wasn't the same after all. He climbed slowly, almost casually, and into my mind came the thought that my feat of strength might have appeared to him more like a panic. I stopped leaping about and sat down on the rock.

'Beat you!' I said in a gay, bright voice. He stood directly below my rock, his head level with my feet; he was breathing heavily with his exertions but his eyes smiling back at me were cool and composed.

'Coming up?' He didn't answer me and he didn't move. My words hung on the thick, still air, discomforting me so much that I had to add, 'Well?' very loudly. Still he didn't answer and slowly as we continued to look at each other it began again. I instinctively gripped the rock with my hands because the vibrations of my heart must surely dislodge me, and his voice when at last he spoke came to me very small because of the blood beating in my ears.

'No!' he said. 'You're coming down here.'

He put his hands around my ankles and pulled me down. His hands moved up my legs, my thighs and my hips until I reached the ground and stood lightly against him. Behind me the rock was about four inches away from my back.

Very gently Leigh nudged me backwards; for a second I was spread-eagled, with him still standing lightly against me, then I could go no further back and I closed my eyes in sudden fear and waited for his body to walk into mine. It came, hard as the rock behind me, blotting out the sun with its shadow, imprisoning me, so that I felt nothing except a hysterical rush of claustrophobia.

I began to push against him but as I did so his body started trembling all over and in an instant my arms went around him and I was no longer pushing, but holding him to me in an ecstasy of desire.

From our shoulders to our knees we seemed to melt into one. He kissed my mouth and my throat and my eyes and my hair, then we lost our footing and fell over into the heather. I opened my eyes to the blue arc of the sky and his strange distorted face, which hung an inch above my own. Very far away there was the high, thin sound of a singing bird. A slow trickle of sweat coursed down his face and fell on to my chin and I said, 'I love you, Leigh.'

Then I looked into his pale, wet eyes, which were framed with the funny eyelashes all clotted together with sweat, and started to cry. Leigh said, 'Oh, my darling,' as though he were in pain, and laid his cheek against mine. And so we lay, side by side, cheek to cheek and told each other that we were in love.

We must have lain there for a long time, as I remember that shadows came and went over our bodies. It was as though I had fallen asleep after four days of mental exhaustion and awoken, neither shocked nor surprised to find that the liberation of my spirit had at last come about not with regaining my freedom, but by sealing its loss. My only wonder was that for four days I could have been so blind.

I talked and talked to Leigh, unburdening my soul to him as I had done in the past, only this time couching my words in the language of love. It is strange to reflect now that it was in that very first moment of love, so perfect just because it neither questioned nor demanded, that I went wrong.

We walked several more miles before we came to the village that Leigh had marked on the map. We walked slowly because every now and then we would have to stop and kiss one another, and go over time and time again the few gigantic moments of the past, when we had sensed that we had been living in the same house together for so long. The few became so many that in the end we got hysterics and further impeded our progress with the pains of laughter.

It was seven o'clock when we reached the little village of Rawley and for Leigh, who was panting with thirst, perfectly timed.

We made straight for the nearest pub, where I drained a shandy and Leigh a pint of beer. It was a dull modern pub and not what we had walked the moors to find, so after assuaging our thirst we retraced our footsteps down the single main street.

The evening had just come and like a benediction was blessing the night for us. I wanted to say to Leigh, 'Do you believe in God?' but I didn't dare because he might say, 'No,' and at that moment I loved God so much that I knew that if he did it would upset me. We walked arm in arm but this time there was no awkwardness. As Leigh had said to me on the moors, 'You'll have to get used to it!' The eternity of this remark kept breaking over me again and again in little flurries of happiness.

We found the pub we were looking for. It stood on a corner of the main street and a rough looking road leading up to the moors. It was blackened and gnarled with age and had no name, just the date carved over the doorway in big numbers, 1652.

There was one communal bar inside, long and low with an uneven floor, but the wide oak benches were set into the wall, making little secret alcoves. I settled myself into one while Leigh got the drinks, a pint of cider in a mullioned glass for me, and Guinness and rum for himself.

'Midnight is nine thirty from the church,' he said, coming back with them, 'which gives us just two enchanted hours.' He smiled at me dizzily and we linked arms and drank and said 'Skol' very seriously.

They were very enchanted moments. Sometimes when I'm feeling sentimental I tell myself it was worth it just for that little while. We sat in our alcove, tight and secure, remote and vulnerable. Remote because we were in love, but vulnerable because by loving each other we also loved everyone else. We looked out through a secret window and found that the world indeed was small and very dear.

We watched an old, old woman knock back pint after pint of stout. She was hideous, with a purple face and no hair, and we both agreed that age had a certain dignified beauty. Two men on our right were discussing their latest offspring, and we listened with fanatical interest and were flooded with tenderness and had to ask questions and see photographs.

From our alcove we held our breaths as we played each emotion-wracked game of darts with the players, and when at last the best man lost, Leigh hurried to buy him a drink. A woman walked round the pub selling heather, and no one in the world had been more favoured than I when she dropped a piece on to our table.

We drank a great deal and we smoked a great deal, and in between we held each other's hands. We laughed a lot and spoke a little and when a drunken man staggered into the middle of the room and started to sing hymns, we nearly had to cry.

Leigh came back again with the glasses filled. I watched him wind his way through the crowd towards me, then lower them on to the table. He stood on the other side of the table and looked down on me.

'We've missed the last bus Ann,' he said.

He held out his watch to me and I saw that it was twenty to ten and said, 'Oh!' then, 'Oh Leigh!' and then, 'What are we going to do?'

Leigh ran a finger round the top of his glass and said, 'We can stay here darling.'

I heard him perfectly but I said, 'What did you say?' as though I hadn't.

He repeated, 'We can stay here darling.'

I said very slowly and carefully, 'We can't afford to stay here Leigh, we can't afford to stay at places, we'll have to go home, staying at places is frightfully expensive.'

'We can stay here Ann, it's not very expensive.'

'Have you asked?'

'Yes!'

'How much?'

He stopped running his finger round the glass; I noticed that a blue vein zigzagged down his forehead. I felt an urgent longing to touch it and a disbelieving wonder at myself that I hadn't noticed it before.

'It's ten and six a night for one double room,' he said.

I didn't say anything at all and he smiled at me and said very gently, 'Don't look like that darling, it'll be just the same as the attic.'

We had sandwiches and tea in the parlour behind the bar. The landlord said, pardon him but we was foreigners, weren't we? Scandinavians, he'd say, and we played up with broken accents and fantastic stories of life in Norway.

'Jewellery,' said Leigh, 'Iss considered wulgar at home, no brooches, no bracelets, no ringss on the fingerss.'

'Is that so?' said the landlady.

I had to stuff a whole sandwich into my mouth as I watched her eyes, heavy with relief, relax their disapproving scrutiny of my hands.

We followed her up a small flight of stairs, pausing on the pitch-black windowless airless landing while she fumbled with the door. I was shivering with excitement. Leigh held my hand and put his lips against the temples of my head. The landlady heaved with her shoulder against the door and it opened and we went in. Neither of us said anything. The last pale daylight illuminated the room with a greenish glow. We just stared at it until she had stopped talking and left us and we could hear the crashing noise of her descending the stairs.

It was a small room under the roof with a sloping ceiling, beams and a lattice window, but it wasn't like the attic after all.

I stood against the door and stared at the double bed. Leigh let go of my hand and walked over and sat on the edge of it and said, 'Feather,' and held out his arms to me. I noticed with sudden distaste and shock that I should notice it, that his legs didn't quite touch the ground.

Leigh said, 'Come here woman,' in a low growl.

I wished he hadn't said it; seeing him sitting on the bed and talking like that jarred me inside. I thought wildly, I wish we could have found a cave on the moors, a big cave with lots of clean white sand and he would have lit a fire and his face would have been all gold and illuminated like it is on stage…

Leigh said, 'What's the matter darling?'

I stood against the door and said, 'Was it… the only room… she'd got Leigh?' like the heroine in some bad bedroom farce.

Leigh said, 'I love you, my darling, darling Ann,' and he kept on saying it, 'My darling, darling Ann,' until I had walked across to him and stood with my thighs against the bed. He kissed me very gently around my eyes and ears and nose and told me not to be frightened.

I said, 'I'm not frightened Leigh, I'm not frightened,' and thought, what's the matter, what's happened, why isn't it the same, why isn't it like the moors and the pub? It is the same, it must be the same, it's Leigh, I love him, it doesn't matter…

I started to say, 'We could put the bolster down the middle,' but I didn't finish it because I felt his hand undoing the zip of my frock and it suddenly seemed a silly remark. My heart gulped… 'Stop it, stop it, please don't, leave it like it is, don't spoil it…' I put my hands behind my back and tried to push his away so that he should know.

He said, 'Don't be childish Ann!' in a brisk voice, as though he had decided that an attitude was going to be necessary to deal with me.

It made me go cold inside. I turned round to him and said, 'Leigh, Leigh!' desperately. I wanted him to look at me and understand, to say, 'Yes I know darling, it's frightful – I didn't want it like this either.' I wanted him to look at me like on the moors, and it to come to him suddenly and him to say choking with excitement – 'We'll hitch-hike darling, there's a moon and we'll hitch-hike, or walk or anything darling. Just you and me, just you and me and the ribbon of white road and on either side the blackness that will be the heather.'

I wanted him to say, 'The moon will glint on your fair hair making it like white gold and we'll sing.' But all he did was give me a playful nudge on the chin and say, 'Silly darling,' in the same brisk voice.

I took off my dress and crept under the cool, white sheets. The greenish glow of light had faded. Leigh stripped off his trousers and shirt in the dark. The whole room was in darkness.

I couldn't see him as he came towards me; a great rush of fear filled me because I couldn't see him. I couldn't see that it was Leigh, I couldn't see that his face was kind and gentle, I couldn't see that his eyes were loving.

I thought in a panic, I can't see if I love him!

I said, 'I want a cigarette, Leigh,' hysterically.

He fetched them over and lit the match. He held it between us, not lighting the cigarettes, and I looked at him until it burnt his fingers, then he blew it out and put his arms around me hard and held me down in the bed.

The shock of discovering that I didn't feel anything was so dreadful that I just lay there passive, while his passion mounted.

I thought, It can't be, it's not possible – there's something the matter with me – in a minute it'll be alright, in a minute it'll be just like I felt in the bus and on the moors. You can't just switch off like that, it doesn't just switch off like that, in a minute it'll be alright.

But the next minute, when he was pulling at my clothes and telling me that he would try not to hurt me, it still wasn't all right and I stopped lying passive and struggled against him, forcing him away from me in a dreadful panic.

He said, 'Darling, darling... Please, please darling Ann... It's alright, you'll be alright, I promise – I love you...'

I shouted, 'Hilda Fellowes says you're married. She says she worked with your wife.' I shouted it at him, hardly knowing what I was saying.

He didn't answer me. He lay beside me with his elbows against my ears. I felt his body stiffen and grow motionless. When he spoke his voice came in rushes, staccato with diverted passion.

He said, 'I'm married. I wanted to tell you... I couldn't tell you... a long time ago... a long time ago. I should've told you. I wanted to. I should've but I couldn't. I couldn't tell you, you wouldn't understand, you're very young Ann, it's different. You see, I didn't want to hurt you, I didn't want to spoil it... It would have spoilt it.

'I wanted today to happen first Ann... I wanted to hear you say you loved me, Ann. It'll be all right though, we'll manage somehow darling! She's an actress, she's a bitch darling, we've been separated for nearly a year... We just rushed into it, you know in the theatre... I never loved her...'

I thought that his voice was a machine gun, riddling my body with bullets in places which made me die slowly.

He said, 'Hilda... Hilda... And the irony of it is we weren't married then, we didn't marry until the end of the season... Living together... she said it looked better in front of the company... Hilda... Hilda... I don't remember, it was just one weekend... yes, yes I do. She didn't remember though, she would have said so, she would have spoken, she—'

I screamed, 'Stop it, stop it, stop it!' I beat at him with my hands and screamed, 'Don't say it, it's not true, stop it, you love me, you love me, tell me that you love me, say you love me!'

They were the sudden horrible last convulsions and when he said, 'I love you, you know I love you,' it was all over and I was dead.

I lay rigid on the bed while he urgently tried to plead with me, tried to understand. He was gentle and kind as before, frightened and unhappy as I had been. He went on and on then suddenly grew wild and desperate and shouted, 'For Christ's sake say something darling, for Christ's sake… For Christ's sake.'

But I didn't. And he stopped being gentle and dragged at my hair by the roots and rained kisses all over my face and body in a dreadful frenzy. And I didn't feel a thing – nothing, except the pain when he pulled at my hair.

Then he rolled away from me and lay on his stomach with his head pressed into the pillow, and I heard the low gasping sobs of his crying. I had never heard a man cry before. It pierced my safe dead body so that I had to clutch the sheets and screw up my face and dig with my heels into the bed.

Everything inside me cried out to turn to him, to take him in my arms, so that he might take me in his arms, so that we might at least cry together. Had he made one movement towards me then it would have been so, but he didn't. And slowly and painfully the danger minutes passed by, and at last against the background of his sobs I began to think.

I thought, I am alone. I am completely and utterly alone. I shall always be alone, quite, quite alone. Everyone is alone. He is alone. Now that I have found that out I must be very brave, I must grow very strong. I'm stronger already, I didn't turn to him, that was strong. It hurts now but it won't hurt later on. It won't hurt later on. It won't hurt later on.

In the morning I shall look exactly the same as I did the night before. No one will know. I'm stronger than he. He's crying, oh God he's crying, I won't cry. I won't cry… I must be strong, I must be strong…

I was pierced right through again and this time it seemed as if the danger minutes would never pass.

There was a pain in my chest which cancelled thought right out, but I hung on, clutching the sheet and waiting, and eventually like the waves of desire I had felt for him on the bus, it passed off.

And so through the long, long night I lay there, thinking and waiting for the next wave to engulf me. When the first light of dawn came I saw that Leigh was asleep.

At nine o'clock we caught a bus outside the church, we would be back in Leek for ten, early down at the theatre. It was a Monday morning, the busiest day of the week with the new show in the evening. We would be steeped in work, hemmed in by work, abandoned to work, to the show which in traditional style would go merrily on. There was just that one hour to get through before we could start, that one hour which civilisation ironically decreed should be spent sitting in exactly the same manner as we had sat the day before.

When the landlady called us we had dressed swiftly and silently and, without waiting for breakfast, had dashed for the bus. Now we sat in an agony of silence and watched the miles crawl by. Leigh held himself stiff and tense away from me so that his body should not touch mine.

And now my heart and mind were quite cold and clipped. I looked out of the window and made dull plans for my life. I thought, now that I know I have no capacity for feelings and have become hard, I shall probably be a lot more successful. They say you've got to be hard to get on in the theatre, to let nothing stand in your way, nothing of course means love. I wish whoever first said that could have seen me last night, they would have been very proud of me. I just threw love off like an eiderdown and this morning it's all right. I'm not feeling heartbroken or even dreadful, not even thinking about him, just sitting here making clear-cut plans for my career. I am a perfect candidate for success. A little, hard cold glow started up in me when I thought about that and I repeated it to myself, 'I am a perfect candidate for success.'

And then I remembered his mattress. His mattress lying there by my bed at number eight, which he would continue to sleep upon every night. And in a flash it all went and my heart cried out, no, no that's not fair, nothing shall stand in your way, okay, and you leave them and move on. They don't go on lying there beside you at night. It's more than I could endure…

I thought again quickly, I am a perfect candidate for success, for success, for success! And slowly a great feeling of cruelness came over me, and out of the corner of my eye I looked at Leigh Peters' pale set face. I thought, yes. Lovely. Very noble. Stiff upper lip! We have nothing to say, but inside it's all a masochistic thrill. You will revel in the fact that you're going to go on lying beside me every night in the attic, and when the season breaks up and you go back to your wife you will be enriched by suffering.

I felt a great surge of hatred for him, as thrilling and intoxicating as the love feeling. I thought, you had nothing to do with my falling in love with you, you were around as you'd always been around, you were kind as you'd always been kind, and the moment I fell in love with you was because if I hadn't, I'd have gone mad with unhappiness. It had nothing to do with you, nothing at all.

I instigated it myself so that now when I don't want to love you any more I can stop it myself and you can't say a word, not a word. Outside the world is beautiful and warm and it's still the beginning. I'm seventeen and I can do anything in the world, go anywhere. I'm hard and strong and powerful and I won't be bogged down by you, by your wife and your love and your goodness...

My blood boiled inside me for a while then gradually cooled down and I thought, I hate you now Leigh, only because I fell in love with you not for yourself but through circumstances, and because I let you think it was the other way round. I know that now Leigh, because I can't feel anything at all for you, because I don't want ever even to talk about it. Because last night as soon as we got into that dreadful room I knew, and not when you told me you were married. You think it's the marriage business, don't you? I shouldn't let you think that, but I'm going to because it hurts my pride to think that I can fall in and out of love within the space of four days.

I feel so free Leigh, I can't tell you how free because it would be vulgar. Had I never said I loved you out loud, had we never come out to the moors or stayed the night together, perhaps I could've done, explained without hurting you that I had gone ga-ga over you for a few days, but had now snapped out of it.

I could have done it like that and then we could have laughed at me and exulted together in my freedom and not lost anything. But perhaps then we couldn't. Perhaps then there would be nothing to be free from. Free? Free? Free? Oh Leigh, when only yesterday I wanted to love you so much that when you kissed me on the moors, I cried.

Oh Leigh, I feel a great ache of loss, not for you but for what I felt for you, the heather and the sky and the summer. The leaping up the rocks and you pulling me down to you and not saying anything. Heathcliffe and Cathy, all pure and beautiful. And the company all sordid and depressing, and Mrs Flood and Mr Dropsey and everything, so dreadful.

But now they're not dreadful but in this bus the thought that I'm nearly back with them is wonderful and very dear. And I don't want you a bit now, but them and life and Mrs Welles and men, we'll find her another, I swear we'll find her another and it'll be great fun all over again. Come on, come on, I want rehearsal and the new play and playing it how she wants it, I don't care…

And so the miles passed by while my innermost thoughts seethed inside me. I wondered what Leigh was thinking. From my hardness I wondered then for the first time how much the moor excursion had been planned with a view to getting me into bed. I wondered then if he really was in love with me or if the way he had spoken had also been planned and if it had, what he must be feeling now. Or if perhaps he had felt genuine love and after the fiasco, like me, had lost it.

I had heard that sex blinded men a lot more than women. I thought about the fact that nothing had happened last night, and should have felt glad about it, and did a bit, but it was swamped by the awful fear that something was wrong with me.

I kept remembering how as soon as he had got into bed with me it had switched off like an electric light, how he could have been a piece of cold fish for all the desire I felt for him. I wondered if I was frigid, and decided that I'd have to have a little talk with Mrs Welles.

Out of the blue and without turning to me Leigh said, 'Do you want to talk, Ann?'

I said in a panic, 'Not now Leigh, not now. We will talk, but not now Leigh.' It seemed to me the most important thing in the world that we shouldn't talk about it.

We never did talk about it. He went on living at number eight and we went on working together and the only awful thing about it was how little the fact seemed to bother either of us. I had thought that although I no longer loved him, his presence would be a constant dragging reminder of when I had. It wasn't. I had thought that he would be noble about me. He wasn't. I realised of course, as soon as we got home, that the atmosphere at number eight was hardly conducive to difficult personal feelings.

The fact that Mrs Welles, where all else had failed, had been roused from her apathy by our staying away the night together, seemed to take away the tragedy angle. She sat round the kitchen table with all her old personality aflame, and instead of Leigh and I being unable even to look at each other, we seemed to join up with Rose again and become moths again dancing around her light.

Down at the theatre too, the important events of the following week tended to drive anything else but work from one's mind. Yet despite all this it seemed to me sad that we should be capable of recovering from each other so quickly. As the days went by and we laughed and joked and were natural together, it made the memory of loving someone for four days appear a little vulgar, a little crude. As though our feelings for one another, he an actor and me an actress, had after all been rather theatrical.

And then there was the loss of excitement, of anticipation. No longer could I wonder what it would be like to wake him with a kiss, to feel suddenly while eating fish and chips that he was looking at me over the newspaper. All the old exciting awareness had gone. The innocent something because it was nothing feeling, swapped for a reality, which turned out also to be nothing. It was in these things I discovered that the sadness lay. I would still stand in the wings and watch his floodlit profile and gold hair, but now my heart could only cry out like Othello's, 'the pity of it Iago, oh! the pity of it all.'

Chapter Sixteen

Important events down at the theatre started the following Friday, when we had all noticed the envelope on our way into the theatre. Mrs Flood and Willy had been late down, so one by one we had all passed by it, laid out on the card table which served as our letter rack. A large brown envelope addressed in a bold hand to Mrs Flood with, 'Script, with care' written in capitals across the top of it. It bore the Leek postmark, which up in the dressing room caused excited speculation.

Through the first half of the show Mrs Flood gave no indication that there was anything unusual in people sending her scripts. But we had to hold the curtain for her after the interval, as she gesticulated madly through the telephone booth that the conversation she was engaged in was of more importance than the show.

This abandoned behaviour caused even further speculation. We dragged through the second half of the show still in the dark, but somehow the ill-omened, deadpan lines of the fated Patrice, for the first time in the week, seemed less irksome to me.

At the fall of the curtain Mrs Flood raised a reticent white hand and briefly exhorted us to be down at the theatre ten o'clock sharp in the morning for the first read through of a new play. She swept off towards the dressing room with Willy in tow and left us goggling behind her. But at the doorway, with a lovely stage turn, she flung out a further careless remark.

'The author will be present,' she said distantly and, disappearing through the door, slammed it behind her. Unfortunately it caught Willy's finger, and the next second she was back among us, screaming hysterically for bandages, Dettol and brandy, which rather spoilt the effect.

We couldn't wait for the following morning. For so long now we had been doing such dated, dreary stuff that the thought of a brand new play with author attached was really exciting. We wondered who he could be, and how anything creative could possibly come out of Leek.

Rose and I were inclined to see him as a young Noel Coward who had nothing to do with Leek but thought it might be terrible, terrible fun to try out his new play on it. Leigh thought he was going to be a decadent great, great grandson of Arnold Bennett, who found it impossible to get anything published outside of The Towns.

We were all extremely shattered when at ten o'clock the following morning we discovered that it was Mr Wynch. Rose nearly fell over.

He was standing with Mrs Flood, pale and nervous, and clutching an armful of straight-from-the-typewriter scripts. We drew chairs up in a semicircle and Willy handed us each a copy. We observed in shocked silence that it was entitled, *The Cut Heart*, a psychological drama by W Wynch.

Mrs Flood eased one foot out of a glacé kid shoe, which she was unnecessarily wearing – from the moment the company had arrived down, Mr Wynch hadn't taken his eyes off Rose – and sent Willy for her slippers. Only when he had returned with them and taken away the glacé kids and returned again did she speak. She was very excited, and, completely ignoring Mr Wynch, spoke to us as though he wasn't present.

'I shouldn't wonder but what this isn't the turning point of the Players,' she said. 'You know – "There is a wave in the affairs of man".'

'Tide,' Willy corrected her. '"Which taken at the flood –"' He stopped short in mid-quotation as the miraculousness of what he was saying broke over him, then burst into wild and delighted laughter; no one could stop him. And after five consecutive minutes of it, by which time he was getting slightly hysterical, Mrs Flood was obliged to send him out for some cigarettes. By the time he had returned, she had informed us in not so many words that despite it being a shocking play, the prestige value of performing the first play from the pen of the author of, *Leek, her Drains and Mains*, would be considerable. We were to go into rehearsal at once and present it with enormous publicity on Monday week.

'And now,' said Mrs Flood, briskly addressing Mr Wynch for the first time, 'Casting. I've read it through thoroughly Mr Wynch, and to my mind – and I'm sure to yours – the casting side presents no difficulties.'

Mrs Flood thumbed through a couple of pages of the script, made a smacking noise with her tongue, and ran an omnipotent finger down the cast list.

'With it being all but a two-part vehicle,' she said boldly, 'you want two people who first and foremost know their job.' She made another smacking noise and fixed Mr Wynch with an unbreakable smile.

'Mr Flood for Vivian of course?' she said, coyly questioningly.

Mr Wynch nodded his head vigorously. 'Yes, yes, Mr Flood of course,' he said, 'exactly who I had in mind, and—'

'And myself of course for Willow,' said Mrs Flood, loudly and not questioningly at all.

In one swift instinctive movement all our heads whipped round to look at Mr Wynch. He was looking horribly embarrassed.

'Well actually,' he began bravely, 'I see Willow myself as... as something almost sprite-like, a thin, dark elfin fey little figure – half-girl, half-child.'

'Half what?' demanded Mrs Flood in a dreadful voice.

'Half-girl, half-child,' mumbled Mr Wynch unhappily.

Mrs Flood gave a short laugh. 'Well, I think we'll just have to forget that little idea Mr Wynch,' she said briskly. 'Having had no experience of the theatre you wouldn't know, but you can take it from me that that type of think just doesn't go, just doesn't pay. The public don't want anythink that's unnatural – not to mention the fact that we don't carry any children,' she finished nastily.

'No! No!' said Mr Wynch desperately. 'You misunderstand me, Mrs Flood – not an actual child. Indeed an actual child would be as wrong as...'

He floundered off miserably and we held our breaths waiting for her to ask him, 'As what?' But she didn't, and instead spoke to him in a sudden resigned voice. 'Well, who had you got in mind Mr Wynch? Ann here is the youngest we can offer you.'

She turned to me with a sudden smile and, in a curiously

eager voice, said, 'It's a long part Ann, would you like to play it?'

My heart warmed to her. All week she had been making tentative difficult approaches of friendship towards me. It was obvious that the fact that she'd been so cruel to me was now hurting her. Her eyes said plainly, if you play the part I'll have made it up to you. It'll be all right then, we'll be quits.

But before I could answer her, Willy spoke.

'Ann's not thin or dark,' he said, 'not a bit fey and elfin. Rose is the one you want really, absolutely right I should say Rose looks.'

Mr Wynch pounced on him in a frenzy of relief. 'Yes, exactly – Mr Flood saw it straight away – who I really had in mind – you must recognise the physical qualities, what I mean by the half-girl, half-child.'

Mrs Flood put up a certain amount of embarrassing opposition, but with Willy backing up the other side, Mr Wynch won the day. It was his play and Rose was to be his heroine.

On reading the play and discovering that it was a very ordinary, dreary little piece about a factory-hand girl (living in a semi-detached house with Mum) and her boyfriend (a floor walker) we felt after the title and Mr Wynch's attitude, rather let down. But we needn't have been, rehearsals were extremely amusing. Mrs Flood had had every intention of producing it as it read, dully.

The only strength of it, she said, lay in the fact that it was so ordinary that people would be able to identify themselves with it.

Mr Wynch however, was of a different opinion, and to Mrs Flood's horror lost no time in explaining to her that the whole thing was fraught with symbolism.

'You see Mrs Flood, when she spits out the chips at her mother she's not just spitting out chips at her mother. It's got to be a great big vomiting rush of nausea, which is more than physical, a revulsion expressed in the everyday things, (chips and mother, etc.) against the system in which she is ensnared.'

'Spitting out chips gets a laugh, Mr Wynch. It doesn't matter how it's done, it gets a laugh. They're going to laugh see, think it's funny – and we're going to play it for a laugh too. Christ knows,' she finished bitterly, 'it's the only one we're likely to get.'

Rehearsals went on till nearly three o'clock every day.

'I'm sorry Mr Wynch but I just don't see it that way. Granted it's the big dramatic scene and he's not going to be just sat down through it, but it doesn't mean you've got to have Mr Flood pacing up and down for twenty solid minutes.'

'But don't you see, Mrs Flood, it's symbolic? In moments of crisis the thing that he is trying to rid himself of is unconsciously exploiting itself in ludicrous and pathetic measures. Remember, he is a *floor walker!*'

Towards the end of the week things began to get better as Mrs Flood suddenly discovered that by agreeing with him that everything was symbolic she got the same results, only quicker. By the weekend *The Cut Heart* was rehearsing smoothly and dully, with all of us rather sick of it; all of us that is with the exception of Willy and Rose.

Rose's attitude was rather unusual for her. She was mostly only really happy in drawing room comedies, the symbolic working girl type of part usually boring her to tears. But for some reason or other, the part of Willow had fired her imagination. She worked really hard at it, studying her part in all her spare time and earnestly discussing it with Willy. They had a great many long duologues together, which Willy took endless time and patience with.

'Can we take it over again Lil?' he'd yell at Mrs Flood after they'd been over a certain scene several times. And Mrs Flood, happy whenever he was happy in his work, would smile at him indulgently from the stalls and tell him that he was a slave driver.

By Saturday morning things had been going so well that Mrs Flood said she felt she could safely leave the rehearsal in Mr Wynch's hands.

'Which means,' she said eyeing us meaningfully, while Mr Wynch settled himself on a chair in the stalls – 'No, Mr Wynch, you want to be much further back than that, at this stage of production it's most important to see the thing as a whole. Which means,' she repeated, 'you go through everything exactly as I've given it to you and if you want to know anything you ask Mr Flood here and not Mr Wynch.'

She made her exit wearing the undyed lion, woollen stockings, and white open-toed sandals, with two shopping bags over one arm and a suit of Willy's over the other.

Left to ourselves, the atmosphere immediately became relaxed and gay. We seldom rehearsed on Saturdays and considered a call for *The Cut Heart* quite unnecessary. We proceeded to bounce through it, completely ignoring Mr Wynch's one or two vague interruptions.

Outside the world was hot and still and it was market day, and with any luck we should be free by twelve o'clock. On stage Willy and Rose were going through their early scenes together almost flippantly. I watched them lazily, waiting to make my entrance as the mother.

Rose, with her black hair and a blue sundress over her sunburn, looked vivid and Spanish; Willy, in a tartan shirt and jeans, looked very young.

In the wings Sebastian and Leigh were playing a hot game of pontoon. Now and again their laughter and delighted yells breaking loud on the air. Hilda sat knitting on a tea chest, and in the corner, upright at the prompt table, Bill Irving laboriously filled in his pools.

All of us were relaxed and gay and united. I went on and came off as the mother, then settled myself against a curtain, sitting on the bare boards (*The Boards!* I told myself proudly) to watch Rose and Willy's big emotional scene.

Rose, as I said, had worked hard at her part and now I could see that her eyes were shining with anticipation as Willy, brutish and suddenly dead serious, moved in towards her.

It was the scene where unable to communicate the feelings of their souls; they just stand and shout at one another. They started off evenly enough, indeed I was struck by the excitation in Rose's voice, and thought with a sudden pang, she can act, I was wrong, she's beautiful and she can act as well.

As their voices grew louder the theatre seemed to become very still. In the wings I noticed that Sebastian and Leigh had left their game and were watching. We leaned forward eagerly, straining to the passion of their acting; and then all three of us realised what was happening.

I felt the old trickle of fear in my stomach as I looked at Willy.

The sweat ran down his face. He swayed on his feet but it was his voice, cracking under its strength and no longer concerned with the play that was so awful. I thought wildly, Rose, Rose, you must see it, stop it, stop it at once... You mustn't shout back...

But even as I thought it, I saw that she had grown instantly silent and was just staring at him. For a second longer perhaps, Willy went on shouting out like a mad, hoarse animal, then he looked at her standing there in front of him all still and pale, and putting his hands over his face he bowed his head and sobbed, 'I can't bear it Rose, I can't bear it, I can't bear it, Rose!' over and over again.

We watched Rose slowly and stiffly put her arms around him and we heard her say, in a curiously tender voice, 'It'll be alright Willy, I promise you it'll be alright, you must just hang on Willy, I promise you it'll be alright.'

I turned away and lit a cigarette. It was nothing to do with us, but at that moment I admired Rose more than I had ever done in my life. I would never have thought of dealing with him as she had done, or answering him back in the same strange way as he had broken down, which, when I turned round again, I saw had worked like a miracle. They had gone back to one of their earlier scenes and were pattering through it as though nothing had happened.

Afterwards Rose was loath to talk about the incident, but the rest of us did with high indignation. Somehow or other it had never occurred to us that our dear funny Willy could feel active unhappiness with his life.

'Though heavens knows!' said Sebastian hotly, 'we must be a thick-skinned lot not to have done. Just imagine not only working, but living, eating and sleeping with her too.'

I don't know what made me come out with the next remark. Perhaps it was because Leigh was laughing loudly about the Floods too.

But I remember that I said, 'You'd be surprised Sebastian Day. They're a great deal happier than anyone would imagine, it's quite something you know for a marriage even to keep going in the theatre,' with surprising defiance.

Monday night went off like a bomb. Mr Wynch had attended to an enormous amount of advance publicity, and for the first time in the history of the Flood Players, when the curtain went up we could see a row of white blobs at the back of the hall which told us that people were standing.

Afterwards we had Champagne on stage with Mr Wynch, with hordes of nasty pseudo-arty friends of his who completely ignored us or made remarks like, 'How nice for you to be able to help darling Wal give birth to his darling play,' or 'And now of course he'll have to get a proper London company to do it.'

Rose was made a slight fuss of on account of her looks, and someone said, 'You must send her to darling Gideon,' and someone else said, 'Oh yes darling, on one of those naughty continental tours,' and everyone shrieked with laughter.

But Mrs Flood of course was in the seventh heaven of delight. She blundered painfully around in her glacé kids from one sophisticated group to another, thrusting Willy in his Harrow blazer before her. Her face was shining, eager and pathetically naïve.

'Mr Flood, my husband – not often he gets the chance to mix with his own kind – so nice for Mr Flood, yes, my husband – to meet you. Quite spoiled for company by Paris, Mr Flood was, misses it something cruelly he does – oh yes, we was on the continent for many years. No, specialised adagio. What? Oh, he won't remember, he's hopeless on dates, no of course it wasn't, Willy, come along darling.'

For some reason or other *The Cut Heart* caught on. Perhaps Mrs Flood was right in thinking that *Leek, her Mains and Drains* had been a best-seller, or perhaps again, the factory girls and floor walkers could identify themselves with Willy and Rose; at any event from Monday till Saturday the theatre was packed and at the end of the week Mrs Flood gave us each ten shillings extra. This meant a lot to Rose and Leigh and me, as back at number eight the money situation had become horribly tight.

All through the time of Mr Dropsey, Mrs Welles had refused to take any money from us for the attic, and the agreement that we should buy our own food had never even from the beginning been adhered to.

If we weren't eating chicken off Mr Dropsey, it was baked beans off Mr Goat; we would bring back the odd delicacy and buy her cigarettes, but so fierce and staggering was Mrs Welles' generosity that never had we really felt the pinch of living on three pounds a week. But now of course it was different.

Mrs Welles had nothing, not even the five pounds a week which Mr Goat had been giving her, and Mr Welles' allowance, she told us, had stopped arriving nearly a year ago. We had all been horrified at this, thinking that it was what she'd been living on before we'd arrived. Leigh had immediately got practical and told her that something could be done about it, but Mrs Welles' had not been enthusiastic.

'Let the dead bury their dead!' she had remarked in a sinister voice, and when we discovered that it had only been thirty shillings, we let them.

But now with all our capital, as it were, finished, we found living on our incomes quite dreadful. We all smoked, and I'm afraid this and tea got priority over food, which consisted entirely of bread and marg, and jam and chips and meat pies. This didn't worry us, particularly as we all had rather a low taste in foods, but the children definitely began to look a bit droopy, and every two days or so we felt compelled to feel their hair and teeth to see if they were getting scurvy. Guinevere's teeth didn't seem any too firm, but we reckoned that she was at the right age to start losing them anyway.

With the success of *The Cut Heart*, Mrs Flood really got under way. She had realised that to get any lasting results from it she would have to make hay while the sun shone, so now we were plunged into a vast publicity campaign.

By Saturday the town was really thick with posters for the forthcoming attraction, (a smart Lonsdale comedy) and practically every house in Leek had had a throw-out shoved through its letterbox. This little distributing job fell to Rose and me. Every afternoon after lunch, armed with the wretched things, we bicycled up and down and in and out and around Leek, 'throwing out' the advertisements.

THE FLOOD PLAYERS (they said)

Will follow up their sensational current success

THE CUT HEART by Wallace Wynch
(yes, your own Wallace Wynch!)

with a very dignified comedy that has only just finished
delighting cultured London audiences.

DON'T BE LEFT BEHIND, LEEK!

Come on Monday night and see for yourselves –

SPRING CLEANING By F Lonsdale

We will all be there:-

MR WILLY FLOOD
In his usual role as The Charmer.

ROSE HART, SEBASTIAN DAY, ANN KING,
LEIGH PETERS

And

MRS LILIAN FLOOD

PLAYING –

Well, that would be telling! But a very daring and naughty
new part.

DON'T FORGET –
MONDAY THE 24TH – SATURDAY THE 31ST

THE TOWN HALL THEATRE, LEEK

7.30 P.M.

Hilda Fellowes   Bill Irving

It was a tedious job, going from house to house, but in a way I enjoyed it. Everyone seemed so pleased to see us. I would hardly have got a throw out through the letterbox and the door would be opened and I would be asked in for a cup of tea.

'Mum!' they'd yell into the recesses of the house, 'it's one of those repertory girls, you know, what we went to see last night. No! The blonde one,' then to me, 'Come on in love, Mum'll love to see you, she did so enjoy the play.'

Rose on the other side of the street did even better, on account of playing the heroine, and came away with bars of chocolate and pieces of cake wrapped up in tissue paper to be eaten 'in that wait you've got, before he tries to suffocate you'.

It was wonderful to be noticed and recognised and admired. Always before we had known that they didn't really like us, that they laughed at us behind our backs. Sometimes we had come down to the theatre in the morning to find rude words written on some of our posters, and some of them torn. And sometimes when we went into the shops the person behind us would be served first. And when we wandered around the market, before we'd even stopped in front of a stall, they'd tell us we 'mustn't touch'. We had always known that we weren't really wanted and although we'd pretended that it didn't matter, it really hurt us quite a lot.

But now in one short week it was different. We seemed to be welcome wherever we went and on the Monday night of *Spring Cleaning* they swarmed in again to see us. We had all been surprised when Mrs Flood decided to play the part of the prostitute. It was a much meatier part than the lead, but knowing Mrs Flood's views on prostitution, we didn't think that that would concern her.

I played the lead and I like to think that she took the other part on purpose, so that I could, but I don't know. She got all the applause and honours and the next day was highly praised in the papers. They seemed to like *Spring Cleaning* as much as *The Cut Heart*.

Sometimes we had to hold the curtain because of people still coming in, and then we would look at each other, not speaking, but smiling with content because it seemed as if it could go on being all right for ever. Mrs Flood said that given time Willy would draw an audience anywhere.

And all the time it was the height of summer. I had never known a summer like it before. It had blazed down on us in June and now we had reached September there was still no let up. The days slipped by one after the other, painted and unreal, all varnished with the glassy haze of intense heat. It made Bill Irving's life a misery and it made Mrs Flood's feet swell cruelly, but the rest of us revelled in it.

Les enfants du soleil, I would exult to myself secretly as Rose and Leigh and I, sunburned and free, would race each other down the hill into Leek. It was our life, an atmosphere, our happiness, us perhaps; we could not visualise the summer ever ending.

After *Spring Cleaning* we began rehearsals for *The Man*. It seemed we were always rehearsing something new so that Tuesday mornings, coming so soon after the first night of the current play, had long since lost their excitement. We noticed mechanically that this Tuesday it was a romantic drama by Ethel Thynne that Willy, as per usual, was to play the lead, with Mrs Flood as his leading lady, and me as his ingénue.

By the end of the morning we had decided that we liked the Parisian underworld setting that everyone was very suitably cast, and that *The Man* stood every chance of being another success. That was all though, nobody had suggested that it would set the Trent on fire. We couldn't help wondering a little then at Mrs Flood's breathless excitement.

On Wednesday we went through Act One again then straight on to Act Three where Willy as The Man, meets Mrs Flood as the fabulous and notorious José de Blanche, for the first time.

A bird had got into the theatre so we weren't paying a lot of attention to rehearsal, and were all craning our necks up towards the flies when Mrs Flood made her first entrance. She gave a screech of anger and we hastily turned to our scripts while she went off to remake it. And that was when we read it.

As the fabulous de Blanche makes her entrance, we read, a hidden tango music starts up and The Man, rushing towards her, whirls her into the centre of the stage where they dance an impassioned tango.

Mrs Flood plodded heavily down the three steps, scratched without penetration at her corsets and said in a gruff voice, her eyes shining with happiness, 'No need to go over this bit, this is where Mr Flood and me is going to do the adagio.'

'Yes,' said Willy. 'Yes, yes, yes! We're going to dance the adagio, at last we're going to dance the adagio again.' His face was wildly ecstatic. I think at that moment watching them, we were all a little moved. But only for a moment. On the way home I thought Rose was going to have apoplexy over it.

'It's wicked!' she said. 'Absolutely criminal, what right has that woman got to make him the laughing stock of Leek? What right has she got to exploit him like a man with two heads in a fairground? Willy,' she said, 'Willy with his wonderful talent made to perform just like an animal with that hideous great hulking old witch.'

'Rose,' Leigh said gently, 'don't be silly, Rose. They were a very famous adagio act, remember.'

'Remember, remember?' stormed Rose, 'I'm sorry but I can't remember back to nineteen-o-two.'

'Anyway Rose,' I said sharply – I thought she was behaving very stupidly – 'I've never seen Willy look as happy as he did just now.'

'Oh Christ,' said Rose in a frenzy. 'Oh Christ, you thick-headed ignorant fools can't you see that –' and then she didn't say any more, but rushed ahead of us up the road.

'Sunstroke,' said Leigh. 'Coupled with an unreasonable jealousy and a sentimental dash of infatuation – remember that night she danced with him on stage?'

'Yes!' I said.

There was a pause while we both looked back, both remembered that it had been the beginning... My heart gave a sad little lurching ache and I saw that the muscles in Leigh's face had tightened. Then he said, rather loudly, 'Beautiful, one of the most beautiful things I've ever seen, their dancing together.'

A month ago I would have added, 'Yes, and dead sexy too,' and we would have laughed together, but now I could only say, 'Yes, beautiful Leigh.'

For myself the prospect of seeing the Floods dance together on stage filled me with an almost abnormal excitement. I was by this time quite fascinated by their past life together and ever since I had had tea with them, and Mrs Flood had for a brief instant talked, desperately curious to know more.

I didn't think that I ever would though. Having fallen out of favour with her I realised that it would take at least another Mr Dropsey to reinstate me to my previous exalted position. Sometimes I found it difficult to believe that I had been entrusted with Willy for a whole day.

But now they were going to dance the adagio together. The same that they had danced all over the world, the same that had made them famous, that had formed their lives for them and held them together. I felt thrilled through and through every time I thought of the forthcoming Monday night.

They never went through it during rehearsals. As soon as we came up to 'A hidden tango music starts up', Mrs Flood would say 'Cut. No need to waste time on that,' she'd say. 'Mr Flood and me will just put it in on Monday.'

We were very curious to know where and when they did rehearse it. We couldn't accept, as she would have us believe, that they would just go cold into it on Monday.

'And it can't be back at the digs,' I told them from my superior knowledge, 'the rooms are like matchboxes.'

And then Leigh did find out. He came rushing back to the digs on the Friday afternoon with the exciting news that the stage door was locked, but that the strains of exotic tango music were emitting from beyond it.

He stood in the kitchen, laughing as he told us. It was really and truly going to happen. It was a huge joke. The Floods really and truly were going to perform.

I said quickly, 'You mustn't laugh Leigh.'

He said, 'Darling Ann, why shouldn't I laugh with delight? I couldn't believe it up to now. I thought it would be "Cut" again on Monday night, but there they are, hard at it on a beautiful summer's afternoon. Your luck's in Ann, they really intend to perform.'

'Dance!' I said coldly. His laughing pricked suddenly the

bubble of my excitement. I wanted more than anything else in the world to see them dance.

'Dance, dance, dance,' I yelled at him. 'For Christ's sake, you criticise Rose, but at least she has no desire to see them "perform", as you call it.'

Leigh looked as though he would like to hit me, then said with gritted teeth that between us, Rose and I would drive him to drink. Rose said that in view of his present financial circumstances she considered this unlikely.

I became contrite and thought that from a man's point of view the household at number eight must sometimes become rather much.

But there it was, the first uncertain doubt, the first uncertain feeling; a still, small voice, if you like, cutting across my excitement and suggesting to me that perhaps after all the ends did not justify the means. I became suddenly aware that alongside myself, several hundred other people would be watching them.

Chapter Seventeen

Monday the ninth of September dawned hot and still. Whenever any date of importance was coming up I would say to myself in bed the night before (prior to anticipating its events), and it will be hot and still. It sort of materialised my imaginings because it always was.

I was awakened as usual with the sun hitting me squarely between the eyes. Very unfair this, Rose didn't get it until eight thirty and Leigh not till nine, an advantage which they exploited fully and which usually resulted in breakfast being ready for them when they came down.

But this morning the first thing I saw was Rose, up and leaning in an abandoned manner out of the window. I looked at the back of her and thought how wonderful it must be to be really slim – 'A drink of water,' Mr Goat had once told her she was – and said to her, 'What's the matter with you?'

Rose answered me out of the window. 'I couldn't sleep,' she said. 'I've been up for hours.' And then she spun round from the window and started dancing madly round the attic. 'Isn't this a lovely day?' she sang.

And I picked up my cue in an instant and bouncing up and down on my bed, sang back, 'Yes, it is a lovely day.'

It was what we called our happy song, and long ago had agreed that anyone who felt that they might burst with this blessed state had a right to sing it in its entire length at any time, and demand co-operation.

'Are you glad I came your way?' warbled Rose, leaping from her bed to mine.

'Yes, I'm glad you came my way,' I sang, heaving my feet about so that she fell off.

'Came my way, lovely day,' we chorused together, then Leigh woke up and joined in.

'Oh you dear one, oh you sweet one, oh you darling, I love you.'

Rose and I started on the second verse but Leigh yelled for *pax vobiscum*.

'No!' he said, 'No Miss Hart, I'm afraid we can't permit its entire length, circumstances are quite unwarranted. Happy?' he said, 'My dear Miss Hart, how you can consider yourself today of all days qualified for that vulgar state is beyond human comprehension. Today Miss Hart,' he said sinking his voice into a sepulchral growl, 'is the first night of *The Man*, today Miss Hart, imprisoned in the wings, you will be forced to watch your Willy dance.'

Leigh rolled around on his mattress in mental torture and beat at his forehead. 'Dance,' he muttered in a delightful frenzy. 'Dance, dance, dance.'

I shrieked with laughter at him, and to my amazement and relief, Rose did too. We finished our song together at the top of our voices, waking up the kids, who came bounding up to the attic with Boysey and threw themselves with delight upon Leigh and his mattress. After that it was a free-for-all-early morning session with Leigh just managing to hold down his title again, i.e. his pyjama bottoms.

Over breakfast I did begin to wonder a bit about Rose's continued high spirits. Although after her first outburst she had said no more about Willy's dancing, it did seem strange that she now appeared not to care a jot.

We bade Mrs Welles farewell and assured her that a ticket would be waiting for her at the box office.

'See 'em dance together?' she'd said. 'Jesus kids, I can't miss a bit of Leek history in the making.'

We walked down to Leek in a ridiculous giggly mood. Outside the YWCA we collided with Miss Fluck, and Rose nudged me and greatly daring we chorused, 'Good morning Miss Fluck' (in a manner which made it just as well that she was an unspoiled Christian woman) before bolting like mad down the rest of the hill.

And it was there at the bottom of the hill that Rose stopped suddenly in her tracks and gazed up at the theatre. It lay just above us in the middle of the High Street, which ran sharply up another hill. Most people would have seen a large ugly town hall, with a few posters stuck low down on the front of it, but not us; it was our theatre and we stood in a line across the pavement and looked at it with love.

Rose said it out loud, 'Our theatre!' in a most un-Rose-like manner.

All around us the everlasting heat lay in its visible, tangible shimmering haze, and all above us the sun beat down in a white glare. The shadow of the theatre lay across it, so deep and so black that I could not determine where it ended and the building began. We had looked at our theatre like this a hundred times, but now on the hundred and first I thought wildly, the shadow is too black, the sun is too white, dear God it can't last, the strain is too much, it must surely break. And then Leigh said it out loud with such accuracy that the goose pimples came up on the outside of my arms.

'It's almost unhealthy looking,' he said uneasily, but when Rose said, 'Whatever do you mean?' he laughed and said he didn't know.

It was Monday morning down at the theatre. We walked into the black shadow, into the stage door and at once the glorious terrifying pace of repertory was upon us.

For me, the theatre seems never more bewitching than during the urgent last rehearsal played out to a background of hammer and saw, to the strong smell of glue and the quick snatches of interval music being tried out on the Panatrope. Feeling emotion that you know perhaps you may never capture again, then hating yourself as even while you feel it, you are aware that you must nip round to Boots for some more leg make-up.

Sharing cigarettes and tea and sandwiches on newspapers, all of us banded together with that fierce, selfless united feeling which only comes in moments of crisis.

And over it all the awareness of time... The precious minutes tick-ticking by...

And today it was intensified because tonight they were to dance the adagio. All morning we had been aching to know whether they would try it out at dress rehearsal.

Leigh had received full instructions on how to work the

hidden tango music, and now only needed to try it with them. Yet when the moment came, it was almost with relief that we saw them merely walk through a few incomprehensible steps, Mrs Flood in her bedroom slippers and Willy smoking.

'Olé!' said Willy without emotion, which was Leigh's cue to take off the record.

Rehearsal went well and by six o'clock, with the stage set and the props laid out, we were ready for the show. Rose and Leigh and Sebastian and myself walked along to the nearest milk bar, discussing with fever-pitch excitement the now almost mythical Adagio Act.

'They've no right to cut it out of dress rehearsal,' said Sebastian. 'No right at all. Anyone would think it was a bloody variety bill, the way they've been carrying on.'

'Willy's probably got to reserve his strength,' said Leigh. 'No joke these days, I should imagine, whirling Ma around the stage.'

But Rose, leaping ahead of us along the pavement, still in the morning's unnatural high spirits, yelled back that the only reason preventing them was that having seen them dance once, they knew damn well we'd refuse to go on tonight.

I sat in the milk bar and thought that the next time I would drink a milkshake could only ever be afterwards.

We made our way slowly into the stifling room, then still with time to spare I sat looking at myself in the mirror; at my face which had gone a bit thinner and a lot darker, at my eyes which had gone a bit smaller on account of continual screwing up, and at my hair, which was now almost white with the sun.

Sitting there with the other two silent, I felt a curious sensation of emptiness. I knew that it was to happen. I knew with all my heart now that it ought *not* to happen, and I knew with all my heart that I wanted it to happen. It was as if by the opposing force of these things, which were of tremendous value to me, they had cancelled themselves out.

I thought of the white glare and the black shadow, which had seemed to me too powerful to go on existing, and then suddenly with a rare lucid painful flash, of myself and Leigh, of Mrs Flood's great cruelty and Leigh's great kindness coming together in the shape that they did, and resulting in nothing.

The silence of our room was shattered by Mrs Flood's voice coming from the other side of the wall. 'Tighter Willy!' she shrieked, 'Tighter!'

The overture finished. The curtain went up and came down on Act One, Act Two... And beyond it the applause of the full audience died down into restless rustling little movements of anticipation.

On stage in the thick-hooped blackness of the wings we waited. My emptiness had gone and now, for the three minutes that must still go by, my spirit seemed to circle upwards so that the speed of my living became incredibly fast yet at the same time still.

I felt as though I was travelling in an aeroplane, dreadfully aware, but only in my mind, of the speed. Crouched on a tea chest, I felt no pain from the sharp steel of its broken edge pressing into my leg, but the gnarled rheumatic-ridden hands of Bill Irving, stiff and tense on the ropes of the curtain, were agony to me. And the thin poised ones that were Leigh's, arched over the dials of the Panatrope like frozen bananas, I wanted with an irrelevant physical pity to massage with oil.

I saw with one eye that was Rose's and Hilda's and Sebastian's and Bill's the white patch in front of us, which was the lit-up area where they would dance, and where Willy, in his purple cummerbund and white silk shirt, stuffed-on-wheels, had taken up his position. Above him, screened from us by the angle of the flats, Mrs Flood stood waiting.

Willy pawed at the white chalk spread over the white patch with a hopeless wooden leg, and in the sixty long seconds that must still go by, I felt passionately and helplessly with him, the numb discomfort of his trussed-up body under its linear belt.

Fifteen slow seconds ticked by. The anaemic white chalk circled and eddied minutely, sucked upwards by the huge, healthy pigmented motes of dust which lay in symmetrical streaks along the shafts of light.

From the secret supply of draught, which they had always possessed, the thick red velvet curtains made three impotent clumsy billows. Rose sneezed, then, 'Right!' came Mrs Flood's voice, and Bill pulled on the ropes and I was no longer riding through the air but on the back of a horse, its magnificent speed the same, but broken down, dissected, and dissolved by the pitiless cameras which were set at slow.

She came out on to the top of the stairs and stood there for a moment. She wore a spectacular short, blue satin dress hung with a thousand silver beads, and on her feet very high-heeled, very sharply pointed matching satin shoes. Around her head, in the style of an Eastern princess, was passed a silver chain from which a large silver cross flopped heavily against her forehead.

Leigh's hands moved on the dials of the Panatrope and as she slowly and proudly dismounted the stairs, the theatre was flooded with the impassioned noise of 'La Cumparsita'. I saw their faces in the two seconds before their outstretched arms met one another. Willy's young and joyous and eager and masculine, hers old and proud and brave and gay.

They danced as they had danced a million times before. The same as they had danced all over the world, the same that had made them famous, that had formed their lives for them and held them together.

A great hush came over the theatre as alongside several hundred other people I watched them dance the adagio. They moved soundlessly in a liquid bundle of colour, but it was not their technique which, although superb, to me may or may not have been as perfect as before.

Watching them, I knew instinctively that I had found what I was looking for. I think perhaps subconsciously I had known where it lay all along. It was not horrible for me to realise that he danced as he had always danced with her, for the very first time. They wheeled in a great arc back and forth across the stage and the expression of love on his face, I had seen in my lifetime equalled only by herself.

Watching him, I understood at last now how it was that he was bound to her as close as with chains. I saw suddenly clear and lucid, like I had taken heroin, the pattern of their dancing life. I saw the eternal beginning and ending forming the tiny circle that renewed itself each night, so certainly that the endings need never be reached but become categorical and it was always the beginning.

I felt a great wave of fear come over me as I saw and understood this, for even as I did so, even as I realised at once and with awe, that it was as deep and good and right and how love ought to be. I knew too, once and for all that it could only have happened with Willy.

Behind me Leigh said, 'My God look at him, look at his face. He has really loved her. I hadn't thought... Somehow, you know... Willy.'

And I was seized with a burning hopelessness because I couldn't cry out to him, No, no you must see it, if he has ever loved her, then he can only love her now. He can give nothing, absolutely nothing, he can neither remember nor anticipate nor create, he can only intercept, ignite. It's dreadful and terrible but I understand it, oh Leigh, I see it all so clear, so clear; she is there all around, all the time, like waves, and in the right conditions he can receive her. He's dancing so he loves her.

He loves her, there can be no 'has', no question of sentimental remembrance. It is happening, it has happened. Oh God Leigh, I've suspected it, I've suspected it like mad and she knows, she knows, she's always known. It all fits in now. The games at the digs, it's the same, it works the same, like dancing, don't you see there can be no beginning or ending...

Leigh said '...completely underestimated him... Christ, his face... Must be dreadful for him, all coming back to him... Normal and human like any of us...'

I looked at them all, crouched there in the wings with a kind of dreadful envy. They were utterly engrossed with the magnificence of the dancing. They who had been ready to laugh, to be humiliated, were moved almost to tears as they watched his face and thought that at least he had loved her.

At least he could remember and remembering recapture, I thought wildly, please, please, they may be right, I want them to be right – I don't know... – and then sharp and clear as an axe, it didn't matter any more because Rose laughed. She laughed long and loud, rearing herself up from the shadow so that the light from the stage fell across her and exposed her face, naked with understanding.

It was almost against his will though, I thought, that Willy's head came round to look at her. But he did look at her and in the short second that their eyes met, Rose acted. She moved so swiftly and urgently that in a dreadful automatic manner we instinctively removed our legs from her way; and there in the space which we had cleared for her, in front of the wide gap through which Willy could see her, in the wings, she started to perform, in burlesque, the adagio dance on stage.

For the three seconds that we did nothing, Willy continued dancing, only looking at her when his head turned naturally that way. Then suddenly, heartrendingly suddenly, the hypnotised look left his face and he stumbled. In an instant Sebastian and Leigh had grabbed Rose and held her to the ground, but it was too late.

As he lifted Mrs Flood across his shoulders, Willy hardly knew what he was doing. We heard her shriek, 'Down, Willy darling – down.'

We saw his desperate, confused face searching for Rose's. He started automatically to revolve Mrs Flood around him. She screamed 'Willy, Willy!' and then with a dull thud fell to the ground. She rolled over and over like an old ball, ending up with a crash in the footlights.

One single gasp of horrified sympathy went through the audience. There was not even a titter of laughter. Behind me, Bill Irving said 'The curtain – shall I? The curtain?'

And Leigh's voice rang out authoritatively, 'No!' and I couldn't put my hands over my face because we had got to bear it.

Willy Flood stood rooted to the spot where he had dropped her, dead from the neck up. And so out there all alone, trembling and blundering like a moth, Mrs Flood, with a great cracked smile on her face, extracted herself from the debris of broken glass. As she straightened herself, without looking for him, she held out her hand and he came down slowly and took it, and as she curtsied, he bowed to her.

The audience applauded as the audience will applause in the face of disaster, and after that there was only a meaningless jumble of time and words to endure before it was the end and we stood lined up for the curtain-call and heard her say, 'My husband... Mr Flood... A blackout... Forgive him... Happens to everyone sometimes... Won't happen again... Forgive him... My husband... Mr Flood...'

They left us. And now that the speed of my living had stopped, my body had grown so irksome to me that my mind could scarcely cope with the enormity of the stairs and my greasepaint and dressing and undressing. And I stayed still on the stage where they had left us and gaped with the others at Rose. They shouted at her and moved about so that they seemed to spin in a kaleidoscope of colour and sound as they had once done, so long ago before.

Leigh said, 'Hurry up and get dressed and we'll go and have a drink,' and took my arm and leaned on me, and so supporting one another like we were very old and delicate, we went to the dressing room.

I sat down and methodically greased my face, and Mrs Welles came rushing round with a flurry of mink and shrieked, 'Christ, if you could only have seen it from –' and I had to grab her and gesticulate madly at the partition, like she had only come out with some vulgar joke. 'Oh yes,' she said giggling and loud, 'oh yes, of course, they must be feeling dreadful about it, the poor old things.'

Rose came into the room. She was singing. I gripped the bench and kept staring into the mirror, but my mind panicked and flitted between the knowledge that I was ready and could leave at once and that if I did I should have to turn round and look at her, and be joined up with Mrs Welles who was saying, 'Hurry up love, Ann and Leigh are ready and we've only got ten minutes.'

Leigh came downstairs and stood beside me, and I heard Rose answer Mrs Welles in a high strange voice.

'I don't think I'll go for a drink Win, I think I'll go straight home. I'm a bit tired Win,' and under the cover of Mrs Welles replying, 'Suit yourself, only don't eat all the pie,' still without looking at her I was able to move in a huddle with Leigh to the door. Mrs Welles joined us and in another instant we would have been through the door, but as Leigh turned the handle Rose shouted, 'Ann!'

I said, 'Yes?' into the door.

But she shouted out, 'Ann!' again, in exactly the same tone, and I turned round and looked at her.

She sat high on her dressing room table, swinging her legs. She still wore her 'loose woman' costume and make-up. The red satin blouse drooped off one shoulder, the red and white striped skirt split up the side from calf to thigh was taut and revealing. Her black hair hung loose, her cheeks burned scarlet, her eyes glittered hard and defiant. Animated and clothed as she was, flushed with her evil victorious power, she looked like some magnificent animal.

We stared at one another then she said, 'Ann!' again, and her voice was high and strange like it had been when she spoke to Mrs Welles.

She said, 'Don't think too badly of me, will you?' and then added, 'Please, Ann?' Her bad taste sickened me. I didn't answer her and she said, 'Please, Ann?' again.

Mrs Welles said, 'Jesus Christ Almighty, Rose, are you sure you don't want us all to come along and put you to bed? It's nothink to us you know, to give up a little dinky-winky for you.'

Her voice was tender and normal and unaware, and I saw it hit Rose so that she cried out, 'Oh Win!' in a husky voice and leaping off the dressing table she ran across the room and threw her arms around Mrs Welles.

Mrs Welles said, 'Get away with you,' in a pleased voice, and examined her mink for damage, then Leigh opened the door and we passed through it and left her.

I hated her; I felt an absolute and vicious hatred for her. Sitting in the pub I found it difficult to get my shandy down because I hated her so much. I had not known that one person, without any gain, just through pure wilful malice, could destroy the most precious thing that two other people possessed.

I thought back to the morning and her extraordinary happiness, which I now understood to be the anticipation of her premeditated action.

Maybe she thought their dancing was going to be a shameful fiasco, which would still have been no excuse. But that she had waited, waited until halfway through, and watched with us and the breathless audience their wonderful, wonderful dancing and the thing they had been to each other, and then to have done it.

My heart tried out these thoughts sweeping aside the small

nagging voice of my mind, which said, that's not quite true, she saw him as you saw him, she understood.

'Oh, Leigh!' I said. 'How could she, how could she have done it?'

Leigh said, 'I don't know.'

We sat there for half an hour, miserably drinking but unable to move, with Mrs Welles bewildered, not understanding, half-heartedly defending Rose.

'So she made him drop her, so it wasn't funny. Well, I can tell you, if I hadn't been sat between a vicar and an innocent child, I for one would have laughed like a drain.'

We trailed home up the hill to Cockton Heath. I thought about them sitting in their squalid house in Commercial Road and wondered what they were thinking, doing, saying; whether she would rail at him or just forgive him as she always forgave him. '...You must forgive him... My husband... Mr Flood...'

Yes, she would forgive him, and they would start all over again or pick up from where they were before, and the only difference would be that her love must become a little more pathetic, a little more desperate, a little more unhappy.

It was a relief to me that Rose was not in the kitchen.

'Well, if you've been talking to her like you've been talking about her,' said Mrs Welles, 'I don't wonder the poor girl went straight to bed. Worn out, she must be.'

She hadn't eaten any of the pie so we had a good supper and afterwards sat talking over tea. It was about twelve o'clock that we ran out of cigarettes. I remembered that I had some dog-ends up in the attic. Leigh offered to fetch them for me, but his leg was never at its best by the end of the day so I went myself. The attic was in darkness and I didn't want to wake Rose but the dog-ends were in a pocket of my coat and I didn't know where it was, so I had to put the light on.

I saw the letter immediately. It lay on top of her neatly made-up bed. It was in a sealed envelope and addressed to me. I read it out once and then again and then I ran to the stairs and yelled, 'Leigh! Win! Leigh! Win!' over and over again at the top of my voice.

They came clattering up the stairs, their faces white and

frightened. I held the letter out to them and they crouched round me on the bed and read it.

It said,

Dear Ann,

I am running away with Willy Flood. By the time you get this letter we shall already be a long way out of Leek. I don't think any of you knew that Willy and I were in love with each other but we are and we have been for a long time. We had planned to run away together some time ago, it was not just on the spur of the moment.

I know that you will think it is a cruel thing for Mrs Flood, but Willy doesn't love her and he does love me, and I'm afraid she will just have to realise it. After all, she is old enough to be his mother. When I said to you, don't be too hard on me Ann, it was because I never meant to spoil the dance like I did. In fact, I never thought about it the whole day except when Leigh brought it up in bed this morning and I couldn't tell him that it was because Willy and I were running away together that I was happy.

We chose today because Willy said he would like to have just one last dance with her and that it would make her not feel so bad about his leaving her as well.

I acted like I did because Willy, being easily impressed as you know, and under her thumb, looked like he was getting sentimental or nervous or something which, with everything planned, must not happen. As you know, it worked.

I am sorry he dropped her but he would probably have dropped her anyway, as he says she weighs a ton.

I would like to have told you about it before and shared the secret with you Ann, but knowing how you feel about the Floods I couldn't. I wish though that I hadn't had to leave with you thinking of me like you must have been.

The two pounds is for darling Win, who I shall never forget and who gave me such a wonderful home. What fun we did have Ann, never a dull moment was there, but there won't be now either, as Willy and I intend to get up a really smashing adagio act like they used to be.

Well, the taxi's waiting at the gate so I must close now.
Cheerio Ann and God bless,
Ever yours
Rose

It seemed to me as if they could never stop reading it, as if they could never get to the end of the cheap piece of lined exercise paper that I had read through twice. It seemed as if they could never know what I knew, as if I would be burdened for ever, alone with my knowledge. I said wildly, 'Rose, Rose has run away with Willy. Rose says she's run away with Willy Flood.'

They didn't answer me. From the dark night outside a wind blew in and rocked the dim electric bulb, making the little circle of light dip about their heads.

Mrs Welles raised her eyes from the paper and looked straight ahead of her and said in a haggard voice, '"Ever yours, Rose." Jesus Christ all bloody mighty.'

There was a long dreadful pause. A piece of branch flapped violently against the window and the wind blew in again with a fierce rush. With awful fascination we watched it lift the white paper from Mrs Welles' hand and drag it a few yards across the floor.

Mrs Welles said, 'Did... you have any idea?'

Leigh cried out, 'No!'

And I, simultaneously said, 'No!'

And then Mrs Welles said, 'Well, I must say I take off my –' and the spell was broken and in a second the attic was reverberating to our excited, horror-struck, hysterical, ghoulish voices.

'What's going to happen? She doesn't mean it... They'll come back... Planned all through the show... I thought in the dressing room... The bitch, the cunning little bitch... We should have guessed it a long time ago... Love him?

'Don't talk such rot... That look in his eyes. She doesn't know what love is... Ever so romantic really... Romantic, oh Win! How can you... Ever such good taste Rose's got... Don't, it's horrible... I could fancy him myself... It's horrible, horrible, darling Willy enticed.

'Enticed away by... Don't talk so soft, you know he's been after her for months... Yes, but not like... Told me so yourself... You don't understand... She's took her clothes, took everythink with her... What about Derrick? She doesn't love him she... What about the show... He doesn't love her... What about the company he can't, he can only—'

'What about Her?' Leigh's voice cut in suddenly, still and

small across our excitement. I looked at him, feeling the sharp sound of my voice falling away, the heat flowing out from my body, hearing myself say as though it were he still speaking.

'...Sitting there in the house... With a note... Like us, only Willy's... on her own.'

We had forgotten. In the drama of the unbelievable letter we had just read, we had forgotten the only thing that really mattered.

I said, all shaking and incoherent on a great wave of anger and fear and ten-horse-power strength, 'I'll have to go Leigh, we can't leave her, we can't leave her on her own the whole night. It's Willy,' I grabbed up the letter and ran to the door.

Leigh said, 'I'll come with you.'

I yelled back, cruel with fear, 'You can't, I'll have to run all the way.'

Mrs Welles said, 'Your coat, you can't go without your coat!'

Leigh shouted, 'Don't be such a fool, for Christ's sake Ann, there's nothing any of us can do till the morning.'

But I was at the bottom of the stairs by then and all I yelled back was, 'She loves Willy Flood more than ten thousand people's love put together, try and work that one out while you're lying in bed.'

They clattered down after me, Mrs Welles shrieking, 'Me flashlight, take me flashlight, Launcelot's planted it among them flowers by the gate.'

By the front door I waited for Leigh and said quickly and ashamed, 'It's not only going fast, Leigh, it's better not with a man really.'

He said he would wait up for me and they watched from the door until I had extracted the torch from its petalled friends and turned the corner out of The Rooley. The night was pitch black, strong, windy and warm, and against it my body burned so fierce that it seemed to eclipse the weak light from my torch and blaze my path for me like a meteor.

I ran faster down the hill than I had ever run before, and the only thought in my brain was that I must run faster still, because it was desperately urgent that I reached her quickly. At the bottom of the hill I stopped and breathed unnaturally in sore, rasping heaves.

Leek was quite, quite empty. There wasn't even a lit-up

window. I jog-trotted up the High Street and my mind became mechanical with such thoughts as the door being locked and her not hearing me, or not wanting me, or having fainted. I didn't think about Willy and Rose very much.

Past the cemetery a man took shape out of the wall and said, 'Seen a ghost, dearie?' frightening me so dreadfully that I tripped and fell over in my running, and his nasty hand shot out and would have got me only his aim was miscalculated.

I twisted in and out of the little slum streets for a lifetime but once in Commercial Road, because it was long and straight, I reached the house quickly. I walked out into the middle of the road and looked up at it, exhausted and fearsome. No lights. I walked on down to the alley and sat in a heap in it to get back my breath.

I thought, she will be hysterical, you must be prepared for her being hysterical. You must be bracing and kind and make tea and tell her that it's only a matter of time before he'll be back. Make it be like he's just taken a little holiday. She will be hysterical; whatever you do you mustn't cry or break down, or be sentimental. If it's fainting you must get her legs up. Oh God! I can't bear it! Don't be such a fool, you should have thought about that before you came...

It was the stillness, the sudden adaptation of my body from its wild, free urgent run through the night to the mean, creeping, shuffling pace of the last hundred yards. To the painful counting along the thick, black fetid dust-path, six protruding lavatories back. I was filled with a drowning sadness and horror that this thing should have happened here; that there were no compensations in life.

The back door was open, swinging soundlessly to and fro in the wind, and on the step my feet crunched broken glass and I swung my torch down and saw that it was littered with the pieces of a broken tumbler.

In front of me the scullery yawned like a black hole and beyond it was the kitchen and the stairs... And still there was no sound.

I didn't like it, nor the open door nor the broken glass. Standing on the step I felt real fear. I told myself, maybe she is asleep, fallen asleep exhausted after the hysterics, and stepped into the scullery, crunching more glass on the inside of the step.

A slow plop of heavy water fell on to me from the dim flapping shape of washed clothes which hung a few inches above my head and I listened again, longing to hear the sound of her crying. But there was nothing. Only the door behind me being dragged on a rush of wind, to shiver and grate against its post.

I walked fearfully up the steps into the kitchen. I thought, I will count three and then shout, 'Mrs Flood.' I counted three, then six, then nine, and had opened my mouth to shout when, tremulous and fine on the air and inexpressively eerie, came the sound of Willy's musical box.

For a moment I couldn't be sure that I'd heard it as the door flung open again and the sound was lost on the wind. But when it closed it was still there, the thin, little piping jabs of his musical box, playing over and over again, '*If you were the only girl in the world*'.

I thought I was prepared for anything, but as the choking lump came up in my throat I told myself that it was the arrow with poison on its tip, that it was the hit below the belt. I groped my way fiercely to the bottom of the stairs then, stumbling in the darkness, mercifully fell against them so that my head came round to face the door to the boarded up room and so that my eyes could discern the faint, faint glow of light which came from under it.

She was lying on a large brass bedstead, which filled the two far corners of the room. She wore a pink silk negligee and lay in a sort of huddle, pushed hard against the wall. She clutched a bottle of whisky in one hand and Willy's musical box in the other and around her, inches deep on the bed and spilling on to the floor, lay Willy's photographs. A lot of the frames had broken and the candle which was lighting the room picked out a hundred pieces of broken glass and reflected them a thousand times in grotesque dancing motes upon the walls.

I stood in the doorway and looked at her and, after a few seconds, she realised that someone was there and said, 'Willy, Willy!' in a slurred, gasping mutter. She moved, still in a huddle, and pushed violently with her feet so that a heap more photographs fell to the floor.

She said it again, 'Willy, Willy!' then moved again.

I said very loud, while the frames crashed down one upon the other, 'It's me, Mrs Flood, I've come to see you, Mrs Flood.'

Mrs Flood said very softly and slowly, 'Yes, yes I know, he told me,' then screamed out suddenly, 'No! No! Willy, you said it was Rose – you told me it was Rose! You must be honest with me darling, you mustn't lie to me darling.'

I was shaking all over. I tried to pick my way between the photographs, but I trod on some of them. I kept saying, 'It's me Mrs Flood, Ann King. It's not Rose, I know about Rose, she left a note for us; she told us she had gone away with Willy. He'll soon be back, but he's not here at the moment, it's just me at the moment Mrs Flood, just me on my own, not with Willy or Rose at the moment Mrs Flood.' I kept saying it over and over again.

Mrs Flood watched me hypnotically and as I approached the bed, pushed herself back up against the wall. I removed a photograph and sat down on the end of the bed.

I said, 'We were a bit worried about you, just called to see if you were alright, Mrs Flood,' and thought, I'll have to go home, get a doctor, get Leigh, she doesn't know what she's saying, doing…

But even as I thought it, Mrs Flood took a great swig from the whisky bottle and said suddenly and heartrendingly, 'Must excuse me… A little upset… Must excuse a little upset… Must have a little drink…'

She thrust the bottle towards me, spilling out whisky on to the bed and I took it from her and drank a great fiery gulp of it and made to put it on the chair with the candle. But she let out a screech and lurched forward for it with an outstretched hand. So I gave it to her and she leaned back again with it clutched against her, not drinking, just with it clutched tight against her.

The musical box had stopped playing and, still holding the bottle, she tried clumsily to wind it up again. But she couldn't manage it and it fell away from her making sharp, jarring musical noises as it rolled over. She made no move to recover it but sat staring at it with a dreadful glassy intensity, and now there was no sound in the room at all except her breathing.

The candle spluttered, sending the dancing motes in elongated streaks up the wall while I gazed at her in terror.

Her face was swollen and blotched almost beyond recognition, ghastly with the coloured, clotted remains of her stage make-up, and horribly and blessedly drunk. Through the transparent negligee her sagging body was heaped and looped about with the unnatural huddle she lay in.

I didn't know what to say, what to do. I could only think confusedly that I had come too late. After a while I couldn't look at her any more and dropped my eyes to the profusion of photographs on the bed.

I saw that they were the ones from the room upstairs and realised that she must have come up and down with great heaps of them, time and time again. I found his note for her crushed between two of them. It was written on a piece of his drawing paper in a clear laborious hand. It said,

Dearest Lil,

I am going off with Rose. I love her so am going off with her. She says she will dance the adagio with me like we used to which I want very much. This is a difficult letter to write Lil as we have never been parted before, but I have not been happy for a long time and Rose says that with you being so much older than me that is why. She says it will be better for you too. I enclose the picture which is the only one took of me you haven't got and which would spoil the collection without.

Yours
Willy.

Pinned to the other side of the paper was the photograph. My heart contracted with love and tenderness, and as I looked at it I felt the tears roll down my face. It was a cheap blurred snap of Willy with his arm round Rose, standing behind the cake at the fête.

But stronger than anything came the terrible feeling of fear for him, for I knew that he had indeed given it her with no other thought than that without it her collection would be spoilt.

I read the note through again, hearing Rose dictating it to him... hearing her giggle with delight as he suggested leaving the

283

photograph... I thought of them riding through the night together, Willy aflame with his mad and long awaited desire, Rose as I had last seen her, flushed and gay, magnificent with her evil victorious power.

From above me, Mrs Flood's voice screeched out suddenly, 'Thass my picture – you got my picture. Give me my picture!' And I held it out to her and she took it and drew it close up under her eyes and said, her voice breaking on sobs, 'I can cut her out of it... I can cut her out of it... So it's only him, nobody would know... So it's only him...'

She kept saying it over and over again so that I shouted out wildly, 'Have a drink, Mrs Flood, have another drink from the bottle Mrs Flood.' But she didn't and kept on saying it, 'So... it's only him, so it's only him,' over and over again in a high cracked voice, with her head rolling from side to side.

And hardly knowing what I was doing, I moved up along the bed beside her and took her shoulders in my hands and blabbered, 'It'll be alright Mrs Flood, it'll be alright. You must get into bed, I'll help you to get into bed Mrs Flood, I'll make you some tea, we'll have some tea together, shall we? It'll be all right, you mustn't talk like that, please, you mustn't talk like that Mrs Flood.'

I guided her hand with the bottle towards her mouth and as though she had found it for the first time, Mrs Flood's eyes focused on it with sudden greed. And dropping the photograph she put both hands round it and lifted it, grunting quickly, to her mouth. She took a gulp then another and another, then fell heavily against me.

I said, 'That's right, that's right Mrs Flood. We'll lie down now shall we? I'll take the bottle and we'll lie down now.'

I extracted the bottle from her and, holding her with one arm, tried to clear some of the photographs with the other. All the time she kept speaking in incoherent mumbles and all the time while I said, 'No! No! Mrs Flood, you mustn't talk, it'll be all right if you're quiet Mrs Flood,' all the time I kept praying to God that she might pass out.

I couldn't move her. I kept heaving at her huddled legs but she resisted me. I said, 'Mrs Flood, please Mrs Flood, you must help me,' when suddenly, sharp and clear through her mumblings, she said, 'He'd never had another woman!'

I turned to her and saw that her eyes were fixed on me, fierce and wondrous and loving. She moved her head in little unbelieving turns as I gazed back at her numbly. 'Never even been kissed by another woman... Just sixteen... I'll never forget that night.'

She never took her eyes off my face; it was as though I hypnotised her the words coming out involuntarily.

She said, 'He'd danced it for the very first time... So little he was, so little and slim... When he come out on stage they drew in their breaths, he was so little and young... So young and lovely and innocent...'

Her voice trailed away for a second and she sagged against me, then I heard the hissing intake of her breath and felt the sharp pain of her nails digging into my flesh, and she shouted, 'And he was all mine, all mine... He wanted me so much. That was the night, that night in the hotel in Manchester and in the morning...' She stopped suddenly, and the thin little tears trickled down her face. 'And in the morning...'

I felt my heart pound sickeningly through me and I heard my voice say even now at the end, 'Yes, yes, go on Mrs Flood, in the morning?'

'And in the morning,' she said in little broken sobs, 'when the papers was raving... We took a tram car up to the prison... To get his mum's permission...'

Again her voice trailed away and now her staring eyes became fogged and vague, and when she spoke again her voice was a secret whisper so that I had to lean close to her to hear.

She said, 'She didn't tell me then... She should've told me then but she didn't... She didn't tell me, not till five years later when I made a special journey up... I had to know... I had to make a special journey up... She come out with it then. I asked her straight and she come out with it then... She told me then that... Willy had been dropped as a baby.'

I held her to me while she cried, fighting not to cry myself, but in the end I laid my head against her thin black hair and we cried together. We sat there for about twenty minutes. Sometimes she moaned and called out, but mostly she just cried against me and called me Willy. She passed out very quietly, gradually stopping crying, then growing limp in my arms, and at last breathing heavily and evenly.

I laid her down on the bed, pulling her twisted up legs straight and covering her up with my coat. I took all the pictures off the bed and put them on to the floor with the others and the empty bottles, then I picked up the one that was still half full and finished it off.

Sitting there amongst the photographs, my mind ticked off into a thousand pigeonhole compartments the thousand dreadful things that must happen in the morning.

In every shape and size they lay... I became aware without emotion that we had played for the last time... 'From the age of sixteen upwards...' That tomorrow night Leigh must stand at the door and give the public back their money... 'So handsome he was then that he took my breath away...' I made my mind keep finding things, dreadful things that were now only little and trivial...

They showed him laughing, smiling, crying. I twisted words round in my brain that we must use: solemn, naughty, sexy... 'personal disaster'... dancing... Mr Flood... dancing... Very sudden... always dancing... Dreadful words that now could only comfort me...

'*Dancing to put thy pale lost lilies out of mind*,' 'Lily Flood and Willy...' I thought about the tragic wake... 'Ten foot high all over the world, wherever they went...' Of helplessness and Guinevere and Bill, of hollowness and Mrs Welles and shallowness and Leigh and me...

'*But I was desolate and sick of an old passion*,' 'Lily Flood and Willy, wherever they went,' '*yea, all the time because the dance was long*,' 'ten foot high wherever they went...' '*I have been faithful to thee Cynara after my fashion*'... I made my mind keep finding things, dreadful things that were now only little and trivial. For I had sat with her the whole night through and although it had come when I was only seventeen, I knew that all the things that would go on happening to me could only be kinder. When I had finished the bottle I felt dizzy, so I pulled myself up on to the bed and lay down beside her

The End

Printed in the United Kingdom
by Lightning Source UK Ltd.
114798UKS00001B/10-12

9 781844 015122